Praise for the novel

The Good Son

"*The Good Son* is one you should immediately pick up and devour because it's so smart and entertaining and beautifully made." —NPR's Alan Cheuse

"[T]he brilliant character development and the labyrinthine plotline . . . make this a provocative thriller that readers won't soon forget." —*Publishers Weekly* (starred)

"[T]hought-provoking, balanced, and smart." —*NewYorker.com*

"*The Good Son* contains all the elements of a bestseller: well-developed characters, a devilish plot, and hairpin turns that keep you guessing and surprised until the very end of the book. . . . Readers will tear through the pages. . . ." —*Bookpage*

"Michael Gruber has never been afraid of difficult topics. . . . His riveting *The Good Son* also tackles thorny questions; at the same time, it's arguably Gruber's most readily accessible novel yet." —*The Seattle Times*

"[S]onia and Theo [Laghari] are possibly the most interesting and multifaceted characters created in recent memory. In placing them within such a rich, layered, and entertaining story, Michael Gruber proves once again that he is one of our most talented novelists." —Debra Ginsberg, *Shelf Awareness*

"*The Good Son* . . . is one of those few and far between complex, intelligent, and insightful thrillers. . . . Gruber's finest novel to date." —Nancy Pearl, author of *Book Lust*

"Gruber . . . weaves threads together masterfully while successfully exploring themes of family, duty, loyalty, cultural identity, and more, without ever slowing the momentum. Smart, tense, and vastly entertaining." —*Kirkus Reviews*

"Admirable. Compelling." —*USA Today*

"Adeptly plotted yet philosophical, worldly yet preoccupied with moral truth, it's a book to provoke comparisons with John le Carré and Graham Greene." —Laura Miller, *Salon.com*

"[T]here are a handful of writers whose narrative skills move them...to the... respected arena of 'literary fiction'—Elmore Leonard, George Pelecanos,... Alan Furst,... and Michael Gruber." —*The Morning News*

"Is there anything Gruber can't write about? In this richly layered tale...there are twists and tension aplenty—ideas, too. If only governments were half as interested in the psychology of violence, maybe war itself might become a work of fiction." —*Booklist* (starred)

The Forgery of Venus

"Tantalizing...Exhilarating. Retains power from the first chapter to keep readers desperate for the suspenseful, addictive fix of every succeeding one. *The Forgery of Venus* is a highly intelligent novel that entertains and educates." —*USA Today*

"*The Forgery of Venus* is the latest in Gruber's series of amazing books. He has applied his deft touch to everything from Shakespeare to shamanism, yielding a finely drawn portrait of an engrossing world every time." —*The Times-Picayune*

"An imaginative novel of psychological suspense." —*The Boston Globe*

"As layered as [a] luminous portrait by an old master." —*The Seattle Times*

"Ingenious...The author owns his subject matter and packs it with well-researched details, making this...a successful, suspenseful examination of insanity, forgery, and reality." —*Chicago Sun-Times*

"Downright delicious." —*Seattle Post-Intelligencer*

The Book of Air and Shadows

"Breathlessly engaging...brilliant [with] energetic writing, compellingly flawed characters, literary scholarship, and mathematical conundrums. Also incredibly smart. We never had this much fun reading *The Da Vinci Code*." —*USA Today*

"If you love books, make room on [your] shelf. Smart, packed with excitement...Gruber mixes in fascinating details about rare manuscripts, intellectual property, and ancient and modern cryptography." —*The Washington Post*

"An intricately crafted and literate work [with] a rich cast of characters who are difficult to leave when the final pages are turned. Gruber is a master of his material."   —*The Denver Post*

"A smart thriller...An engaging adventure."   —*The Boston Globe*

"It has quirky, flawed characters, tricksy first-person narration, some knowing references to the cinematic nature of its own plot, and nimble, witty prose—a dash of Nabokov and a dollop of Amis. Gruber is the real deal."   —*Salon.com*

"A crackling whodunit. Characters [with] rich inner lives that transmute genre fiction into literature."   —*The Dallas Morning News*

"Finely honed prose, ambitious structure, and captivating characters...This is a whip-smart adventure that surpasses its competitors with dexterity."
                                                      —*Rocky Mountain News*

"A gripping literary thriller. A taut novel that offers ingenious puzzles plus murderous threats along the way."   —*Seattle Post-Intelligencer*

"Ingenious...engaging...The mysterious murder of a Shakespeare scholar, shootouts in the streets of Queens, and an unlikely romance all combine to make for a gripping, satisfying read."   —*Publishers Weekly* (starred review)

"[With] intelligence and engaging style...Gruber raises the thriller stakes and accelerates the plot while still creating convincing personal journeys for his characters. All that and a tantalizing imagining of Shakespeare's personality, too."   —*Booklist* (starred review)

"Not since A. S. Byatt's *Possession* has an author so successfully combined literary puzzles, tempestuous duplicity, human adventure, and good storytelling. In a thriller written with remarkable flair, Gruber serves up an elaborately layered and devilishly detailed masterpiece."   —*BookPage*

"A fast-moving tale about the world of rare books. A wonderful story with absolutely superb casting"   —*Kirkus Reviews* (starred review)

Night of the Jaguar

"Michael Gruber...joins the elite ranks of those who can both chill the blood and challenge the mind."   —*The Denver Post*

"(A) highly entertaining thriller . . . hotly spiced with hit men and guns, demon gods and piranhas." —*Publishers Weekly*

"Superior entertainment that raises sincere, provocative questions of intellect and faith." —*The Seattle Times*

"Compellingly original. Gruber gives more to ponder than intriguing clues to the identity and motive of the killer—both of which, when they arrive, are as satisfying as they are unthinkable—and he does it with prose that is efficient yet rich and hip. His characters have lives, they care about issues in ways that compel them to wax enthusiastic as they are sucked into the labyrinth of the case." —*The Oregonian*

"A worthy addition to this heretofore terrific series . . . the novel fires on all cylinders, once again displaying Gruber's skill at blending genres." —*San Francisco Chronicle*

Valley of Bones

"The Stephen King of crime writing." —*Denver Post*

"*Tropic of Night* and *Valley of Bones* [are] miracles of intelligent fiction, and are among the essential novels of recent years. . . . *Valley of Bones* challenges the reader to accept the reality of an unseen world. . . . Emmylou Dideroff is one of the great characters in recent popular fiction." —*The Washington Post*

"Grade: A. A feast of rich characters, an intricate, globe-hopping plotline, and an exploration of faith's place in our world." —*Entertainment Weekly*

"After his dazzling, literate, and downright scary debut thriller *Tropic of Night,* Michael Gruber proves he's the real thing, and then some, with *Valley of Bones,* his equally mesmerizing, multilayered, page-turning new novel. Gruber is nothing less than masterful. . . . Don't miss this book." —*The Plain Dealer*

"Gruber has not only written another winning tale but also deepened the reader's interest in the complex, compelling Jimmy Paz. . . . *Valley of Bones* and the series [are] worth savoring." —*Los Angeles Times*

"First there was *Tropic of Night,* one of the strangest, most original crime novels in recent years. . . . Now there is *Valley of Bones,* another startling and equally original thriller about faith and evil and the line of madness that can run between them.... Gruber is a gifted and natural storyteller."

—*Chicago Tribune*

"A writer ... who takes genre conventions and bends them to his will.... An ambitious foray into the nature of evil ... and the clash of the rational and the irrational."

—*The Sun*

"Gruber more than fulfills the promise of his dazzling *Tropic of Night* (2003).... Evocative prose, an erudite author, spellbinding subject matter, and totally original characters add up to make this one a knockout."

—*Publishers Weekly* (starred review)

"Gruber has drawn even with John Sandford and has power to spare.... Gruber intersperses the Miami action with scenes from Emmylou's possibly confessional notebooks detailing her at first lurid and then heroic past, tossing in searing sex, African civil-war carnage, wonderfully serious religious thought, great tenderness, and some of the snappiest byplay since William Powell and Myrna Loy."

—*Kirkus Reviews* (starred review)

Tropic of Night

"A blockbuster ... Just when it looks as if detective fiction has plowed every gory, suspenseful possibility, along comes a novel that raises the stakes on the genre.... Gruber creates a hallucinatory atmosphere as unsettling as it is exciting."

—*People*

"Bold, provocative, and frightening ... An extraordinary debut." —*USA Today*

"Sorcery, magic, witchcraft—by whatever name, no matter what you think about it now, you will take it more seriously after you've experienced this mind-bending novel.... The author wields his own sorcery as he lures us into the hallucinatory world of his imagination. No summary can do justice to the richness and fascination of this novel...."

—*The Washington Post*

"Michael Gruber has written a book with such intelligence, confidence, dazzling bits of arcane knowledge, and downright page-turning scariness that other novelists are going to want to just smack him. Absolutely mesmerizing ... Equal parts literary novel and thriller ... Gruber has an astonishing way of pulling in the reader. "

—*The Plain Dealer*

"No ordinary thriller . . . Brilliant." —*St. Petersburg Times*

"We hate Michael Gruber. Nobody should be that good. . . . *Tropic of Night* is one of those brain-frying, sorry-your-water-broke-honey-but-I-can't-take-you-to-the-doctor-'til-I-finish-this-chapter thrillers—the sort that soon will occupy that rarified cerebral air associated with such litero-thrillers as *Smilla's Sense of Snow*, . . . *The Secret History, Mystic River*, and, basically, the entire canon of James Lee Burke." —*The New London Day*

"A fresh, intelligent thriller that will alter the way you see the world. . . . [O]ne of the most absorbing and original novels I've read this year. . . . [Gruber's] unforgettable heroine, Jane Doe, is a rare and remarkable creation—smart and fearless, loving and vulnerable, at home in the world, at home with power." —*The Times-Picayune*

"Reminiscent of Peter Hoeg's *Smilla's Sense of Snow* . . . original, unconventional, and intricately plotted . . . a gritty, edge-of-the-seat crime novel." —*Sun-Sentinel*

"A superbly written story by a new writer, and one that lovers of good suspense should not miss." —*Vero Beach Press Journal*

"An intricate thriller . . . perfectly balanced . . . [a] finely crafted, intelligent, and original work." —*Publishers Weekly* (starred review)

"Monstrously entertaining . . . what would be overripe overplotting in lesser hands becomes wonderfully credible here, with cleverly drawn characters (Paz and his most excellent mum must surely return), trunkloads of ethnobotanical factoids. . . . The climax is pleasantly apocalyptic." —*Kirkus Reviews* (starred review)

"A dark, brilliant book with as indelible a central character as Smilla from *Smillia's Sense of Snow*." —Martin Cruz Smith, author of *Gorky Park*

The
Good
Son

The
Good
Son

A NOVEL

Michael Gruber

 ST. MARTIN'S GRIFFIN ◢ NEW YORK

THE GOOD SON. Copyright © 2010 by Michael Gruber. All rights reserved. Printed in the United States of America. For information, address St. Martin's Press, 175 Fifth Avenue, New York, N.Y. 10010.

www.stmartins.com

Designed by Meryl Sussman Levavi

The Library of Congress has cataloged the Henry Holt edition as follows:

Gruber, Michael, 1940–
    The good son : a novel / Michael Gruber.—1st ed.
      p. cm.
    ISBN 978-0-8050-9128-1
    1. Political kidnapping—Fiction.   2. Pakistani Americans—Pakistan—Fiction.   3. Pakistan—Fiction.   I. Title.
    PS3607.R68G66 2010
    813'.6—dc22

                        2009036955

ISBN 978-0-312-67494-6 (trade paperback)

Originally published in hardcover in 2010 by Henry Holt and Company

First St. Martin's Griffin Edition: February 2011

10 9 8 7 6 5 4 3 2 1

For E.W.N.

The Prophet was asked:

Whom should you befriend most?

He replied:

"Your mother. Then your mother.

Then your mother.

Then your father."

SAYINGS OF THE PROPHET MUHAMMAD

The
Good
Son

1

The phone rang at a little before one in the morning and I knew it was my mother. I didn't even have to look at the number there on the little cell-phone screen, I just said, "Mom."

Next to me, my not-really-girlfriend, Gloria, heaved over and jammed a pillow on her head and said nasty stuff about people calling in the middle of the night. I ignored this and added, "Anything wrong?"

My mother said, "No, of course not. Why do you always ask that when I call you?"

"Because that's what people do when they get a call at one A.M. You forgot about the time zones again."

"I didn't forget. I thought soldiers always rose at dawn."

"When they're on duty," I said, "which I'm not. I'm at Gloria's place. What's up?"

"I'm at Heathrow on a plane for Zurich. I'll be gone for a couple of weeks. Could you tell your father?"

"Why don't you tell him yourself? I think they still have phone service in the District of Columbia."

"Please, Theo. If I call him we'll get into a big argument, and I don't need that just now."

"Because you're going to Zurich for a few weeks? Why should he object to that?"

"Because I'm not going to Zurich. I'm just changing planes there. I'm going to Lahore."

That stopped me; sweat popped on my arms where they stuck out of the quilt. I said, "Lahore? Mom, you can't go to Lahore. There's a fatwa out on you. You can't go to the Muslim world anymore."

"Oh, don't be silly! In any case, I'll be traveling on my Pakistani passport; no one will bother S. B. Laghari, the Pakistani begum, the professor's wife, in a proper head scarf. Besides, I'm not going to Iran. It was a Shi'a fatwa anyway. No one is going to pay any attention to it in Pakistan."

"You know, that's right," I said. "Only thirty million Shi'a in Pakistan and the ayatollahs are right next door and Sunnis and Shi'as have been killing each other in Punjab for the last twenty years and there's a heavily armed Shi'a militant group based in Lahore.... Are you fucking *out of your mind*?"

"Please don't speak to me like that, Theo," she said, after a pause. "It's unseemly. I'm your mother."

I felt my face flush. She was right. The army messes with your manners. I said, "Look, could you just, like, think about this like a rational person? Why don't I get on a plane, we'll sit down, we'll talk—"

"Darling, there's nothing to talk about. I'm going. I'll be back before you know it."

"No, this is *insane!*" I shouted into the tiny perforations. "How can you do stuff like this to me? You've always done it and you're *still* doing it. For God's sake, I'm wounded! I'm your wounded son. You're supposed to be here, taking care of me, not going to Lahore."

This was disgraceful, I knew, pathetic, but it was one of my buttons. Unfortunately, my mother has guilt handles the size of a little girl's earrings. She said, "Well, if you'll recall, I did come to your side when you got back. But it was made perfectly clear that I was in the way."

Not true, although what she meant was that she was not up to much in the nurturing department. My father is the main nurturer in our family, and she knows it and it makes her feel bad.

"I have to go," my mother said. "They're closing up the plane. I'll call you from Lahore. Remember to call Farid."

I was still trying to talk her out of it when she said a firm good-bye and I was listening to the ether.

I cursed in a couple of languages, and this brought Gloria into full wakefulness. She sat up, rubbed her eyes, and smoothed her long hair away from her face. She said, "That's the one problem with the cell phone, in my opinion. You bring some bozo home with you and he can talk to other women when he's actually lying in bed with you. Which one was that?"

"It was my mother, Gloria."

"That might be even worse. Why does she call you in the middle of the night?"

"She was calling from London. My mother is a famous world traveler who doesn't get the whole time-zone thing."

"And this is why you started screaming?"

I told her why.

"So what? She's a grown-up. Why shouldn't she go to Lahore? Where *is* Lahore anyway?"

"It's in the Punjab. In Pakistan."

"That's where you're from."

"Originally."

She'd propped herself up on one elbow and she had that look, her pumping-for-information look, on her smooth, tan, flat face, with that hair hanging loose and thick on either side. Maybe you have to grow up in a Muslim country to understand the erotic appeal of long black hair. It still knocked me out to see American women just walk through the streets with their hair hanging down for anybody to see, a little fossil of my upbringing. Especially this kind of hair, Asian hair, thick, glossy, blue-black, although Gloria is a Latina and not from where I'm from.

I said to the look, "It's a long story."

"You say that a lot," she said. "Mr. Mysterious. If you think that makes you more, like, attractive, you're wrong."

"You're delving, Gloria. I thought we were going to keep it simple and shallow."

"Asking about your *mom* isn't delving. Delving is who did you go out with and what did you do with them? Or, you know, what you did in the war."

"You want to know this? It's interesting to you?"

"Yeah. We have to talk about something. I told you about my folks, my brother, and all that shit, so you tell me about yours. It's what normal people do. We can't have sex *all* the time."

I snaked my hand under the quilt. "We could try," I said.

She moved her legs to make a space for my hand. "Yes, but tell me: Why can't she go back to Pakistan?"

"Okay," I said, and suppressed a sigh. "My mother is Sonia Bailey."

"Who?"

"She used to be pretty famous back in the seventies. When I was about three she left me in Lahore and traveled through what was then Soviet Central Asia, disguised as a Muslim boy. She wrote a book about it that got a lot of play, especially from the feminists. Then she hung around Lahore for a few more years, and when I was ten she went off again, but this time she went on the haj, the pilgrimage to Mecca."

"Also as a boy?"

"Yeah, and that was the problem. She polluted the holy places with her transvestism. The Muslim world went crazy. Death sentences got issued."

"Like that guy, what's-his-name?"

"Salman Rushdie, but this was way before that."

"And nobody found out she was a woman?"

"No, not until she wrote a book about it. She's small and wiry, like me."

"No tits, huh?"

"Pretty flat. Narrow hips, too. And she had an artificial dick."

"Seriously?"

"Uh-huh. She had it made in Lahore. She could pee through it, so when the guys saw that, it closed the deal; she was one of the boys."

"Did she take you along on *that* trip?"

"No, she left me again," I said and I didn't want to talk about it anymore then so I got to stroking her in the way she liked, which she'd already told me about. Gloria is good with the details. She lives a very controlled life, and after a few minutes of this she said, "Jump on me, quick," and I did.

After we finished, she popped immediately out of bed. I always thought women liked to cuddle after—that's their favorite part, is what I understood—but not Gloria. She was getting ready for her early shift. I heard a shower going for what couldn't have been more than ninety seconds and got strobelike sightings of brown skin and sensible underwear, and there she was in her pink scrubs with her long hair coiled and pinned into a shining black bun.

She leaned over—a quick kiss—and said, "Toss the key through the mailbox; don't forget, okay?"

I said I wouldn't and she was gone in a flash of pink. A minute later I heard the sound of her old beater starting up, and off she rattled.

Gloria is a nurse at Walter Reed Army Medical Center, in the north end of Washington, D.C., where I'm being treated, and she was a soldier too, once, and is now a civilian employee. She is the child of Mexican immigrants and a big striver, which I am definitely not. I am what they call a lifer; I will probably be in the military my whole life. When your average troop says this, it means twenty-and-out or thirty-and-out, retire on the pension, maybe get another job, and have a pretty nice life—what with the benefits and all—but I will probably get killed, considering what I do, so I will really be in the army my whole life.

I fell asleep and awoke at dawn like a good soldier. Then I took a lot longer than a ninety-second shower and helped myself to some of Gloria's coffee and cereal. The milk was bad, so I ate the cereal dry, washed down with the coffee, which was some store brand I never heard of. Gloria doesn't spend freely. She has a plan, which she explained to me on our first date. She was working two shifts a day, seven days a week, and going to school on top of that, so she could become a nurse-anesthetist, and really rake in the money, and she thought that in ten years of doing this she would have enough to finance medical school. She also explained, on the same first date, that she wasn't after a regular boyfriend, she just wanted someone nice who was out of town a lot and wouldn't try to control or otherwise fuck up her life, which, as I say, she had all planned out.

I was planned too, so that was cool. How I hooked up with her was I go for physical therapy three times a week at Walter and a while ago, on one of those days, Brenda Crabbe, my PT, had handed me a piece of paper with a phone number on it and said that Gloria Espinosa wanted to meet me. I asked her who she was and why me, and she said, "Half the doctors in this place been trying to get into that girl's pants for a year and she won't have anything to do with them. This is your lucky day, Sergeant." She had no idea why, she said; she said, "It can't be your face."

So I called the number and we arranged for a date and I got cleaned up and drove my rental to her house, which was in Riggs Park, a section of D.C. I had not been in before. Hamilton Street, where she lived, was rows of two-story brick buildings that someone built for people who needed a roof and could pay but who didn't have much of a choice. Her building had a sagging metal awning in front and a pile of plastic lawn furniture under it, designed so that the people who lived there would have a place to sit when the Washington summers made it impossible to stay inside. That was before AC and TV; the furniture looked like nobody had used it in a while.

She opened the door and she was beautiful: the cheekbones, those plush lips, and a curved nose with all kinds of character. She was smaller than me, which was nice, because I am not a large man, and she had a neat figure-eight kind of body, which appealed to my Middle Eastern tastes, that and the hair. And she gave me a beer, a National Bohemian, as a matter of fact, and I thought she was being funny, because Natty Bo is the beer soldiers in the Washington area drink by the case to get drunk, because it's really, really cheap.

So we had a beer each and talked, or she talked mainly, and she gave me the plan; she had to be careful about dating because she absolutely could not get involved, not seriously involved, with anyone. It was a little like being interviewed. She was looking intensely at me, to see if I was maybe concealing a guy who would give a shit, and I told her that was fine with me; I just wanted someone to go to a movie with and I didn't want to get involved either.

She said, "You're career-oriented too?"

I said, "In a manner of speaking. I'll probably get killed, and I don't think it's fair to saddle a family with that."

Her eyes got wide when I said this and she asked me what I did in the army and I was going to use the lame one—I could tell you but then I'd have to kill you—but she was not the kind of woman to be put off with that so I said what I was allowed to, which was some bullshit about long-range scouting.

"That's why you're working with Brenda. You got hurt in Iraq."

"No, Afghanistan," I said, our first lie. I'd known the woman for twenty minutes, so this was something of a personal best.

I'm in an organization called the Tactical Intelligence Support Detachment, which is its name just now. It's had a lot of names, but what it's been doing for the last twenty years or so is going into various places and gathering military intelligence, mostly what they call comint, which is eavesdropping on telecommunications but also just looking around and getting the feel of a place that the army might want to go into. Running agents too. The unit has three kinds of troops in general: knob turners who get the signals or whatever, spooks who gather the humint from live local types, and shooters, people who make sure the others don't get caught doing it. Sometimes—rarely—the shooters are ordered to commit some other form of necessary violence. I'm a shooter. The army is officially not supposed to do stuff like this. It's covert operation, which is supposed to be the domain of the CIA. But the CIA doesn't belong to the military, it does not salute and say *hoo-ah* when the army wants something from it, so the army decided it wanted its own little CIA, which is us.

Obviously, we've been busy since this whole terrorism thing started, although not as busy as we could've been. One thing a general hates is risk. The way they got all those stars is by not taking a risk and not ever getting a bad grade on their report cards, so when they get up there in the Pentagon the last thing they want is a bunch of cowboys in disguises slipping into some supposedly friendly country and listening to guys plotting bombings or, even worse, taking the guys out, as they say, extrajudicially. What if someone got caught: scandal, questions in Congress and the media? So half our missions get scratched, but the one I got hurt on didn't.

As it happens, I'm fluent in Dari and Pashto and Urdu, languages spoken in Afghanistan and the tribal areas of Pakistan, which was where this abortion actually went down. The target was a guy named Hamid al-Libiya, a comrade of Mr. bin Laden, who was tracked via comint from his dwelling place in Waziristan to Riyadh in Saudi, where he apparently picked up some funds from our wonderful allies there and went back to Waziristan. I guess al-Q has learned by now that they can't just send messages via sat phones because we're all over that, and they don't have broadband cable yet in Waziristan, so in order for the bad guys to keep their operations together they have to travel from time to time. They can't seem to stop using cell phones, though, so that's how we triangulated in on Mr. al-Libiya, who was in a place called Baggan, which was all Taliban all the time.

I was with two other guys, and we were posing as militants, armed to the teeth and so forth; we had beards and we smelled right and we blended right in; we had our own house and everything. After a day or so, we observed the arrival of several tinted-glass SUVs during the day, and from our house the knob turners are picking up intercepts of the subject's cell phone, and they learn he's meeting with a couple of senior Taliban commanders. So we got set to run in there that night and snatch the bunch of them.

We ran into a little problem, which is really part of a big problem. Okay, the army hates Special Ops, but it's like the bad girl on the block;

they know she's bad but they can't keep their hands off her. So instead of being a self-contained operation there's levels of sign-off on every mission, which tends to compromise our security and slow things down; also, when we actually get clearance to go in, everyone in the area wants to be involved in this real exciting stuff and get part of the credit, if any. For this thing, they gave us a reinforced platoon of Special Forces guys, under a Captain Lepinski, who were supposed to hover in the area and provide backup and extraction in case we got into trouble.

We actually didn't get into trouble. Everything was going okay; we snatched up our insurgents and a little firefight broke out, nothing we couldn't handle, but Captain Lepinski got his signals crossed and the fuckhead painted the house with his laser target designator, and an F-16 loitering way up high dropped a 250 kg GBU-12 bomb on it. The explosion caught me and Billy Olin going out the door and killed eighteen people inside including women and children. Rittenhouse died too.

It could've been worse for me, I guess. My left leg was broken in three places and my right shoulder was smashed up some and my right wrist was cracked. Fred Rice and Buck Claiborne and the LT came running back and dragged me and Billy and Steve's body out of there, not that I was personally aware of anything at the time.

We got air-evacuated to a hospital, first in Afghanistan and then in Germany. They covered the whole thing up per usual, because as a unit we don't exist, and the story that surfaced was internecine fighting between insurgent factions, and the Pakistanis lied too because they never admit that the U.S. has boots on the ground in Pakistan even though we do all the time. No one said a word about the blue-on-blue shit.

None of which I told to Gloria then, and she didn't press me for war stories—she probably got her fill at work—so we chatted and drank our beers and I asked her if she wanted to go out for something, drinks, a movie, a club, but she surprised the hell out of me by saying, "No, why don't we stay here and have sex?"

I have to say that I have not had much experience with regular women. I was too young in Pakistan and I grew up in the middle of a war surrounded by men. Then I was in jail and then in the army. There are plenty of women available around army bases, and not only whores; there is a particular kind of woman who is a groupie of the elite formations, they like being around lethality and hard bodies, and a small number are interested in marrying someone with a short life expectancy and G.I. insurance.

I'd been with groupies enough, and lots of fun too, but we all regarded them as a kind of gym equipment. Maybe they felt that way themselves, I don't know. Anyway, I'd never had a direct invitation like this and it threw me; what was the catch? I asked her, *why me?* and she said she liked my look, I had what she called the wolf look; I was a loner basically and so was she, and she said she used to stand in the doorway of the PT suite and watch Brenda torture me and also she would get a whiff of my sweat and she liked it; she thought it was chemistry. Which I guess it was, but confusing a little, American women being so much like boys are where I come from and not like women in that country at all. So that was our first date, and it became a couple-of-times-a-week deal, always the same.

After I left Gloria's I drove to the PT clinic at Walter Reed Army Medical Center for my date with Brenda Crabbe. I'm renting a junker while I'm in D.C. I don't care what I drive, unlike many of my comrades; that's another thing I didn't get growing up, the whole American you-are-what-you-drive thing. I get in, it goes, I get out, and I could care less what it looks like.

It's strange, driving in the real world again. You never get your cherry back; I mean, except for the odd drunk, driving long distances in the U.S. is pretty safe. But I still keep my foot on the brake most of the time and my eyes are scanning like a motherfucker, looking for death on wheels. Like just this morning driving up Georgia Avenue a woman in a Dodge van swung out of a side road and cut me off and I practically ran off the road, and what I was thinking was that if someone had done that in Iraq the grunt on the fifty cal above me would've trashed her and her little van, probably killed her and six kids. It happens all the time over there and no one even slows down.

And I look at the neat rows of houses here and imagine them with their fronts blown out and all the domestic shit exposed: the TV and the couch, dishes, letters, and photographs all strewn like leaves in the fall; also, I can hardly look at my fellow citizens, like in a mall or on the street, without imagining them lying in blood, nicely dressed bureaucrats or businesswomen, reading their *Posts*, with their clothes blown off, no legs, a long streamer of guts running down the street and people stepping daintily over it.

They tell us that we're over there so it won't happen *here*. High strategy is not in my job description, but you know, when you come back, you kind of secretly want your fellow citizens to get blown up a little; we don't admit it but it's true. How the fuck can they be so—I don't know, *normal*, like in a dream of shopping and careers and ordinary daily bullshit, while what's going on over there is going on?

Brenda gave me a big smile when I showed up at her station. She spends all her time with guys who are resentful and bitter because their bodies are fucked up beyond repair, and I try to ease the tension some by a little flirting through the pain, although she is a large powerful woman and plain as a manhole cover.

So for an hour I lit up her life and she made me wish I was dead, and afterward I had some lunch in the cafeteria and walked over to Building 18, where they had Billy Olin. This is one of the crappy old buildings where they keep soldiers who are too busted up to fight but who the army hasn't got around to kicking out yet. Peeling paint, black moldy walls, really decrepit; they were supposed to fix all this up but they haven't got around to it yet. Personally, I'm not surprised or shocked. This is how the army is. What surprises me more is that people think they'll get anything different from an organization whose main purpose is to kill people and whose leaders are easily distinguishable from Mother Teresa.

There's a couple of squashed water bugs on the floor of Billy's room and he's sitting in his wheelchair watching an animal show on a portable TV. I mean the show was playing, but I couldn't tell if Olin was watching. He's got a dent in his skull now, from a chunk of debris probably, and it's hard to tell if anyone's home in there. I try to go see Billy when I come for my sessions here; I've known him for a long time and I feel bad about what happened to him. I was the senior guy so I should've been the last man out, covering his back, but I went out first. Stupid thing to think, really, a bomb like that goes off and it's more or less random what happens, but still.

It's not like we're a band of brothers or anything. There are about three hundred of us, I don't know for sure, and they arrange us in task forces for special missions, mix and match, shake and bake. Also, we're not really soldiers, we're spies, and spies have a different standard of unit cohesion and comradeship. We're not warriors either, although that's the bullshit they pass out in the kind of training people like me go through—elite warriors, Special Forces, SEALs, Delta: each level more elite warrior-ish than the one before, until you're so elite you can't get killed or shrunk down to a husk like this poor sucker. As it happens, I've fought with actual warriors and there's a difference. The warrior's an individual before anything else. Sure, he has a family, a clan, and a tribe, maybe even a national movement, but the main thing that drives him is personal: his honor, his fame. A soldier is a whole different thing. I take the silver solidus from the Man and I kill on command, nothing personal about it. The reason there are a lot more soldiers than warriors nowadays is that soldiers will beat warriors every time, if they're well led and paid on time. This whole warrior thing is a sick fantasy to protect guys who've grown up secure in the burbs from realizing what business they're in. I could give a shit, myself. I've been killing people since I was nine years old; it's the only thing I'm really good at. And like I say, I'm not even much of a soldier anymore, given the outfit I'm in.

I didn't even know if Billy knew I was there, but like I always do I pulled up a chair and talked to him awhile. I talked about what was on my mind, which was mainly about my mother and the crazy thing she was doing. I guess I really didn't think he could hear me, because this is a subject I would never bring up with the people I work with. As far as anyone knows, my life began at age eighteen when I enlisted. People ask where I'm from, I say D.C.: my mother's a writer, my father's a college professor. *How come you know all those languages?* I tell them I grew up bilingual in Urdu, and that Dari and Pashto are related languages I picked up as a kid on visits to relatives. A little exotic, yeah, but I'm not that forthcoming, I don't expand, I don't share those amusing family anecdotes that people seem to have, especially in the South, where so many of our troops come from. It's not a big deal because most of what you talk about in military circles besides the strictly professional stuff is sports, fucking, and the shit the army pulls. I'm not known as a conversationalist, which is sort of okay in my part of the service. An advantage, in fact.

So I went on about my mom, how she was traveling to Lahore

from Zurich, probably on PIA. A good airline and it helps get her into her Muslim head. She'd be traveling as a Pakistani, in the full costume and the head scarf, and she'd ask to be seated next to a woman, which of course they oblige if they possibly can. She flies business nowadays; she's got the money and she's paid her dues. She'll fly east over the hot dry lands she crossed years ago, on foot, in rattletrap buses, and in trucks loaded with oranges or wailing sheep, back when she was a man, a rubber dick strapped to her crotch.

Billy made no response when I got to this part, which kind of convinced me he was somewhere I couldn't get to, although you do hear about guys in his condition who pop out of it years later having heard every word people said when they were in the vegetable state. I told him, just for background, as it were, that in 1979 she decided that she wanted to go on the haj. I didn't have to explain to Billy what the haj was because he's done the cultural sensitivity course too, just like me, although I didn't need it. She went on haj not by plane direct to Mecca the way people do nowadays but overland and by coastal sailing ship, like they used to in the olden days. That's why she went as a man. And when she got to the holy city, she switched and saw what it was like for women too, slipping into a burqa and hanging out with the ladies.

And then she wrote a book about it and got essentially barred from the *umma*, the Islamic world. Infidels are prohibited from setting a toe on the sacred soil of Mecca, so that was one thing they had her on, although she always maintained she was a Muslim and would recite the Shahada at the drop of a hat, and had whole chunks of Qur'an memorized and could spout Hadith like a sheikh. So then they got on about how she'd violated the rules about the separation of the sexes, she'd shown her face outside the family, and her reply to that was since no one knew she was a woman how could she inflame the lusts of men? A fine point there, a little too fine for the ulema, because it's also *haram* for one sex to wear the clothes of the other, and the Iranian ayatollahs issued a fatwa against her shortly after the book took off in the States.

Our family in Pakistan said it might be a good idea if she made herself scarce for a while, maybe a century or two, until things quieted down, and Farid agreed, but despite the family's wishes he stayed married to her. So after various other catastrophic incidents they eventually moved back to D.C. and my father got his post at Georgetown, and she stayed there for a while, but she started feeling antsy in the city and pinched by the life of a faculty wife and author, so a couple of years back she got a little adobe house in the Huerfano Valley of Colorado, and she works part-time at a mental health clinic in Pueblo, probably the only Zurich-trained fully loaded Jungian therapist in the poverty zones of southern Colorado. I wonder what the meth freaks and drunk Indians she gets in there think of that. Probably that she's writing a book about them. Probably true.

I went on that way for a while. It's better talking to Billy than to the assholes at the post-traumatic stress disorder clinic I'm supposed to attend. I don't have PTSD. Civilians think PTSD is what you get when something bad happens to you. It isn't. People get scared and neurotic when something bad happens to them, or if they're in stress too long. It's a physical thing, really; the body fluids are telling you to run away, and if you get out of the stress you'll pretty much recover. For example, speaking of amusing family anecdotes, my mother has had some pretty traumatic things happen to her, but each time she pulled up her socks afterward and went on to live what most people would call a successful and interesting life, if you don't count risking her neck whenever the opportunity arises as a defect. Or the way she treated me.

Real PTSD, on the other hand, is from doing bad things to *other* people. It's what gives you the nightmares and sends you to the drugs and booze and makes you shoot your wife, kids, and self. Most of us aren't designed to do the kind of shit you have to do in a war zone, especially in a war zone with lots of civilians. Or even to see what you see. Little girls in embroidered dresses lying by the side of the road like dead dogs, cars full of some family that was in the wrong place and they're sitting there—Dad behind the wheel, Mom holding the baby next to him, three kids in the backseat—and they're all roasted meat, teeth grinning out from the char. And so on. A small number of people don't seem to get PTSD—a group that includes your basic concentration camp Nazis, your gulag operators, your professional secret police torturers—and obviously our own service has any number of such people, of which I am one. I haven't cracked yet, is what I was explaining to Billy, and he kept quiet and listened, nodding and drooling a little.

Sometimes I think I will kill someone, my CO maybe, or my mother, or a bunch of strangers in a public place, and then kill myself, but these thoughts fade, like they belonged to someone else. I love my mother, and if anyone harmed her I would definitely kill whoever. I have been through a lot of hard shit, but I believe I have a solid base and maybe, if you have that, nothing life throws at you can really touch you in your core; there'll always be a magic circle you can hide inside. My mom always said that, and looking back I think I had it in the house of my grandfather, Bashir Bilal Muhammad Laghari, in Lahore, where I spent the first nine years of my life.

I ran down after a while, said good-bye to Billy, and went over to the pharmacy. I was waiting for my pain pills, when something on a sign they had there reminded me it was a Thursday. Thursday is a big deal in Lahore, as in most Muslim places, kind of like Saturday night is for the infidels, party time, and that got me thinking about Thursdays at the Laghari house, my grandfather's *haveli*, as they call it, on Bhatti Street near the Urdu Bazaar in Anarkali, in Lahore. Most Thursdays he would hold a *mehfil*, a gathering of his friends, who were the cream of Lahore society across all political factions. B. B. Laghari Sahib, Baba as we called him in the family, was a judge and a legal scholar. A more or less honest judge in a society where corruption is the national sport, he was respected by both the Sharifs and the Bhuttos, the major clan factions in Pakistani life, and his Thursdays were one of the few places where the warring tribes could meet in a halfway civilized way. I felt a little bad about not recalling what the day was. If you grow up in a religion your interior clock is geared to the holy days and the cycle of the festivals, but I don't practice Islam much anymore.

What they mainly did at the mehfil was listen to people sing *ghazals* in Urdu, to the music of the sitar, the *surbahar*, the *sarangi*, and the tabla—Indian versions of the guitar, bass, cello, and drums. Ghazals are all about heartbreak and longing, feelings familiar to me from an early age. My colleagues have country music and I have the ghazals. I often sing them to myself, and sometimes to girls. Laghari Sahib entertained most of the famous ghazal singers of the day, people like Muhdi Hassan and Ghulam Ali, which would be like us having Madonna or Pavarotti to a private party. I started getting invited to these things when I was around seven, along with my foster cousins and Wazir, my best friend, who was the son of my grandfather's Pashtun bodyguard. While my contemporaries were watching Bullwinkle, I was listening to geniuses sing the poetry of Háfiz and Ghalib.

So that was a kind of base, that house full of beauty and love and the most amazing generosity. It was unheard of in the social circles the Lagharis moved in for a man like Baba to take in a waif, a woman like a wild fox, my mother, and let his oldest son marry her, and love their half-breed child, me. And look what I did with it! As I walk out of the pharmacy clutching my dope, there in my head Ghalib is singing:

> *I am neither the flower of song, nor the tapestry of music,*
> *But the sound of my own breaking.*

2

Sonia puts her cell phone away and looks out the window as the plane begins its taxi. She is wearing Pakistani clothes, a *shalwar kameez* of dark green embroidered silk and a black cashmere *dupatta* draped around her upper body and head. She had considered taking a coat, but then she would have had to lug it all through the trip and she likes to travel light.

Next to her in the caressing business-class seat sits a young well-scrubbed businesswoman, reading a thick report. The young woman has not said a word to her and will not, Sonia thinks, for the duration of the flight. Even the flight attendant's smile is gelid when it falls on Sonia in her Muslim dress. They fear the Other, although neither of them would admit it. They mistrust the woman still bound by the patriarchy from which they have so recently escaped; more than that, even, they think her a possible sympathizer of the new enemy. The umma is not popular on international flights nowadays. Sonia doesn't really mind; she is not a chatterer on airplanes, although in a Central Asian second-class train carriage she would be the life of the party.

Sonia opens her briefcase and looks through the papers of the conference she has organized, the reason for this trip to Lahore. She has booked a conference room in a Lahore hotel, but she would really like it to take place in Leepa House, the Lagharis' vast summer home in Pakistani Kashmir. Leepa House belongs to her husband, technically, but she has not asked him. He would not approve of her traveling to Pakistan in the first place, and certainly not to Leepa House, with all that is going on in that part of the country. But his brother Nisar has the use of the place, and she will ask him when she gets to Lahore.

The plane passes ten thousand feet and there is the usual announcement; she reaches into her bag, extracts her iPod, and fills her head with the music of Abida Parveen, the famous throaty voice weaving the patterns of the ghazal in between the tap of the tabla and the whine of the sarangi. She sings about going away to build a house in a lonely and forsaken spot, never to see a human face, a house with neither roof nor walls nor doors. . . .

The song makes Sonia cry, as always. She wipes the slight tears away and feels a pang of regret and a passing self-contempt. She is like the bourgeois couple in the Anatole France fable, who stroll by a suffering match girl without a glance and then weep real tears watching *La Bohème* at the opera. She did not cry when she departed from those she presumably loves or when recalling the horrendous events that have marked her life. She puts this thought from her mind—she does it easily, a well-practiced skill—and thinks again of Lahore.

How will the family deal with her? She's sure of Rukhsana, Farid's sister, an actual friend: they e-mail several times a month and Rukhsana visits when she's in Washington on a story or just to go shopping and see Farid. Nisar, the middle brother, will exhibit the typical inoffensive charm of the businessman and politician and hide the person, if any, behind the smiling mask. Seyd, the youngest, the soldier—he must be a major by now at least—an ornament of the Inter-Services Intelligence Directorate, the dreaded and wonderfully incompetent ISI. Seyd, if he even bothers to meet her, will be cold, formal; he disliked her twenty years ago and has not changed his opinion. If Baba had not died, things might have been different.

A deeper pang here, the old wound, intensified by the sound of the ghazal and the memory of listening to that music in his presence. Self-torment is a part of her personality; it is why she plays that music on these long trips, so that the reverie of the stratosphere might be infused with some contact with that time. She has been analyzed by an expert in Zurich, the whole Jungian treatment, and the result is she still suffers but at least knows why, suffers like a human and not a dog, and she can use the suffering in her work; the wounded healer reaches deepest into the psyche, below the level of history and anamnesis to the dark core where the devils play.

The drone of the music blends with the noise of the plane's engines.

Hypnotic: the persona is alert to the immediate surround but beneath this the true self breaks loose of time and is transported back to a former existence as a nineteen-year-old ex–circus performer with a suitcase full of cash and nowhere to go.

℘

In those days you couldn't fly direct to Lahore, you had to go to Karachi and take the train, so there she was with that suitcase pressing against the back of her knees in a first-class carriage. Farid had insisted she was not to undergo the rigors of a second-class Pakistani train. Still, the sights of Karachi were exotic enough as they traveled by cab from the airport to the train station; it was like an endless circus sprung free of the big top and smeared across a whole land, a boiling mass of brown people in exotic dress and, like the circus people she knew, seemingly possessed of a more intense existence, a striving desperation not to sink and be lost in the cruel stew.

She recalls Farid on that journey, sitting next to her on the sticky-hot seat, more formal than he had been in New York, a different being in his own land. They spoke little as the train rushed onward; she'd ask a question, he'd answer in his precise way and fall silent. He was nervous, she could tell, and no wonder, bringing a strange woman—a girl, really—with a pile of dubious cash into his father's house. It was only later that she understood what a colossal act of kindness and generosity it was. He never touched her during the entire trip. He'd purchased Pakistani clothes for her in the bazaar in Karachi and showed her how to wear them, her first time in shalwar kameez, but she was used to costumes, to being someone she was not. It was at least not a spangled leotard and a feathered headdress and she was not on a horse under the spotlight.

IIe said it was fate that had brought them together, and he was not just uttering a banality, as might have come from the mouth of an American. She had just happened to be in Central Park that day, in the middle of the morning, after several exhausting and unsuccessful days of seeking secretarial work, and she was not looking forward to the bus ride back to Paterson, having to tell Guido that she had failed and hear his mockery: Why can't you get a job *cleaning*, for God's sake; who do you think you are?

Who she thought she was—who her mother thought she was—was

not someone chained to the rough life of tiny failing circuses, doomed to live in trailers, fifteen shows a week during the season and scrabbling at menial jobs in the winter, no education, no culture, living with stupid, larcenous people. So Marta Kracinski of Warsaw, from a murdered family—an aristocratic family in the Polish manner, proud as bishops, poor as dirt—sat every evening of Sonia's young life and, by the light of a dim bulb or a hissing gas lantern, put her girl to her lessons, conveying an eclectic, idiosyncratic education: the classic books of Europe, whichever of them happened to turn up in small-town used bookstores; the French language; the Catholic religion; mathematics up through plane geometry; and more than American girls usually get of the glorious and tragic history of Poland. And typing. Marta was big on typing. If you could type, you could get an office job, you could meet a man, a *distinguished* man—that is, not like Dad. Sonia could type over sixty words a minute by the time she was fifteen and handled all the small correspondence of the circus office.

Sonia rarely thinks of this part of her life and what came after. She has come to terms with her past, as she learned to say in her therapy. *Coming to terms*: a curious phrase, she thinks, a metaphor from the military and affairs of state. Armies and governments at war come to terms—who will yield and who will gain—and the use of the phrase in therapy supposes a war in the psyche that must be ended. But it never ends; it is like the War on Terror.

Her first meeting with Farid, on a warm day in late May: sitting on a park bench, her belly hollow and griping, with not a dime for food, watching a woman feeding bread to a flock of pigeons and wondering, in a hysterical way, what the woman would say if Sonia got down on her knees and scrabbled for the bread among the filthy birds. A man sat down on the opposite end of her bench, took a bag out of his brief-case, opened a Styrofoam container, and began to eat from it. From which the most wonderful odor arose, spicy and rich with the promise of stewed meats. She felt the spit well up in her mouth and felt also the blush of shamed anger. She looked at the man—stared, really—and after a while he looked up at her. He was dressed like a student, in chinos and a checked short-sleeved shirt, sneakers on his feet. He met her eyes, then looked nervously away.

The pigeon fancier dumped her bread bag, shaking out the crumbs, and left. Sonia sat wretchedly in place, thinking about money, about what she would and would not do to get it, about the man on the bench, heedlessly eating, when with a clatter of wings the whole flock of pigeons rose into the air, and within that clatter came another, stranger sound, a flat noise, like a bat hitting a pillow.

In the center of the asphalt path a small tan hawk clutched a pigeon, from whose open mouth a small ruby of blood shone. The next moment the hawk flew off with slow flaps of its long wings, straining to lift its lunch.

Sonia said, "Wow!" and looked at the man on the bench. His face was transformed by wonder and he smiled at her, white teeth flashing in a face that was almost the same color as the hawk's plumage. He said something in a bubbling, throaty language she did not recognize and, at her puzzled expression, recited in slightly accented English:

"This was fated from the beginning of the world,
That this pigeon should meet her hawk.
So, we too, from the moment I saw your coils of black hair
And let your talons tear my heart.

"It's a poem from my country," he added. "Originally in Urdu."

"Are you an Urdu?" she asked, and touched her black hair, half consciously.

He laughed sweetly. "No, Urdu is the language of the poet. I am Punjabi, from Pakistan."

"Is that like India?"

"Very unlike," he said, still smiling. "We are neighbors, however, like that hawk and the pigeon."

Then he introduced himself formally, and she did the same, and they chatted there on the sunny bench. He was Farid Laghari, a law student at Columbia, just finishing his degree. She hid her own life from him then, ashamed, and the shame surprised her. She was ashamed of being an ignorant horse girl in a failed circus, speaking to this polite and educated man. Now she recalled her mother speaking of manners and breeding, and how the carnival people had none, and Sonia had not understood what she meant; she had imagined it was part of the fantasy world called Poland or an oblique way of nagging her husband.

But this was the thing itself, here on this park bench: manners and good breeding. She turned toward it like a flower to the sun.

After a time he looked at his watch and told her he had to go. They stood up, and the world spun and she fell clumsily against him.

"What is wrong?" he cried. "Are you ill?"

She was starving. She had breakfasted on a cup of coffee and a doughnut at six that morning and had then cleaned the stalls and exercised the horses before cleaning herself and dressing for the city. She confessed this and he stared at her, shocked.

"Horses?" he said. "You are a *groom*?"

And then the whole story came out, what she did: the stranded circus, her disgraceful poverty, though never disgraceful before now, but she could not stop talking to him. After listening to the tale he insisted on buying her something to eat; he took her to a restaurant on Madison Avenue, bought her a meal such as she had never eaten, and watched her consume it with evident pleasure. During the meal it emerged that she was looking for work as a typist, and he said, "This must be fate again, because I am just now seeking a typist. I have whole notebooks that must be transcribed for the law review, and later there is my thesis to be typed as well."

So they agreed. She would begin working for him the next day.

At Zurich Sonia boards the Pakistani International Airlines flight to Lahore. It is another red-eye, scheduled to arrive in Lahore at seven-thirty the following morning. She is seated next to a bulging Lahori matron of a familiar type, a real begum who, on spotting Sonia's getup and learning her name, immediately engages her in conversation or, rather, monologue. She begins in a thick subcontinental English but after the plane has ascended switches to the Mahji dialect of Panjabi. Sonia has not spoken Panjabi for some years and at first she picks up barely one word in three, but the flight is long, the begum tireless, and in a while the old synapses start firing again and she can appreciate in full the perfect banality of the discourse.

Little response is required in any tongue. The woman drones on and Sonia's thoughts are free to drift, carried back by the flow of Panjabi to her first entrance into Lahore and her first meeting with B. B. Laghari.

↬

There he was in his white suit and his British school tie, behind a rose-wood desk in his study with the fan turning slowly overhead. She stood in front of him like a schoolgirl and he stared at her out of his hawk face, although not unkindly, and said, "My son tells me you have an interesting story. I would like to hear it. Please take a seat."

She did. "What part of the story?"

He answered, "All of it, if you please. I have a great love of stories. Start with your family. Farid tells me they were performers in the circus."

So she told him a story, one that would entrance him, one that would make him have sympathy for her and, more than that, make him think of her as an interesting person, because she had nowhere else to go and he was the power. Some of it was even true.

She started with her parents. Tadeuz Bielicki is a stage magician in Poland, working in a provincial town. It's wartime. Marta Kracinski is in the Polish resistance, on the run from the Gestapo. Tadeuz saw her in the freezing little theater of some miserable town and approached her after the show; they spoke; she asked for help: You're a magician, she said, make me disappear! And he did. He used the hidden compartments of his apparatus, and they escaped to Yugoslavia. It turns out that he was some kind of minor Allied agent, and after the war, as payback, the visas appear, first for Britain, then for the United States, where Sonia is born.

The pair make their living in the small touring circuses of the era: Tadeus is a juggler and magician, Marta sews costumes, takes tickets, and performs as an understudy where a beautiful woman is needed to replace one of the regular performers. Of course she can ride, like any Polish aristocrat, so she rides the circus horses and atop the elephants; she is the lovely lady in the cat act who holds a flaming hoop: the tamer cracks the whip and the tiger leaps through it. She is of course entirely fearless; she walks among the lions like a queen, pink tights, red spangled costume, plumes nodding on her golden head.

Sonia saw she had him now; he leaned toward her, his large liquid dark eyes aglow.

The show traveled all around the country and as Sonia grew she joined its marvelous life, becoming a true child of the circus. She learned to ride a horse and to stand on its back as it circled the ring, on one foot or on her hands; she learned to sit on the elephant's trunk and be lifted high; and she learned especially her father's tricks with coins, scarves, cups, and cards. Her little hands were clever; she worshipped her father and lived for his praise; she excelled at legerdemain: her father said often he had never seen her like.

From her mother she learned everything else, especially about Marta's favorite subject, her own distinguished family: ancient, deeply cultured, wealthy, ruined.

Sonia saw this part hit home as well; she knew the Lagharis were a family like that: Indian Muslims expelled to Pakistan, heads packed with memories of lost glory.

Sonia lowered her eyes. Now a theatrical pause, a little catch in the voice: here begins the tragic part. One night, Marta is performing in the center ring. The lions and tigers are leaping about, the whip is cracking; the finale calls for a static display, all four cats must sit up on their platforms while Marta ascends an empty platform between two lions. Each lion rests a paw on one of her shoulders. Marta raises her arms in salute; her smile shines in the pink light. The lion tamer bows, a fanfare from the band, the lights go out, and the band strikes up the music for the march of the elephants.

Sonia was up on an elephant waiting in the dark wings, watching her mother finish the act. She sees Marta take her bow and the lion tamer do the same, and she is watching as, just before the first chord of the fanfare, the right-hand lion, a young male named Odin who has done this a thousand times like a lamb, leans over and grabs Marta's head in his jaws.

At this Laghari Sahib gasped and uttered what must have been an oath in Urdu. "My God," he cried, "how very dreadful! What did you do?"

"I rode in on my elephant and did the act," said Sonia. "The show must go on. They had blacked out the cat ring immediately so the crowd thought it must be part of the act, a fake, and of course the circus went along with this error, which is what they always do when there's an accident in the show."

She resumed the rest of the story. Marta was killed instantly; afterward, Tadeuz was never the same: he pined, he became ill, it was TB, he hadn't the will to fight it. He died that winter, and Sonia continued with the circus, whose slow decline accelerated after Marta's disaster. The end came one autumn in a muddy field outside Paterson, New Jersey, when the circus awoke to find the owners had vanished, leaving the troupe owed a month's pay and having sold the vehicles and livestock for ready cash.

Everyone had to find work because winter was coming. Each day Sonia took the train to New York, looking for office work. She could type but she had no references, and that was when fate intervened more kindly: she had met Farid in the park and become his secretary, and he had fallen in love with unsuitable her.

So she spent her days working for Farid and her nights in a spare bedroom in his apartment, but every Thursday she would get on a bus in Chinatown and travel with the Chinese gamblers to Atlantic City. This was from loyalty, because after her parents died, Sonia had been taken in by a large family of aerialists, the Armelinis. Guido, the patriarch, had visions of a new show based on his family act. But where would the funds for this come from? It turned out Guido knew some people in Atlantic City who ran high-stakes poker games. They were always looking for a mechanic, and Guido thought Sonia would be perfect for the job.

Here Laghari Sahib interrupted. "Excuse me, what is this 'mechanic'?"

"A card sharp. My father had taught me all kinds of sleight-of-hand with cards, you know, for amusing tricks. But the same skills can be used to cheat."

"Please explain this."

"Well, when the cards are exposed after a play, the dealer sweeps them up and shuffles the deck. It is possible to mark the location of the cards in your head and then arrange them in any order you like during a riffle shuffle: that is, arrange them undetectably while you are apparently giving them a good shuffle. You can also compensate when someone else cuts the cards afterward. If you are very good you can do what is called a double duke, where you deal the mark a very good hand, maybe a full house—tens high, say—and deal your partner a higher full house or a flush. So the mark bets heavily and you win a lot. I had learned to stack cards from the time I could hold a deck, perhaps five or six years old, so I was quite good at it. At first I refused, but we were in a bad way, all the circus people, we hardly had enough to eat, and so in the end I agreed. He said no one would suspect a girl dealer."

So she worked the weekend games in Atlantic City and no one did suspect, and the money accumulated. But unfortunately the people who'd set up the cheating games wanted more, as those kinds of people always do, and not only did they refuse to pay Guido his share but they wanted Sonia; they wanted to take her to Vegas like a portable cash machine. So one night in a cheap motel in Atlantic City, when Guido demanded his cut and the men started to beat him, Sonia had grabbed a suitcase full of cash and gone out the bathroom window, hailed a passing cab, and paid five hundred dollars for a trip to New York, where she had told Farid all and thrown herself on his mercy. And here she was.

‰

The plane is asleep. The begum has at last stopped talking—how different her story was from Sonia's own! Sonia has naturally made up a similarly harmless tale in exchange, she was an American student who fell in love with her Pakistani teacher—scandalous, of course, she could see it in the woman's eyes, but also fascinating; the woman would dine out on it for months. And there was a happy ending, for with remarkable generosity the father embraced the stranger, brought her into the family, and they were married and the young infidel became a Muslim: God is indeed merciful and compassionate, although Sonia could see that the woman had arranged her own affairs quite differently: three children, all professionals, and three carefully arranged marriages.

I attest there is no God but God and Muhammad is the messenger of God. She had recited the Shahada right there in Laghari Sahib's study, and that was all there was to it, so easy to become a Muslim; she thought she had been as good a Muslim as she had ever been a Catholic, nor were the Lagharis a particularly religious clan. She suspected that Baba had seen his son's marriage to an American as another mark of modernity and a glancing blow at the stuffy conventions of his social set. In any case, she had been taken into the family and married to Farid; had borne Theo, the necessary male heir, in Lahore; and later on she had produced two lovely if somewhat less satisfactory girls, Aisha and Jamila, and fulfilled the duties of a wealthy Punjabi matron, deferring to Noor, her mother-in-law, and worshipping her father-in-law as a demigod.

A secure enough life, constrained but more luxurious than anything she had ever imagined, her mother's aristocratic fantasies lived out on a far shore, until it ended. Until she ended it by an act of outrage. Again she shifts her thoughts away and rests her head against the cool glass and looks down into the dark. They are probably over Turkey now, only a few scattered lights mark Anatolia below. She stares at the sparse twinkles until her eyes grow heavy and she joins the other sleepers.

℞

Something wakes her in the night—turbulence in the air or in her spirit, she can't tell—but she has been dreaming. Sonia takes her dreams seriously, and while the rags of it drift from her mind she gropes in her bag for her notebook, opens it, and flicks on her overhead light. The notebook is thick, quadrille ruled, European; she has had it for nearly twenty years; its black pasteboard covers are scarred, gouged with travel and use, its pages marked with grime, wine, tears. She writes down the dream: She is in a farmyard—no, a circus encampment; there is a boy there, who is not quite right, subtly deformed, a crablike stride, his head too large, an avid look on his face. He holds up something for her inspection, a nest of tiny birds or squirrels, she can't recall which: small, warm, helpless things. He begins to smash them on the ground; they explode with soft pops and gouts of vivid red. He offers her one; she takes it and smashes it. She knows it's wrong but she can't help herself; she is carried away by the transgressive excitement. There seems to be an endless supply.

Then a presence appears, dark, powerful, a woman in a spangled costume. The odd boy cringes before her, hands over the nest. Sonia feels horrible, she wants to undo the carnage. The spangled woman embraces her and tells her she is forgiven; it was the boy's fault, and Sonia is shown the nest and sees it is still full of tiny birds. Or squirrels. The boy will be punished, but Sonia is loved; she will not be punished, only she will have to take the place of the boy, will have to be deformed too. The dream becomes horrible; the kind stern woman wants to turn Sonia into ...

Sonia finishes writing down what she can recall. It is a significant dream. She often has such dreams when she travels, travel being symbolic of the psychic journey, releasing the collective symbols up through the quotidian sludge to illuminate, to terrify, sometimes to foretell. She wonders what old Fluss would say about it. Not much, he never interpreted but pushed and prodded her into doing the hard work, and she recalls how she resented him and loved him during that year in Zurich at the Jung Institute when he saved her life and became her mentor. Remembering him and neat, snowy Zurich, she smiles; she is going to the opposite of Zurich now, where the archetypes walk the streets in the blazing sun of day. Is this also the reason for taking this somewhat inconvenient flight, instead of going straight from London? She switches off her light, puts in earplugs, falls asleep again, and wakes only when the cart comes around with tea. It is six-thirty in the morning, and an hour later they land in Lahore.

꒜

She sees Rukhsana waiting for her on the other side of the customs barrier, looking nearly the same, a woman ten years younger than Sonia, maybe grown little plumper over the last year or so, startlingly like her father in drag. She is wearing a dark Western suit and blouse with a chiffon scarf draped loosely around her head as a sop to propriety. Expensive sunglasses perch above her broad brow. She is a reporter for the liberal English paper *The Daily Times* and has seen no reason to quit this job just because she is married and a mother.

The two woman embrace warmly. Rukhsana says, smiling, "*Lahore Lahore hai*," Lahore is Lahore, which is how residents of that city greet one another after a long absence, as if to affirm that there is no other place fit to live in. Rukhsana fights Sonia over Sonia's bag, wins, links arms with her, and carries her out of the terminal. A sprightly blue Morris is parked right at the curb, in violation of traffic regulations but protected by a large card on the dash that reads PRESS in English and Urdu. The two women drive off into the insane Lahore traffic, west on Durand Road, through the death-defying intersection by the Lahore Press Club, past the Provincial Assembly, and down Egerton Road to the Mall, which no true Lahori ever calls by its new properly Muslim name.

While they drive, Rukhsana talks; family first. The children, Hassan, Iqbal, and Shirin, are fine in health and accomplishments; husband Jafar is fine too, in health and accomplishments; she speaks also of his defects, which are numerous, both physical and mental. Her brother Nisar remains chubby and sly, mistresses galore, richer than ever although a little nervous now, trying to maintain his place on the spinning circus ball of Pakistani politics. Seyd, the baby brother, recently made major, still a pompous pain in the you-know-where, dreadful politics, a supporter of the recently deposed general. Sonia asks what Nisar thinks about the conference they are organizing, the reason Sonia has returned to Lahore.

"Oh, you will hear that from his own lips. I suppose he is as interested in it as in anything else that does not immediately put money into his pocket. Or votes."

From which they pass to a précis of the current political situation in her nation and the familiar defects of the foreign policy of the United States.

"No wonder you are losing!" Rukhsana says. "Pakistan is stupid enough, but we are all Bismarck compared to you. Why is this, Sonia? People ask me, because I was educated in America, so I am the expert. What can I tell them?"

"You can tell them that not one American in ten thousand can distinguish Iraq from Iran or find Pakistan on a map. We are not a subtle people."

"Oh, you can say that again! The British were bad enough, but at least they made the effort to understand. They spoke the languages, they knew the history, and still they made terrible errors. But nothing like this. Our country is coming apart, and it all comes from what you are doing. You know how I know this? My brother is moving funds out of Pakistan, so when it collapses we will not be standing in our shirts. This is what we've come to."

She pauses to honk at a motor rickshaw driver who has swerved into her path, a long blast nearly unheard over the continuous honking of the other traffic.

To change the subject, Sonia observes, "The traffic has gotten worse. I wouldn't have believed it possible."

"Yes, Lahore is unlivable now, but we still live here. I'm glad I have this Mini. Jafar wants me to use the Mercedes, but can you imagine trying to steer that boat in this mess? Look, there is the High Court. Do remember when you used to drive us children to meet my father there when we had half days at school, and he would take us to the bazaar for ice candy?"

"Oh, yeah, and other sweets. He had a sweet tooth himself, and your mother would always complain that he was ruining our appetites. And he would let himself be berated and give us a sly wink."

A painful silence after this; then Sonia said, "I'm sorry about your mother. I'm sorry I didn't come to the funeral."

"Yes, you should have been there with your husband. She was not very nice to you, but you should have come."

"I didn't think I'd be welcome."

"Oh, what nonsense! Because of something that happened twenty-eight years ago? A book? But *now* you come."

"I'm sorry," she says, and is.

"I forgive you," says Rukhsana, "although others may not."

"Does that include Nisar?"

"Oh, no, with Nisar everything is negotiable, even forgiveness. Otherwise we would not be here. Move your ass, you stupid monkey!" This is shouted out the window at a van that has stopped in a traffic lane to make a delivery.

"Besides, in the family you know what we say: *Sonia Sonia hai.* You are horrible but we still love you. Here we are."

She honks at a gate in a whitewashed wall and a servant opens it and they drive into an enclosed yard shaded by two arching *peepul* trees, the paving of the courtyard scattered with blue jacaranda petals.

Sonia climbs from the little car and pauses. "I assume he's in your father's library."

"It's *his* library now," says Rukhsana, bitterness touching her voice; Sonia walks slowly down the crushed stone path to the house.

℞

When Sonia comes out of Nisar's house an hour later, the heat and the ordinary odors of Lahore—spices, jasmine, traffic fumes, sewage, rot—feel welcome, like real life. Nisar has fitted the house with air-conditioning, including a back-up diesel generator, and he keeps his office as cold as his heart. Or so Rukhsana says as Sonia slides into the car.

"It wasn't too bad," says Sonia. "He said we can use Leepa House for the conference. He'll call ahead to the caretakers."

"In return for what?"

"As you predicted, he wants a meeting with Bill Craig to pitch a scheme for making computer components in one of his Karachi plants. It's a good deal."

Rukhsana starts the car, drives out the gate, and turns north, up to the Mall and beyond it to Ravi Road, passing through heavy traffic along the western edge of the old city. They are going to the studios of Ravi TV to record interviews.

Rukhsana asks, "And how did he treat you? Was he nasty?"

"No," Sonia says wearily, "he was polite and businesslike. He doesn't seem to dwell in the past."

"As I do, you mean?"

Sonia sighs. "Honestly, Ruhka, I don't want to dredge up old family fights or take sides."

Undeterred, Rukhsana continues. "That's easy for you to say. You don't have to live here. Farid is the eldest son, he's supposed to be the head of the family, but Nisar always gets his way, and—"

"Yes, but as you well know, Farid has no interest in being the head of anything. Look, there's the cemetery. Can we stop for a little while?"

"We'll be late."

"Please."

Rukhsana twists the wheel violently and cuts across two lanes of traffic, prompting a chorus of horns. She spits out a skein of curses in the street language of Lahore, and turns into the gate of Gau Shala, the old burial ground of the city.

She parks. Sonia asks, "Do you know where they are?"

"Of course," says Rukhsana stiffly, and leads the way through the thick, dusty, monumented ground, walking ahead like a soldier.

Sonia stands for a while in front of the simple stone slabs that mark the graves of her father-in-law and her two daughters. Jamila would be thirty and Aisha thirty-four, she calculates, but this thought does not summon a sense of loss. Like the markers, that part of her heart is stone now. Grief among traditional Muslim women is operatic, but they are not allowed to attend funerals. They wail at home. She wailed in the streets of Zurich when she heard the news, when someone (it was in fact Rukhsana) remembered to call her. Farid had suffered a complete collapse and was hospitalized for a month after the event. She has long forgiven him, for that lapse and for what happened at about that time to her son. The many catastrophes in her life have marked her, but not by the manufacture of grudges. She recalls a Yeats line Baba often quoted: "Cast a cold eye on life, on death. Horseman, pass by!" She does that, has done that, for years. The two women walk back to the car, arm in arm. Rukhsana's cheeks are wet, but she makes no comment.

After they have taped their interviews, they drive to the Avari Hotel on the Mall. Sonia checks in and learns from the desk clerk that the rest of the members of the conference, except for William Craig, have already arrived. The Avari is a perfectly anonymous luxury hotel of the type found in any major city. One might be in Singapore or Toronto, Sonia thinks, upon seeing her room, except for a discreet plate marking the *qibla*, the direction of Mecca for prayers. She has selected this hotel on purpose; there will be culture shock enough for the Western conferees when they get to Kashmir.

Sonia orders tea from room service and sits on the bed with the conference papers spread about her. The conference is called "Conflict Resolution on the Subcontinent: A Therapeutic Approach." The meeting is actually her idea, although the official sponsor is Amin Yakub Khan, a wealthy Pakistani, once a friend and protégé of B. B. Laghari and now the president of Pakistan's largest charitable trust. Sonia and he had put together the conference in a flurry of phone calls and e-mails last winter, keeping a low profile because of its controversial nature, designed to discuss the possibility that the kind of ethnic and confessional violence that had characterized the region since the exit of the British Raj was in fact a kind of mass insanity and that the analytical tools that had been used to help many individuals recover from madness might be adapted to the peacemaking process. When Sonia first suggested the project, Amin had laughed and said it might be easier to flood the Indus, the Ganges, and the Brahmaputra with Prozac.

But she wore him down. It would be interesting, she said. It's always nice to meet people who are not in the tedious mold of one's everyday acquaintances, it would be a week out of sweltering Lahore in May, and it would be a sort of memorial for Baba, who was always a partisan of East-West cooperation and a lover of peace. They were coming up on the twenty-fifth anniversary of his death. They could write a dedication to him when they published the proceedings. So he agreed, in the end, and it only remained to choose the participants and obtain funding.

For the latter, Sonia made contact with William Craig, the famously eccentric telecom billionaire, who owned a vast ranch on the New Mexico border not far from where she lived for part of the year. His foundation had been supporting a network of mental health clinics in the region for years; she worked at one of these, and they sat together on the organization's board. They were not exactly friends, but she was able to reach him directly and thus to have her proposal stand out from thousands of others. He immediately agreed to pay for the thing but he wanted to attend, which she had not expected. Perhaps he would cancel at the last moment.

The other invitees were a mixed bag. She had let Amin pick them, insisting only that at least one of them be an Indian national. He'd selected Manjit Nara for that slot, a psychiatrist and ethnographer from Delhi, an expert on Kashmir. Besides him, they invited Father Mark Shea, a Canadian Jesuit who had been prominent in several Latin American peace negotiations; Porter and Annette Cosgrove, American Quakers, who had worked to end the conflict in Angola and written some important books on nonviolent political change; and Karl-Heinz Schildkraut, from Zurich, an old friend of hers and a psychotherapist with a long-standing interest in the history of India and Pakistan.

When the funding came through, Sonia had called her sister-in-law. Rukhsana would be a good choice for the conference rapporteur and could also help Sonia back into the good graces of the Laghari family. Rukhsana had suggested another invitee, Harold Ashton, an Englishman, a former foreign service officer and an expert on the diplomatic history of the subcontinent, who also accepted. Sonia drinks her tea, when it comes, and reads the papers prepared by the attendees until jet lag seizes her and she sleeps.

She awakens three hours later to the sound of the *azan*, the call to Maghrib, the prayer at sunset:

> God is great God is great God is great, I attest there is no God
> but God, I attest Muhammad is the messenger of God, make
> haste to prayer, make haste to welfare, there is no God but God.

The wailing song floats in from a nearby mosque loudspeaker and cuts through the international air-conditioner hum. She has not prayed as a Muslim for a considerable time, but after hearing the azan she finds herself almost reflexively reciting the *du'a*, the supplication before prayer, and then she ties up her hair in her scarf and goes to the bathroom and performs the ritual ablution, washing her feet and her hands and arms and running her wet hands over her face.

She takes the prayer rug the hotel provides and arranges it to face the qibla. Silently she goes through the proper intention for the Maghrib prayer and then enters the prayer state easily, without friction, the ritual words and the prescribed movements, the hands up next to the face, the hands folded, right over left on the belly, the kneeling, the full prostration, the cycle of one *raka'ah* after another until the three ordained for the sunset prayer are done. Sonia has always been religious in her own fashion. In America, she attends a Catholic church in whatever neighborhood she finds herself, as her mother trained her to do. In Muslim lands she follows her adopted religion. In Europe she presents herself as an adherent of Carl Gustav Jung. Nor is it hypocritical, she thinks, not merely a case of When in Rome. She doesn't see why her worship should be restricted to one faith, especially as she is devoted to all of them and believes that God understands this peculiarity and approves.

Now it is time to get ready for the reception. She showers, washes and dries her hair, dresses in her best shalwar kameez, a black number shot with silver threads, and arranges a black silk scarf over her short hair. The wall mirror shows her a thin, slight woman with graying black hair atop a deep-tanned face out of which shine dark, bright eyes. She thinks she looks like an American in costume, so she takes a breath and shifts the tension in her muscles, especially the muscles of her face. She looks again and smiles shyly for effect. Now she is a Muslim lady, probably a Pathan, at home in Pakistan. She is very good at this, and it gives her an absurd and infantile pleasure.

The hotel has provided a small room set up with a large round table and a bar. As she enters, Sonia sees Rukhsana speaking to a couple of men. One is a slight elfin figure in a cheap tan suit, his blue eyes bright and cheerful behind rimless glasses, his narrow skull clothed with a thatch of sand-colored hair going gray; the other towers over him, a really huge old man, his face decorated by a noble nose and a white brush mustache. Rukhsana gestures her over and embraces her; Sonia can smell liquor on her breath, although the glass she is holding appears to be fruit juice. Rukhsana introduces the smaller of the two as Father Mark Shea, S.J.

"And of course you know Dr. Schildkraut."

"My dear Sonia," Schildkraut says, embracing her. "You have not changed even a little bit."

"Nor have you, Karl-Heinz," she replies, a lie. Schildkraut is twenty years her senior and now looks it.

"We were just discussing religion," Rukhsana says brightly. "Perhaps Sonia can add something. She claims to be a Muslim and a Catholic simultaneously."

"That must be fatiguing," says Shea. "You actually practice both?"

"I practice," Sonia replies, "but I'm not good enough to perform either on the professional stage."

Father Shea laughs, throwing his head back so that he almost faces the ceiling. Sonia thinks he must be a man who likes to laugh but doesn't get much of a chance in his ordinary work. He says, "I'd be interested in how you get the statement in the Qur'an—that God begets not, neither is He begotten—to play nice with the clear declaration about the nature of Christ in the Nicene Creed."

Sonia says, "Well, clearly either the Church Fathers were mistaken or the Prophet, peace be unto him, was mistaken, or else—and I think this is most likely—that any statement about God falls short of the ineffable truth and therefore neither is mistaken, but we mortals are incapable of resolving the differences with our puny minds."

Shea laughs again, more loudly. "Thus you defy the theologians. Well, good for you! We Jesuits, you know, are supposed to be all things to all men, but you put us to shame."

A man comes by with a tray of drinks. Shea snags a champagne; Schildkraut and Sonia take soft drinks; Rukhsana ignores the man and his tray entirely. Instead she is looking across the room at something, and when Sonia follows her gaze she sees that it is a man heading toward the bar. Rukhsana mutters a brief excuse and walks off in that direction. Soon she is deep in conversation with the man, whom Sonia now recognizes as Harold Ashton, the face familiar from a photograph on a book jacket and a similar one she acquired as she organized the conference. As is usual with authors and their book jacket images, he is jowlier and more worn by time than the image testifies but still handsome in the English style, with a bony high-colored face, long dark hair combed straight back and hanging raggedly over his collar, a strong nose and jaw, and pale imperial eyes. He leans over Rukhsana from his considerable height and touches her arm lightly from time to time.

Now uniformed waiters are passing through the room and laying the first course on the tables, so the conferees do the usual shuffle to find their place cards. Sonia has seated herself between her fellow convener, Amin Yacub Khan, and the Indian psychiatrist, Manjit Nara. Of the other seats, two are occupied by Rukhsana and Ashton, two by Porter and Annette Cosgrove, two by Father Shea and Dr. Schildkraut, and one is empty, its plate of tiny kebab appetizers cooling. Sonia turns to Amin and asks, "Have we heard anything from Craig? Is he going to make it?"

Amin finishes off a kebab, sucking its stick clean. "Yes, as a matter of fact, I heard from him just now on my mobile. His plane is approaching Lahore International as we speak, and he will be here before dinner is over, God willing. I've arranged for a car to pick him up and also a police escort."

"That was thoughtful," says Sonia.

"Well, yes, we would do the same for any Pakistani billionaire—do we have real billionaires in Pakistan? I suppose we must. I know you have billionaires in India, Manjit."

The two men banter across Sonia for the next few minutes about the relative wealth of their two nations, which persons have hold of it, and whence it comes. Then the talk moves to globalization, how the free flow of capital is affecting the two countries, how after a long period of stagnation the Pakistani economy seems to be taking off, like India's did in the final decades of the past century, and what this means for their future relationship. Sonia listens to them talk, glad that they seem to get along so cordially. She is pleased also by their contrast in size, the opposite of their respective nations. Amin is a bear with the shaved head and aggressive mustache of a Mughal aga, a solid cylinder of expensive cloth stuffed with the best Punjab beef. Dr. Nara is a wisp, Gandhi-gaunt, with a flat modest face and the huge liquid brown eyes of a lemur. His motions are quick and precise, birdlike, but like a nice bird in a children's cartoon, not a bird of prey. The two men seem to be purposely avoiding anything controversial, speaking generalities. Sonia hopes the conference will not be all speaking generalities.

Then Porter Cosgrove speaks up from across the table. "What do you think the effect of all this will be on the Kashmir situation? I mean, there's no point in becoming increasingly prosperous if you both continue to spend such an absurd amount of your nations' wealth on arms. Especially as you're each other's only likely enemy. I mean, doesn't anyone in either country think it's absurd, given present conditions? It's like France and Germany in nineteen hundred, you know? Anachronistic."

There is a pause. Then Amin chuckles and says, "Well, you are certainly outspoken, sir. But the actual situation is not so easily dismissed."

Ah, thinks Sonia, they have already stumbled on the K-word.

"No, the plight of the Muslim majority of Kashmir is not so easily dismissed," Amin continues, and then smiles down at the Indian. "But perhaps Dr. N and the rest of us can solve it where so many have failed."

"Stranger things have happened," says Nara, with his own shy smile. "Although I cannot help but agree with what Mr. Cosgrove says. My thought is that until we recognize violent nationalism as another sort of mental disease we will get nowhere."

"Yes, but where is the cure?" says Amin. "Who has ever cured it?"

"Well, as to that I have some theories," the Indian replies, "which I daresay you will hear enough about during the coming week to make you quite ill with the sound of my voice. And while I am not such a fool as to credit the inevitablity of progress, I think that if one hundred years ago you had predicted that Western Europe, the greatest hotbed of nationalism of that era, the very source of the contagion, if you will, would be converted less than a century later into what amounts to a single great country, with a tiny armaments budget and utter peace among all its parts—well, people would have thought you a lunatic. But it occurred. And it can occur in South Asia as well."

"Yes!" says Amin, "I will drink to that," and he lifts his glass of soda water.

Sonia appreciates the way Nara has defused the topic and she turns to him and draws him out on his practice of psychotherapy. While she chats, her glance falls frequently across the table, where Rukhsana is sitting next to Ashton and directing nearly all of her energetic attention to him, the two heads leaning at each other like flowers in a bed.

Nara seems to pick up on her thoughts. Quietly he says, "Mrs. Qasir seems to have made a conquest."

"Yes, or the other way around. Of course, they are old acquaintances."

"Yes, Harold knows everyone. I myself know him reasonably well."

"I don't. What's he like? I know his books, of course."

"Yes, a great expert on the subcontinent is Mr. Ashton. As he should be. He is almost the last of his breed, you know; he descends from nabobs, from the white Mughals. I believe his family came to India in the eighteenth century, and they waxed great; his ancestors doubtless ruled mine with an iron hand, though in the famous velvet glove. Very fair, but stern. When we kicked them out in 'forty-seven, some few could not quite give us up, and so we have the Harold Ashtons of the world. Speaks all the languages, of course, chats in the bazaars and the chancelleries with equal aplomb, and informs the world of our mysterious Eastern ways."

"You sound like you don't care for him."

A delicate shrug. "Nothing personal, I assure you, and at least he is not an ignoramus in his chosen field. It's only that...have you ever noticed that when an English person of a certain type—I mean the type represented by Ashton—enters a shop kept by an Indian or a Pakistani, here or abroad, something happens to the shopkeeper or clerk? As soon as that pukka accent emerges the air changes, the clerk stands straighter, he becomes more attentive, perhaps a bit fawning, and other customers are ignored. The clerk is in a sense hypnotized by what we must call racial memory. Colonialism still inhabits our unconscious, even now, fifty years on."

"And yours too?"

He smiled and sniffed a laugh. "Oh, yes, mine too. I find I start sounding like an old babu, and my English becomes a little tangled. It is humiliating."

"How do you know him?"

"I am one of his informants. He considers me an expert on the psyche of the various subcontinental races. Which is, I suppose, why I am here."

He abandons this uncomfortable subject and addresses Amin. "This really is an excellent curry, properly spiced. I always find, don't you, Amin, that when Westerners are at a dinner they always make the curry tastelessly bland."

"Yes, indeed!" says Amin. "But not here. All the Westerners must be vetted for proper curry, or they can't come. Mr. Cosgrove, for example, is passing the test. I see you are enjoying your dish, Mr. Cosgrove."

Cosgrove swallows his mouthful of incandescent mutton and says, "Yes, delicious. We both like spicy food, don't we, dear?"

And without waiting for his wife to reply he launches into a presentation of his thermophiliac bona fides. They have been in Haiti and Angola, in Mozambique and Guatemala, all zones where people have learned to mask the taste of slightly off meat with chilies. He actually quotes this theory, unconscious of the pained expressions growing on the faces of the Pakistani and the Indian at the table. "We eat anything," he asserts with a smile.

A man who enjoys the sound of his own voice, observes Sonia, as Cosgrove reels out a series of amusing and gently self-deprecating anecdotes about culinary disasters in the world's hellholes. His wife listens with the sort of gelid expression often seen on the faces of loyal wives with older loquacious husbands, even though much of the deprecation involves her: skinning and cooking the capybara, mistaking ipecac for baking soda, and so on.

Sonia has not had much to do with Quakers before now and had imagined them to be severe, taciturn, and dreamy. Apparently not, if the current example is typical. Annette, however, is a little dreamy. Perhaps, she muses, Cosgrove is a Quaker by marriage and Annette is the real thing. Cosgrove has the bland, unobtrusive, forgettable face one sees often in white America, the fruits of genetic homogenization. Annette is from the same stock, but hers is unforgettable; she does nothing with it, but nothing is required: the cheekbones and the clear, lightly tanned skin are marvels. She has a wide mouth, unreddened by lipstick, but red enough without, and an endearing little overbite that enhances her smile. They are both blue-eyed, with fine corn-silk hair, Cosgrove's neatly trimmed in a ten-dollar haircut and Annette's kept long but bound up in a crown of braiding. She is slim; he is not, perhaps from eating everything. Sonia wonders what their intimate life is like, whether they have a family or if, instead, they have devoted their all to the peace of the world.

After Cosgrove runs down, the conversation becomes general. They speak of Lahore and the problems of Pakistan; then the issue of America, the great bull of the planet, and how it can be made to tread more lightly upon our common earth. The curry is cleared away and a deep-fried *rohu* follows, a local fish much prized by the Lahoris, bland and emollient with greases, a rest stop for flaming pharynges, and then a chicken tikka that proves even hotter than the curry. Sonia sees that Annette has become flushed and sweaty but continues to eat manfully, like her husband, soaking up the fiery stuff with handfuls of naan, wisely abstaining from ice water.

The chicken is cleared and dessert arrives: *gulaab jamun*, pyramids of deep-fried dough balls soaked in rose-flavored syrup. Sonia tastes it and smiles at Amin.

"You remembered," she says.

"Yes, you reminded me when we were setting this up how Baba used to serve it to his guests, and I thought it would be fitting. Ah, I see they are wheeling in my cross, so to speak."

Hotel staff have rolled away the bar and set up a podium. When the dessert is finished and the coffee poured out into tiny cups, Amin rises. He is a good speaker, strong-voiced, and the style of his subcontinental English reminds Sonia powerfully of Laghari Sahib, which, together with the taste of roses in her mouth from the gulaab, brings a stab to her throat and a pressure of tears to her eyes. He speaks, in fact, of that gentleman, describing him to those in the assembly who did not know him, his charity, his integrity, his devotion to peace and lawful ways.

It is a bland speech, and short, and after it Amin introduces Rukhsana, who takes his place at the podium and speaks briefly about how happy her father would have been to see this assembly and its mission and to know it was going to pursue its deliberations at his beloved country house. Then some logistics for the following morning: they will drive to the Leepa Valley in a convoy of two minibuses and a car. It will be a long drive but it will pass through some of the most beautiful scenery in the world, and this rarely seen, because the area is normally barred to foreigners. The government has arranged for transit through the military zone.

As she speaks, a thin, ungainly white man dressed in a pair of wrinkled chinos and a short-sleeved blue shirt walks into the room. He peers around through thick glasses, as if unsure that he has come to the right place, until his gaze falls on Sonia, at which point he nods and walks over to her and sits down at the table.

"You missed a good dinner, Bill," she says. "Spicy, just what you like."

He smiles and rolls his eyes. William Craig famously lives on cups of yogurt and jam, washed down with Diet Coke.

"I'm sorry I'm late," Craig says. "I got tied up in Dubai. You know how it is."

"Exactly. I've often been tied up in Dubai."

Rukhsana has seen Craig enter and now she announces that the author of the feast has arrived after the feast and would Mr. William Craig like to make any remarks? Craig declines. Rukhsana finishes her logistics talk and answers a few questions, after which the meeting breaks up, but not before all the attendees have gathered around Craig to pay their respects. It is perfectly feudal, Sonia thinks, and quite appropriate for the country. As she leaves, she observes Rukhsana and the Englishman, Ashton, again in close conversation. Perhaps there is something going on there, perhaps Rukhsana had a liaison with this man. Sonia understands that she herself has little interest in this sort of thing and is always the last to find out who is sleeping with whom. She hopes it will not affect the conference and is oddly saddened by the knowledge that her sister-in-law may be betraying her husband, a kind but emotionally oblivious physicist. Why the mullahs want to lock up all the women, she thinks as she leaves.

🙢

Their departure is scheduled for dawn the next day and she knows she should try to sleep, but she is restless and she is in Lahore. On impulse, she takes from her suitcase a garment she has not worn in over twenty years, a black burqa, and drops it over her head. Now she is invisible. Once she had a fight with her sister-in-law about burqas. Sonia had said casually that she didn't mind them and Rukhsana had snarled, "Oh, it's fine for you to say that, you're a tourist. But imagine having it forced on you!" She understood Rukhsana's point and was suitably abashed, but she doesn't think she is a mere tourist. A tourist belongs somewhere and goes elsewhere for amusement, but she belongs nowhere and amusement is not why she has come to Lahore.

She slips out of the hotel, a darker shadow in the gathering dusk.

When she enters the alley at the side of the hotel she hears Amin's voice. Coming closer, she sees him standing next to a wonderfully painted minibus, one of a pair parked there, and speaking to a squat, balding man in a mechanic's coverall. She waits in the shadows and listens. This is the man Amin has hired to take them to Leepa. Amin calls him Hamid.

They are negotiating the fee in the old-fashioned manner, as formal as prayer. Hamid offers his two sons as drivers and guards and five cousins and in-laws as additional spear carriers. Amin says they don't need a platoon of guards, nor do they need their own small army. After all, they will be traveling through one of the most militarized regions in the world, and there are real soldiers everywhere.

Agreeing to cut the crew down to the sons and two cousins, they shake hands, and Amin hands over a pack of English cigarettes to show grace and favor. Sonia slips away, curiously heartened by the scene she has just observed, the more so because she has done it in secret. Eavesdropping has been a habit of hers since childhood, born in the circus, nourished by Lahore.

She tours the streets, still bustling even now, distributes alms to beggars, and then, suddenly exhausted, returns to her room and packs for the following day. She lays out her traveling shalwar kameez. This is made of stain-resistant burnt-almond fabric and has numerous small pockets in it, some sewn in unlikely places. She fills these with various items, chosen from long experience in traveling through South and Central Asia: a Swiss Army knife, a small flashlight, matches in a waterprooof case, hard candy, a compass, a sewing kit, and, for luck and remembrance, a new deck of cards and a Sufi rosary. She strips and crawls naked between the stiff hotel sheets and is almost instantly asleep.

The next morning, just after sunrise (a tomato-red smear barely visible through the scrim of brown filth in the air) they all go, sleepy and cranky, to the buses. Although there are only ten people to transport, Amin has decided to engage two minibuses, to allow for stretching out a little and to leave room for the considerable load of supplies necessary for a week's stay in an isolated area. On Sonia's bus are Amin, the two Cosgroves, Father Shea, and Dr. Schildkraut. Hamid's son Azar is the driver, and Hamid sits in the shotgun seat with a stockless AK stuck in the footwell. Leaning against an old Land Rover are the cousins, who will lead the way, and Hamid's other son, mustached and hung with webbing gear and toting the same kind of weapon. Ashton, Nara, and Craig are on the second bus with Hamid's other two sons as driver and guard, but Rukhsana is not; she calls at the last minute. She has an emergency meeting: someone is suing her about a story she wrote and she has to attend to it with her employer. She will follow in her own car; of course she knows the way perfectly well.

So they set off under a yellowish-pink sky, traffic blessedly light at this time of day, and soon they are on the famous Grand Trunk Road, which stretches from Kabul to Calcutta, heading north out of Lahore. As they pass through the outskirts of the city, Schildkraut says, "So this is the Grand Trunk Road! I had somehow imagined that it was, so to speak, *grander*."

Sonia says, "Yes, it would be a county road in the U.S. or Europe, but then it's over four hundred years old and hasn't been widened since. Except for the motor vehicles, Kipling would feel right at home. On the other hand, you'll think it pretty grand when we get up into the mountains, where the standard is a one-lane dirt track."

They drive on amid frantic honking traffic. Before Rawalpindi, they turn onto a secondary road, barely a lane through high brush, that Hamid promises will be a shortcut. Dust soon coats every surface. The heat builds up and there is hardly any breeze coming through the windows because of the closeness of the roadside vegetation. The passengers fall into the somnolent, jouncing discomfort of the road traveler in South Asia. This too would be familiar to Kipling.

Now the road is perceptibly rising, leaving the dusty plains behind. Immense mountains loom violet in the distance and evergreen trees appear on the low ridges. They pass through Azad Pattan and Rawala Kot, Bagh and Dungian. The air clears, it becomes positively cool. In the backseat, Schildkraut sags, gently snoring. The Cosgroves converse softly or read. Father Shea is snapping photos with an expensive-looking digital camera, exclaiming at the increasingly sublime landscape. Past Chikar they enter the Jhelum Valley. Shea's exclamations increase and Schildkraut awakens to join in expressions of wonder at the steep slopes, covered in cedar, fir, and pine, and at the crystalline air, the waterfalls, and the rushing river far below.

Past Naili they enter the restricted zone and stop at a blockhouse, where Amin gets out to converse with an officer and show him papers. When he returns, he says, "We should be at Leepa House by three at the latest. It is just twenty kilometers up this road."

"This road" turns out to be a track cut into the side of a mountain. Riding on it is like flying a small plane, so vast is the view; at one point they have to back up almost a kilometer to allow for passage of a convoy of troop carriers and armored vehicles.

They enter the Leepa Valley. The road makes a sharp hairpin bend to the right. The Land Rover in the lead disappears around it.

Now comes a flash of orange light. The shock of an explosion shakes the bus, followed by a cloud of acrid smoke. Hamid cries out an oath and stamps on the brakes. They come around the bend and there is the Land Rover on its side, burning. Hamid yells in despair and jumps from his seat. He runs wailing toward the ruined vehicle and is immediately cut down by a burst of automatic fire. Azar unlimbers his AK and leaps out of the bus. He gets off a string of shots and then he is hit too and falls next to his father.

More firing. Sonia tells her fellow passengers to get onto the floor and they do. Everything seems to be moving in slow motion. A random bullet shatters one of the side windows. The firing stops. They can hear the wind sighing in the cedars and the sound of running footsteps.

The side door of their minibus is flung open and a man stands there. His face is masked and he points a Kalashnikov at them, shouting in Pashto: Out, out!

They stumble from the bus and stand in the smoke of the burning car. Sonia sees that the other bus is being similarly treated. The windshield there has been blown out and Hamid's two promising sons are still in their seats, slumped and dead.

More masked men come down from the hillside. The passengers are surrounded, their hands are bound in front of them, and they are pushed into a close group by the rifle butts of their attackers. Other men loot the baggage in the second minibus.

Then the passengers, the former conference on mental disease and violence in the subcontinent, are roped into a coffle and marched off the road up a footpath. No one on either side has said a word after the initial rough commands. The conferees have left, for a time at least, the domain of speech.

3

The army is generous with dope, I'll give them that; I walked out of there with enough OxyContin to stagger a platoon. I know a number of my fellow wounded sell it on the street, but not me. I take it as prescribed, no more, no less, whether I need it or not. I am not supposed to drive or operate heavy machinery when dosed, but I take this as a suggestion and not a rule, so I drove my rental home to my parents' brownstone in the pricy Washington neighborhood called Kalorama. The house was empty, my father being at work and my mother in Lahore. I live with my parents on the few occasions when I find myself off duty. It's cheap and saves a lot of hassle and it's traditional.

I changed into sweats and opened a beer, which I also wasn't supposed to do on the dope, and plopped down in front of the TV. I do this a lot now. Really, the worst thing about being wounded is the agony of time passing with nothing to do—no, the second worst thing. The worst thing is being weak, slow, off balance, the body no longer the spear and shield it once was. It gets me to the core, makes me nasty at times. I'm not a good patient.

Also, it's hard to get involved in American television now. There's no war here; all that horseshit about everything being changed by 9/11 lasted around two months and then back to sports and game shows. I don't know, maybe that's all right; maybe obsessing about money and sex and celebrities and celebrity sex and the teams is a sign that the terror has failed to bite, which is great, but if it's no big deal why the hell are we breaking the army into pieces over it? Once again, not in my job description. But still, it's another thing that makes me snap and get pissed at my fellow Americans.

I switched over to Ary, the Urdu channel out of Pakistan that my father likes, and I watched a news program, mainly about corruption scandals and unrest in the tribal areas and whether there were going to be elections and would they be honest or not. They interviewed a general who lied about the recent killing of a terror leader outside of Quetta; the guy's car vaporized and the general said it was a Pakistani army op, although children in diapers knew it was a Hellfire missile from a CIA Predator drone. Not even that good of a liar; his eyeballs flickered and you could see the sweat on his face.

After that came sports, cricket and football, and a longer piece about a *desi* golfer on the pro tour, and after that a talking-head thing and I was about to switch over to Geo, looking for a cultural program, maybe hear some ghazals, when I saw my mom on the screen with an interviewer.

He introduced her as Sonia Laghari, which is her usual nom de umma, a writer and psychologist, a Pakistani-American, daughter-in-law to the late, much-mourned jurist B. B. Laghari, and one of the organizers of a conference on solutions to the current mess in the country. No mention of her famous books. There was text on the screen; my reading Urdu isn't up to much anymore but I thought it said that this was a tape of an interview made the previous day in Lahore.

They were speaking Urdu. The interviewer's name was Jamil Babar Khan, and he started off by complimenting her on her Urdu, and that was as nice as he got because, although Mom was in full Pakistani rig, he started right off on America and its many sins against the Muslims.

My mother smiled at him and agreed. America was not good for the umma. Mr. bin Laden was perfectly correct in his goals, although his methods were deplorable, and in her considered opinion he was destined to fry in the hottest flames of Hell for causing the deaths of women and children and of many, many Muslims. Therefore, she said, America should completely withdraw from the Muslim world. It should close its embassies and prohibit its citizens from working in Muslim nations or trading with Muslim nations. It should expel from its shores all foreigners from Muslim nations. This would eliminate the source of any conflict with Muslims and save a great deal of money, since aside from Muslim terrorists, America had no natural enemies. It should be of no concern to America how Muslim nations governed themselves.

"But what about the oil, Mrs. Laghari?" the man asked.

My mother made a dismissive gesture. Oh, the oil. That's not a problem, she said. America and the West could become independent of Middle Eastern oil in a decade if they put their minds to it, using existing technology. The price of oil would collapse and the principal exports of the Muslim world would go back to being dates and rugs. The Saudi princes would become simple camel drivers again, no one in the West would care what happened in Iraq or Afghanistan or Pakistan, and all would return to the wonderful days of the early caliphate. Men would be simple and just, women would be chaste, sharia law would prevail throughout the umma and Osama bin Laden and his followers would no longer rage. When that happened, Westerners could return as tourists to the quaint crumbling cities of the new caliphate. They could buy rugs and dates.

Jamil Khan said, "Forgive me, madam, but that is a ridiculous position and patronizing as well. It assumes that the majority of Muslims worldwide are supportive of the mullahs and people like bin Laden. They're not. They want the same freedoms and the same opportunities for self-improvement as people in the developed nations."

"Yes, I believe that too," my mother said, grinning, "with all my heart. I'm afraid I was being a bit facetious. Forgive me. But the truth is that America has poisoned the well through her clumsiness and stupidity. As it stands now, every Muslim father who wants his daughter to get an education, from Morocco to Bengal, can be portrayed as un-Islamic and a tool of the Americans. If you want democracy and free speech and secular law, that's un-Islamic because America wants all those things too. It demoralizes the whole umma. But if America became less aggressive, the mullahs would fall on their faces, because they really cannot provide people with what they want. The Iranians would throw them all out next week if they couldn't keep pointing to the Great Satan. Thousands of Pakistanis tolerate the Taliban, thugs who practice a religion utterly inimical to the Pakistani tradition and spirit, and why? Because American troops are occupying Afghanistan and Iraq, and killing and torturing Muslims, and bombing civilians in Pakistan itself."

"But I thought it was the American withdrawal after the Russian war that enabled the Taliban to take over Afghanistan."

"Yes, and so what? No American would have given two pins about how Afghanistan was ruled if bin Laden had not been based there and attacked America, and he would not have attacked America if we hadn't been up to our armpits in the politics of Muslim nations. It is not our responsibility to decide how others should live, and whenever we try we fall into the most arrant hypocrisy. And lies. The Americans say, 'Oh, we're fighting to preserve our way of life; the mujahideen hate our way of life, just like the communists.' But as bin Laden says, al-Qaeda has no interest in changing the Western way of life; he doesn't attack Sweden. All he wanted from the 9/11 attack was the withdrawal of U.S. troops from Arabia, and he got that almost immediately. He won; the war is over. Why are we still fighting? Look, I am a Pakistani *and* an American. I love both my countries, but one of my countries, America, is incapable of rational action in the other country. When little boys fight with sticks, the mother must separate them and keep them in separate rooms for a while, and that is what I am suggesting."

"The Israelis would not be happy with what you suggest, and as we all know the Americans do what the Israelis want."

"Yes, except when they sell arms to the Saudis," she said. "I'm tired of hearing about Israel. Israel has the only modern economy in the Middle East, the most powerful army, and over two hundred nuclear weapons. Israel can take care of itself. What keeps that ulcer raw is not only the land hunger of the Israelis, about which we can do nothing, but also the stupidity of the Palestinians, and I would say here that America is fortunate in the Palestinians, because otherwise America would be the stupidest nation in Middle Eastern affairs."

"You think that wanting freedom and an end to a brutal occupation is stupid?"

"Of course not, but look at how they resist! They could have had their own state and an end to the occupation twenty years ago by using the same methods that were successful against the British, right here where we're sitting. India defeated the greatest empire in history using Gandhian noncooperation and nonviolent resistance. You think that Israel's nasty little empire cannot be defeated in the same way? But they don't do that, they love their posturing and their face masks and the rifles waving, and the people are controlled by bandit gangs who are constantly selling one another out to the Mossad. It would be ridiculous if it weren't tragic."

The interviewer seemed not to want to pursue this line so he asked her about the conference and they talked about that for a while, and it was here I learned that they intended to meet not in Lahore, where there was at least some security, but in Leepa House in Pakistani Kashmir, which was a long fly ball from the Northwest Frontier Province, otherwise known as Jihad Central.

The rest of the interview was about who she was supporting in the coming elections, but I hardly listened, and as soon as it was over I switched it off and dialed my mother's number on my cell phone. It was past midnight in Lahore but I didn't care.

I got a not-available recording and left a message. I was pretty calm, considering that she had just pissed off on international television every bunch of armed maniacs on the planet except the Basques. What was she thinking? Did she *want* to get blown up?

As soon as I had that thought it hit me that maybe she did, maybe that was part of what made her Sonia, what my father called her trapped-fox part. I had that too, if I was honest with myself; I got it from her and from how I was brought up, maybe an adrenaline deficiency, the whole dicing-with-death thing. Or maybe not. I know guys who do sport jumping, motorcycle racing, whatever, but it's not like that. There has to be an opponent; death has to show himself in human form; you have to beat the angel on its own terms.

These old thoughts were boiling into froth, and under them the thrill of real fear. I kept calling through the evening, the last one at eleven-thirty, and still nothing, even though it was now morning in Lahore. My mother never turns her cell phone off during the hours she's awake. I left a message demanding an instant call-back. Then I called my Auntie Rukhsana, who keeps hers on even when she's asleep. Also no answer. I left a similar message. Then I took another pill and had another beer, after which I conked out in my room upstairs. I'd been out a little over three hours, by my watch, before the ache and thirst and the need to go to the can got me up, which was a pretty typical night for me, and when I was up and around I heard the sound of the TV in the living room. I recalled switching it off, which meant that my father was up.

He was sitting on the couch watching Pakistani cable, and he didn't take his eyes off the set when I came in, which was funny to begin with because my father is a formal guy, always stands up and gives a hug and a kiss when we happen to meet. I sat next to him on the couch and asked him what he was watching. The screen showed a couple of talking heads, the usual morning anchorperson and a guy with the familiar sleek and sneaky look of a Pakistani pol. He didn't answer me and I looked at him and saw that tears were streaming down his cheeks and I knew what it was and cursed.

"Something happened to Mother," I said.

He pointed mutely at the screen: a shot of a mountain road with a burnt-out Land Rover on it and two empty minibuses with their doors hanging open like a dead bird's wings and Pakistani military swarming around them, looking pretty helpless. There were big patches of what had to be blood on the ground and the glitter of spent brass scattered around.

The announcer was saying that a party of foreigners had been abducted on a road in Pakistani-administered Kashmir; they had no names yet and no knowledge of what had happened to them. Then back to the anchor and the interior ministry official, who dispensed empty assurances and more ignorance.

I said, "They don't know it's her group."

He replied, "But we do. My sister just called and woke me up with the news. It is Sonia's group without question. Rukhsana recognized the minibuses. She would have been there herself had she not been delayed. She was entirely devastated." He stared for a moment at the repeating images on the screen. "Apparently they killed the drivers and the guards."

He threw his arms around me and sobbed and I comforted him as best I could, which to be frank wasn't all that much. A breakdown like the one he pulled after Baba and my sisters were killed wasn't what I needed now.

But in a few minutes he recovered himself, went away to the bathroom, and came back, composed again and grave.

I asked, "Babu, did you know she was going to Lahore? She called me and asked me tell you."

"Of course I knew. Your mother is a wonderful woman, but she derives an infantile pleasure out of sneaking. She kept the whole thing quite dark, as she imagined, but naturally Rukhsana has kept me apprised throughout. As has Nisar. I told him I did not approve of allowing them to use the house at Leepa, but he ignored me. As he usually does, of course. He very much wanted a meeting with William Craig, and I understand this was part of the arrangement."

"Who?"

"William Craig, the electronics billionaire. It is astounding, you know? Your mother has no regard for her own safety but surely a man of such acumen might have considered it foolish to ride without adequate security into the most terrorist-infested place on earth."

"Maybe he wanted the thrill, like those rich guys who like to break records, ballooning around the world and like that."

"Perhaps," he said and gave me a funny look. "But his character is not, after all, our most pressing concern at the moment. You seem to be taking this disaster very well. Aren't you worried about her?"

I shrugged and answered, "I don't know. Maybe I'm in shock. It doesn't seem real yet. Maybe it's just a ransom gang after Craig and they'll let the others go."

I kept thinking that, telling myself it was true, and we sat there for hours together, not speaking, one or the other of us going for food or to the john, the other staying put, watching the tube, until the kidnappers delivered their tape and the station played it. There she was with the others, surrounded by masked men with guns. There was a statement by a man in a ski mask. After the routine condemnation of the infidel Pakistani government and their crusader allies, and the routine grievances, the murder of innocent civilians by the military forces thereof, the torture of prisoners by the authorities and the Americans, he declared that the present act was meant to provide hostages against these infamous behaviors. The captives would receive decent treatment, unlike the brothers rotting in American and Pakistani prisons, but should any more innocents be massacred by the infidels, on each day that such an event took place, one hostage would be executed. God is great! All the masked men waved their weapons and shouted this too, and the camera did a slow cruel pan across the strained and exhausted faces of all the hostages.

My father was like ice then, strangely enough; it was me who howled and cried like a baby on my father's shoulder. And while I was crying, with the tears and snot running down my face, all I could think of was them taking her out on some hard-baked patch of ground and cutting her head off with a sword. I'd seen it done in Afghanistan more than once. The fuckers who cut people's heads off now aren't that good at it; it's a lost art, one of the many things the Muslims have forgotten how to do, not like the glory days of the caliphate, when they had professionals. It turns out that beheading with a sword is harder than you would think.

My father comforted me awkwardly, like you do a child who's bumped his nose. We're not close. I still blame him for the way he behaved during the previous family disaster; forgiveness doesn't come easy for me. So I pulled away from his hugs, a little abruptly, and we sat there watching the tenth rerun of that fucking tape, me thinking it was the last sight I'd ever have of my mother alive.

After a while he picked up the remote and muted the television. He said, "Will you be all right? I want to make some calls."

"Who are you calling?"

"Well, family first. Nisar may know something, with his connections in Islamabad. We'll see if he can find out anything that's not for public consumption. Rukhsana too. She has sources as well, from her work. And Seyd, although I doubt I'll get anything from him outside of the official line from ISI, especially if . . . no, I won't think about that, not yet at any rate."

I asked him what he didn't want to think about.

"Well, you know these mujahideen groups up in Swat and Kashmir and so forth all have Inter-Services Intelligence connections. Suppose an ISI-sponsored group carried out this kidnapping?"

"But why wouldn't that be a good thing? Seyd could help get them out."

"Oh, Theo, I'm talking about *Seyd*. He's my little brother and of course I love him, but he is a monstrously ambitious and ruthless man, who has always felt that having a famous apostate for a sister-in-law put a blot in his copybook. I don't say he would be happy to see Sonia decapitated on television, but he would not weep bitter tears either. No, we will get no help from Seyd. My greatest hope is that he will not actively hinder plans to rescue them, if any."

"I should go over there," I said.

"And do what? Wander through the hills calling her name? Don't be foolish, Theo!"

I gave him a hard look, but he stared right back at me, which was a bit of a surprise. I guess in the lives of fathers and sons there's a moment when the kid understands his father is not some kind of god but just a guy and then he has to decide whether he likes him or not, and, if not, how he's going to handle it. That came a little too early, in my case, and while I've always treated him with respect, more or less for my mother's sake, I've always considered him something of a pussy, and fairly early on I arranged another father for myself, a man of unimpeachably violent barbarian credentials, every little boy's dream.

I thought Farid would've crumpled under this disaster too, but he hadn't; he was standing tall. It was me crumpling, and it pissed me off.

"You know, I have some contacts too, in the hills," I said, snapping.

I couldn't read the expression on his face. Shame? Sorrow? I've never really talked to my father about what I did between the ages of nine and seventeen, up in Afghanistan, but he knew, or could imagine it, and I know he thought it was his fault, my entire fucked-up life. So that was between us, like a big black sack of garbage stinking up the room, and there was a silence and then he looked at his wristwatch and said, "I must call now. Will you be all right?"

I said I would and he left and I turned on the sound again and flipped through the channels. After doing this for a while I learned that the group claiming responsibility was called al-Faran, which some expert commentator explained was a blowback from the Kashmiri jihad, an organization the Pakistanis had set up to give the Indian occupation grief but which had now joined with the general insurgency in the Northwest Frontier Province. The guy said that this bunch was distinguished for their media savvy and had pioneered a small but growing videotape niche market: decapitations of kidnapped Westerners. Wonderful.

The hostage tape produced a lot of media activity, mainly because of Craig, and we thought it was a good thing for us because no one was paying much attention to the other hostages. My mother's peak of fame had been a couple of decades ago, and she had never gone in for the public intellectual business: no interviews, no talk shows, no magazine articles about the plight of women in Islam, and so forth. She hadn't even had an author photo on her books, so the upshot was that for all anyone knew she was a regular Pakistani-American writer and no big deal, and we were anxious to keep it that way.

A senator who wanted to piss off the administration about its policies in South Asia organized a hearing about what, if anything, the government was going to do about the three-and-a-half captive Americans—Craig and some missionary couple and Mom—and they brought in a few undersecretaries who told elaborate lies—What, a rescue? Oh, shit, no, senator! We respect the territorial sovereignty of our ally Pakistan; we would never think of going in there even if we knew where they were, which we don't—and they stood a major general up who underlined that point: there's nothing harder than a rescue mission in hostile territory, especially with faulty intel; remember the Iran fiasco, we don't want another one of those, oh, no.

As it happens, the unit I work for was founded right after that fiasco just so we *could* do shit like that on the sovereign territory of whoever, but they didn't ask me and anyway we don't officially exist.

꩜

Within twenty-four hours after the hostage tapes aired, we understood that as far as the Pakistanis and the Americans were concerned, the hostages were on their own. Nisar reported a stir running through the highest levels of the Pakistani government; generals had approached him in strictest confidence about moving large sums of money offshore. Everyone felt the loss of face. A party of foreigners, including an American billionaire, snatched in daylight from the heart of a district supposedly under tight army control? Questions in parliament, angry editorials from opposition papers, everyone a-tremble about what the Americans were going to do.

Which was nothing, as it turned out. Rukhsana found out from a usually reliable source in the U.S. embassy in Islamabad that the Pakistani government had been assured that no incursion whatever was being planned or even considered.

The worst thing about an event like this, besides the hell of not knowing what's happening to the victims—the loved ones, as they always call them—is that life goes on. Traffic flows, the noble buildings still stand whitely there in Washington, people go to their jobs and eat and to bed, and after the shock is a little past, so do the not exactly bereaved, carrying on in a suffering somewhat worse than an actual death in the family, because of the torture of hope.

Me too. I thought I would go nuts if I had to hang around the house, so the day after they showed the hostage tape I went to my regular PT session and sweet-talked Brenda Crabbe into filling out a report that said I had got all the benefit out of PT that was there to be got and, if the docs agreed, I was good to go.

٭

The following day I drove down to Fort Belvoir in northern Virginia to return to my job. Fort Belvoir is a sort of military mall that the army uses to house units that they can't figure out where else to put, stuff like the Defense Logistics Agency and the Institute of Heraldry. *Soldier Magazine* is there and so is the Tactical Intelligence Support Detachment, which is us. You would think that an organization as secret as the TISD would want to stay anonymous, but no, we have a sign and a shield too, a sword cutting a chain and a Latin motto. I showed my special ID to the guard at the desk and he ran it through his computer. My army records are completely fraudulent. I'm supposedly serving in some regular unit somewhere if anyone wants to look, which suits me okay. I'm kind of a fraudulent character to begin with.

I went in to see our first sergeant, whose name is Cheney, Ronald D., although everyone calls him Dick and blames him for Iraq, in one of those boring jokes that stick to any unit. Big guy with a narrow horse face and a dimple in the middle of his chin, a lifer like me. The first thing he said when I went in there was, "What's wrong with your eyes? They're all red."

I said something about getting soap in them in the shower, and he asked me how the PT was going, and I said I should be yelling hoo-ah in a matter of weeks. Then I asked him where our guys were and he said, "Team One's in Iraq; Team Two's in Afghanistan; Team Three's in transit somewhere, they didn't tell me where yet, but I'm guessing Pakistan;

and Team Four's on stateside rotation for rest and training. Did you hear about Claiborne?"

"Not hurt?"

"Shit, no. He's leaving. He came in here and I had his reenlistment papers all ready and he said to run them through the shredder; he was going to take a job with some security outfit. Blackwater or one of those."

"That's fucked up," I said. "God, Buck Claiborne! Why would he do something like that?"

"He said they were going to pay him over a hundred grand a year plus benefits, and no army chickenshit either. He didn't say anything to you?"

"No. He was always talking about telling the service to go fuck itself, but I thought it was just talk. Well. That's a kick in the ass."

"Roger that. Funny he never mentioned it. You guys were pretty tight."

Yes, we were. Buck Claiborne saved my ass when the house fell on me. He was probably the largest person ever to successfully complete Special Forces training, which tends to favor moderate-sized people like me. I was a little hurt that he hadn't told me he was getting out. I don't have many close relationships with the men I work with, but I thought he was an exception and I was obviously wrong. I wanted to change the subject.

I said, "I guess we weren't that tight. By the way, has there been anything down about this terrorist kidnap yet? The Craig thing?"

Cheney said, "No, nothing. That's up in Pak, no?"

I said it was. Our unit is descended from the one that rescued General James Dozier in 1981, when the Red Brigades snatched him. Organized for tight coordination of comint and action, we led the carabinieri commandos right to the apartment where Dozier was being held and they rescued him without firing a shot.

If no one had alerted us on the kidnapping it was more bad news. If it wasn't us it was probably nobody, which meant the U.S. was really not going to lift a finger.

"Could you keep your ears open on that, Top? I'd like to know if anyone gets an alert on an op, anything they have going to spring them."

He didn't reply for a moment, looking me over. "Sure, no problem. What's your interest?"

"Oh, one of the victims is someone I know," I said, and then I said I'd sure like to go downrange and he said, What, you can't wait to kill again? and I said, Yeah, it's an all-consuming need. He laughed and said I was getting pretty short myself, and was I planning to do a Claiborne when my enlistment ran out next month? and I said, Oh, sure, like they'd let me go. As a matter of fact, reenlistment is a formality with me; the army has this little catch that they can extend you indefinitely if you have a vital skill essential to national security, which I do with my languages and cultural knowledge of South Asia, so I might as well get the re-up bonus. I am a well-paid slave soldier, like a Mameluke or a janissary.

We bullshitted for a while about army stuff, and he gave me some paperwork to fill out, and as I was leaving he said, "You know, I saw an old pal of yours the other day, Captain Lepinski, only he's a major now. They assigned him to JSOC staff, the fuckhead."

I said, "I'm glad to hear it. You can always trust the army to reward good work. What've they got him doing?"

"I don't know. Shuffling paper. Personnel assignments, the usual shit."

I thought that was a good thing to learn about Lepinski, because the Joint Special Operations Command staff is the outfit that cuts all our orders. I said, "Well, he probably won't kill anyone doing that."

I sat down at a spare desk and looked over the crap that had accumulated for me during my time away from the unit, the usual army chickenshit, but there was one item that drew my interest. It was an evaluation form for a course I'd been to just before the operation that had got me hurt, a course about how to handle a situation where terrorists had got hold of a nuclear weapon.

⁊

I recalled it pretty well, although it must've been six months back. I'd been called in to see Captain Stoltz. Brian Stoltz is not a bad guy for an officer, he's a wiry little son of a bitch like me, fair but cruel. I wouldn't say we like each other, but we get along. He's a runner—set some kind of record when he was at the Point—and likes to take us running carrying heavy equipment. His nickname in the army is Flyin' Brian, but we usually say the Fly. Mine is Ice, as in Ice Tea. Billy's was Rowboat. Is.

I knocked and walked in and saluted and he sat me down in a side chair and asked me how I was, by which I knew I wasn't in trouble and he was going to stick me with some pain in the ass that someone had passed down the line. So after the chat, he said, "Congratulations, you're our new CBR NCO."

I said, "Thank you, sir. I appreciate the honor."

He said, "And fuck you very much. There's a course, starts tomorrow."

I said, "What kind of course? I already had CBR training."

"This isn't a bullshit course," he said. "It's about nuclear weapons, very high level. I'm going too."

I asked him if I should be worried and he said the brass was and had sent the word down that every unit with clandestine insertion capability had to have one officer and one NCO down to the company level familiar with the design and appearance of nuclear explosives.

He said, "I can see their point. I've never seen a nuclear weapon. Have you?"

"Sure. They're pointy at one end and have a little screen with red numbers on it counting the seconds down."

"Uh-huh, and they have the spooky girl's voice, *This device will detonate in . . . forty-three seconds . . . forty-two seconds.* Well, apparently not, so they started this course. Be here at oh-six-thirty tomorrow, BDUs, bag for three days."

"Where's it at?"

"They didn't tell me and I didn't ask. It's local because we got ground transport."

The next day we drove off into the Virginia woods to some no-name facility. They had us in pretty nice quarters, a campus kind of arrangement, with maybe fifty people taking the course, three-quarters military and the rest various kinds of civilians. I had the sense it was a CIA site, but I could be wrong on that. Stolz went off to a higher-level course with the officers, and I went to what I guess was the dumbed-down version for the NCOs.

Basically it was all about nukes, a little history with some films the general public doesn't get to see: some background about how they work, how an amateur would go about making one, some sketchy stuff about how, if we found one, to make sure it didn't detonate, various means of sensing the radiation they give off from a distance, and some information about the government operations devoted to preventing bad guys from getting nukes and what would happen if they did get one and we had to go in and take it away from them.

They had a guy named Morgan come down from the National Security Agency to talk about communications intel—he ran a special section at NSA that did nothing but listen to intercepts and filter them for any sign that nuclear materials had gone missing—and a woman from something called the Nuclear Emergency Support Team, which was responsible for recovering lost or stolen nuclear material, and which I'd never heard of, and she went on about the various forms of nuclear material and how hard or easy it was to make something that would explode from the various types. A man from Langley gave a briefing about al-Q capabilities in this area, and about the ease and difficulty of stealing nuclear material, and how the bad guys would handle it, and there was a special mention of terrorists who were supposedly nuclear experts, and there were pictures, in case we ever ran into one of them at the mall. The main one I recall was named Abu Lais, but they didn't have a picture of him yet.

It was pretty interesting in a not very real way, and the impression I got was that a terrorist nuke was not all that likely, but if it happened then all bets were off; it would immediately become the only thing on the agenda of the U.S. government, balls to the wall, and so on. On the trip home me and Stoltz were in the back of a van with some SEALs and other guys we didn't know and they were all sacked out and he turned to me and said, "What was the NCO course like?"

And I told him, and he said the officers' course was like that but also they talked about the tactical aspects; if you knew some terrorists had a bomb, how would you go in there and get it out? It was an impossible problem, really, and they were still working on the doctrine.

"You see why," he said.

"Oh, sure," I said. "If the bad guys hear you coming they'll flip a switch and take out everything within a couple of miles, including all your guys and the whole civilian population."

"Right. So you'd have to have totally accurate pinpoint intel about where the bomb was, and you'd have to get a team on that spot without anyone raising an alarm. It would have to be perfect, no do-overs, first time right. I mean, you've been on enough missions—when did anything ever go perfect? I mean, we can do tactical surprise, fire superiority, sure, but that wouldn't be enough. We would have to be on the bomb before they knew we were there. I don't think it can be done."

"It can be done," I said.

"How?"

"You'd need a guy on the inside, to pinpoint the device and keep the bad guys away until the good guys got there."

"Right. And how are you going to infiltrate a nuclear terror cell?"

"I don't know, sir," I said, "but at least it's doable in theory. For that matter, we pass as bad guys all the time. But any other way is instant mushroom cloud, game over."

He thought about that for a while and then he said it was above his pay grade, and we starting talking about sports and shit.

Now, checking through the little boxes that rated how valuable you thought the course had been, I recalled it pretty well, and especially that conversation with Captain Stolz. By the time I got back to my folks' place I had the sketch of a plan that might get my mother out of where she was with her head still on her neck.

I was anxious to talk to my father about it, not so much because I wanted his advice or because I thought he'd encourage me, but because it was the kind of thing I couldn't pull off alone. Or maybe I wanted him to talk me out of it. I'm not much of a planner.

When I walked in he was sitting in the living room with Mohammed Afridi. My father said, "Oh, good, Theo, you're back. Come sit down and listen to what Mo has to say."

Afridi is about the same age as my father, wears his hair long, and has a short graying beard. He's a Pashtun of the intellectual class, a fairly rare bird in America, and he teaches at Georgetown. He's supposed to be one of the big academic experts on Afghanistan and the Northwest Frontier Province. My father thinks he worked for the CIA during the Russian jihad, but he doesn't talk about it to us. Which is fair because we don't talk about my own involvement in that war either.

Afridi was talking about the situation around where my mother had been taken, and he rolled back a little to bring me up to speed. He confirmed what we already suspected, which was that the group involved, al-Faran, was pretty much a creation of the Pakistani ISI, and that up until now they had been operating in Indian-occupied Kashmir. Why they had suddenly decided to kidnap a group of foreigners was something of a mystery, but Mo thought that they never would have done it without a wink from the ISI.

"So why did ISI wink?" I asked.

He shrugged and spread his hands. "Well, that would depend on who in ISI you mean. Like all of Pakistani society it's riven by factions, some more aggressive than others, some religious, some out for the main chance. That they have kidnapped a billionaire suggests a ransom is in the offing, although, as you know, kidnap for ransom has never been a Pashtun specialty. Hostages, yes, but taking people and exchanging them for money is a little . . ." He sniffed and touched his nose.

"Punjabi?" my father said, and the two of them laughed.

"You have said it, my friend, not me. No, ransom is not a Pashtun thing; it goes against the idea of hospitality. It is hard for a Pashtun to give someone food and shelter and then sell him. There is a price of twenty-five million dollars on bin Laden's head but no one has collected it, and the same rule applies, in general, to this kind of kidnapping. It is different from stealing women for wives, which was practically the Pashtun national sport in the old days. On the other hand, Alakazai is a peculiar man."

"Who?" I asked.

"Bahram Alakazai, the leader of al-Faran. I knew him during the war. His mother was Punjabi, so perhaps that explains it."

My father said, "Explains what?"

Afridi was silent for a moment, stroking his beard. "He was not a man at peace with himself. You know, the Pashtuns have many vices but one vice they have avoided, and that is the divided heart. You cannot, of course, trust a Pashtun, but you can trust a Pashtun to be himself, to do the things demanded by the Pashtun code, to seek revenge, to offer hospitality, and so on. Alakazai was not like that. We could never quite understand his goals. He seemed to enjoy playing with people just for the sake of the game. And he was good at it, a master manipulator, far more subtle than the Pashtuns, Pakistanis, and Americans with whom he typically dealt. An educated man, naturally, he studied in both Pakistan and the U.K., and I believe he was in America for a time, in the eighties."

My father said, "He seems an unlikely fellow to lead a mujahideen band."

"Oh, for that he has Idris Ghulam Khan, his field commander, an entirely different sort, the usual fanatic. Bahram negotiates with the Pakistanis and plans grand strategy and Idris does the shooting. It seems to work, and now they have pulled off this coup. It is just the sort of affair that Bahram is good at. He likes to keep the world guessing."

"Can you get to them?" I asked. "Find out what they intend to do with the hostages?"

He frowned and shook his head. "I can leave messages with people who might be in contact with them, but I could not guarantee that al-Faran would receive them. I feel so helpless in this matter."

"You could do something," I said, and my father looked at me with interest.

"Anything in my power."

"You consult with the U.S. government, don't you? On politics among the mujahideen?"

He smiled faintly and replied, "Officially, no, I'm afraid. But should I be asked to consult, what would you like me to do?"

"Someone must be following the terrorist chatter about this kidnap, in the CIA and the NSA. There can't be that many people fluent in Urdu or Pashto or Dari working on this end. If you could find out who they are and what they're talking about over there, it could give us a better idea about what's going on."

After that there was some polite protest from Afridi that he was a very small fish and could not pretend to penetrate very far into the guts of the national security establishment, but I pressed him a little and he promised to keep his ears open. I believed him. He's one of the many my mother has charmed.

When he left, my father asked me why I'd made that request and I told him it could be helpful in our plan.

"What plan?"

"The plan to get the U.S. Army to invade Pakistan and rescue Sonia."

And I laid it all out for him, just like it had popped into my head while I was filling out that eval form on the conference in the Virginia woods. It would involve my going to Pakistan, yes, but not just wandering around at random, and it would have to involve our family. I thought he would object, being a lawyer and having that legal-procedure cast of mind, but he didn't. He thought it was a good idea, and I thought this was another example of what so often happened when my mother was in the picture, people cranking it up to do for her what they never thought they would or could do.

4

Shortly after six in the morning, with the sun just a pink promise over-head, Cynthia Lam left her apartment on California Street in the Adams-Morgan district of Washington, D.C., entered her Taurus, and began her commute. She worked at Fort Meade, Maryland, the head-quarters of the National Security Administration, and it would take her a little more than forty minutes to drive there at this hour, instead of the ninety that would be required by a later departure. Cynthia liked living in the city and did not mind rising before dawn. She went to sleep early; like many young people on the make in Washington, D.C., she had no appreciable life outside of her job.

Cynthia Lam was the product of a Vietnamese father and a French-Canadian mother. Her father, Colonel Lam, late of the air force of the late Republic of Vietnam, had emigrated to the United States after a spell in a reeducation camp and an extremely trying voyage on a small boat, and like many boat people he had cast ashore in the capital of his former patrons. Like many of his colleagues he had been corrupt, but not very corrupt, for the money he had managed to sequester was just enough to buy a small dry-cleaning establishment on the wrong end of Massachusetts Avenue, a mile or so southeast of Capitol Hill.

The shop did not flourish but survived anyhow, and toward the end of its first year of operation it received the custom of a pretty young woman named Celeste Moreau, a French-Canadian employed as a nanny in the wealthy zone. Colonel Lam was ordinarily morose behind the counter but he had an eye for beauty and a certain look in women's eyes, which Celeste had, and one day the woman forgot herself and addressed him in French, at which he lit up and answered her in kind, and the kinship of shared language led to other things, and eventually to the birth of the girl Chau-Thuy, who called herself Cynthia.

The small family lived above the dry-cleaning shop, but their life there was not a happy one. Colonel Lam had never got over not being a colonel anymore, with an orderly and a staff to command, and Celeste bridled under the quasi-military discipline. She thought she might as well have stayed in Montmagny and endured the fists of her dad, so it often happened that she ran from him into the streets of southeast D.C., where crack was as common as dog shit and there were plenty of enterprising fellows to teach her how to smoke it and how to pay for it too. The colonel wasn't having any of that, and at the age of three little Chau-Thuy found herself motherless.

The next Mrs. Lam was a plump, dull Vietnamese girl obtained through an ad, who knew how to follow orders and press shirts. She raised Cynthia with care but without much love, reserving her affection for her own baby, which unhappily never arrived. Colonel Lam's contribution to this rearing consisted of ignoring the embarrassing fact that Cynthia was a girl. He applied rigor and discipline and was rewarded with a brilliant and beautiful not-quite-son, who won all the prizes and got a full scholarship to Stanford, the most distant school that made an adequate financial offer. (She did get offers from schools closer to home, but she trashed them before her father learned of these successes; at seventeen she was already an expert in disinformation and the keeping of secrets.)

Now Cynthia worked as a translator for NSA, although she did not translate from the Vietnamese. Her usual joke was that although she was Vietnamese and a translator, she was not a Vietnamese translator. Her languages, besides her native English and Vietnamese, were Modern Standard Arabic, Urdu, Dari, and Pashto, and she could do Persian in a pinch as well. This was an unusually rich and useful suite of tongues for an American citizen to own. Cynthia had planned it this way, starting in her days as an undergraduate at Stanford, for it answered the question of how to distinguish herself from among all her frighteningly bright peers, to make C. Lam into a unique product that someone would want to buy.

She'd been amused and contemptuous when the dorm chatter turned to selling out. No one, it seemed, wanted to sell out—all the computer geniuses, the science geniuses, the artistic geniuses said they had a horror of selling out, or so they claimed—but Cynthia wanted nothing more than to sell out, although at a very high price. And since the only thing she had going for herself, besides her startling Eurasian looks, was a facility with languages, and since in the late nineties it was obvious that the languages that would count in the future were those spoken in the contested areas of the earth—the Middle East and South Asia—she had set herself to master them.

This had worked as planned. NSA snatched her up right out of graduate school. She was now the senior translator in her section, but she did not intend to remain a translator forever. She intended to ascend through the GS ranks to the Senior Executive Service and beyond.

Because she understood that if she knew the languages she would know the secrets, the subtle hints, the nuances that could only be communicated in a native tongue, and this would give her an unassailable advantage over her monoglot rivals in the perilous world of national intelligence. Eventually she would be one of the mandarins who actually ran U.S. foreign policy behind the shadow-puppet politicians. She would write the critical memos, she would accompany the figurehead on the secret mission, she would propose the options, trade or boycott, peace or war, carefully crafted to force the choice she desired, she would leak the career-destroying indiscretion to the press, she would exercise the power of the anonymous, from which there is no redress.

She counted rising before dawn and working eighty-hour weeks a trivial price to pay for this future, and such thoughts were frequently in her mind on these mornings when she drove through the half-deserted streets of the capital. She had been with NSA for three years and had made herself indispensable to her section chief. It was time to think about making a move. She'd had several tentative offers but she wanted the move to be a big one, and for that she needed a coup, something that would make her name known to the people who could really advance her career.

She was considering idly what sort of thing that would be, and how she might position herself so as to be more likely to have access to something like that when her cell phone rang, an austere chime.

She groped in her bag and pulled it out, frowning with annoyance. She was not a good driver, she was over the speed limit on the Beltway, and her exit was coming up, but when she looked at the glowing face of the thing and saw who was calling, she pushed the button.

"What is it, Ernie? I'm in traffic."

"Drive faster," said the phone. "And could you meet me in my office before you talk to anyone else?"

She agreed, suppressing her curiosity about what had caused Ernie Lotz to call her at that time in the morning, which he'd never done before. But naturally she hadn't asked him to elaborate. Employees of NSA don't discuss work on their cell phones. She increased her speed as much as the traffic allowed, perhaps a little more than that, and so arrived quickly at the Fort Meade Military Reservation, or the part of it that its residents call Crypto City, the headquarters of the National Security Agency. She parked her car and entered the security lobby of the enormous black glass Headquarters/Operations building. She put her blue card into the access control terminal, passed under the big NSA shield, and walked through a set of hallways until she came to Building OPS-1, an A-shaped 1950s building where the actual business of the NSA was accomplished, the working quarters of thousands of cryptographers, eavesdroppers, signals analysts, and linguists like her. She reached Lotz's office, knocked, and Ernie Lotz appeared, with a big smile on his pink face that faded a little when he saw the expression on hers.

"Okay, what's so important?" she asked.

He ushered her in and relocked the door.

"Abu Lais has surfaced," he said.

"What! When? Are you positive?"

"I'll let you decide. Have a seat, I'll bring the files up."

They sat next to each other on rolling chairs while he punched his computer keyboard. "This intercept came in last night from Fort Gordon, and NSOC routed it here. Obviously, the filters picked up the name mention, and—"

"Did they get both ends?"

"Yeah, they did, and that makes it more interesting. He's talking to Khalid al-Zaydun."

"Holy shit! Are you sure?"

"Wait a second, I'll let you listen to the sound files." Cynthia slipped on a set of headphones. He pressed several keys. A conversation entered her headset.

It was the refined product of an immense eavesdropping program, millions of cell-phone conversations a day sucked out of the Asian ether by satellites and beamed down to the antenna array at Fort Gordon, Georgia, inspected at microsecond speeds by the most sophisticated filtering software in the world, reanalyzed by secret machines and programs, and then sent, as an ultimate distillate, to Crypto City's own ultra-secure intranet. Cynthia and Ernie were both part of NSA's W Group, the Office of Global Issues and Weapons Systems, one of the big units that had replaced the old geographical-specialty divisions the agency had used during the Cold War. W Group was largely about international terrorism; within W Group was the N Section, a multidisciplinary team devoted to tracking terrorist efforts to obtain nuclear weapons. N Section was rich in comint experts, who were constantly improving the collection and filtering apparatus. At their command, spy satellites shifted orbit and recommendations were generated that might send teams of spies to penetrate fiber-optic cables on the other side of the world. But ultimately, the information thus collected had to pass through the human brain of someone who spoke the languages the terrorists spoke, and this sort of brain was the very rarest commodity at NSA's disposal. Cynthia was such a commodity, as she had planned, and was much caressed in the agency.

The voices she was now hearing, filtered and cleaned to the technological limit, supposedly belonged to two of N Section's prime targets. The first was Khalid ibn Hammad al-Zaydun, a longtime associate of Osama bin Laden and the leader of al-Qaeda operations in Pakistan. The second man—who, she noted, spoke Modern Standard Arabic with an accent—was known as Abu Lais. They had no idea what his real name was, but they knew that, three years ago, someone of that name had tried to make off with nuclear material from a former Soviet depot in Tashkent. That plot had been foiled, but there was no reason to believe that Abu Lais had stopped looking. Since that time trickles of information about the man had come in, from informants, from prisoners, from the web chatter that NSA combed assiduously. He was a Pashtun, of Pakistani origin. He had fought against the Russians in the eighties, and so must now be around fifty. He was educated as an engineer, probably somewhere in Europe or America. He had continued the association with al-Qaeda first formed during the Russian war but seemed to have no operational responsibility. It was suspected in the U.S. intelligence community that obtaining a nuclear weapon was his sole task.

It was a short conversation. She listened to it once straight through and then went through it in short segments, seeking nuance.

> AL-ZAYDUN: Abu Lais, it's good to hear your voice, but this is dangerous.
>
> ABU LAIS: I know. I will be brief. Tell them I have achieved the first phase.
>
> AL-ZAYDUN: That's wonderful. Is it definite, then?
>
> ABU LAIS: Yes. I will have the package in my hands within three days, if God wills.
>
> AL-ZAYDUN: The sheikh will be very pleased. Do you need anything?
>
> ABU LAIS: I will in some small time—money, men, and vehicles at the location we discussed. I will let you know.
>
> AL-ZAYDUN: Courier only.
>
> ABU LAIS: Of course. Good-bye. God is great!
>
> AL-ZAYDUN: God is great! Good-bye, and the blessings of God be on you.

Cynthia slid off the headphones. "This is hot," she said. "Abu Lais! And the sheikh they mention has to be bin Laden. Does Morgan know yet?"

"He might have transcripts from Speaker ID by now, but you know what they're like."

Cynthia did. Speaker ID was NSA's application of the Berger-Liaw Neural Network Speaker Independent Speech Recognition System developed at the University of Southern California, designed to pluck words or phrases from electronic cacophony and convert them into printed text. But in the nature of things, there were a lot of false positives, innocent conversations, and jokes swept up, and these still had to be perused by humans. It was a work in progress, and NSA's human linguists thought it would be a while before it replaced them at NSA.

"So this catch wasn't off Speaker ID?"

"No," said Lotz, "we got it the old-fashioned way: the bad guys slipped up. They've got a million cell phones and they usually use them once and toss them, but we had a watch on the one al-Zaydun used to receive that call. I think it came from a number on a SIM card that got picked up in a raid on a safe house in Kandahar. Maybe they didn't realize it was compromised. It's hard for them to keep ahead of that kind of thing. I mean, they're fairly smart, but they're a couple of hundred guys and we're the United States."

"Don't let that get out, we'll lose our jobs."

"Yeah, but that's why they call it asymmetric warfare. We can win on every single day but one and then we lose. Meanwhile are you thinking what I'm thinking? The *package*?"

She nodded. "What's the point of origin of the cell phones?"

Lotz turned to his computer screen. "It looks like al-Zaydun's is out of a cell tower in Peshawar. Abu Lais's call came out of Kahuta."

"That's not good," she said, and they stared at each other. Ernie's look was bleak, but she felt a growing thrill: shameful, of course, but there it was. Kahuta is the Los Alamos, the Oak Ridge, of Pakistan, where they refine fissionables and manufacture the weapons.

There was something about a secret like this, Cynthia thought, looking into Ernie's face, that was like nothing else, almost an intimacy: they were probably the only two people in the country right now who knew about this. Ultimately, only a few people would ever know about it, but just now, for these few moments, it was theirs alone—or, rather, they shared it with a few violent men in Pakistan, whose voices she had just heard. Another intimacy, between the hunters and the hunted. And she was the hunter here, the girl with the languages.

The two of them sighed in unison and smiled, like they had just shared a kiss. Lotz said, "I guess it's time to hit the red button."

This meant bringing in Lloyd Morgan, the head of N and their boss. He had made his reputation in signals intelligence, tracking Soviet missile launches, although he had seen earlier than most of his peers that NSA had to change: unwrapping Russian ciphers and tracking their missiles was not going to be as important as formerly, there was a future in electronic eavesdropping on terrorist cell phones, and to do that successfully you needed linguists. He had pulled in Cynthia straight out of her initial orientation and brought her into N Section when it was formed.

Cynthia called him, asked for an urgent meeting. The name Abu Lais cleared all previous appointments. They went to Morgan's office immediately.

Morgan had enough status to rate a TV set in his office, and it played continually. Just now it was running CNN silently, a grim-faced anchor talking to a correspondent on a dusty tan street, the logo on the upper right of the screen showing the subject: the kidnapping of billionaire William Craig and others by Islamic terrorists, now in its second day.

Cynthia launched into her report without polite preliminaries. She described the situation for him, played the message on his computer speakers, translated it line by line as it played.

Morgan listened without comment. He was a good-sized fleshy man, pleasantly ugly, with dark-red straight hair combed back from a large pale freckled face. Colorless eyes. In anger, red bars appeared on his cheeks and the eyes turned to lead slugs, merciless. She liked that about him, in the way that attractive women of a certain stripe like men who are impressed by power rather than beauty. Cynthia had gone through enough of the other kind.

She'd gone through Morgan too. He'd put a heavy make on her from her first day in the office, nothing annoying or actionable, just a slow intense burn. Two months after she started working for him he'd taken her along to San Diego for an academic conference funded by NSA. It was about advances in natural language filtering, and neither of them really needed to be there. And the usual: they drank deeply, they told stories about their lives, and a good-night clinch in the elevator led naturally enough to his bed.

It hadn't developed into a passionate affair, neither of the parties being that kind of person, but after San Diego she was the one he took along on junkets and to important meetings, so her name would circulate at the higher levels. She had not failed to notice that many men at these high-level conferences had attractive female assistants. Out of town, sex was on the menu, but they never engaged in anything around the office, no assignations at local hotels, all very discreet in the tradition of the inhabitants of the secret world. Cynthia regarded the liaison as a reasonable career move and a useful relief of workplace tension, one of the things a good-looking young woman did to get ahead, like earning a first-class graduate degree. She had no idea how Morgan felt, nor did she particularly care. He was married, with a couple of grown kids, well settled; she thought he rather appreciated her indifference.

After she finished, he thought for a full minute in silence. A deliberate man, Morgan; she'd never quite decided whether it was because he was extremely smart, and was calculating chess moves off into the distant future, or because he was playing outside his league and had to compensate. Morgan was another of the closely guarded secrets of the NSA.

At last he spoke. "What do *you* make of this, Cynthia? I mean, just from the languages." He had a deep baritone voice, the kind they use in commercials to convey reliability.

"Well, both of them are speaking Modern Standard Arabic," she replied, "indicating that they're not from the same Arabic-language area or they'd be talking in one of the colloquial forms. We know al-Zaydun's home dialect is Eastern Saudi, and it shows here in the substitution, in a couple of words, of the *g* sound for the *q* and a few other details. The other man isn't a native Arabic speaker at all. He messes up the *'ayn, gayn,* and *ha'* sounds, like almost all non-native speakers do."

"But not you." A smile here.

"No." No smile.

"What's his native language, do you think?"

Cynthia had spent thousands of hours listening to recordings of dozens of Arabic dialects, and of native speakers of several score other languages speaking Arabic. "It's hard to say exactly. I'm inclined to think a South Asian language. Dari or Pashto. Maybe Panjabi. Maybe Farsi. But Abu Lais is supposed to be Pashtun, so that fits. I could tell more with a longer colloquy."

"Yes, and it would be nice to have their cell-phone bills with the address printed on them." He turned to Lotz. "What does the voiceprint say about the recipient subject?"

"The voiceprint?"

"Yes. We have a recording of al-Zaydun's voice. Is it the same?"

"I haven't ... I mean, we thought we should come to you ..."

"Go do it."

"Now?"

"No, next Easter. Go! No, wait! Lotz, this catch stays with us three alone until further notice, understand? I mean *no one* else." Lotz said he got that, and Morgan made a shooing motion.

When the door had closed on Lotz, Morgan leaned back in his chair, laced his hands behind his head, and grinned. "Well, finally!"

"You think it's genuine?"

"Fuck, yes! We have the right guys—I fully expect the voiceprints to check out—and the right place, and what the hell else could it be? They're not shipping bananas." He gave her an inquiring look. "Why, don't *you*?"

"Not just yet. As a matter of fact, I've been waiting for them to try something like this. I mean, don't you think it's a little funny that the most elusive al-Q operative on earth, who as far as we know hasn't used a cell phone in years, should call a senior al-Q leader on a compromised device, which leader immediately identifies him by name?"

"People make mistakes," he said. "The history of intelligence is full of boners."

"Yes, Lloyd, we both know the history of intelligence," she replied. "But I'm more concerned with *recent* history. This country is involved in two wars right now, and both of them are the result of massive systemic intelligence failures: we missed 9/11, and that's the war in Afghanistan, and we screwed up on WMD, and that's Iraq."

"I'd hardly call Iraq an intelligence failure. There was no evidence of WMD because there weren't any weapons."

"No, but our intel on the Iraqis was so piss-poor that any bunch of bozos could make a temporarily plausible case for an invasion. Now we're making noises at Iran. So I ask you, who would benefit from a stolen-nuclear-weapons scare in Pakistan? Who would love to see us involved in yet *another* attack on a Muslim country?"

"Iran?"

"For starters. The mullahs would *love* it. Plus, any hints that the Paks are not reliable custodians of nuclear weapons drives a wedge between us and them. Actually, al-Q would like nothing better than a U.S. involvement in northern Pakistan. The country would come unglued. Half the population would go jihadi. A big chunk of their military and intelligence service are sympathizers already; so we have to make absolutely sure that this is the real thing before we pass it upstairs."

"There are no absolutely sure things in intel," he said. "That's one of the things you learn when you've been in the business as long as I have. I got a good feeling about this one, Cyn. And I'd like to win one for a change."

As he said this Morgan leaned back in his chair, and Cynthia saw his eyes pass across a souvenir of a lost one, a framed North Vietnamese battle flag Morgan had brought back from his tour as a junior army intelligence officer in 1968. That was one of his object lessons: we had tried to fight a war where the enemy knew everything about us and we knew practically nothing about them—or, rather, we had all the information we needed but wouldn't use it.

After a moment, Morgan continued. "Look, get off anything else you're doing and tell Ernie to do the same. Focus on the intercepts from Peshawar and the Kahuta area. I'll make sure all that material is routed to you. If you get any confirmation, anything at all, come direct to me."

They spoke about details for a while, and Cynthia asked if he wanted to open a permanent file on the intercept. Morgan said he did and, after consulting his computer and a list of available code names, he told her to call the file GEARSHIFT.

As she left she reflected once again on Morgan's perfect discretion. Within the bounds of the institution, even when they were alone in an office, never did he indicate by a look or an action that they were anything but subordinate and superior. In this too was Morgan a career model.

Cynthia went back to Ernie Lotz's office and found him hunched over his keyboard.

"Are you recovered?" she asked.

"My shorts are still smoking, but I'm fine. He never yells at you like that."

She ignored this. Cynthia didn't really know how widespread was the intel that she was sleeping with Morgan, but gossip usually filled in the blanks

"Actually, I should have thought of checking the alleged al-Zaydun voice against the files. Sorry, my bad. Did you have any luck with it?"

"I did some preliminary checks. The software says it's the same voice. So it's the real deal."

"It could be. Morgan certainly thinks so."

"And you don't?"

"I'm reserving judgment."

Lotz made a face. "Yeah, but if it's real and we don't blow the whistle, we're in deep shit. Why do you think it's a fake?"

"I didn't say it was a *fake*. I'm a little suspicious, is all. And I didn't like that cat-eating-cream look on Morgan's face. He's been waiting for this for years. It justifies his whole existence. So let me play devil's advocate for a while. Anyway, this intercept is now GEARSHIFT, and just for the three of us until further notice. You didn't tell anyone else about it, did you?"

"No. I put it up on my Facebook page, but no one ever looks there. I have three friends, and one of them is my mom."

Cynthia let this go by, and there was the kind of silence that occurs when someone has made an inappropriately facetious remark. Ernie was prone to these little high-school-level comments, excusable as office banter, self-deprecating remarks about his social life, although why he should have trouble in that department was beyond Cynthia's comprehension. The sad-puppy thing did not suit him, she thought, or maybe it really did and it didn't suit her. Irritating, at any rate.

After a moment, she said, "We need some way to refocus the comint screens around voiceprint catches off these two subjects," and they began to work in their usual easy professional way, planning how to lay off their current duties on others and roughing out communication intelligence protocols.

Afterward, Cynthia went back to her own office and started to read through recent transcripts from relevant areas. Now that they had this lead, she thought, maybe other conversations that seemed innocent at the time might appear in a different and more interesting light. She searched for *package, first phase, sheikh*, occurring in the same intercept and also for that odd locution, *some small time*. Not an idiom, the phrase was more likely to be used by someone not at home in Modern Standard Arabic.

As she worked, she thought about her paranoia, if that was the word. She knew Morgan didn't think that their enemy's psychology ran to this kind of deception. They were true believers, not at all like the cynical gamesmen of the late Soviet regime. These people were perfectly frank about their aims. They felt that God was on their side and, while they were crafty enough, they were not crafty in that way. On the other hand, there was always a first time. The events of 9/11 had drilled that lesson deep into the minds of the entire U.S. intelligence community.

So she would try to keep a lid on Morgan's enthusiasm. And as she thought about this she considered the possibility that his enthusiasm, his desire to be at the center of the largest conceivable kind of national security crisis, would lead him to overstep, to push the evidence further than it warranted. And if he did that, and if she was the one who reined the whole thing in, who prevented America from falling into yet another blunder fueled by faulty intel—well, that would be it, the much-desired coup. She would be made. Morgan would be destroyed, of course, at the same time, and as she reflected on this she found, a little to her surprise, that she didn't mind at all.

5

B ound together in a line, the Conference on Conflict Resolution on the
Subcontinent: A Therapeutic Approach is herded through the night
over rocky trails, across drifts of sand and shale that drag at their feet,
through ankle-twisting boulder fields, across freezing streams. Sonia is
tied behind Karl-Heinz Schildkraut and in front of Annette Cosgrove, who
is the last of the coffle. Schildkraut is wearing European slip-on shoes and
in the waning daylight Sonia can see they are coming to pieces. Sonia herself is wearing sandals made of buffalo hide, of local manufacture, and she
has complete confidence in them, although her feet are now soaked and
numb with cold. Schildkraut stumbles often and several times falls heavily. When this happens their silent captors jerk at his rope and prod him
with the butts and barrels of their rifles until Sonia and Annette grab him
by his arms and help him to his feet. He is ashen and wheezing, and Sonia
tries to suppress useless feelings of guilt. She thinks he might not survive
this travail.

A military helicopter flies low overhead, and at the first sound of its
engine their captors shove and club them all into the convenient over-
hang of a rock wall until it has passed. Then they are on the move again,
driven like animals. Sonia feels herself descending into animal mind: the
future fades, the past fades, there is nothing but the next step, the pain
from her many bruises, and the chafing cords. She is barely conscious of
the passage of time, until she becomes aware that the sun has sunk below
the mountain ridges and color has leached out of the surrounding landscape. Still they are pushed along relentlessly until it is hard to see their
footing in the gloom, the captives are tripping at every other step, and at
last someone at the head of the line falls off the trail into a shallow ravine

and the whole group is yanked off their feet. The kidnappers call out to one another as they attempt to get their captives back on the trail. Sonia crawls forward from where she has fallen to where Schildkraut lies.

"Karl-Heinz, are you all right?" she whispers.

"I am alive, at least. I would have worn my hiking boots if I had known this was part of the conference program."

"I'm so sorry," she says and then one of the kidnappers comes along and tells her to be quiet and get to her feet. When she doesn't move quickly enough to suit him, he jabs her in the ribs with the muzzle of his AK. She stands up and looks him in the face. There is still just enough light to see he is a young man, in his late teens at most.

She says, in Pashto, "How dare you strike me, you little pisser! I'm old enough to be your grandmother. Does your mother know you're out in the night beating women?"

The boy's eyes widen. He raises his weapon to firing position. "Move!" he says.

Sonia raises her voice. "How? I am tied to this man."

The boy kicks at Schildkraut, producing pitiful groans. It is unbearable to watch and Sonia throws her own body over his, crying out for the abuse to stop. A moment later, Annette Cosgrove rushes forward and also flings herself down to protect the old man's body. "Don't hurt him," she shouts, and she has a carrying voice. Sonia hears Annette's husband call out her name from forward on the line. The other prisoners now also call out; there is a commotion, guards and prisoners shouting. Their cries echo from the now-invisible rock walls of the gully.

Sonia adds her voice, louder still: "Look, this is an old man. He must rest, or if you want him to move at this pace, someone must help him, and we can't if we're tied up like this. Do you think we'll try to escape? How could we? From twenty armed men when we don't know where we are? If you untie us, the stronger will be able to help the weaker ones and we won't fall as much and you will go faster to wherever it is you're taking us."

Sonia hears a voice calling out in Pashto, "Patang! What's going on back there? Shut that woman up!"

Sonia says, "Patang, talk to him! Tell him what I said! Believe me, you will move more quickly. Otherwise, you might as well shoot us all now."

The boy hesitates, then leaves briefly and returns with a thin man in a large black turban and a sheepskin jacket. Sonia listens while the boy

Patang explains the problem as she had expressed it, to which the other man replies, "Cut them loose and shoot the old man. We can't afford to waste any more time."

Sonia cries out, "Oh, I see I was mistaken—I thought you were mujahideen. I prayed you were mujahideen. But now I see you are only bandits, and accursed of God."

With that, she drops down again on Schildkraut, covering his head and shoulders with her body while Annette Cosgrove lies across his legs and lower back.

"Now you will have to kill three of us," Sonia says, in the same loud voice, "and then you will have to kill her husband too, and that will be four of nine hostages you won't have, and who will make up the ransom for them? Think, man! Nine hostages delivered on time in reasonable condition against five, and maybe fewer than five, because no one can walk through this country tied together with their hands bound. What will you do if there are broken legs or broken necks?"

Sonia cannot see the man's face, but she does not think he will shoot them, nor does she think he will order the boy to shoot them, or that the boy would obey such an order. She has spent a good deal of her life among violent men of this type and she is betting three lives that she has judged them correctly. A minute passes. She can hear Schildkraut's heavy breathing and the lighter breaths of the other woman. She is deeply grateful that Annette backed her play. That was another quick assessment that worked out. She hears low voices and the sound of retreating footsteps and then shouts from the head of the column.

The boy bends over her and grabs her arm. She sees the flash of a knife and her hands are free. The boy says, "You women will support the old man. If he cannot keep up then we _will_ shoot him."

Now he stares at her, because she is not moving to help the other woman. Instead, she has broken a branch off a small bush and is sweeping the dust from a flat area to the side of the trail.

The boy looks baffled. "What are you doing?"

She says, "Since you have taken my prayer rug, I must clean a portion of the ground, as is permitted."

"You're going to pray?" the boy asks, staring.

"Yes. The sun has gone down and it's time for the Maghrib prayer." With that, she begins the ritual ablutions, using sand, as is allowed in the absence of clean water. Patang observes this in silence for a moment and then runs off. Sonia rubs the designated parts of her body with the flinty sand, reties her head scarf, and, facing east, prays the du'a.

She hears footsteps, whispered conversation, and then the murmur of two dozen men praying. Interesting, she thinks, when the prayer is done; they were going to skip it to save time, and wonders what fallacious reasoning had been put forward to allow that grave sin of omission.

Schildkraut is somewhat revived by the brief rest. Sonia and Annette throw his arms over their shoulders to support some of his weight, and with the rest of the party they move off down the narrow track. The kidnappers have taken all their watches, but the sky is clear and full of needle-sharp stars and by observing their motion Sonia can estimate the time elapsed after sunset. She thinks it is about four in the morning when they reach what appears to be an actual road, narrow and rocky. The mujahideen assemble their prisoners along the road, commanding them to be silent and once again binding their hands. They wait; the stars wheel overhead, the captives shiver where they sit. Sonia discovers that the man sitting next to her is William Craig. She can see his glasses glitter in the starlight as he shivers.

She asks him how he is.

"Terrific. I twisted my ankle and I'm freezing to death. Who the hell *are* these people?"

"They're mujahideen. Self-proclaimed Islamic warriors."

"What do they want with us? Is it ransom?"

"I think they want to make a political point. We're from the West, and the West is the enemy. So we're fair game."

"But who do they answer to? Surely they're open to negotiation at higher levels."

His voice has risen and this attracts the attention of one of the guards, who comes over and tells Craig to shut up, and although Craig does not speak the language and has not recently been told to shut up by anyone, the message is conveyed, and Craig falls silent. Sonia hadn't a good answer to his question anyway.

After perhaps an hour, they hear the sound of an approaching engine. It is a five-ton truck with the high arched frame typical of the region standing above the truck bed. The mujahideen swarm around the truck, speaking softly and working at something Sonia can't quite make out but which involves off-loading large bales and crates. Then the prisoners are made to stand, and they are gagged with rags and hustled into the empty bed of the truck. There they are arranged to lie supine in three rows, head to toe, like sardines. Ropes are passed over their bodies securing them to bolts in the truck frame so they can't move at all and then a plank floor is laid over them, and on this floor the men reload the crates and bales.

The truck starts. After a few minutes, the discomfort of the prisoners becomes real pain, then what seems unbearable pain, as the motion of the truck on the rough road smashes them up against the false floor and then down on the unyielding ribbed steel of the truck bed, but as the hours pass they discover that more can be borne than they had imagined. Sonia hears muffled weeping, but she can't tell who weeps.

It is like being in a coffin, without the peace of the grave. She fights the instinctive panic, controls her breathing, welcomes the pain, concentrates on freeing her hands; it takes what seems like hours to do this, and when they are free she pulls the gag from her mouth and reaches out. Annette Cosgrove is next to her and she pats the young woman's thigh, which is all she can do for her; she is still lashed rigidly to the deck of the truck, and even if she were free there is not enough clearance above her face to enable her to move from her slot.

They roll on and, as night passes into day, tiny dots of light appear, cast through holes in the truck's bed, but there is nothing to see except the planks lying inches above their faces. Sonia is thinking about entombment, the physical kind that she experiences now, and the other kind, the psychic kind, the closed hell of unhappy families, of addiction, with which she has had much to do in her work, in her own life.

She recalls reading that the pain of a toothache will drive all so-called psychological suffering out of your head, but now, suffering physically as much as she ever has, she thinks that is cynical and not true. The suffering, even the torture, imposed by one's enemies can be borne because it *is* imposed, the sufferer is not responsible for it; the enemy acts through hate, and the answer is the same one Jesus gave from the cross: they don't know what they are doing. Yes, they can break your body, but also aren't they a little foolish? Aren't they like little boys pulling the legs off insects?

And also one is inspired by the famous tortured ones who did *not* break—Saint Joan, Mandela, the survivors of the camps—so there *is* a model, and these examples shine light into the darkest cell.

But it is different, she thinks, when the suffering is imposed by those who are supposed to love you, whom you are supposed to love. Then there is no escape, then you must learn to love the lash, and then there are no noble examples to follow; there is no nobility at all. And the worst torturer is the most beloved of all, the self, for who knows better where the knife must twist to yield the most exquisite agony?

♫

Tea with Farid's mother, Noor, and her lady friends, and her three sisters: what could be more calm, civilized, elegant? Oh, Farid, my husband, she thinks, and laughs inwardly, would it surprise you to know that I would rather be captured by terrorists than sit through another one of those endless afternoons? Women like Noor, upper-class Lahori begums, had only two functions in life, keeping their husbands contented and marrying off their children in a satisfactory way. Sonia's arrival, she gathered (and really gathered in hard-earned bits, since no one ever bothered to explain it to her) had presented Noor with an intolerable conflict: Baba wanted Sonia accepted into the family home, so of course she had to be accepted; but this meant that Noor would forever after be saddled with the most unsatisfactory daughter-in-law imaginable, a shame to her distinguished family and friends.

Until she met Noor and her circle, that house of staring women, the subtle, unchallengeable knives of their looks, Sonia had never been exposed to naked contempt. In the circus life the rubes admired the circus people, of course, and within the circus family a strict hierarchy ruled; everyone knew their place, and while there was certainly enough nastiness and petty intrigue, this did not break the essential solidarity of their lives, which was the show, their show, against the world.

But in her father-in-law's house Sonia was all alone. She didn't speak the languages, she didn't know the rules, and she hardly knew her husband, who seemed like a different person in his father's house from the one she had known in New York. The air in that house seemed to have shriveled him; he did nothing in her defense; he told her, Sonia, just be nice, they'll get used to you and you'll learn how we do things here.

So she learned. She was bright and observant and soon discovered she had an ear for languages, and when she could understand a little she was able to comprehend the full extent of the contempt in which she was held. She started to get the little asides at the tea parties now, the comments on her physical appearance (a corpse, a skeleton, a demon), on how she held a teacup, her utter lack of any family.

Her status rose considerably when she gave the Lagharis a grandson. Now she was tolerated by the women, although it was made clear to her that she knew nothing about rearing a child, that Noor would make the decisions about how to raise him, that the actual daily care would be provided by an ayah whom Noor would choose. The only fight she won in that period was choosing the child's name: Theodore, after her own father; Laghari Sahib, from whom there was no appeal, agreed. He thought it distinguished to have a grandson named Theodore Abdul.

Gradually, she came to understand the power of the weak. She cultivated Baba, she flattered, she learned reams of poetry, both English and Urdu, for his delight, she became another prized exotic pet, like his parrots, his Yorkie. And she suborned the servants with bribes and gifts, she listened to their tales of woe and injustice and sympathized, she learned the various languages of that city. She sought allies and found one in Nasha, the wife of Gul Muhammed, Laghari Sahib's Pashtun bodyguard. From her Sonia learned Pashto and something about the way of the Pashtuns. The women became friends of a sort. They were both isolated from their native cultures, lonely and vulnerable, so they had a basis for companionship. Here also she made her first connection with Nasha's son, Wazir.

In fact, it was Wazir, more than anyone else, who taught her Pashto. He was three or so when she was pregnant with Theo and it was love at first sight, the way it sometimes happens between a child and a woman who is unsure about being a mother. After Theo was born, and it became clear to Sonia that raising him would be a perpetual battle for control against Noor and the dread weight of Punjabi culture, she found a kind of release in being a second mother to little Wazir. And this was possible because there was something wrong with the first mother. Nasha was sickly, she had endured a series of miscarriages, and the one baby she had produced besides Wazir had died in infancy. Her chief terror was that Gul Muhammed would divorce her and send her back in disgrace to her village in Afghanistan. Against this, there was only one possibility for survival—that her son would become a great and powerful man. It was Sonia who convinced her that the road to power for a man in the late twentieth century was through education, and Sonia had gone to Laghari Sahib and told him that Wazir was unusually bright and deserved an education equal to that which his own sons had received and which his grandson would receive. She used every circus wile she possessed to do this, to sell the proud old man on the idea that it was part of his own uniqueness, and part of the debt he owed his bodyguard, to send the young Pashtun to Aitchison College, the Eton of Pakistan.

So it was done, and Gul Muhammed agreed, for he was a sworn servant of Laghari Sahib. It was Sonia's first real victory in the house of Laghari. Later, she continued her interest in Wazir's education, making him into something neither Nasha nor her husband could ever have conceived, and whether it was a prize or a curse had still not been established.

With effort, Sonia turns her thoughts away from this line; she does not want to think about Wazir just now. Instead she thinks of how she managed her escape from the house of Laghari and its whispering women. From the bazaar, secretly, she had obtained the clothing of a Pashtun boy: worn and faded shalwar trousers, a kurta, a long Pashtun waistcoat, a turban wrapping her hair. At dawn one morning, dressed in these clothes, she slipped from the sleeping house, down the back alleys of Anarkali to the Urdu Bazaar and felt free for the first time in she could not recall how long it had been, since at least her girlhood in the circus, once again feeling the superiority of the show people over the rubes.

It was not invisibility. For a large part of any male Muslim population, a smooth-faced boy, especially one who appears poor and unattached, is as attractive as a woman, something Kipling didn't bother to mention when he described Kim's adventures, and as she strolled through the bazaar there were whispered invitations. But she found these easier to dismiss than the ones she got on these same streets as a woman.

She was just avoiding a particularly importunate *bazaari* when she turned a corner and saw Ismail Raza Ali on his mat. He was telling a story to a small group of men and boys sitting or standing around him. The public storyteller had almost disappeared from Lahore's markets in those days, drowned out by recorded music, unmuffled scooters, motor tricycles and trucks and unable to compete with the attractions of film and TV. She was surprised to see even one survivor, so she stopped and listened.

He was telling the story of the fisherman and the demon, and the magical fish the demon taught him how to catch, in colors red, blue, green, and yellow, and what happened when these fish were brought to the king and fried: the mysterious woman who appeared though a wall in the palace kitchen and asked, "O fish, have you kept the pledge?"

Like all stories from the *Thousand Nights and a Night*, this one has no end but blends into another one, and another. The storyteller stopped his tale at the point when the king journeys from the enchanted lake where the colored fish are caught and finds the palace with the unfortunate prince inside it, half man and half black stone.

A sprinkle of small coins and crumpled rupee notes fell into the man's profferred brass bowl and the little crowd dispersed. But Sonia stayed.

The storyteller placed his takings in a leather purse and, leaning on his staff, stood and wrapped a patched gray cloak over his shoulders. Sonia saw he was only as tall as she herself and just as wiry, his face the color of an old saddle and curiously saddle-tight and smooth over the high cheekbones. His eyes had the Asiatic fold in them, she noticed, when he turned them on her, and they had in them a look that combined amusement and penetration. He said to her, "That is thirsty work. How about a cup of tea down the road?"

She followed him to a tiny stall, where he was known and salaamed amid smiles by the host, who served them sweet milky tea and small cakes twice as sweet as the tea.

Sonia was a little shocked because the man had addressed her in English. In Pashto she asked him why he had spoken thus to a Pashtun boy. He said, laughing, "Because you are not a Pashtun boy but an English girl."

"American," she said. "How did you know?"

"Wrists. The line of your neck. The way you listened, which is the way a Westerner listens and not the way a Pashtun boy would listen." Here he produced on his face an expression of dull amazement and laughed when she did. She introduced herself as Sonia Laghari, and he wished her peace and announced himself as Ismail Raza Ali.

She pointed to his cloak and asked, "And are you really a Sufi sage or are you as fraudulent as I?"

He answered, "Indeed I am fraudulent or I would long since have overcome my *nafs*, what you call the ego, and would be conversing with angels instead of fake Pashtun boys. But I am also a sincere Sufi, of the Sufi order Naqshbandiyya. I have been in the south, in Sindh, where the shrines of our saints are thick on the ground and where the Sufi *pirs* are even more fraudulent than I, being very rich and driving around in limousines while the peasants starve. So I am going north. There are shrines and tombs I must visit, and I especially want to visit the shrine of Hazrat Shah Azar Basmali again. It was there many years ago that God spoke to me and set me on this path I am now upon."

"North," she said. "As far as Pindi?"

"Farther."

"Peshawar?"

"Farther."

"Beyond the passes? Afghanistan?"

"Beyond Afghanistan."

"But there is no going beyond Afghanistan," she said. "It's the Iron Curtain."

He smiled. "It's rusty nowadays. People do pass. The guards are ill-paid and lazy. They like tapes and tape players as much as anyone, you know, and the eyes of Moscow are far away. Also, I am a very obscure person, no one notices me. I leave one week from now."

She said without thinking, reflexively, like a knee jerk, "Take me with you!"

Another, thinner smile. "And why would you want that, 'boy'?"

She said, "Because the life of a little begum does not suit me. My husband is a fine man whom I do not love. My baby is cared for by many hands, all more skillful than my own. My mother was eaten by a lion. I wish to find God and ask him why. If I don't get away, I will kill someone, or disgrace myself in some hideous way, which I don't wish to do, for it would harm people who have been nothing but kind to me. Yet kindness is not enough."

"No, it is not. But unfortunately, *you* would attract notice, even as a boy. Perhaps even more as a boy. You know the Pashtun song that goes, 'I know a boy with a bottom like a fresh peach, but he is across the river'?"

"They would not notice me if I was your *murid*. I would wear my sleeves long and a Pashtun scarf around my neck. And I would make sores on my face with flour paste and rouge. Although I will be ugly and contemptible, I will still be of use, for you must have a disciple like other Sufis do. What if you got sick or hurt? Who would care for you?"

"And how would you care for me? How would you earn bread? Would you tell stories in languages you cannot speak?"

"No, I will be mute. But I can do this." So saying, she tossed some small coins into her empty teacup, covered them with the saucer, shook them to a rattle, and then upended the cup on the saucer. She lifted the cup with a flourish. The coins were gone.

"A useful trick," he said, after a short pause. "Although it is more useful to make money out of nothing than to make it vanish, which I can do all too well by myself. But you are right in that it is traditional for someone like me to have a disciple, and I have none. Regrettably, I do not attract the more devout youth, ah . . . what shall I call you? Not Sonia; but Sahar is a good Pashtun name; we met in the morning, after all, and that name means *morning* in Pashto. So, Sahar, I have no murid because I am not very holy. I drink, I run my fingers under the buttocks of devout youth, I eat the food of unbelievers—well, many Sufi do that—but I also say disturbing things about Islam."

Ismail shoved his stick in the path of a genuine street boy.

"Ho, you, boy! Stop!"

The boy paused, wary as a fox.

"Here is ten rupees," said Ismail. "Take a message for me to the house of Amu the goldsmith on the street of the jewelers, and you will get another ten. Here is the paper. Go!"

The boy ran off through the crowd.

"That is a messenger," said Ismail. "He carries a message to my friend Amu; Amu reads it and carries out my instructions. What he does not do is to treat that ragged, ignorant boy as if he were me, filled with however little wisdom and sagacity I have been able to gather in a long life. Amu would be a fool to do that. Yet the Muslims treat God's messenger as if he were God Himself; every remark someone heard fall from his lips is sacred, as if it were Qur'an itself. As for the noble Qur'an—I was not there when it was written down, nor was the Prophet, peace be upon him. Who can tell what was slipped in or revised or mistranslated? Arabic is in any case a slippery, allusive tongue. They say, you know, that any word in Arabic can be made to stand for *camel*. So I believe that God wants us to pray and fast and give to the poor and help those in need and be compassionate, yes? But what interest can the Lord of the Day of Judgment possibly have in eating pork or drinking wine? And did He who created women with the same hand really want their witness to be worth half that of a man? When anyone with eyes can see that the world is full of women more truthful and penetrating than the mass of men? But the Muslims don't want to hear this, for they much prefer their religion to God. In this, all men are the same: Hindu, Buddhist, Sikh, Christian; they say, Lord, Lord, here is this little ritual, be content. O God, do not love me out of existence! God, however, is not religious. God is the flame of love. He desires us to love Him as He loves us, but all human things, including Islam itself, stand in the way of this love, for all human things strengthen the nafs. Even fighting to supress the nafs strengthens the nafs. And piety strengthens the nafs more than anything else. I am good, they cry, so God must love me. But there is no 'because' with God's love."

"Then why be a Sufi?" Sonia asked. "Why not sink into drunkenness and lechery and forget the whole thing?"

"I *do* sink into drunkenness and lechery," cried Ismail. "I *do*. But that only makes me remember the more, not to forget." He gave Sonia a grin that demonstrated the latter vice. "And as my murid will you warm my bedroll in the cold of the hills, as a good murid should? Perhaps you have a bottom like a ripe peach."

"If you like," replied Sonia, and he laughed in delight.

"But," he said, "we must first supply you with a thing which, once seen, will establish your identity as a boy beyond question. All boys love to shoot their stream off bridges and down precipices, and so must you. Therefore we must visit the false-penis-wallah and have one made."

"Is there such a thing?"

"In Lahore? City of utter depravity? Of course, and his name is Harun Elahi, and if you let him, he will tell you how his ancestors made such things for Babur Moghul at the beginning of history."

"So I conclude that when I have been fitted with this item you will take me as your murid."

"I will. It is our fate, just as it was my fate to be at the shrine of Hazrat Shah Azar Basmali with my heart twisted and full of poison, where God was waiting for me like a cobra on a rock and struck me in the heart and filled it with His love. All my life since then I have been trying to recover that moment. I think that at the next shrine He will be waiting again, or the next. In the meanwhile, I struggle to wear down the poisonous nafs with the exercises and devotions of my order. These I will teach you, Sahar, my murid, and, God willing, by the time we arrive at the sacred place, He will have mercy on both of us."

"Where is the sacred place?"

"In Chechnya."

"*Wa-illa!* That is a long way."

"Longer than you think, murid, for we must retrace my journey in a great circle and pass through all the Muslim lands now under the Russian boot. Do you still want to go?"

She did; and she went.

ℛ

Her reveries are interrupted by a change in the motion of the truck. They seem to have moved onto a smoother road, they are traveling faster, and there is a wonderful hot dusty breeze coming up through the holes in the truck's floor.

The truck stops several times and they hear the voices of men and the sound of other motors and once the unmistakable clanking of an armored vehicle. They are passing through military checkpoints. It grows hot, then roasting, in the narrow space. The road grows rough again and the angle of the truck changes so that they slide against their restraints, first one way, then the other. The heat diminishes and then the light. It is nearly dark again when they stop at last, and they hear the sounds of male voices and movements of the truck's load. The false floor is lifted and the prisoners are dragged off the truck. None of them can stand but all have survived the journey. They have all pissed themselves, and there is a distinct odor of human waste in the chill air. They are unbound, and armed men half-carry, half-drag them into a building.

But the two women are not touched at all; they are allowed to support each other and totter down a dark hallway and into a small room. The door is shut behind them and they hear the squeak of an antique lock turning. Sonia is shining a penlight around the room.

"Where are we?" Annette asks, and then, startled, "Where did you get that light?"

"I have pockets sewn into my clothing," she says. "An old traveler's trick."

The thin beam shows them a room about eight feet by ten, with tile floors and roughly plastered stone walls. The ceilings are high and there is a tall window closed with thick wooden shutters. The only furnishings are two wooden rope beds—charpoys—with quilts and, in one corner, a galvanized bucket. On a shelf sit a brass kerosene lamp with no chimney and a brown earthenware basin. A large brass ewer with a long spout squats on the floor nearby.

Sonia turns off the penlight, retrieves a match case from a pocket, and lights the wick; the lamp yields a dim and smoky flame. Sonia says, "Well, that's better. We can see where we are."

"Where are we?"

"We're in a *hujra*, a village inn, probably somewhere in the Northwest Frontier Province, up by the Afghan border. We certainly were on the road for long enough. My God, you look terrible; your face is all banged up. Come here by the light."

Sonia uses a corner of her dupatta and water from the brass ewer to clean the livid bruises on Annette's face. After this, Annette breaks down and Sonia holds her while she cries. It is a fairly short breakdown, given what has happened to her, and after she has recovered herself she asks, "How come you didn't get banged up? Your face looks fine."

"Because I wasn't tied up. I could brace myself with my hands."

"How did you do that?"

"My dad was a circus magician. He had an act where he'd get some guy in the crowd to tie him up and he'd get free. It's not hard if you know how, and if the person who's tying you up is in a hurry and working in the dark. Excuse me, I'm dying for a pee."

Sonia uses the bucket and the ewer, washing in the manner prescribed for Muslims. Annette uses the bucket too, and afterward says, "I hope we don't have to do everything in that."

"No, there's going to be an earth closet somewhere on the premises, and we'll be taken to it. These people may kill us, but meanwhile you can expect them to obey all the traditional sanitary laws of Islam to the letter."

There is a pause. Then Annette asks, "Do you think they *will* kill us?"

"They're certainly prepared to. That's why we're in a hujra and not in someone's house. The hospitality laws of the Pashtuns would make us guests, and guests are sacred to them."

They both start as the lock squeals and the door swings open. They see a dark figure appear for a moment and lay a tin tray on the floor and then the door is shut and locked again.

"Speaking of which," says Sonia, "there's our dinner. By God, I'm starved!"

They eat ravenously, scooping up clots of dal with chunks ripped off book-sized loaves of naan, topped with yogurt and washed down with milky tea.

After they finish, Annette laughs and says, "What was that, a hearty meal for the condemned?"

"No, just what they usually eat in places like this. I don't think they intend to starve us. We're probably quite valuable to them in one piece. By the way, don't eat with your left hand. It's vile."

"I forgot. I'm sorry."

"You've never worked in a Muslim country before?"

"No, we've only been in Latin America and the Christian parts of Africa. Are you really a Muslim or is that an act?"

"No, it's real, although I'm not a very good one, theologically. I try to make up for it by being scrupulous about prayer and the various prohibitions. The Prophet, may he have peace, was very big on prohibitions. It's an interesting religion, very simple and pure. I enjoy it when I'm feeling that way. I assume you're a Christian."

"Yes, but not a very good one, theologically." Here a nervous laugh. "I come from an evangelical background. I was saved when I was fourteen but I drifted away in college, not that I lost my faith, really, but I got turned off by the way the evangelical kids on campus behaved, a lot of looking for the mote in their brother's eye, and of course politically they were all to the right of Attila the Hun. Then I went to South Africa with a do-good operation, teaching in these unbelievably poor townships, kids sharing pencils and so on, and that's where I met Porter."

"And fell in love."

Annette bobbed her head and let out a surprised giggle. "Yes, you could say that, although he's not very romantic and, you know, he's quite a bit older. I was impressed by his devotion to helping all the suffering, trying to stop people fighting, and I guess I wanted to share that life. And also ... well, he really needs my help. I mean he's a wonderful speaker and much better with people than I am, you have no idea, he just looks for the best in people and most of the time they respond. But he can't cross a street without getting lost and he forgets things and his papers would be a mare's nest if someone didn't keep them in order. He's a Friend, you know, what you call Quakers, and I suppose I'm a Friend now too. Also a very simple religion, which consists mainly of being quiet a lot and working for peace." She sighs and chews on her lip. "I'm so worried about him. He must be devastated that this happened, and those nice boys shot down in front of his eyes. Do you think they'll let me see him?"

"Well, they'll certainly assemble all of us for the video."

"The what?"

"The video they're going to make to show the world that they have us and to announce their demands. It'll be all over the Internet by midday tomorrow."

"Oh, God, I can't believe this is happening. My mother will die!"

"I hope not," says Sonia. "Mothers are often tougher than you think."

"But what will they demand?"

"Hard to tell. Probably something like the release of prisoners held by the Pakistanis and Americans."

"Will they do that? I mean, trade us for the prisoners?"

"They might get some of their people released by the Pakistanis, but meanwhile they have the whole world watching. Terror is essentially public relations. Also, they've got one of the richest men in America; that might be the reason we were lifted in the first place. Craig is worth a lot of money alive, so I suppose that's a consideration."

"If they just want him for ransom, why don't they let the rest of us go?"

"Because we're all useful as hostages. They can make a threat—we'll kill one of the infidels every day until you do what we want—and they get to make videos of the executions. There's a vast audience out there for videos of Muslims murdering Westerners; it's a recruiting tool for them."

"So they *are* going to kill us!"

"Possibly, but we're not dead yet. A lot depends on who these people are. Islam is a very decentralized religion. Anyone can call himself a mujahid, a holy warrior. The movement attracts lots of people, from the sincerely religious to the insane or just bored kids looking for action. In the West they race cars drunk or knock off convenience stores. Here they become mujahideen. At the edges they blend into simple bandits, which this part of the world has always been famous for, but I don't get the message that our guys are like that."

"Why not? They certainly seemed brutal enough when they shot down Hamid and his boys."

"Oh, well, brutal is the base coat in these parts. They kill very easily. What I meant was, are they sincerely religious? Are they moved by some kind of moral impulse?"

"I don't see how you can put moral impulse together with murder."

"That's because you're not from around here. The fact is that we're being kept in what to them are quite comfortable quarters, we've been fed decent food, we haven't been molested. I think they're trying to make a point: Americans and Pakistanis torture people, but real Muslims don't. That's a hopeful sign. It means they may be looking forward to releasing us, so we can tell the world how well we've been treated, in contrast, for example, to Abu Ghraib and Guantánamo. On the other hand, a prize like Craig is going to draw attention from every mujahideen group in the Northwest Frontier, from the Taliban, and from al-Qaeda itself. Our fate may not be in the hands of the group that captured us."

"But what do we *do*?"

"We could wash your hair," says Sonia with a grin. She reaches into her garments and flourishes a tiny tube of green gel.

"You're kidding."

"I'm not. We happen to have plenty of water and a basin and shampoo, which may not always be the case. And you want to be pretty for your close-up tomorrow. Seriously, take off your shirt."

She does so and Sonia washes the filth, dried blood, and dust out of the long golden hair, and then uses a comb from another of the many pockets to pull the knots from its shining length. She dries it with her dupatta and then, to Annette's surprise, cuts off a wide length of the material with the scissors of a Swiss Army knife (drawn from yet another pocket) and ties it around Annette's hair.

"There!" she says, when she has it right, "you look like a good Muslim wife." She pauses and cocks her head, thinking. "I don't suppose you'd consider converting?"

"What, to Islam? Seriously?"

"Yes. It would give them an immense propaganda victory if the bunch of you did, I mean besides me and Amin, who are already believers, and it would almost guarantee your survival."

Annette considers this proposition for a few moments and then says, "No, I couldn't in good conscience, and I'm sure Porter would feel the same." She laughed. "If they kill me I guess I'll be a martyr to the faith. That will surprise them back in the Friends Meeting in Cannondale, Missouri. I don't think they've had one recently."

"Well, it was just a thought," says Sonia. "By the way, speaking of martyrdom, I wanted to tell you how splendidly you behaved back on the trail, backing my play with Dr. Schildkraut."

"Oh, that! I can barely recall why I did it. It was a sort of spasm of…I don't know what. Toxic charity, maybe. I just couldn't bear to see them shoot that nice old man, or stand by while you were being so brave. To be honest, it surprised the heck out of me. I mean, I'm used to what most people would call hardship, with our work and all, but as a matter of fact international peace work's not really that dangerous. It's not like we're actually throwing our bodies between warring armies, although maybe that would work better."

As she speaks she is taking off her shoes, high-topped sneakers, and her filthy socks. Her bare feet are dirt-stained and bleeding.

She says, "Do you think I could soak my feet in that basin?"

"Sure. That's what it's for, more or less."

Annette does so and groans. After some silent minutes, she says, "This is so—well, strange. I mean, we're chatting together like we're in an airport, the words and the intonations…. Why aren't we gibbering or using some other kind of, I don't know, more elevated language?"

"That's an interesting question," Sonia says, and then laughs. "Speaking of conventional phrases. But it turns out that people who are grounded and secure don't change very much under stress. That's what being grounded means. The frauds tend to fall apart and the tough guys, too. In the Korean War, they found it was the well-brought-up middle-class kids who resisted the communist torture best, not the ones from the slums, whom you'd have expected to be tougher."

"Oh, in that case I'm going to be fine," said Annette, and laughed too. "I assume you were nicely raised too—you're unbelievably cool about all this."

"As a matter of fact I had a terribly traumatic childhood. But afterward I sort of reraised myself."

Annette seems about to ask for an expansion of this statement but checks herself. "So are we completely helpless at this point? Does it all depend on what kind of people are holding us?"

"No, not completely," Sonia answers. "Do you know what Stockholm Syndrome is?"

"Where the prisoners start sympathizing with the captors. Patty Hearst."

"Yes. Well, it works the other way around too. We'll see if we can make that happen. With God's help, of course."

After that, they both take to their charpoys and fall into instant exhausted sleep.

Sonia, however, has always been an early riser, and the events of the past days have not changed that. Dawn is just dribbling through the slats of the shutters when she slides out from under the quilt, performs her ablutions, and, searching under her charpoy, finds what she expects, a worn but clean prayer rug. She prays the two raka'ah of the dawn prayer, the Fajr, and then goes to the door, intending to knock on it to summon the guards. But she hears voices in the hallway outside and instead places her ear against a crack in the rough boards. She recognizes one of the voices and listens with interest.

More footsteps outside and the door lock squeals open. A guard enters and looks around. Sonia sees it is the boy, Patang, from the incident on the trail. He backs out and an old woman in black enters. She deposits a tray with naan and tea on it, picks up last night's tray, and leaves without a word.

Sonia awakens Annette and they eat and drink. They have barely finished when Patang returns with another guard, also masked, this one with a bushy dark beard sprouting out from under his ski mask. Both are armed with Kalashnikovs. Patang says, "Come," and the two women leave the room.

They are taken to the courtyard of the hujra and made to stand against the wall. In a few minutes, the male captives enter, accompanied by guards. They are all bruised to varying extents and covered with dust. Schildkraut can barely stand and is supported by Porter Cosgrove and Father Shea. When Annette sees her husband, she calls out and tries to go to him, but the guards bar her way with pointed Kalashnikovs.

The captives are now lined up against the wall. Across the courtyard the mujahideen stand in small dark groups, hefting their rifles. It is the classic scene, familiar from the movies, the pathetic last moments of the hostages: up against the wall. Sonia starts to wonder if she has been mistaken, whether for some tactical reason or on orders from a higher level of the insurgency they are all to be executed now. She steps away from the wall and looks down the line of her fellow prisoners, to the left and the right. Next to her, Annette is rigid, her expression a startled one that says, *This cannot be happening to me.* Manjit stands on the other side and seems to be engaged in some kind of breathing exercise; his brown face is calm. William Craig has lost his glasses and peers out at the morning with the face of a terrified rabbit. Father Shea is moving his lips in obvious prayer. Amin next to him looks like he is waiting for a bus, as if the doings in the courtyard are of no concern to him. Ashton is paper pale but slouches against the wall, hands in his pockets, showing the natives class. Porter Cosgrove, last in the line, seems ready to break down in hysterics, his face contorted like a baby who's about to bawl. Sonia is ordered back to the wall with shouts and hostile gestures,

Now a man comes out of the hujra carrying a tripod, but instead of a machine gun, the tripod mounts an expensive-looking video camera. Sonia releases a breath she didn't know she was holding. The man sets his camera up some distance from the wall, peers into the finder, makes adjustments. Then the leader of the band appears, the man in the black turban, masked with a scarf wrapped around his face. He stands in front of the prisoners and reads from a paper. As Sonia expected, it is the usual terrorist want list: removal of infidel troops from Muslim lands, release of prisoners, and then the threat—the infidel spies will be executed if any more Muslims are killed by the crusaders. God is great. Fade to black.

After the video session, the prisoners are allowed to use the latrine behind the hujra and are then returned to where they came from. Patang escorts Annette and Sonia back to their room. Just as they are about to enter the doorway, Sonia stops short and turns to the boy, looking him in the eye. She says, "I can tell you what your dream means: the black horse, and the white, and the cliff."

The gape of shock on his face as she closes the door on it gives her a good deal of satisfaction.

6

The next day, I was in the kitchen drinking coffee and watching the news on TV when the doorbell rang. It was a reporter from the *Washington Post*. For the past couple of days we'd had some press interest, reporters wanting to know how we *felt* that our wife and mother was in the hands of murderous fanatics, but we didn't talk to any of them. I guess this particular woman was more hard up for a human-interest story than the others. I spoke to her in the doorway, long enough to brush her off, but she gave me her card anyway in case I changed my mind and decided to bask in the glow of public sympathy. I was going to toss it away, but then I had a thought.

I needed some time off and the army wasn't about to give it to me because our unit was due to start our rotation downrange and there was no leave, so when I looked at the reporter's card and had that thought I got my Washington Military District directory and looked up Major Lepinski. I typed out a friendly note and clipped the reporter's card to it and called a courier service and had it sent over to his office. The note said I'd just had a visit from a reporter who was doing a story on the blue-on-blue incident we'd both been involved in out in Waziristan, where we weren't supposed to be in the first place. I said the reporter didn't know it had gone down across the Pak border but she had a lot of details. She'd heard that a certain Special Forces captain had called down a big bomb on his own side and one guy had been killed and one ruined and one (me) wounded and would I confirm that such was indeed the case and did I know the captain's name? She'd heard that this officer had not only not been reprimanded for the blunder but had been promoted to major.

I said I hadn't told her anything; I'd said I'd call her back, because I wanted to talk to you first, sir. And later that day my phone rang and it was Major Lepinski and we had a nice chat. He explained that the whole mission had been secret, national security at stake, and the army had held a full (secret) investigation and cleared him of all wrongdoing; it was just the fog of war; and I said I understood, sir, and I would keep it tight for the good of the service. And now that I was his very favorite trooper in the whole army, I thought I could impose on him for a little favor, because I didn't want to go along with my unit on this current rotation; I had a few weeks of urgent personal business I needed leave for and could he help me out? And he could, he would take care of it, he would cut orders for a couple of weeks of temporary duty at the Special Operations Command HQ (that is, a no-show assignment); I could rejoin my unit whenever. I thanked him and assured him, Sir, I would definitely shine my reporter the fuck on. I told him I might be going out of the country for a while starting tomorrow, and he said, Go, he'd be happy to cover for me, and I could hear the relief in his voice.

Gloria had called me when the news of the kidnap broke and she was pretty good about it, being a trauma nurse and used to dealing with people on the edges of catastrophe. She asked if I wanted her to come over, and I said no and told her I was going away for an indefinite time. There was a pause on the line. I could tell she was waiting for some kind of good-bye, and I thought about my mother just taking off on me without a word and found I couldn't do that, even though we'd agreed to no commitments and all.

So I took her out to dinner at Citronelle on my father's plastic, using his name to get a reservation. Farid is a pretty modest guy, but he's still a Punjabi mogul, and he's known at the nice places around town. I've never taken a nickel off him but he wanted to do this and I agreed. He assumed I would be going out with a woman who would expect a luxurious dining experience rather than scarfing takeout from local taquerias in bed, as was the case. There are deep veins of misunderstanding in my family, and lately I have started to find them amusing, although it was not always so.

So we had a nice meal, not my favorite kind of food but she seemed to like it, and she spotted some celebrities eating there, and the celebrities looked at us and wondered who we were to be sitting there at one of the good tables in Citronelle. Then I took her back to Kalorama and showed her around the house.

She ooed a little. "I didn't know you were rich," she said.

"I'm not rich. My father's rich."

"Same difference."

"No, it's not. I live on my E-Seven pay."

"Why? Is he stingy?"

"It's a long story."

"Everything's a long story with you," she said. "If I knew you had this kind of money I would've hit you for some. You could keep me in style."

We were in my bedroom at this point and she wandered around looking at things, opening closets, checking out the books and CDs.

"Where's all your stuff?" she asked.

"This is it. I don't have a lot of stuff."

"I mean when you were a kid. I've got more shit than this in my room at home, and we were piss poor."

"I didn't live here very long. Until I was seventeen I lived in various places in South Asia."

"Yeah? You said you were born in Pakistan but I figured you were raised here. I mean, you're an American."

"Am I? How can you tell?"

"He walks like a duck and talks like a duck, he's a duck."

"The duck would like a drink," I said, and went downstairs and came back with a bottle of Glenlivet and two glasses. She was lying on my bed with her shoes off, paging through a high school yearbook. "You're not in this," she observed.

"No, I never graduated. I have a fourth-grade education." She rolled her eyes the way people do when I say that but declined to comment further.

I poured out a couple of drinks. We drank and smooched a little. I said, "Do you really want this story? I mean, I can go on for quite a while about my sad life."

"I'll tell you when I get bored," she said. "No, honestly, you have no idea how uninteresting most people I know are, especially men. They get poured into a mold in high school and they set up and that's it for life. It's TV shows, sports, and gossip, what they're buying and what they're planning to buy, and bitching about how everything's not perfect in their lives. And meanwhile they're working around dying, smashed up people. It drives me nuts. But you ... I spotted something about you the minute I saw you getting worked over. I thought you might have something else going on, which is the real reason why I dragged you into this relationship. So spit it out, Buster! You were born in Pakistan. And then what?"

℞

And then what? I can tell the story, but will she understand what it means? Like all Americans, her whole thing is about privacy, pulling away from the parents to be yourself, whatever that happens to be, and I get it that's the way things are here in the Great Satan; you reach age thirteen and suddenly your parents don't know shit and you can't wait to get out of the house and hang with the kids.

But that's not the way it is where I come from. There, in Lahore, and later in Pashtunistan, boys still want to grow up to be like their fathers, their grandfathers. To be young is nothing. To be young is not to have a job, a wife, to be broke all the time; if you're a Pashtun, it's not having a gun. When I was a kid in Lahore, I thought my grandfather, B. B. Laghari, was God on earth, and I thought Gul Muhammed was, besides Baba, the greatest man in creation. And Farid, my father, and my uncles and my aunt thought the same about their father.

When I got to the States and started going to an American high school, which I did for an extremely short time, I thought everyone around me was insane, the way they talked about their parents. I thought the parents were insane too, they way they handled their kids, like every request they made was a bargain they weren't sure would be kept. That little whiny tone at the end of every statement: "Be home by ten, *okay?*"

A traditional society. We say the words but we—I mean Americans— don't get what it stands for. Here's an example. My grandfather considered himself a modern man, and in a lot of ways he was. He didn't boot his son out when that son showed up with a strange American woman he wanted to marry. He installed flush toilets—that was a big deal in Lahore at the time—and he gave his daughter the same education he gave his sons. But he wouldn't allow TV in the house and he was strict about movies. His wife, Noor, was a traditional Panjabi begum, stayed in the home, didn't mix with his male guests, and so forth. The main point was that he was in control; he was living the life he thought a traditional Muslim Punjabi of the higher kind was supposed to lead, but he was like Timothy Leary compared to Gul Muhammed.

Grandfather used to have his high-class ghazal evenings, and after the children got sent away, before they sang the more erotic stuff, we would sneak out of bed and go to the servants' quarters in the back of the yard, and there we would listen to Dost Yacub tell Pashtun stories for Gul Muhammed and his pals. In the winter they met around a fire pit and in hot weather they moved up to the roof of Gul Muhammed's house, or under the *barsati* if it was raining.

Dost Yacub was probably over seventy at the time, and one of the last traditional Pashtun storytellers in Lahore. He'd been a warrior in his time and had probably taken shots at people Kipling had known. He told stories about the wars and feuds he'd been in, too, all about *zar, zan, zamin*—women, gold, and land—and in my child's mind the stories of his adventures and the stories about princesses and jinns and man-eaters all blended together to make a picture of a different kind of world than my contemporaries in America were having pumped into them through the tube, none of that *Sesame Street–Mister Rogers* stuff there around the fire or under the hissing lantern. The fairy tales they tell American kids always end with "And they lived happily ever after," but most Pashtun tales go out with heads rolling "And thus he had his revenge." I mean, that's the *point* of the stories.

So we would sit there and listen to Dost Yacub, me and Wazir, propping up our eyelids as it got late, and later on we'd play out the stories, the way American kids do with cowboys and Indians. We had tin swords and Pashtun clothes and sometimes we could talk or bribe one of the servants' kids to play a princess or an evil man-eater. Wazir was four years older than I was, which is a lot when you're a kid, so he was the master of the games. Technically, Gul Muhammed and Wazir were servants, but they weren't treated as servants, more like members of the family. The story I heard was that Gul Muhammed had rescued Baba during a riot in Srinagar after the partition of India. He'd been cornered with his wife by a gang of Hindus and they were going to rape her and slaughter them both and Gul happened on the scene with a pistol and drove off the gang and so after that they were like brothers, and Baba brought Gul into his home and Gul became his sworn protector, because when you save a life you are responsible for it ever after.

We played that out too, in our games, Wazir haughty and brave as his own father, and my sister Aisha, two years younger than me, was our grandmother, Noor, and I was Laghari Sahib. The marauding mob of Hindus came out of Wazir's imagination, and he was good, lots of violent threats, screams of rage, twisted face, clutching hands, and I would fight the Hindus with my tin knife while Aisha cowered behind me, until I was borne down by all the fiends Wazir was impersonating, and then switching back to his father again, a fine Pashtun speech here, elaborate threats and boasts, and then he would draw his pistol, an angled piece of pipe that contained as many shots as an Armalite, and slaughter the bestial Hindus. These sessions often left little Aisha in tears, which Wazir considered proof of their authenticity. When we wanted to play again, she always refused, and it was Wazir who had to cajole her to enter the game once again. This always worked: no one could resist Wazir, beautiful, masterful Wazir, the prince of our yard and, when we got older, of the neighborhood beyond.

In the afternoons, when I was eight and he was twelve, we would throw off our school uniforms and put on shalwar kameez and embroidered caps and walk through the Urdu Bazaar. Wazir, who seemed to know everyone, would flatter and joke and insult our way into free candies and hot fried dumplings and sticks of sugarcane, which always tasted sweeter than the ones bought for us. I followed him around like a dog.

That was my Pashtun life but I had another, or maybe it was two other lives. I was the grandson of B. B. Laghari Sahib, and I was being raised as a Punjabi gentleman and a citizen of Pakistan, a Lahori. As soon as I could read well enough, I was required to stand before him and recite Urdu poetry and also Wordsworth and Tennyson, because the heritage of the Raj was not to be despised. And Yeats. The Sahib was a little nuts about Yeats, I have to say; I think he identified with the old lunatic genius, the fact that he mastered the English language better than anyone else of his era yet was not himself English, that he was a statesman as well as a poet, that he had a view of the decline of the ordered world similar to Baba's own. In any case, I was made to memorize huge chunks of Yeats's poetry, which I did with a good will because I revered my grandfather and wanted his approval more than anything else in life except maybe the attention of my mother.

I went to the mosque on Fridays with the men and learned the prayers, although it was clear to me at an early age that Baba's Islam was sentimental rather than devout. He didn't, for example, serve wine at meals, but he had a decanter of whiskey in a locked cabinet, which he shared with select friends in the privacy of his study. At seven I was sent as a day student to Aitchison College. Wazir had preceded me there, and I was amazed to find the wild Pashtun boy transformed into a decorous scholar in blazer and shorts. Being several forms ahead of me, he could not officially recognize my existence at school, but I remember once asking him why he put up with it, and he said, "My father expects it and it is a matter of honor. I would be shamed not to do well before these Punjabis." I did poorly myself: slow to read, the fat paragraphs of prose impossible to untangle. I was punished often and resented it. The only thing I was good at was memorizing poetry.

The third life was the one I shared with my mother, a secret life. For one thing, although she prayed conventionally enough with the other women, each Sunday she would wake me early and dress me and take me out of the house. We mounted her little 50cc Honda motorbike, me on the pillion behind, hugging her tight, and drove out of Anarkali down the Mall to Hall Road, where we parked in front of the Roman Catholic cathedral and went to mass. I can't quite recall what I thought of this at the time. I knew my mother was strange and not like the other women of the household. I saw that Laghari Sahib treated her almost like an honorary man, so I guess I assumed she had a special God that was peculiar to her. There were statues of women in the cathedral but none in the mosque, and when I was very small I thought that these were statues of my mom. I didn't take in much doctrine, but I was happy to have her to myself for a morning and grateful to the Catholic Church for providing it.

I have to say she was not a nurturing kind of mom, no great soft breast to hide in, the last resort of comfort; not at all like the other women I knew in my early life—Wazir's mother, Nasha, or my old ayah, Faiza. Hugging Sonia was like hugging a boy.

Not that I lacked hugs. From birth I had Faiza, who bathed and dressed me and kissed away my little hurts and spoke to me in the languages of that country, so that I spoke them like the native I was. The awkward part of this traditional arrangement was that Faiza worked not for my mother but for Noor, my grandmother, called Bibiji by the household. It was apparent to Bibiji that a crazy American woman couldn't possibly be trusted to raise the heir of the eldest son, so when I was small she took over my rearing entirely.

This was wonderful and terrible at the same time. It was wonderful because I was the little prince among the begums, Bibiji and her per-fumed gold-jangling court, the aunties and the friends, all cooing and pinching and hugging and stuffing me with sweetmeats: *barfis*, gulaab jamuns, *jalebis*. Lahore is one of the world centers of sweetmeats, and I would have blown up like a football had my mother's lanky genes not turned out to be proof against that. It was also horrible, because the hugs were too hard and the pinches too painful and the perfumes often smotheringly dense; the talk, too, mainly knocked my mother and the foolishness of my father for bringing such a one into the Laghari family.

My mother left us for almost two years, starting when I was three and Aisha was one, so I spent those formative years unprotected amid the poisoned candy. I should have become one of those plump and indolent Punjabi men, spoiled in the way that only tyrannized women can spoil their sons, but for some reason it didn't happen. I remember very well when she returned to Lahore, tough, lean, and burned as black as a Sindi peasant, shocking the pale aunties and me, too; I ran screaming from her embrace. But after some days of thrilling, nervous courtship she lured me back pretty well, with little treats and presents and the gift of her attention, making me her slave until she was ready to tie on her rubber dick and ditch me again.

I suppose you'd have to call our relationship romantic, in that it involved secrets, like our slipping away to church, and a kind of yearning pursuit on my part. I know she hid from me. There was on our roof an assembly of huge ceramic vases that contained a collection of palms and cycads. It served as sort of a backdrop when we had parties up there and shielded part of the roof from neighboring windows. I once found her there, after a frantic search, behind the palms, sitting on a charpoy, writ-ing in a notebook. I recall spying on her in her hideout and then tiptoeing away, coming back again and again when I couldn't find her elsewhere.

Eventually I must have made some sound because she caught me and invited me into the tiny space. I asked her what she was doing and she said she was making privacy. She said, "Lahore is wonderful and the house is wonderful and the family is too, and don't think I'm not grateful, but they haven't invented privacy here yet and I need it." Then she told me about how when she was in the circus and she wanted to get away from everyone she would crawl into one of the trucks and burrow down into the piles of packing mats and make a little cave for herself where no one could find her.

I liked it when she talked about her time in the circus and I asked her questions about it, only some of which she answered. Later that day I think we played with cards. She always had a deck on her, and she amazed me with card tricks and taught me, when I was old enough, how to rig a deck and deal from the bottom. She could deal from the middle, too, but I was never good enough to do that. Anyway, the next time I went up to the palm cave she wasn't there. I never found her new hiding place.

That first absence was when she went to Soviet Central Asia and came back and wrote a book about it, which nearly caused a war. In 1974 it was one of the most secret places in the world, studded with nuclear facilities and rocket sites, and somehow this twenty-three-year-old girl disguised as a boy slips across the Afghan border—the Iron Curtain!— seems able to go anywhere she wants, and writes a book about it, actually an amusing, charming book, describing no rocket sites, a book about all the lost people up there and their crazily corrupt society: *Up in the Stans*. It made her famous, they called her "a modern Kim," as if she had really been a boy and not a mother of two children, and people came to the house to interview her for American and European TV—which she refused.

Naturally, the Soviets said it was all a CIA plot, and I think Pakistani intelligence was a little miffed, but Laghari Sahib cooled everything down and after that, for about five years, we had what I look back on as the most peaceful period of my life. I put all this together a lot later, when I was grown and curious about what had contributed to the disaster of our lives. When you're a kid, it's just a succession of days; you're happy or sad without much context. My mother had been gone, now she was back, and things would once again revolve satisfactorily around the fixed center of the universe, me.

Mom got pregnant after that and later in the year she had another girl, Jamila. I thought we would be a regular family from then on, and we seemed to be, with only the usual discontents. My father could not have been more kind and generous to me, but the fact is I gave him nothing back; I disdained him and ignored him when I could. My sense of what a real man was had been formed by Gul Muhammed Khan and Laghari Sahib, and Farid didn't measure up.

I think I picked up some of that disdain from Baba himself. Looking back, I can see that the old man was dissatisfied with all his sons, each of whom had inherited only one of his own characteristics. Farid, the eldest, had got the kindness and generosity, but he lacked ambition and the edge necessary to flourish in the tiger pit of Pakistani politics. He'd been handed a job in the foreign ministry, as the basis for a brilliant career in government, but he did not distinguish himself there. His real desire was to be an academic, studying the laws other men had written. Nisar, the middle son, had the brilliance and ambition, as well as the appreciation of art and culture, but he was mean, with a cruel streak. He went into business, which Laghari Sahib considered only one cut up from actual theft—as it sort of is in Pakistan. Seyd, the youngest son, had plenty of edge, and he was generous and loyal to those he considered his friends—among whom my mother and I did not figure—but he was dull. It was all he could do to get through the military academy they sent him to when he bombed out of Aitchison.

Rukhsana, being a girl, did not figure in this algebra, but in the strange way of families, being a girl and the oedipal horseshit being moot, she was closer to Baba than any of her siblings, and he would often ask her to sit by him during the weekly mehfil gatherings, with my mother on the other side.

How do I know all this? Another part of my secret life. My mother used to sit me down, usually in the afternoons after I got back from school, while I ate my tiffin, as they called it, and the girls were out with Faiza, and she would explain my family to me: the tensions, the rivalries, the disappointments, the resentments, all anatomized and poured into my small pink ears. I think now it was cruel to do that to a child, loading me with the kind of insights a kid can't really absorb, just as bad in its way as Bibiji's bad-mouthing. I think it warped me, or maybe I was just warped to begin with. She probably did it because she was lonely, despite

Baba's and Farid's kindness, and she seized on me as the one who could fix it. Or maybe it was *because* of the kindness. It's harder to accept charity than to give it, especially if you're half wild like she was, the way they say a wild animal kept for years and seemingly tame may one day without warning turn on its keeper and chew him up.

That's one excuse. The other, which she actually told me when I asked her years later why she did it, was that she wanted to protect me from what might happen to me if anything happened to her, that this kind of knowledge, that penetration of motive and hidden interpersonal combat, would help me survive.

These séances were usually interrupted by the return of Faiza and the girls from wherever they'd been, to a public garden or the bazaar, and the change of air was astounding, like sun breaking through a muggy day. Aisha was seven at the time I'm thinking of, to my nine; she would arrive in a whirl of gangly legs and a spate of bright chatter, and instantly all the dark plots were blown into flying ash and dispersed. *There was an elephant and the man let us feed it, but Faiza wouldn't let us ride. A lady crashed her bicycle into a man and everything spilled and the pigeons escaped, oh, Theo, it was so funny!* They brought halvah home, and news of the halvah-wallah and his tribe, in detail, with opinions and then comments on everyone who'd talked to them, and this was not a short list, because Aisha was the princess of the Urdu Bazaar; she could hardly go ten steps without someone calling her to talk, offering her a sweet. If a family is lucky it has someone like Aisha in it, the clearer of the air, the one for whose sake quarrels are stilled, the lens through which all the family's love is refined and focused.

She loved me too, the big brother, the strongest, bravest, most handsome of brothers, as she would tell me in Urdu, where you can say things that would be ridiculous in English, and I wanted to cut off a finger every time I hurt her, times more frequent than I can now bear to think about. Farid worshipped the shadow of her passing, and my mother ... well, there was a distance between them, I felt it at nine, and I suppose it was because even an angel child has to be disciplined and my mother was the one to do it, because Farid would give her anything she wanted.

Then my mother left again: I must have been nine or ten; one morning she was just gone without a word. My father said she had gone on haj, which I knew was a good thing to do, so I wondered why all the adults in the house were angry. That week in Bibiji's court it was the only topic of conversation, mainly in nasty whispers so I couldn't hear, but I heard enough, and when my grandmother said that my mother was no better than a *fahisha* I pulled away from her and stood up and said my mother was not a fahisha and I wouldn't stand for hearing her called one; the fahishas lived in Tibbi, what Lahoris call the Hira Mandi, where Baba went to see them every Saturday night with his friends. I don't recall how I knew that Baba visited the famous courtesans of Lahore in their special district; I guess I had picked up the servants' gossip or maybe Wazir's, who knew everything.

Whatever, we had a screaming match and I ran out of the perfume fog into fresh air. After that, I was not invited to sit with Bibiji and her friends; I had joined the camp of the enemy. After that, Aisha was the favorite, though a girl.

Because of these events and because my mother was gone, Aisha got indulged more than she would have. Not that she wanted much, a kid surrounded by that much love doesn't need a lot of stuff, but one thing she wanted got me into the most trouble I was ever in while I was in Lahore and also saved my life. The thing was a Polaroid camera. She'd seen it at a party and she conceived a fierce desire for one and uncharacteristically nagged our father about it, and at her next birthday he gave her one, with a warning to be sparing of the film, hard to get in Lahore at the time, and never to take it out of the house.

Which of course she did, how could she deprive her friends throughout the bazaar of a look at her treasure? Besides, she wanted to give them each a Polaroid portrait of themselves. So she went out with it concealed in a straw market bag that she always carried in imitation of Faiza's big one, and she was able to slip away from the ayah and down an alley. She met the ice-candy man and did his picture, a crowd gathering to see this wonder, and then, with the camera slung around her neck, she trotted off back up the alley. By that time some big kids were waiting for her, and they roughed her up a little and took the camera.

It was Wazir who told me who did it. Up as he always was on the gossip of the bazaars, he came into my room on the night after it happened— I could still hear Aisha weeping at intervals, being comforted by Faiza to not much avail—and told me it was the Barshawi brothers. These were a trio of teenage mopes, the sons of a local butcher who was also a ward-heeler type who did low-end political thuggery. The boys were in the habit of grabbing stuff without paying for it, and the father's political connections made it hard for the bazaaris to get any redress. That's Pakistan.

As it happened, Laghari Sahib was in Islamabad for a couple of days on judicial business, and Gul Muhammed with him, so we boys decided that the honor of the family had been damaged and like good Pashtuns we had to make it right. This was Wazir's idea, naturally, but I took to it without much argument. Somehow, it never occurred to me to go to Farid. Anyway, Wazir was able to sneak off with one of his father's guns and that evening the pair of us went down to the Urdu Bazaar. As the injured party, I got to carry the thing, a fully loaded .455 Webley Mark VI pistol jammed in my waistband under my long shirt. Arriving at the street of the butchers, we found the oldest Barshawi boy, Amir, in the act of unloading a live sheep from a motorized cart. I pulled out the pistol.

I was nine years old and small and this piece weighed two and a half pounds, a hunk of black steel the size of a leg of lamb. I could hardly aim it at all, and the single-action trigger pull is hard even for a grown man, but in the service of honor I got off my shot. *Boom!* The sheep gave a shrill despairing bleat, Amir let out a similar sound and went down, and the pistol's mighty recoil snapped my skinny forearm back like a door hinge, sending the hammer into my forehead. I went down too with a face full of blood.

Wazir hauled me to my feet, picked up the pistol, and dragged me out of there bearing my first wound on the field of honor, blinded, deafened—not unusual conditions where honor is concerned—but reasonably satisfied. Fortunately, as it turned out, I'd whacked the sheep and not Amir, so Laghari Sahib was able to smooth things over when he returned the following evening. Then we had an informal judicial hearing in his study.

In my military career I have been chewed out by experts, people who do it for a living at the highest levels of out-chewing, but I have to say that the reaming I got from my grandfather that night was well up there among the top two or three. He had me stand in front of his desk, him erect in his big tufted leather chair, my father sitting at one side, looking pale, as if he were getting some of the back blast himself, while Grandfather called me a fool, a coward, a moral imbecile, a disgrace to the name of Laghari, a curse on his house, a bazaari guttersnipe . . . and on and on in the same vein. I'd never seen this side of Laghari Sahib before, and for the first time I felt a spark of sympathy for my father.

Then he went on about how day after day he labored to bring law to a lawless, violent land, how the law was the only thing that kept this misbegotten country from falling into murderous anarchy, and now to find it flouted by a child of his own house? Unspeakable! Intolerable! He asked whatever had possessed me to do such a thing and I said I had heard that the Barshawis had beaten up Aisha and stolen her camera and—

And what? My voice choked off. There is a kind of thinking so stupid that little boys and leaders of nations can't actually bring themselves to articulate it when the jig is finally up, but Laghari Sahib knew very well what it was.

He said, "So on the basis of a bazaar rumor, you proposed to murder a human being? Instead of calling for the police?"

"The police don't do anything to the Barshawis."

"Yes, the police are corrupt, but corruption has a limit, even in Lahore. Didn't it occur to what I suppose I must call your mind that stealing from the granddaughter of a supreme court judge and offering her violence is a different matter from swiping a piece of fruit or a roasted chicken from a bazaari shop table? It is grand larceny with violence, you blockhead! I could have directed the police to arrest those dreadful boys and I would have seen them prosecuted to the full extent of the law. They would be in prison this minute, and for years. Now, instead, I must go hat in hand to the butcher Barshawi and ask him please not to press charges of attempted murder against you and Wazir, and I will be in his debt. Can you even conceive of what it will mean to be in debt to such a man, of what evils I will have to ignore in my official capacity? Oh, stop your sniveling! Farid, give him a handkerchief. Disgusting behavior! I tell you, young fellow, it is a good thing for you that I do not believe in corporal punishment, or you would not have a single bit of skin left on your backside. As it is, your allowance is stopped from this instant. You will be confined to your room except for school and meals. No excursions and no treats until further notice. House arrest, do you understand? And you are very lucky to escape the boys' prison at Rawalpindi, you and Wazir."

"It was my idea," I said. "Wazir just got me the gun. It's not his fault."

"No, his fault was greater because he is old enough to know better. And let me tell you, I would not be Wazir tonight for a crore of rupees. Farid, get this creature out of my sight!"

My father stood and put his hand on my shoulder, but I shrugged it off and ran out, my eyes streaming. As I came into the courtyard I heard, mixed with the usual sounds of the night—a bulbul twittering, the pump generator, distant music, the rustlings of the peepul tree—an unfamiliar addition: a sharp whistle ending with a snap and then a sharp, stifled cry of pain: Gul Muhammed whipping his son.

I found I didn't care much, my own misery being too all-consuming, although I recall a perverted envy. Wazir would bear manly marks of suffering, while mine were all in the pride of my heart and unavailable for boasting inspection. Once in my room, I descended into rage, not because of the ridiculous, insulting, infantile punishments, but because I had been injured in my conception of myself as a hero, and by the man whom I wished to impress more than anyone else. I hated Baba in that hour, as only a boy can hate, without the tempering of a lifetime's experience or the constraints of adult responsibility. I took it out on the furnishings and on my possessions, overturning my bed and dresser, flinging the lamp against the wall, and so on. I had a collection of beautiful British lead soldiers, given to me by Baba for a succession of birthdays, all the regiments of the old Raj, horse and foot, and these I carefully destroyed, one by one, the tears and snot gushing forth.

Then my sister Aisha appeared at the doorway, in her nightgown, clutching her stuffed bunny, her face still bearing the livid marks inflicted in the mugging. She was worried about me. She thought I'd been whipped too and wanted to comfort me.

I snarled at her. I told her it was all her fault, she'd been told not to take her stupid camera to the bazaar. I said I wished they'd killed her. I used English obscenities, which were the only ones I had on hand. Her little face collapsed. She fled. Perfect.

The next day she painted me a picture and slid it under my prison door. She was a wonderful artist, and the picture showed me and Wazir and her and Jamila playing in a green field under deodars. I tore it up and scattered the pieces out the window.

In the next few days I ate breakfast with the family in silence, went to school, ate again in silence, and stayed in my room. The servants had repaired the damage to my room, of course. One night, later in that awful week, I was awakened from an uneasy sleep by a repetitive clinking sound. I looked out my window—nothing. So I climbed out on the balcony and hitched myself up on an iron trellis full of bougainvillea, and from there I could just make out, through the peepul's branches, a group of men at the end of our street, where you had to make a sharp turn to get onto Lahore Road, who seemed to be repairing the pavement. I wondered briefly why they were working at night and decided it was so they would not interfere with traffic. I went back to bed.

The next day was March 23, 1980, a date forever burned into memory. This is Pakistan Day and a public holiday. The courts were closed, and on such holidays Laghari Sahib liked to take us children in his Rolls-Royce to Gawal Mandi to stuff ourselves with sweets and then to Shalamar Garden to play and fly kites and later wander among the thousands of candles in the dusk. The Rolls was the old kind with a massive chrome bumper in the back, and the local street kids had learned that when Daud, the driver, slowed to turn the tight corner on the end of our street they could jump up on it and, crouching down, enjoy a ride to wherever we were going. I recall envying them their freedom and wanted to ride that way myself, instead of in the plush interior.

Of course, neither Wazir nor I was going this year. I was therefore able to watch as Baba and the two girls, my sisters, mounted the big Rolls along with Faiza and Daud and set off. I was at my desk, doing my homework, long division as I recall, when the house shook with the blast. I ran out on the balcony and saw the Rolls engulfed in black smoke and flames, right at the place where I'd watched the men the previous night.

I think of that every time I smell the blast stink of high explosive, which is a lot, considering what I do for a living. And that was the end of all those lives—I mean my multiple lives—and of my childhood.

℞

Gloria had listened to all this without asking anything. By the time I was finished, the bottle was nearly empty.

"That's quite a story," she said. "And I thought *I* had a hard life."

"What was your hard life?"

"Oh, you know, the barrio, the agony of poverty and prejudice, yadda yadda. My kid brother became a junkie and got shot in the street. The usual. So what happened next?"

"I'm sorry about your brother."

Her face closed down. This was delving, apparently. "Yeah, but I got over it. Anyway, the car blew up and your grandfather and your sisters got killed, and . . . ?"

"I'll tell you, but first."

"Oh, I have to put out to get the story? Like what's-her-name, Scheherazade?"

"The reverse," I said. "It's an Islamic thing. You probably wouldn't understand."

We took off each other's clothes with our mouths locked together, like in the movies, and I found it was harder than it looks on the screen. She seemed to have been aroused by my story, and I felt myself riding on her excitement, drowning the guilt to an extent, which I figured out about then was the reason for the nice meal and this terrific dessert while my mother was tied up in some cellar. My excuse was that—honestly—I thought it might be the very last time.

7

Sonia awakens to the sound of a heavy truck rolling past the inn and up the narrow village street. The room is perfectly dark; her eyes register nothing but their own energy, little points of shifting false light. She hears Annette's soft sleep noises, snores, whimpers, the creak of charpoy ropes as her fellow captive turns. From the street comes a shout; other voices join—it's amazing how sound travels on a still night in a village in the mountains—there is a scraping sound and more voices, rhythmic now, as if a group of men are carrying out some heavy task. A door closes, and then silence, except for the hiss of the night wind blowing sand against the walls.

Some time passes. Sonia wishes she still had her watch but laughs secretly to herself. She has no need anymore to tell time; captivity makes time irrelevant and so is curiously liberating for a denizen of the frenetic West. After an uncertain interval a new sound begins, a deep muffled growl, which she recognizes as a diesel engine, a big one. Sonia rises and walks carefully to the wall under one of the windows. There is an irregularity in the masonry there that enables her to boost herself up to look through the shutter slats. She can see the black bulk of an adjoining building and a thin triangle of sky, specked with small chilly stars. Then, for just a moment, she sees a flash of light from the direction of the diesel sound, unmistakable evidence that someone is generating electricity in the village.

She drops lightly from the wall, landing with a little bounce, the early training still in her nerves and muscles so she can never forget the circus, and lies on the charpoy again, waiting, thinking about the boy's dream and what she will say to him, if he comes.

And about her own dream, the deformed child, the slaughtered little creatures. Is the boy Patang, are the creatures the hostages? It's possible; she has had clairvoyant dreams before this, but at the same time she knows that everything in a dream relates both to her own personal history and also to the deeper history of her species. That's the great problem with the Jungian approach: everything can mean anything. It requires colossal discernment to tease meaning out of the tangle of archetypes, memory, synchronicity. The psyche knows, but the psyche is not telling; the psyche is subtle and not entirely of this world.

She'd learned that from Joachim Fluss in Zurich, her therapist, teacher, friend, and tormentor, the last in a series of father figures in the skein that began with the horrible Guido and included B. B. Laghari and Ismail Raza Ali but not her poor actual father. Fluss was gone now; he was in late middle age when she met him, one of Jung's original students, present at the creation of analytic psychology back in the teens and twenties of the last century, a stalwart of the Burghölzli and still serving there on the day she'd arrived, near catatonic with grief, strapped to a bed so she wouldn't hurt herself. Her head was bandaged; she had tried unsuccessfully to bash her brains out against a curb on the Bahnhofstrasse.

They had sedated her, and she came up out of the welcome oblivion to find him staring down at her, his appearance so startling she let out a little cry of alarm. They had opened the blinds so the room was full of winter's pure light, and he was sitting at such an angle that this light reflected off his round gold-rimmed spectacles, so she saw only two glittering disks and a halo of untidy, flossy, gray-tinged wheaten hair. Then he moved slightly and she saw his face: round, red-cheeked, knobby-featured, the brush mustache, modeled on the Master's, still yellowish, and those deep-set, humorous, penetrating blue eyes.

He introduced himself and asked how she was feeling. She turned away from him, told him to leave her alone. But he did not. Instead he began to talk, in a pleasant baritone, slightly accented. He said she'd been unconscious for two days, during which time the authorities had determined her identity and gathered information on her recent catastrophe. He extended his condolences. He said further that inquiries had been made of her family in Lahore. There seemed to be much confusion in Lahore—understandable in the circumstances. He was obliged to inform her that, regrettably, her husband had also suffered a severe breakdown and was at present himself in hospital in Lahore. Whoever had spoken to the inquiring administrator had been quite adamant that the family wanted nothing whatever to do with Sonia Bailey.

She had not responded at all to this information. She recalled wishing that he would go away. She recalled wishing for more sedation, another plunge into dreamless sleep. But he did not depart. Instead, he told her that he was an admirer of her work. He'd read both her books: a fascinating view of a little-known world—unknown to the average Swiss, at any rate—he himself had always longed to travel, as she had, as Jung had, of course, and immerse himself in different cultures, but aside from the usual conference-going he'd only managed two trips, one to Brazil and the other to China, both too short, and he hadn't known the languages and was a victim of translation, unlike herself. How remarkable her facility with languages! He had very few himself, alas, just the usual Swiss mix. To what did she attribute this gift?

No answer, but he plowed along as if she *had* answered, as if they *were* having a conversation. He talked knowledgeably about her books, including his favorite passages, and about other travel books he'd loved: Saint-Exupéry, Beryl Markham, Rebecca West, Bruce Chatwin, Gertrude Bell. Intertesting that so many great travel writers were women, especially given the limitations faced until quite recently by women traveling on their own. Why do you think that is?

No answer to this either, or to dozens of other questions over the following week, but he is not put off, every day in the late afternoon he arrives, pulls up a straight chair, and begins again, as if they are old friends, as if she is a willing partner in their conversation. Later she understands that he is using language to bring her back into life; he does the same with people who have not spoken to anyone in years, and sometimes even they respond.

When eventually she spoke it was with anger: How dare he interrupt her grief with this chatter? She told him to go away. He ignored her. He beamed. She speaks! Wonderful!

She shouted, cursed, threw a water glass at his head.

He picked it up, smiling, and she saw he dragged his left leg; he had a built-up shoe. He tapped the cup: plastic, he said, inelegant, but many patients throw cups at my head, and the staff dislikes clearing away the broken glass. How did you come to marry into a Pakistani family?

If I tell you, she answered, will you leave me alone?

Of course, he said. I promise to skip tomorrow.

She told him the story, the murdered family; he listened, asked no question, bid her good day, and left.

He did not come the next day, true to his word. When he arrived again, she told him she wanted to leave. He smiled. Of course you can leave. This is a madhouse, you know, and you are not mad. Anyone would break down under a load of such grief. But now you have recovered yourself. He called an attendant: Bring Madame Bailey's things, if you please. He shook her hand and turned to go, but paused. He said offhandedly, with that hint of slyness she would come to recognize, You know, it is really a shame.

The attendant entered with her clothes and she sat on the bed, clutching them on her lap. The blouse was stained with her dried blood. She felt a pang of nausea but not because of the blood. She was fine with blood; the nausea was existential, as in Sartre.

She asked him what was a shame?

He said he had reread her books. He said she had a remarkable ability to penetrate foreign cultures; she was a listener; she accepted the concrete existence of the unseen world. All these abilities were desirable in an analytic psychotherapist, for the mad are a different culture, each one a sole member of that culture, each speaking a tongue incomprehensible to others; thus their dreadful isolation and pain. We have drugs and shocks and all that now, but here we also believe that you must enter that world, the culture of the insane, speak to them in their own language, and gently bring them back to our world. I believe this is something you could do.

She was amazed: did he seriously think she could be a therapist? I can barely take care of myself, she said.

Actually, that is an advantage, he said: the wounded healer. He tapped his bad leg. Polio when I was fifteen. I was a football player, a mountain climber. I thought my life was over. I was at zero, you understand, as you are at zero now. The ego is all eroded. There is nothing worse than a therapist full of himself, and we both have avoided that. Besides, you must have work. I expect you are no longer interested in traveling the world and writing, and you are cut off from your family. It is just a suggestion....

Thus she began her therapy, which, if it did not entirely cure her, had at least provided a direction for her life, a vector that had led to this locked room. Thirty years to go from locked room to locked room. Fluss would have been hugely amused.

℞

She hears soft, scraping footsteps outside the door and a liquid sucking noise, hard to identify until she smells the sweet reek of lubricating oil. Smart Patang, to oil the squeaking lock. A soft click and a little breeze on her cheek and the loom of another human presence in the room. Close by, on her charpoy, Annette Cosgrove murmurs and turns in her sleep.

His voice close to her ear. "How did you know about my dream?"

"Never mind that now. Do you want to know what it means and why God, the compassionate One, has sent it to you?"

A considerate pause. "Yes, tell me."

"Then in the name of God listen! You dreamed that your father asked you to bring him two horses, a black stallion and a white mare. He told you to ride the white and lead the black on a line. You headed up a high mountain along a narrow path with a precipice on one side. The mare was calm under you, but the stallion was unruly and kicked and bit at the mare, so you decided to disobey your father and ride the stallion instead. The path grew steeper and narrower, and then to your horror the stallion bolted and plunged off the edge. You were suspended over the void by the line but did not fall, because the white mare held it. The line stretched and came near to breaking. Then you heard a voice saying, 'Cling to the line and cut the stallion loose.' But you were afraid to cut the line because of what your father would say if you lost a valuable horse. Again the voice called, 'Save yourself, my son, and cut the line!' When you realized it was your father's voice you cut the line, the black horse fell screaming into the abyss, and the white mare pulled you up to safety, but as you rose you wounded your heel on a rock. That was your dream."

"Yes," he replies with a quaver in his voice. "What does it mean?"

"The narrow path is the way of Islam; the white horse is the teachings of the Prophet, on whom be peace. The black horse is the horse of pride and the violence that comes from pride. The abyss is the gate of Hell, to which the prideful are condemned. Your father is your father. He is dead, is he not?"

"Yes. He died in the jihad, when I was a baby."

"God sent him to you out of Paradise then, as a warning, to keep you safe from Hell, by making you return to the path of Islam and the certain guidance of the Prophet, peace be upon him."

"But I *am* on the path of Islam. I am a mujahid."

"Your father was a mujahid. He fought the Russians, who denied Islam, stabled their troops in mosques, murdered women and children, and defiled the holy books with their filth. But you murder good Muslims, which I saw with my own eyes, and make war on the innocent."

"Not true! Idris Ghulam says we must do the lesser evil for the greater good."

"Which is what?"

"Driving the *kafiri* out of Kashmir and Afghanistan and building Islamic states."

"If you wish to drive the Indians out of Kashmir, you should be shooting Indian soldiers, not Pakistani Muslims. And Pakistan and Afghanistan are already Muslim states."

"They are not proper Muslim states. They are allied with America, and they don't follow sharia law."

"Tell me, what is the year?"

"What do you mean?"

"The year! What is the year, counting from the hegira?"

"It is 1429."

"Yes, and why do we count from the hegira?"

"Because it is when the Prophet, peace be upon him, fled with his followers from Mecca to Medina."

"Yes. Don't you find it interesting that the birth of Islam is counted from a retreat? Not from a victory, not from the victory at Badr or at Ohod or from the conquest of Mecca, but from a retreat. Why do you suppose we do that, Patang?"

The boy is mute, baffled, and so she continues.

"Because the Prophet, peace be upon him, was reluctant in the highest degree to shed human blood. He did not form a secret society in Mecca to assassinate idolaters and their women and children and burn down their homes. Instead he retreated to a place of safety. And even when the idolaters attacked the Muslims at Badr and God gave the faithful their victory, the Prophet, peace be upon him, released all his prisoners after the battle and warned his followers not to molest the harmless or destroy their dwellings or their means of livelihood. And this was when Islam was a mere handful of families, not a billion people and two dozen nations. No, child, you ride the black horse of pride, you and your Idris Ghulam, and it will lead you to the flaming pit. Your father warns you from Paradise. God warns you. Heed the Prophet, peace be upon him; ride his horse on the narrow path. Thus says the Prophet, peace be upon him: 'He will not enter Hell who hath faith equal to a single grain of mustard seed in his heart; and he will not enter Paradise, who hath pride equal to a single grain of mustard seed in his heart.' "

"That is not true!" the boy shouts. "Why should I believe you? You are a foreign woman and a witch!"

"I am not a witch," says Sonia. "You asked how I knew of your dream. I could have lied and put fear in you and say I divined it with the help of the djinn, but God hates liars, and so I say now that I heard you tell your dream to the other guard. But my interpretation is true, as you will see, for you will be wounded on your foot and then recall your father's words and mine."

The boy utters a frightened curse and leaves, locking the door behind him.

In the dark, from the other charpoy, Sonia hears Annette stir. "Did we disturb you?" she asks.

"No. What was that all about? The guard didn't seem too happy."

Sonia summarizes the conversation. Annette gives an astonished whistle. "Wow! Do you think it's wise to annoy our guards?"

"The truth is often annoying. Besides, just now it's our only weapon. I've penetrated his self-righteousness, just a little. He sees himself as a holy warrior, which is why he can bear to serve in a unit with men from other tribes, and take orders from men from tribes with whom his tribe or *khel* has a blood feud. This is how Pashtuns are: they can join briefly against a common enemy, but they always tend to pull apart after that enemy is defeated. That's what happened in Afghanistan after the Russians left. This so-called jihad is all that holds them together now, so we have to break them of the idea that they are fighting in God's cause, which of course they are not. Let's see what happens when young Patang hurts his foot."

"But what makes you think he's going to hurt his foot?"

"Because he dreamed it and I interpreted the dream that way."

"What? That makes no sense."

"No, not rationally, but we're not in the rational world here—or in our dreams either. Patang will be thinking about his foot all the time now.

He'll be extra careful for a while, but it will gnaw at him, he'll grow clumsy, because, of course, you can't really do any of the things we normally do with our feet using conscious thought. So he'll trip and sprain an ankle. Or he'll become so obsessed with the idea that he'll unconsciously discharge the tension by 'accidentally' dropping a load of bricks on his toes. Then, naturally, he'll blab the whole thing. Pashtuns are fascinated by this kind of stuff; it's threaded through all their folk tales—the prophetic dream. We should get some attention after that."

"My God! Isn't that incredibly dangerous?"

Sonia laughs softly. "Well, we're not exactly in the lap of safety as it is. No, first we have to draw their attention to us—to me, actually—as something other than a victim. Once I'm established as that, I'll have to challenge them from the heart of their religion, which I've already started doing with Patang. I told you before, hostage and captive are in a relationship and we have to control the tempo of that relationship, even though we have no power. Think of the Romans and the original Christians. The Romans murdered them for three centuries, and with every murder the Christians grew stronger and the Romans weaker. Why was that? Because their faith allowed Christians to die with nobility, even though they were slaves, and that struck at the heart of the Roman idea of how the world was constituted. *Dulce et decorum est pro patria mori.* Any belief that allowed a slave to die like a Roman general had to have some underlying reality, so every martyrdom in the arena made a hundred converts."

"But what if they kill you?"

"Oh, they're going to kill me. I was doomed from the moment they stopped our convoy. But I'm going to make it hard for them, and maybe that will save some of you."

Sonia can now make out the shape of her companion across the room. The gaps between the slats in the shutters have gradually become visible as slate-blue strips.

"What do you mean you were doomed?" says Annette. "Why you in particular?"

Sonia laughs again. "Well, maybe that's an exaggeration for effect. I have a tendency to oversell. It comes from being raised in the circus. Tell me, do you know who Sonia Bailey is?"

"Some kind of explorer, back in the seventies? My roommate in college had her book."

"Ah, that's a welcome answer. Let's hope our friends out there share your ignorance."

"I don't understand. What does Sonia Bailey have to do with us? Anyway, isn't she dead?"

"Not yet. I'm her."

"*You're* Sonia Bailey?"

"Yes. Pleased to meet you. Anyway, it's not like Superman and Clark Kent, although I try to keep it quiet. Back when I wrote those books I declined the usual celebrity perks: I didn't give interviews or do book tours, I wasn't on TV, I didn't even have an author photograph. The mysterious Sonia Bailey. Obviously, my family knows, and several members of our group here, but for the past thirty years I've been Mrs. Laghari, a Pakistani-American therapist, a respectable lady who did not travel the haj to Mecca disguised as a man. If these jokers find out they'll snuff me like a candle."

"Jesus!"

"Just so. Crucifixion is one of the traditional punishments for blasphemy, although, for women, chopping them into pieces is more common. On the other hand—"

She stops. A thin wailing has begun outside, hardly distinguishable from the whine of the eternal wind, announcing that the night is ended; it is time for morning prayers. Annette watches Sonia as she washes and performs the ritual gestures and prostrations, so different from her own private, silent, liberal religion.

Sonia finishes the Fajr, the shortest prayer of the day, and becomes aware that the other woman is staring at her. She smiles and says, "It must seem strange to you, this kind of prayer. Primitive?"

Annette blushes. "Yes, frankly, a little. I realize it's not politically correct, but I tend to be suspicious of highly ritualized religion. It's too easy to punch in all the rituals and then feel you're right with God, meanwhile feeling free to be as nasty as you like in daily life."

"Spoken like a true child of the Reformation," says Sonia, and they both laugh. "On the other hand, we're animals, we have bodies, and what our bodies do is important. That's one reason God gave them to us."

"Don't you find it hard to practice back home? I mean in the States."

"Oh, no. Back home I go to church. I'm a Catholic there."

This knots Annette's smooth brow. "You mean it's a *pretense*?"

"Not at all. I'm perfectly sincere at the moment of prayer in either tradition. Surely you don't think God *cares* how we worship Him? And a mass, with its ritual motions and responses, is very much the same as *salat*, in the sense that humanity is one family, whether you call it the umma or the Body of Christ, and it's important for us all to do the same thing with our bodies at the same time. Every believing Muslim in this time zone just did what I just did, and as the earth spins around today so the tide of Fajr will flow with the light of day, and then another prayer at noon, Dhuhr, and then Ashr, Maghrib, and Isha, five in all, today and every day. It's a pretty neat feeling, being engulfed in prayer and, despite individual differences between people, to be united in that one thing."

"Yes, well, it doesn't seem to have helped the Muslims get united any more than it's helped the Christians."

"No, it's a scandal. We're none of us what God meant us to be. But on the other hand, if you suppress that kind of ritual you atomize the faithful even more. Islam has a small number of divisions, and the Catholics are still hanging in there, but anyone with a Bible and a good speaking voice can start a Protestant church. Recent history suggests that when you cast off all that uncomfortable ritualistic stuff your religion tends to collapse into mere sociability and niceness, and then it fades away. Then some joker comes along and says, Believe in *me;* we can make Paradise here on earth; we don't need God. All we have to do is get rid of the capitalists—or the Jews, or make everyone into a capitalist—all we have to do is make everyone rich and have lots of sex, and life will be perfect."

Annette says, "Surely you're not saying that religious fanaticism is better for the mass of humanity than civil rights, clean water, health care, and a decent income."

"No, of course I'm not saying that," Sonia replies, but any further clarification is interrupted by the sound of the door. In comes a woman carrying the usual food tray with tea, chapatis, and dal. It is not the old woman who has served them before, but a younger one, just a girl. Her shape under the concealing robe is slender, her face is veiled by a fold of her dupatta.

Sonia takes the tray, smiles, and says, "May God be with you," and the girl answers, "May you live in peace," in a voice curiously distorted. Sonia says, "My name is Sonia. What is your name?" The girl says, "Rashida," and immediately turns and leaves the room. A guard, the one with the bushy beard, glares at them for an instant and then closes and locks the door.

The two women sit and eat their breakfast. Annette asks, "Why did she keep her veil on? The other woman didn't."

"Oh, I think she was embarrassed. Didn't you hear her voice? Her nose has probably been cut off."

"Good God! By who?"

"Probably her father or a brother. It's less common than it used to be, but it still happens. It's common enough so that among Pashtun boys it's a coarse flirt line, like 'Show us your tits' among drunk frat boys in the States. You accuse a girl of having her nose cut off, and maybe she'll flash her face to show it's not true. Risky, but it does happen."

"But why would they do that to a girl?"

Sonia shrugs and takes up another chapati. "It could be anything. She was seen talking to a boy; she exposed her leg or her face to a strange man. Or it could have been just suspicion—maybe her family thought she was too seductive-looking."

"And I'm sure the man who did it thinks he's right with Allah because he says all his prayers."

"I'm sure he does, although that kind of thing has absolutely nothing to do with Islam. Every culture has fetishes, and among the Pashtuns it's on the one hand hospitality and on the other the chastity of their women. Among the Americans it's on the one hand money and on the other sexual hypocrisy."

"Surely you can't compare that to mutilating a girl!"

"I can and do. Businesses and factories are closed down, people are discarded, whole communities are destroyed, with all the catastrophes that follow—crime, suicide, domestic violence—just so a firm can get a bump in the stock market, and we think that's perfectly okay; that's how capitalism works. We keep the poor in festering ghettos. If you can't pay for health care you sicken and die. It's rational, we say, because return on investment is our highest good. Well, to the Pashtuns honor is the highest good, so it's rational to cut off the nose of a girl who's compromised your honor."

"You can't possibly believe that."

Sonia pauses as a loud vehicle grinds up the hill outside the hujra. It soon stops and they hear shouts and clankings from a nearby building. The diesel engine from the night before roars anew.

"It seems to be a busy day in the village of no return," observes Sonia. "But it's not a question of what I believe—or, rather, it *is* but in another sense. If you believe in God, you're inclined to take the world as it comes, rather than impose a system on it. The problem with both the Pashtun way and the American way is that they each worship something other than God: honor and money. The Pashtuns shouldn't cut off girls' noses for honor, and the Americans shouldn't destroy lives for gain, especially since the Prophet preached extensively against pride, and you'll recall Jesus had some harsh things to say about loot. But what you seem to be implying is that the Pashtuns are inherently depraved because what they falsely prize is different from what we falsely prize. And that can't be true."

"I don't prize money," says Annette.

"No, you fly into dangerous places and try to make peace. It's very noble."

"Are you being sarcastic?"

"Not at all. But you know, people devoted to good works are in exactly the same danger of spiritual pride as people who concentrate on doing the rituals properly. There is absolutely nothing more dangerous in the world than self-righteousness tied to power. Those idiots out there are one example, and the recent foreign policy of the United States is another. The world is beyond fixing. That's why we pray."

"But surely, faith without works is sterile—" Annette begins, and then is stopped by a shrill scream, followed by shouts and more screams. A door slams and all becomes silent again, except for the wind and the diesel.

"I wonder what that was all about," says Sonia. "I'm sorry... you were saying?"

But Annette has dropped her theological point, as though the cry from outside has pressed upon her with renewed force her present dire circumstances. She says, "Excuse me. I'm very tired right now; I need to rest," and she lies down on her charpoy and pulls the quilt over her head.

Sonia observes this and understands. She herself slept a good deal after her mother was killed, twelve or even sixteen hours a day, for weeks. There are life events that can destroy the personality, which is a lot more fragile than most people imagine, constructed as it is from bits provided by others in the most haphazard way. People can be torn down to the core, "shattered," as the expression goes, and then they seek sleep. And dreams, which provide the ground for the construction of a new and more integrated self. Providing there's a core, and providing they're willing to do the work.

Nor does insight help much. Fluss was always calling insight "baby steps." During her first year in therapy, she had balked; she was tired of going over the sad stories, she thought she was done, and he'd said, You aren't even started, my dear. Yes, now we have the dynamics, the demanding mother, the ineffective father, the shattering accidents, the insecurity, the rejection of offered security, the purposeful disruptions, the running off, the guilt and what results—all fine. Write it on an index card and stick it in your wallet. But now we must start on the *work*. Now we must get you to *awaken*!

Yes, work and awakening. That was the hard part, and Sonia is not sure that even now she has achieved it. More than Annette, perhaps. She can handle the Jungian jargon, she can do the dream work, but there is a blockage, a drag, a secret standing in the way. Perhaps that dream with the horrible boy is a clue. She wonders if she will figure it all out before she dies.

Annette has fallen asleep. Sonia feels a certain sympathy for the collapsed, naturally, but at the moment Annette's collapse means there are more chapatis for her. She eats them all greedily and drinks the rest of the tea.

She spends the next hours writing in her notebook with a tiny pen. She is writing to her son, an apology, not just in the commonplace sense of a petition for forgiveness but also, mainly, in the older definition, an apology for her life, an explanation of why she has lived it as she has. She hopes it will somehow survive her death and that he will read it. She is a fluent writer, but this is a hard thing to do. It is easier to tell the truth to the world than to people you love.

There comes a point when she can't write anymore. She puts the notebook and pen away in their small pocket and from another one takes a deck of cards. She shuffles, does fans—the peel-away, the reverse, the one-hand—then fancy shuffles—the waterfall, the hindu—then deals out the four cards from the top of the deck, all aces: *snap, snap, snap, snap*. She wishes she had a mirror to check her passes and lifts, for she has not practiced in a while and feels rusty. On the other hand, now she has nothing but time.

The hours pass; the light from the window becomes rosy, then white.

She wonders about the others, especially Karl-Heinz, who is so frail. She knows him from the Zurich days, he and his wife, Elsa. She had met Elsa before she met Karl-Heinz; Elsa was an almoner at the Burghölzli. Fluss had sent her in because of the blood on Sonia's clothes, and Elsa had taken the clothes away and brought fresh ones, a characteristic act of kindness. Afterward, when Sonia had become Fluss's student, she had taken Sonia into her social circle along with Fluss, who was divorced, and a changing circus of other lost souls: the formerly mad and their keepers and a good portion of the psycho-industrial complex of Zurich. A salon, but cozy in the Swiss manner; it was probably this kindness more than the precepts of Jung that had saved Sonia in those first months. She had a cozy deficit of vast proportions and drank it in like water in the desert.

Elsa was dead too. Karl-Heinz was the only one from those days with whom Sonia had retained contact, and she was determined that he would survive.

℘

Sonia is still practicing a changing-card trick, deceptively difficult because it has to be done very slowly to be convincing, when the door opens again and the bearded guard sticks his head in. Sonia wishes him peace in Pashtun, and he seems startled to hear his language on her tongue. She wonders what the troops have been told about their captives. He mumbles something and withdraws, allowing the girl Rashida to enter with another tray of chapatis, dal, and tea.

"Peace be with you," says Sonia, as the girl sets down the tin tray and picks up the old one.

The girl responds, "May God be with you."

Sonia flicks the cards into a fancy double fan, catching the girl's eye. "Would you like to see something magical?"

Without waiting for a reply, Sonia performs a card change. She cuts the deck and holds it up, the long side parallel to the ground, exposing the queen of hearts. Slowly, she moves her free hand over the card face and away. Still the queen of hearts. Again she caresses the queen but when she draws her hand away again, the card showing is the ace of spades. Rashida gasps behind her veil.

"Do it again!"

Sonia does, and then asks casually, "We heard someone scream this morning. I hope no one has been hurt."

"Only Patang," says Rashida. "The men were unloading from a truck, and a heavy box fell on his foot." She hesitated. "He was crying out that this was foretold from a dream he had. And you foretold it."

"That's true."

"Can you really?"

"I can. I am an interpreter of dreams, with God's help."

"Ya-Allah! We had such a man here in Paidara once, but he died. I must leave, I am not supposed to talk to the foreigners."

She leaves. Sonia returns to her charpoy and plays solitaire for a while. She dozes, waiting for what will happen next. The azan sounds distantly, and she washes and prays the Ashr. The bars of light from the shutters glide across the floor and the walls, turn red, and fade. She has just lit the kerosene lamp when the door opens and the bearded guard comes in. She greets him politely but he does not answer her greeting. He says, "You come with me!"

She is led through the courtyard of the hujra and out a wooden gate, then down a narrow street to a large house surrounded by a mud-brick wall. She is taken through a gate into a small courtyard, where armed men give her hostile looks and mutter as she passes. Inside the house, in a room at the back, she finds the man in the black turban, Idris Ghulam, reclining on cushions with three other men, all of them dressed in dusty shalwar kameez, Pashtun waistcoats, and green or black turbans. They all wear full beards, black on two of them and, on the other one, white, dyed orange with henna. Weapons lean against a wall. The room is lit with a single lightbulb suspended from the ceiling by a wire. Close by she can hear the diesel generator rumbling. There is a whiff of its exhaust in the air.

Sonia looks the leader in the eye. He doesn't like this, she can see, and also sees something else, a redness in the rims, bags beneath them, bloodshot, unhealthy-looking whites. She says, "May you not be weary, Idris Ghulam."

He scowls. "How do you know my name?"

"All the world knows Idris Ghulam, and all believers praise his many feats of courage and daring."

He ignores this and demands, "Do you know why you are here?"

"Yes. I was driving on the highway with a group of scholars who wished to find ways to peace, in accordance with the will of God, the compassionate One, when I was kidnapped by a group of armed men."

"No, I mean why you are here now, standing in this room."

"Because you wanted to talk with me," she says. "It is one of the unpleasant things about being a prisoner, you can no longer choose with whom you must converse."

"You are here because you have bewitched one of my men."

"Witchcraft is forbidden to believers. I bewitched no one."

"You prophesied he would hurt his foot, and he hurt his foot today."

"I interpreted a dream and told him that, if he did not keep on the true path of Islam, his foot would be injured as a sign from God. And so it has happened."

"This is sorcery," says Idris, "and the penalty for sorcery is death."

"The interpretation of dreams is not sorcery, as you must know. Yusuf, may he rest in peace, interpreted dreams for Pharaoh. The Prophet himself, peace be upon him, interpreted dreams for his Companions. And did he not say, as the Hadith of Sahih al-Bukhari reports, that true dreams are from God?"

"But the Prophet, may he have peace, also said that bad dreams are from Shaitan."

"But this dream of Patang's was not a bad dream. It was a warning from God, and the warning in the dream has come to pass. God controls all things."

At this, the three mujahideen at the side of the room murmur and pass looks.

Sonia has considerable experience with the body language and facial expressions of such men. It seems to her now that Idris is unsure of his position. The three men are all older than he, and age counts for much among the Pashtuns. They talk among themselves. Idris darts quick glances at them after he speaks, as if to confirm that he has spoken properly. She concludes that he may be a tactical leader, in temporary command even, but he is not the sworn chieftain of these men.

He returns to the attack. "But your interpretation was false. You told Patang that the path of jihad was a false path."

"Untrue. I said his dream told him the truth, that the path he was on was not the true path of Islam. I said nothing about jihad."

"But Patang is a mujahid."

"Is he indeed? I wouldn't know. I have not seen him fight those who seek to oppress the Muslims, but I was taught that such is the task of the mujahideen. I have not seen him shooting Indian soldiers in Kashmir. I have only seen him murder a family of drivers, all good Muslim men. I have only seen him making war on innocent people, guests of a Muslim land."

"This is not a true Muslim land," Idris says. "Its leaders are kafiri and puppets of the Americans."

"How terrible for you, then, to be ruled by kafiri! The Pakistanis are kafiri, the Saudis are kafiri, the Syrians, the Pashtuns who rule Afghanistan are kafiri; undoubtedly the Persians are kafiri. Everyone is kafiri except you. How shrunken is the umma! You have pronouced *takfir* upon nearly all of it. How sad it must make God and His messenger, peace be upon him, to look down from Paradise and see that His only true believers now are small groups of murderers."

Idris shoots to his feet and punches Sonia in the face. She sees it coming and manages to turn her head, but the blow strikes the corner of her jaw and knocks her off her feet.

"Blasphemer!" cries Idris. "Whore of a blasphemer! You will die. We will stone you tomorrow and send you to Hell."

Sonia shakes her head to clear it of ringing. From where she lies she says, "As I said, you are a mere murderer. I have not been convicted of blasphemy before a *khazi* on the testimony of two witnesses, and therefore you have no right to execute me. Besides, the punishment for blasphemy is not stoning, but the cutting off of a hand and a leg from opposite sides, or banishment. In any case, a woman cannot be executed for blasphemy, according to the Kitab al-Hudud. She must be imprisoned until she repents and shall be beaten at the times of prayer."

"Be silent, whore!" Idris shouts. "I will judge you."

"Yes, and if the scales of justice were in your hand, you would count your mule equal to another's horse."

At this line from Rahman Baba, the great poet of the Pashtuns, laughter breaks out among the three older men, and now she knows that Idris is not their chief or they would never have laughed at the sally.

She raises herself up and points a steady finger at Idris Ghulam. "You have forgotten the wisdom of Rahman, who says, 'Do not be fooled by the outer appearance of a man; look at the inside of the nut to see whether it is soft or hard.' I am not a man, but I am hard as steel inside. And I tell you that if you kill me except by the letter of the *fiqh*, my blood will be upon you, and my son will avenge that blood according to the law of the Pashtuns, upon you and your brothers and your father and your sons. Be warned, Idris Guhlam. This is not an idle threat, for I have no ordinary son."

She turns and stares at the man with the hennaed beard.

"Sir, forgive me for addressing you, but I require your witness. You were in the real jihad against the Russians, were you not?"

The man slowly nods his head.

"And when you fought there, did you hear of a certain Kakay Ghazan?"

Again he nods, and says, "Everyone has heard of Kakay Ghazan. He was a famous warrior, although a boy."

"He is still a famous warrior," says Sonia, "but now he is a man, and I am his mother."

Consternation. The three men all begin talking at once, but Sonia's voice rises above theirs; now she is on her feet, her head aching, but speaking directly to Idris. "And he is a Pashtun of the Barakzai, of the Taraghzai, of the tribe Kakar, and all these he will raise against you, if you kill me outside the law, so beware, Idris Ghulam! You thought you had a load of fat geese, ready for plucking, but one of them is a scorpion."

For a moment Idris seems mesmerized by her revelation, but then he comes to himself, resumes command, gestures to the guard, and says, "Take her away! Lock her in the stable! Now!"

The guard grabs Sonia roughly. She points again at Idris and says, "Nor will you sleep easily, Idris Ghulam, until the day *you* repent."

Sonia is hustled out, but she can hear the sound of violent argument coming through the door. She shakes her head and works her swelling jaw. She thinks it has been a very successful interview and looks forward to one with the real leader of the group.

8

Cynthia often lost track of time when she worked with sound files, a habit that originated during her language studies in graduate school. In the language lab, eyes closed in concentration, in the little soundproofed cubicle with a big padded Bose headset on her ears, the uncomfortable syllables of a conversation in Arabic or in Dari filling her mind and her foot on the replay pedal so she could hear the same phrase over and over like some kind of rap sample, she would fall into a strangely delicious state, bordering on intoxication, although her auditory senses, at least, were strung to the last notch. She loved it, she supposed, because of the element of control. She had always been a good girl up until then, which is to say she fulfilled the expectations of others—her father, her teachers, her peers, society at large—but in the lab she was the queen of time; with the headset on, the various external pressures on her seemed to dissolve in that universe of perfect feedback, the voices starting, stopping, repeating at the tap of her foot. She spent more time in the lab than she had to—it was a kind of addiction, she supposed later, as was her pursuit of perfection in the shaping of sounds in her own throat. They had a machine that gave you a word or phrase and you had to repeat the phrase perfectly, if you could, and then the machine showed you a sonogram that told you how well you'd done and gave you a score. Cynthia had reached the maximum score in all her languages.

Here was something.

She played the sound file over again. Two men were speaking over cell phones in Urdu. She checked the source notation and found that one cell phone was in Kahuta and the other was in Lahore. They were young voices, and the one in Kahuta was obscured by what sounded like wind and motor traffic; the man was outside, at any rate.

KAHUTA: Hello, is that you, Walid?

LAHORE: Please! No names!

KAHUTA: Sorry. I am told to tell you we have the shipment on board.

LAHORE: Excellent. You can leave immediately?

KAHUTA: Absolutely. I have the directions.

LAHORE: No trouble at all? No alarms from the . . . the facility?

KAHUTA: Nothing. It went as we planned.

LAHORE: Thank God! Everything is ready at the destination; all the equipment arrived today. They should be setting it up now. How long do you think—

KAHUTA: No more than three days, God willing. I will call in on the way.

LAHORE: Then peace be with you, brother, in God's name.

KAHUTA: And peace unto you. God is great!

Cynthia typed out the translation on her computer, removed her headset, and sat for several minutes in thought. There was something wrong with the colloquy. For one thing, the conversation was in Urdu, which was fine—Urdu was the official language of Pakistan—but in general, when Pakistanis conversed with people they knew they spoke in their cradle tongues, of which that land had hundreds: Panjabi, Lahnda, Pashto, Sindhi, and on and on. That these two were speaking Urdu to each other meant they were from different origins and the transaction was a commercial one, which didn't seem right. Terrorist groups were famously tight, especially in that part of the world, with its endemic mistrust of the stranger, one reason why they were nearly impossible to infiltrate. And there was something else: the tone and rhythm of the talk were a little off; there were none of the minor hesitations and repetitions that appear in natural conversations, no *ah*s, no *hmm*s. It was almost as if they were reading a script.

Or maybe she was losing it. She attached the source header, the sound file, and her translation to an e-mail and zapped it off to Ernie Lotz: READ THIS AND LET'S TALK.

She put the headphones back on and returned to the stolen etheric whispers. Even with the most sophisticated electronic filtering, there was still an enormous amount of dross to get past. A lot of people in South Asia were talking about shipments, many of which were illegal but were of no interest to NSA or to her. The listening at this point was automatic, and her mind was free to drift above the chatter. As she often did, she thought about her career and where it was going. N Section was a fine place to learn the ropes, but it was a dead end. Vital, yes, because obviously terrorists could not be allowed to obtain nuclear weapons, but it was vital in the way that night watchmen were vital. You didn't want the factory robbed or burned down, but you also were not going to offer the guy with the square badge a seat on the board. No, N was a springboard to something better, a wider scope....

Something touched her shoulder and she yelped, tore the headset off, and spun around in her chair.

"Jesus, Ernie! Don't come in and *touch* me when I'm listening!"

"Sorry," he said, "but you have to see this." He handed her a piece of paper.

"Did you get my message?" she asked.

"Yeah, but that's nothing compared to this."

It was a few lines of typescript in English.

"Who translated this?"

"No one. It was English in the original. Read it!"

She did.

> MAN: Hello, it's me. Don't be angry, my dear, but I have to tell you I will not be home tonight.
>
> WOMAN: What? Are you mad? Tonight is the party for Shira and the Sajjids.
>
> MAN: I am sorry, my love, but it is quite impossible. We have an emergency at work.
>
> WOMAN: God help us! Not the reactor?
>
> MAN: No, thank God. But it is almost as bad.

WOMAN: What then? What is more important than your daughter's happiness?

MAN: I can't tell you. It is a security issue.

WOMAN: Before God, if you do not give me a proper explanation I will never speak to you again. This is the most outrageous thing I ever heard of. The Sajjids will think it is an intentional insult.

MAN: Be calm, for God's sake! Look I may be able to get away, we may find the blasted stuff in the wrong place, but I must be here to supervise.

WOMAN: What stuff? What are you talking about?

MAN: I am talking about thirty-three kilograms of ninety-four percent enriched uranium that has gone missing.

WOMAN: Thirty-three kilograms? Is it that valuable?

MAN: Not as such, but it is enough to manufacture several nuclear weapons, and we must find it. If we don't, I could conceivably be sacked.

WOMAN: Oh, God protect us!

"What's the source here? Who are these people?" she asked.

"The source tap is from a cell phone out of Kahuta belonging to Jafar Baig Qasir. I looked him up in the database. He's a nuclear engineer who works at Kahuta and lives in Lahore. He's one of the people in charge of refining and casting weapons-grade uranium. From the context, I assume he's talking to his wife."

"Why are they speaking English?" she asked.

"I don't know, Cynthia," replied Lotz, a hint of annoyance in his voice. "Why shouldn't they? A lot of upper-class Pakistanis use English as their second language."

"Yes, but not on intimate family subjects to their wives. Besides that, don't you notice anything fishy about the conversation?"

"No. What do you mean?"

"It has the same phony tone as the one from the supposed trucker. Did you listen to that one?"

"Yeah, it sounded fine to me, and it just adds to the case. Cynthia, I don't understand why you're—"

"And on top of that, don't you think it's funny that a senior scientist should talk to his wife on an open cell-phone line about something that should be the most top secret thing that ever happened: a theft of weapons-grade uranium? He makes it sound like a fender bender or a coffee spill on his pants. What's the traffic like from Pakistani security?"

Lotz said, "I haven't checked it recently. I wanted you to see this right away."

"Well, check it. They should be running around like chickens with their heads cut off if this is real."

"I will, but don't you think we should get Morgan in on this?"

"No, I don't. The last thing we need is a premature orgasm, and I can tell he's ready to pop."

"You would know," said Lotz, half under his breath. She didn't call him on it, and he left her office. Yet another reason for getting the hell out of N Section.

She put her headset back on, but she was too restless to focus on the voices. Instead, she switched to her music collection. The Allegro of Mozart's Concerto for Clarinet and Orchestra sounded, in her ears, so much more soothing than the chatter of conspirators, a souvenir of a less dangerous, more orderly world.

If they were conspirators. *If* they had stolen enriched uranium. *If* they could make a bomb. Cynthia had been through a secret course given by some people from Los Alamos. She knew that making an effective nuclear device was a lot harder than most people supposed. Yes, there was a lot of public information available, but the devil was in the details and in the technical skills through which they were applied, and these were not so generally available. Could a group of terrorists actually steal nuclear materials and manufacture a weapon in some mountain village? Not very likely. Nevertheless, even the possibility was sufficient to provide employment for her, the rest of N Section, and the other parts of the government that worried about such things. On the other hand, a nuclear *scam* could be mounted with a lot less effort and, if America fell for it, it might be nearly as damaging to its cause as a nuclear explosion. American boots on the ground in some Pakistani village, civilian casualties, the erosion of what little trust remained between the two governments: a cheap victory and intensely embarrassing for the already embattled intelligence community. Cynthia would have recommended such a scam herself, had she been on the other side.

She listened to the music, the familiar melody of the clarinet, soaring, glorious, but always returned to earth by the repetitive thrum of the full orchestra, each phrase sculpted to fit, each original but grounded in its form. That's how she wanted her life to be, soaring but under control. Her thoughts drifted for a time, lost in Mozart's structured beauty, and then settled on the figure of Abu Lais.

If there was such a person, if this whole thing was not an elaborate ruse. Here was the paradox of espionage, and especially of the type NSA practiced. NSA snooped; everyone in the world knew NSA snooped; everyone knew that electronic communications were not secure; therefore, anyone with any brains would send into the ether only those things he wanted NSA to know; therefore, what NSA learned with its multibillion-dollar investment in snooping was essentially valueless. But such thoughts, although they occurred to everyone who worked at the agency from time to time, were distinctly not profitable, and Cynthia had no patience for the unprofitable.

As often when she listened to music, an idea coalesced. She considered it, turned it around, found it potentially profitable, if not strictly a part of the normal order. After some browsing on the Internet, she worked for a while until she had covered half a dozen sheets of paper. With these in hand she left her office to violate the spirit, if not the letter, of Morgan's prohibition. She walked down many a sterile hallway and up several flights of stairs until she came to the part of NSA devoted to scouring the Internet for terrorist chatter, and specifically to the office of Walter Borden.

Borden was in. Borden was rarely out. On his own admission, he had no life, was a self-proclaimed nerd of the pear-shaped rather than the pencil-necked variety, and his office door was covered with a collage of Dilbert cartoons, beer coasters, and dozens of tiny strips from fortune cookies. A bumper sticker proclaimed, NERDS DO IT DIGITALLY. Cynthia had a history with guys like Borden, having learned early how easy it was to obtain intellectual favors from desperate misfits—math tutoring, computer repair—in return for a modest investment of smiles and badinage. And she enjoyed the hopeless worship.

She knocked and without waiting for a response entered the usual nerd nest—wrappers and cans on the floor, science-fiction posters on the walls, cartoons stuck to his whiteboard with magnets. It had a peculiar smell, too, like someone had cooked an unsuccessful dessert featuring caramel and canned mushrooms. The origin of Borden's smell was a topic in the local hallways.

His job was keeping abreast of the innumerable Web sites, most of them ephemeral as mayflies, that the international jihad used to keep its real and prospective membership up-to-date and to recruit new members. One reason they were ephemeral is that Borden and his section took them down by technical wizardry nearly as soon as they arose, except for a rotating number of favored ones, which they filled with misinformation or embarrassing pictures. Borden often remarked that he could hardly believe that they were paying him to do this work.

His office, as usual, was dark except for the glow of a huge flat-panel screen. Borden had his headset on, so Cynthia had to tap him on his Spiderman T-shirt to get his attention. He swiveled in his chair and brightened when he saw who it was.

"Hi, Lam," he said. "Look, we can't keep on meeting like this. People are starting to talk."

"Let them, Borden. My passion for you knows no bounds."

"I don't think so, Lam of my heart. I think you're fascinated by my unearthly intelligence, but you don't love the real me deep inside."

"You got me, Borden. I'm a faithless slut." She glanced at the screen in front of him. It was blue and covered with dense lines of code. "What are you up to? It looks like work."

"Yes, but it's nothing I could put in girl language. It's part of the AMICUS project."

The name stirred a vague memory. "This is the thing about intel coordination? I didn't realize it was up yet."

"It's not. It's years away. Decades, even."

"I'm surprised. I thought that was a big DCI priority."

"Yeah, right, like anyone cares what the DCI thinks. Look, in the first place you have dozens of different systems, all mutually incompatible, a lot of them written in languages no one uses anymore. You could never get them to talk to one another. So let's have a single system that everyone uses, right? I mean, we could just agree on a commercial database system and tweak it a little, but oh, no, the government can't do that, it might save too much money, so there are endless committee meetings about agreeing to formulate a plan to plan for developing a data plan. It's like riding on a glacier. But you didn't come down here to talk about data set coordination. Tell me you want to sit on my lap and coo sultry songs in my ear."

"I'll have to take a rain check on that. Actually, I was interested in Pakistani sites, any chatter about a big coup, any approaching major blow to the infidels."

"This is nuclear, right?" Borden knew where she worked. "Someone lifted a bomb."

"No one lifted a bomb, Borden. Get real. If someone lifted a bomb there'd be red lights flashing in the hallways and a whoop-whoop sound would be playing over the hall speakers. I'm just following up on some suggestive comint, and rather than send it through the usual channels I thought I'd come down here and get it from the unearthly intelligence himself."

"Or itself. But now that you mention it, there was this little beauty. It sprang into being, as near as we can figure, at 9:53 P.M. our time and immediately went viral in the jihadi Web world."

He pressed keys, and the screen of code shrank to a window and another, larger window popped up. Borden pulled out his headphone jack and the sound of a Pashtun song filled the room, a man singing, with tabla and *rubab* in back, a war song about jihad and how sorry the infidels will be when the Muslims take their revenge, how they will wail. The screen showed quick cuts of European and American cities, interwoven with shots of nuclear explosions and devastated cities: Paris, explosion, Hiroshima; New York, explosion, Hamburg '44; and so on. Cynthia watched it twice.

"No idea where this came from, of course," she said.

"Well, they try to mix us up, the usual anonymous cutouts, run it through Moscow and then Kiev and then Iceland, et cetera, but I'm pretty sure this one comes out of a server in Peshawar. There are technical similarities with some stuff we know was produced there, so odds-on it's the same guy or group. Their production values are coming right along, I have to say."

"They've mastered production values? Why fight on?"

"I agree," said Borden. "You should order your burqa before the rush."

"Seriously, though, the real reason I came down here was I need a favor."

"I'm listening."

"Suppose the Pakistani Ministry of Trade wanted to do a survey to see if certain items had been purchased domestically or imported into Pakistan over, say, the past three months, and because they're an up-to-date country they would send an official e-mail to these firms, with a form attached, which I've designed for them, and the merchants would fill out the form and send it to a link at the official Ministry of Trade Web site but really—"

"Yeah, yeah, I'm all over it like a cheap suit," said Borden. "The e-mail part is trivial, of course, and obviously you don't want the Pakistanis to know you've doing this survey in their name. Interesting little problem." Borden looked up to the ceiling and his eyes started to glaze as the unearthly intelligence cranked up.

Cynthia said, "So you can do it?"

Borden glanced at her, rolled his eyes upward, and mimed typing. "Mozart on the keys. Tonight too late?"

"Tonight would be perfect. " She handed him the sheets of paper. "Here's the apparatus list and the company list. Thanks a million, Borden. I owe you a big one."

"Indeed you do, and yet I surmise that the payback would not include, say, sexual favors of any kind."

"Correct. But I will allow you to fantasize about me all you want. And by the way, there are women on this floor who might not find that kind of remark amusing."

"Well, *those* women can kiss my pimply ass," said Borden. "I happen to be very selective about whom I fantasize about."

"I'm glad to hear it. I was starting to feel like, you know, cheap? Oh, and Borden." Cynthia was now moving toward the door. "Let's just keep this little project between the two of us, okay?"

"What project?" said Borden, and swiveled his bulk back to the screen.

Cynthia stayed at work until eight or so that evening, long enough to determine that Borden had set up his phony Pakistani Web site and sent the e-mails, and then went home. The next three days passed without any significant intercepts. On the fourth day, a Friday, Cynthia received an e-mail from Borden with an attachment containing the catch from their fake Pakistani government survey. She was perusing the information on her screen when Lotz burst in.

"We got another one. It's dynamite. So to speak." He handed her a paper, a sheet from the NSA's machine translation service.

She read it, put on her headset, and called up the referenced sound file. The Urdu conversation had been recorded off the same cell phone that Cynthia's original trucker had used outside Kahuta.

KAHUTA: Peace be with you, brother.

PESHAWAR: And with you be peace. All is well?

KAHUTA: Yes, we are on the road. We have the birdcage concealed under sacks of wheat.

PESHAWAR: And it's satisfactory? No leaks?

KAHUTA: No, we tested it. We used one made by the same plant that manufactures birdcages for Kahuta itself.

PESHAWAR: It might have been better to dispense with the barrel and just bury the material in a sack of wheat.

KAHUTA: No. It has to be shielded. It may be a while before the theft is discovered, but we can't take the chance that an alarm will go out and the authorities will be watching with ... ah ... special equipment.

PESHAWAR: Well, you know best. You have done wonderful work! How long will you be?

KAHUTA: Not long. A day or two at the most. Tell our friends they will have their birdcage by Thursday evening at the latest. God is great!

PESHAWAR: God is great! Death to the enemies of God!

She listened to it three times, making notes, and then removed the headset.

"What do you think?" he asked.

"Speaker ID was fairly accurate for a change. I assume the search term was *birdcage*."

"Yeah, we have a priority on it. Anytime anyone mentions a birdcage on any of the phones we're tracking we generate a translation. They use the English term."

"Yes, people there often do with technical words," said Cynthia. She stared at the transcript and recalled the care with which the trucker (if he was a trucker) had mentioned the word. He'd used it three times. Cynthia didn't think he would've done that if he'd been talking about structures for confining fowl rather than the fifty-five-gallon steel drums with internal bracing that were used throughout the world to transport highly radioactive matter.

Lotz's attention had turned to Cynthia's computer screen. "What's that stuff?" he asked.

"Just a survey I did. Four days ago, M. K. Chupa Metal Fabricators Ltd. purchased from Lahore Foundry Supply Company Ltd. a Morgan Mark IV dual-energy bale-out furnace and a used Bridgeport Series One manual milling machine, plus graphite crucibles and various other casting and machining accessories, for the equivalent of ninety-three hundred dollars and they paid cash. Before you ask, Pakistani tax records have no record of any M. K. Chupa Ltd. *Chupa*, by the way, is Urdu for "hidden." Could be just a coincidence, I guess."

"The bomb factory," said Lotz. "That would seem to be the closer, along with that line in our conversation here where the Kahuta guy says, 'It has to be shielded. It may be a while before the theft is discovered, but we can't take the chance that an alarm will go out and the authorities will be watching with ... ah ... special equipment.'"

"Yes, and that's to make us believe they're worried about radiation monitors," said Cynthia. "And yet they're not worried about blurting the whole thing out over a cell phone that might be compromised. And they bought their supposed equipment on the open market in Pakistan instead of smuggling it into the country, even though smuggling is half of Pakistan's GDP. It's absurd, Ernie! At the levels of al-Q we're talking about, they smuggle *everything* they use, including cell phones, which they typically use once and then ditch. No one involved in a plot like this would use the same phone day after day to report on the progress of a load of stolen weapons-grade."

"Abu Lais did. And we know for sure that he was talking to al-Zaydun; we have the voiceprint. Do you think *that's* a fake too?"

"No, but one ambiguous conversation does not a nuclear conspiracy make."

"So what *would* convince you, Cynthia, a mushroom cloud? You know what I think? I think you've got stage fright."

"What are you talking about?"

"I'm talking about us, N Section. For years we've been sitting in our tiny offices, forgotten, more or less, watching for something that nobody really thought would happen, and now it *has* happened and suddenly we're going to be the most important people in the whole government. This intel is going to go from our hands straight to the president's people, and they're going to want to make damn sure it's right. And you've got butterflies."

She looked at him coldly. He seemed a different person now, hectic, avid, like a frat boy planning a date rape. She said, "You're wrong. It has nothing to do with my personal shit. The tapes are *wrong*. The people on them are reading scripts. And if you'd spent as much time listening to real conversations as I have you'd know that."

"Yeah, well, maybe that's why we have analysts and why the munchkins in the headsets don't get to make the decisions."

She stared at him, stunned by the nastiness of this remark from the ordinarily genial, flirty Ernie Lotz. The supposed plot must have unleashed some kind of testosterone storm in the men involved. She had little hope that Morgan would be any different.

❧

Nor was he, later in the day, after Lotz had briefed him on the latest intercepts and the commercial information, what he insisted on calling *Lam's bomb factory*.

The three of them were in Morgan's office. With every bullet point on Lotz's briefing paper, Morgan seemed to expand, his face to glow, his bright blue eyes to send forth sparks. The grand finale was the playing of the Qasir intercept. He didn't need Cynthia to understand that. Lotz concluded with a recommendation that the GEARSHIFT material should be passed up the line for an executive decision. When it was finished, he turned to Cynthia and said, "That should satisfy even you, Cynthia."

They both looked at her. Seconds ticked by in silence. She said, "What do we know about this guy Qasir?"

"What do you mean?" said Lotz. "He's legitimate. He checks out. He's in Kahuta; he handles nuclear materials for their bomb program. What more do we have to know?"

"His politics maybe?"

Morgan said, "Oh, please! You think he and his wife are in on your conspiracy too?"

"I didn't say that," she replied, trying to keep the snap from her voice. "I have reservations, I won't deny that. I still believe this could all be a clever provocation. But I concur with Ernie's recommendation. There's no way we can come to a conclusion just on the basis of comint. We have to have people on the ground. Besides that, if there's one thing we learned from 9/11, it's that if intel agencies don't share all their data it leads to disaster. It may be a provocation, but if it's not, and someone detonates a nuke and it comes out that we had this data and did nothing... I don't even want to think about it. So let's get everyone in the same room and find out whether this thing is real."

It was a reasonable finesse, she thought, and was satisfied to feel the tension drain from the office. Morgan favored her with an amused smile. She was a team player again. This is why empires collapse, she thought: Vietnam, 9/11, Iraq. Everyone wants to be a team player, to bask in the respect of their peers and the favor of their superiors. She was no different.

"Okay, generate a briefing," Morgan said. "Fifteen minutes. Just the data and our conclusions. I'm sure I can get a meeting with both Holman and Spalling on the strength of this. After that, I think it'll move very quickly indeed. Don't plan on going anywhere until this is resolved."

Interesting, that. He'd given her the responsibility for pulling together the briefing: *her*, not Ernie. She could see the brief wave of disappointment pass across Lotz's face. Morgan was rewarding her for caving on this; besides, she was a lot better at putting together briefings than Lotz was. She had the language skills.

℞

While the meeting was being organized by those at levels far above her, Cynthia returned to her office and worked on the PowerPoint presentation Morgan had ordered. When it was done, she e-mailed it to him and an hour later it came back with a note requesting some corrections, all weakening the caveats, which she duly made. After that she noodled. She read some technical articles, answered e-mail from colleagues, and stared blankly at the door and the wall clock.

At ten of six her phone rang and it was Morgan's secretary telling her to be in front of the building in five minutes. She was, and in a few moments Morgan came down the drive in a gray government car. She got in, hauling her special NSA laptop and a stack of copies of the presentation and tapes of the source material.

"We're going alone?" she asked, as he drove off.

"No, of course not. Spalling and Holman are coming in their own car."

Yes, she should have known that. The iron law of bureaucracy insisted that no one can talk to anyone several rungs higher in the chain of command without the intermediate rungs being in the room. James Spalling was the deputy director of operations, NSA, and Ken Holman was the head of W, Morgan's boss.

Anticipating her next question, Morgan said, "We're going to Liberty Crossing."

Cynthia nodded. The Liberty Crossing Building in McLean, Virginia, was where the National Counterterrorism Center had its headquarters. The main purpose of this tiny organization was to encourage the mammoth organizations that actually countered terrorism on behalf of the American people to talk to one another and to avoid the ignominy that attended upon one counterterrorist mogul having to actually visit the lair of another. She asked Morgan who would be there and he said, "The usual cluster-fuck," which did not encourage conversation, so they drove the rest of the way in silence.

She looked out the window at the uninteresting traffic and the bland suburban scenery, the golf courses and homes of a peaceful nation at war. She had been a government employee long enough to understand what Morgan's salty term implied. Another iron law of bureaucracy: no one in government will take seriously a command from anyone who does not directly control his budget or hiring. For counterterrorism in general there is no such person other than the president, who has a lot of other stuff to worry about. The director of national intelligence is supposed to speak with the voice of the president on these matters, but this person certainly does not control the budget of the secretary of defense, who spends 80 percent of the intel budget and personnel and who, like the president, has many things other than intelligence to worry about. Even within the defense empire there are intel rivalries; all the services have direct connections to Congress and to their contractors, who also have direct connections and generous lobbyists, which is why the U.S. Army has a navy and an air force, and the U.S. Navy has an air force and an army. Everything that's done has to be negotiated with many layers of people, all of whom see their particular organization as the center of the national effort or would like to build it up as such, and nearly every office with "intelligence" or "terrorism" in its title wants to directly control guys with face paint and silenced submachine guns. All these important people were about to make, she thought with growing dread, a terrible mistake, one that she would be helpless to stop.

Unless. For the rest of the drive she concentrated her thoughts on how to derail this onrushing freight train without throwing her own body onto the tracks. Most government mistakes can be stopped if someone is willing to sacrifice a career, but Cynthia knew she was not that sort of person. The art of bureaucracy is to crawl through garbage and end up smelling like a rose. As this thought crossed her mind she thought of the man who had taught her that—and also provided her with the image of N as a pathetic, if necessary, night watchman: Harry Anspach. That was what she would do. She'd call old Harry and seek advice. Maybe something could be done. Maybe the mighty coup could still be extracted from this disaster.

℟

Morgan and Cynthia arrived early, as befitted their relatively junior status. They busied themselves connecting the laptop to the apparatus that would project their presentation on the conference room screen and testing to make sure that it worked. It was one of those ultrasecure conference rooms, windowless, carpeted, low-ceilinged. Cynthia hooked up her laptop to the room's speaker system and played some of the sound files she had brought along. She walked to different parts of the room, to make sure of the acoustics, and found that sound bounced in odd ways. In one far corner of the room she could hear Morgan breathing and turning the pages of his notes, as if he were close enough to touch. Strange, but not uncommon in such hyper-sealed rooms, not significant.

She had just finished with these chores when the attendees began to arrive, first a woman, the deputy director of the counterterrorism center, their nominal host; then the CIA man, the deputy director of operations; then another woman, this one the deputy director of the Department of Energy's Nuclear Emergency Support Team, the people responsible for finding lost or stolen nuclear material; then their own bosses, Spalling and Holman; then a full colonel from the Defense Intelligence Agency, representing the Pentagon—the real Pentagon. The National Security Agency, although formally part of the defense establishment, was obviously not deemed representative enough. Cynthia thought it was because the NSA had no personnel with face paint and silenced submachine guns.

Each of these people brought along an aide, it being another iron rule that no senior person go unaccompanied to any meeting of his peers in other agencies. These aides sat in chairs against the wall, along with Cynthia. Then, finally, the ostensible senior person, Thomas Bettleman, the deputy director of national intelligence, a tall fit-looking man with black horn-rims and an academic air. He had *two* aides. He sat down at the head of the table and, after introducing himself and asking the others to do the same, briskly turned to Spalling and said, "Jim, I believe this is your meeting."

Spalling made some introductory remarks to the effect that NSA had uncovered evidence that an agent of al-Qaeda had stolen nuclear material from Pakistani sources, that this meeting had been called to determine whether a response by the United States was warranted, and, if so, what form it would take. With that, he introduced Morgan, described the duties of his section, and motioned to him to begin. Morgan stood up, the lights dimmed, and the screen immediately shone with the NSA seal.

Morgan was a good briefer, Cynthia thought: concise and positive, an avoider of hems and haws. Everyone in the room, she knew, was a good briefer, that's how they had risen to their current positions, since the ability to put complex issues into a form politicians could understand without making them feel stupid or putting them to sleep was the golden road to power in Washington. The other thing they all had in common was that none of them had ever made a mistake they could be blamed for, which meant they were each of them either perfection itself or unusually skilled in avoiding blame.

As Morgan went through the evidence, the Abu Lais connection, the quality and reliability of the comint, the confirming conversation of the trucker and the man from Peshawar, Cynthia was able to turn her attention from the screen and study the people in the darkened room. She had never attended a deputy-director-level meeting before, and it gave her a certain chill to realize that these were the people chiefly charged with keeping America safe from terrorism. She was not impressed. Although she actually worked for a national security operation, her imagination had been formed by movies, and none of these people looked heroic enough for their roles.

This opinion lost nothing when Morgan presented the transcript of the Qasir colloquy and played the tape over the room's speakers. She thought she saw fear on some of the faces; yes, there was a palpable sense of fear in the room when Morgan wound up his spiel, with the appropriate (weakened but still ass-saving) caveats. It could be a scam, a provocation designed to further erode the shaky relationship between the U.S. and the Pakistani government, but in order to explore that they would either have to confront the Pakistanis with this evidence, seek clarification using significant human intelligence, or bet that it was a scam and not rise to the bait.

Morgan now had the options up on the screen. Three options, two impossible, which was the usual way in which junior people manipulated and controlled government policy. No one was prepared to enrage the Pakistanis and make the Afghan insurgency even more disastrous than it already was, and no one was going to contemplate lying doggo while al-Qaeda got a nuke. But they were going to have to decide something now, and whatever way they decided would generate a high-risk situation. These were not people who sought risk.

After a pause, Bettleman turned to the woman from the Department of Energy.

"Doris, if they really have thirty-three kilograms of weapons-grade uranium, could they build a working nuclear weapon?"

This was a neat dodge. It provided the opportunity for some technobabble, during which all the important members of the group could gather their thoughts and prepare their responses. Doris Ames, the NEST person, was a thin, pleasantly ugly woman with a mass of springy black hair escaping from a silver clip. She wore a fuzzy purple dress, the only note of color in the room besides the men's ties and the colonel's ribbons.

She cleared her throat. "Well, the short answer is yes, with thirty-three.

But a lot depends on how they're going to use it and how skillful they are. What we call 'bare crit' for metallic uranium at ninety-four percent U-235 is fifty-two kilograms. That means it'll go off if you just drop one half on the other. But obviously weapons aren't designed that way. They use shielding to contain and reflect the neutron flux, and shielding can be anything that's dense enough: steel, lead, graphite, even water. With the proper shielding the critical mass drops by around half. That said, the real answer to your question depends entirely on how good your guys are. A crude gun-type bomb would use all their metal and produce something like the Hiroshima bomb, say fifteen kilotons on detonation, if everything worked right. They apparently have a furnace for melting and machine tools for shaping the target and the plug. They can probably steal or buy lithium and polonium for the initiator. On the other hand, if they had a fair weapons designer on board and they wanted to build an implosion device, say a levitated pit design, with an aluminum pusher and a depleted uranium tamper, they could make three bombs out of what they have, all with approximately Hiroshima yields. If they didn't care about optimum yield, they could make a whole bunch of five kilogram fizzle devices that would yield, say, a hundred tons of TNT. Or if they were *really* good, if they had a professional weapons designer and skilled machinists, they could make half a dozen linear implosion devices, the so-called suitcase bomb, yielding one to three kilotons each. In general, the smarter you are, the smaller and more lethal the bomb. Does that answer your question?"

Cynthia thought that the woman sounded more satisfied than the grim occasion warranted. It must have given her considerable pleasure to have all these big, important men hanging on her words. She felt a sisterhood: Doris and Cynthia both had jobs that were almost silly until the bad day came; they were the night watchpersons who never got to sit at the big table, but on the bad day they got to tell the boys in charge the evil tidings, and the boys had to listen! Cynthia looked at the NEST woman and thought, That is *not* my fate, a job like that is *not* where I intend to end up, a middle-aged minor supergrade wearing a purple dress so people will notice her.

Bettleman thanked the woman and opened the room to discussion, of which there was very little. The main conclusion was that the material should be put before the president for his decision. Bettleman responded by asking for more detailed options, from both the Pentagon man, Colonel Brand, and the CIA man, Wayne Price. Price was the youngest person at the table, a man in his forties, and his smooth face had the constipated look of someone operating out of his depth. In years gone by the deputy director for operations of the CIA was one of the most powerful men in the world. He ran legions of spies and dozens of front organizations, he was the world's biggest briber, he played with the rulers of nations like pawns on a board. But no longer. This guy, Cynthia knew, had been recently shot into his job by the resignation of three people senior to him, in the great political revolution that had also stripped the central intelligence coordinating power from the CIA director and given it to Bettleman's tiny office. The national government believed that what the CIA could not do—coordinate national intelligence—with a multibillion-dollar black budget and twenty thousand troops could be done by one man and a corporal's guard of bureaucrats.

They all listened to what Price had to say. He had sent a message to his Pakistani operation to gather anything they had on a nuclear theft or on the whereabouts of Abu Lais, but so far there hadn't been any incoming humint that such a plot was in the offing. Colonel Brand did not roll his eyes, and no one passed looks. The CIA still retained some resources and had some good people, but as an organization capable of meeting the intel needs of the United States it was finished. Bettleman said something diplomatic, a head pat, to Price and then turned to the colonel.

They all turned to the uniform, like flowers to the sun, because everyone understood that the military was the big player here. Colonel Brand talked about assets and intercepts and operations. The Defense Intelligence Agency had its own little NSA for monitoring certain communications, the kind you couldn't get with the big antennae or the satellites, and it had its own little CIA too, although that bordered on the illegal. It seemed DIA knew all about Abu Lais and his nuclear plotting. There had been indications—buzzing on the terror networks—for some time. The colonel thought Abu Lais was the key; they should all forget about the Pakistanis and find Abu Lais. Cynthia found it hard to follow the colonel; the buzz in her head was like the buzz on the terror networks, obscure, threatening, boiling with many tongues all saying wrong wrong wrong.

"Ms. Lam?"

She started. Spalling was calling her name, not for the first time, she realized, and she became aware that everyone was looking at her. She felt herself blush.

"Sir?"

"Ah, you're back with us," Spalling said, which provoked a titter around the room. "Yes, Ms. Lam, I understand you have some linguistic evidence you derived from the Abu Lais interception."

"Yes, sir. He was speaking Standard Arabic with a Pashtun accent. I also detected a softening of the Arabic gutterals characteristic of someone who has spent time speaking English."

"You're sure about this?"

"About the Pashtun accent? I'm fairly certain about that. On the English, it's more or less a guess. The colloquy wasn't long enough for me to make a definitive call."

Colonel Brand asked, "Is this kind of speech what you might expect from a man with Pashtun as his cradle tongue, who had later been educated in the U.K. or the U.S., and then learned Arabic as an adult?"

"It's possible, sir, but his Arabic was pretty good. He could have learned it as a child, like many people in that part of the world. . . . But also—"

This was the moment. They'd all heard the tape. Why couldn't they hear the phoniness? Why didn't anyone ask the obvious questions about a senior scientist chatting casually about the theft of nuclear materials to his wife—if it even *was* Qasir and his wife? But no one did. They were all team players too.

"Yes, Ms. Lam?" said Spalling, but she shook her head and mumbled, and Bettleman nodded vaguely in her direction and began to sum up the meeting. He said the obvious: The White House would have to be informed and he would undertake to do that this afternoon. There would have to be a fuller analysis of the situation in the president's daily intel brief tomorrow, and he would be sure to ask for options, so the Chiefs would have to get that rolling right away. Colonel Brand could be trusted to do just that. Then he passed compliments all around, expressed optimism, and was about to close the meeting when Morgan spoke up.

"What are we going to call this? I mean, the incident and the intel that comes in."

"Let's stick with GEARSHIFT until further notice, shall we?" Bettleman said.

℞

The meeting broke up shortly afterward, the attendees assembled in transitory clots around the room, the principals and their aides mostly, speaking in confidential tones as they filed out. Cynthia was pulling up her cables when she heard, as if from someone standing right next to her, a fragment of a conversation. Startled she looked up and saw that the deputy director for operations of the Central Intelligence Agency was deep in conversation with another man, halfway across the room. That she could hear what they were saying was a trick of the safe room's peculiar acoustics.

She turned away, still coiling her cable, and listened. The DDO said, "Anything new on Ringmaster?"

"Only that it's confirmed; Ringmaster's definitely a hostage. Do you think this business here is connected to Showboat?"

"Has to be," said the DDO, "but I'm goddamned if I know how. Look, when we get back to Langley..."

But Cynthia couldn't hear what was planned when they got back to Langley, because they had moved away from the acoustic pocket. She continued her packing up, keeping her inner excitement from showing in her expression only with difficulty. She had by accident snatched the gold ring of intelligence work: she had learned something she was not supposed to know, and from the highest levels of the CIA. This slip established that there was more to GEARSHIFT than the CIA was willing to share with the rest of the intelligence community: no one had mentioned anything called Ringmaster or Showboat at the meeting, so she assumed they were names of assets or operations so secret that not even the highly cleared people at this meeting were allowed to know about them. But now *she* knew, and it remained only to determine how she could use the knowledge to her best advantage. It never for a moment occurred to her to share this knowledge with Morgan or anyone else at NSA.

9

The guard takes Sonia to a small outbuilding near the hujra. Inside, she smells the dense odors of animal waste and fermenting silage; they kept goats here. The man opens a trapdoor and points down into the darkness. She descends a rickety ladder and the trapdoor slams shut. She waits for her eyes to adjust to the dark. The blackness resolves itself into a room not quite high enough to allow her to stand upright and about the size of a decent bathroom in an average suburban American house. The only light comes from a narrow slit in the ceiling where the exterior wall does not quite meet the beams supporting the floor above. By leaning down she can see the dusty ground and the foot of the building across the street. The floor is mud, covered with rotting straw and archipelagoes of goat turds.

She clears a place on the floor with her foot and sits down with her back against the wall. Within a few minutes she feels the first hot prick of a fleabite. The place is infested with them, and they clearly have not fed in some time. She spends the next hours trying to catch and crush them. She waits for the sting, gives the beast time to become involved in its meal, and then places a finger over the point of pain. Then she rolls her finger carefully but firmly over her skin and onto the ball of her thumb. Then she holds her hand up to the dim light and slides her finger back, and if she has been successful she can see the black dot of the flea, which she then crushes with the index-finger nail of her other hand. It makes a satisfying pop. She supposes she gets in this way one out of fifty that bite her, but it serves to pass the time. She has done this before.

The light beams from the slit move across the floor and up the opposite wall; they fade to red, and then she hears the call to pray the Maghrib, the evening prayer. She cannot pray because there is nothing clean here to wash with, and in any case she knows she will be otherwise occupied. She hears footsteps above. The trapdoor opens and the guard, the same man, looks down and tells her to climb the ladder. She pulls her dupatta around her head and shoulders and goes up.

The guard has a length of rope, and with this he binds her hands in front of her and leads her out of the hujra and down a narrow street, and another, until they come to a wider road, the main street of the village. The mosque is there with a crowd of men just emerging from it. They stand in their dust-colored clothes and stare at her, a sea of black beards and eyes. Sonia sees Idris and the other men from her recent interview at the front of the crowd, which now stirs and makes way for the mullah. He is a thin, dark man in early middle age, dressed in a peach-colored shalwar kameez, a long black Pashtun waistcoat, and a black turban. Sonia's guard presses down on her shoulder and kicks at the backs of her knees, until she kneels.

There is a farm cart there, with high solid wheels, painted with fanciful designs. The guard secures Sonia's leading cord to one of the uprights at the tail of the cart. The mullah climbs on the cart and addresses the crowd. He says that this woman—pointing a finger at Sonia—has blasphemed before reliable male witnesses and shall now be punished according to the sharia. She will be confined and whipped at the times of prayer until she repents her blasphemy. He jumps down from the cart.

Sonia cries out, "I am no blasphemer, but a good Muslim wife. I have not been convicted of anything before a khazi."

The guard now wields a bamboo stick about four feet long, split at the ends, and with this in hand he sets himself and strikes her across the back. The pain is colossal, like breaking bone. An involuntary scream issues from her mouth.

"I have not blasphemed. I have not been convicted," she cries, and the next blow falls. She calls out this sentence after each of the next four blows and then the power of speech deserts her. She can only howl like a dog. She loses count of the blows after the tenth and something happens in her head and her vision narrows to a tiny reddish dot and then goes out.

When she returns to consciousness she is back in the cellar. The trapdoor is open and the guard is about to climb the ladder.

"Wait," she calls out. "Give me water, for the love of God."

He pauses, not looking at her. "There is water in the plastic."

She looks around and sees a ten-liter plastic jerrican on the floor. There is a cloth nearby wrapped around some loaves of naan. He starts to climb.

"Wait," she says again. "Tell me your name and lineage."

"So you can curse me?" he says, climbing higher. "I can't be caught that way, witch."

"I am not a witch. Please, because if I am beaten like this five times a day I will be dead in two days, and when the Day of Judgment comes and you are being cast down to Hell, I want to say to God the merciful, the compassionate, 'My Lord, You know all things and You know that this Yousef Muhammad, or whatever you are called, has murdered me against Your law, with his whip, but it was not his fault; he is ignorant and was betrayed by the wicked, who kill falsely in Your name, so in Your mercy let him inhabit the cooler parts of Hell and do not place his murderer's hands forever in molten lead.'"

The man snarls a curse. Sonia says, "Very well. But I would rather have my back than your dreams to come. I wish you peace, man with no name, but I doubt you will have any. Beware the Day of Judgment."

The man makes a gesture, an averting sign against the evil eye, and scrambles up the ladder with unusual speed. The trapdoor closes again.

Sonia drinks from the jerrican, groaning as she lifts it to her mouth. She carefully removes her tunic, an agonizing process, and pours water down her back, writhing as the cool liquid washes her cuts. She sees that the whip has sliced the back of the tunic into ribbons. She wraps her dupatta around her and collapses back onto the earth, lying on her right side. The fleas feast at will, but now she barely notices them against the wrenching agony of the wounds across her back.

She falls into a paradoxical state, not quite conscious yet too fitful to be called sleep. The pain is like a drug, squeezing her mind into unaccustomed hypnagogic regions. Is that her life passing before her eyes, is this death? No, or not yet, at any rate, but she experiences a series of intense sensory impressions. Her mother, the gleam of a gas lantern making a golden halo behind her head; the smells—gas; her mother's smell: perfumed powder, the smell of greasepaint and cold cream; the stink of the great cats, of the grease from the concession stands, of cotton candy, the cigarette smell of her father—the woman in her dream, the spangled costume, a mother image? No, her mother had dark hair, Sonia sees the woman clearly now, a stranger yet familiar, maybe not a woman at all, some kind of androgyne, an angel or demon. It is an animus, she decides, the representation of the Logos in the female, as the anima is the representation of Eros in the male. In its negative aspect it is opinionated, conventional, banal, self-righteous, argumentative, the caricature of the gabbling woman that is the dead spirit of the father rising to hideous life in her. In its positive aspect, it conveys spirit, feistiness, the capacity for reflection and self-knowledge, the capacity to handle philosophical and religious ideas at the higher levels.

Sonia hears herself laughing; the laughter rises to a hysterical pitch, breaks down into sobbing. Yes, part of her is saying, You are doing Jungian analysis in this stinking pit; what good has it ever done you? Are you *cured*? Are you *happy*?

This is the animus speaking; it has never been integrated. Fluss said it and it was true, and how she had fought him on the subject. Of course, she argued, that is what the disintegrated animus does, it bitches. But this dream is important, she knows that; and now in this fevered state she struggles to make sense of it. The awful boy-thing from that dream floats into her mind. The crusher of tiny helpless creatures. She thinks of Farid, her husband, whom she has tortured, whom she has crushed. The boy-thing cannot be Farid, who has never hurt anything in his life; that's his problem: He has no edge, his anima is toxic, inert, Eros and its holy power does not flow from him, poor man. The Mother is too strong, Noor has done her work well, all unconscious, of course, all of them are asleep, and she thinks of the sons of Noor, classic examples of the three main types of animus-ridden men: Farid, the softy; Nisar, the voracious mogul and philanderer; Seyd, the fascist.

She holds the monstrous boy in her mind's eye, he floats in the dark sparkles under her eyelids, and as she watches he changes; he grows tall, strong, beautiful: her son. She feels a pang of love. She calls out to him; he smiles at her and begins a careful kind of stepping, almost like a dance, and she sees that he is crushing under his feet the small helpless creatures from her dream, tiny birds or squirrels. She calls again, suddenly panicked; this is not right. She calls out, *Theo, don't! This is not how you were raised!* And he smiles again, the flash of white teeth in a tanned face. It is not Theo at all but Wazir, and now she sees that the deformed boy is still there, crouching in the shadows; he has Theo's face. Wazir speaks; he says, *I'm just doing what you taught me*. And she *has* taught him, nurturing him over the years; she's spent more time with him as an adult than ever she spent with Theo after he was grown. As this thought enters her mind, and with it a profound sorrow and regret, her deformed son leaps at her, wraps his arms about her waist. She calls on him to stop, she says he's hurting her, but he does not stop; he is climbing up her back, he is pinching her, he is clawing at her back with his nails. Wazir does nothing to stop this; he seems amused. The pain is horrendous, she writhes with it. At some level she understands this is a just punishment for what she has done.

Then she is out of the dreamlike state; she is back in the stable, and her back is covered with rats, their sharp teeth tearing at her open wounds.

She rises with a scream and the rats fall off her and vanish into the straw. She knows they will return, attracted by the smell of her blood. She wedges herself into a corner and sits trembling in terror, with her penlight in her hand. Its little beam wavers, grows yellow, fades to a tiny glow.

Sonia is still in this position when the trapdoor opens again, revealing a figure holding an oil lamp. She lets out a sob. It cannot be time for dawn prayer already, time for her next beating; it is still black outside. Then she sees it is not her guard but the girl, Rashida. She has not covered her face for once, and Sonia can see that she has a nose after all, and that she is a beauty.

The girls clucks when she sees that the naan has not been eaten, that it has been gnawed by the rats. She says, "I have brought you a new kameez. Here, let me help you put it on."

"No, it is too painful to have anything next to my skin. And besides, they will only tear it again, and you are not rich enough to afford five new ones a day."

"But they are saying you will not be beaten in this way anymore. The mullah says it is immodest for men to see your body through the rips in the cloth. So, God willing, they will beat you on your feet."

"Thanks be to God," says Sonia. "I will be a cripple, but not shamed."

The girl does not detect any irony in this statement, and says, "Yes, thank God. I have some grease my mother gave me. We put it on burns.

I will dress your back. I also have some cloths that my mother says will keep the cuts from turning bad."

"Thank you. God will reward you for this mercy."

Rashida rubs grease on Sonia's back with a delicate hand and ties on the cloths. The pain seems to diminish a little. The girl helps her on with the new kameez and says, "Is it true that you cast the evil eye on Mahmoud Saiyed?"

"Is that his name?" says Sonia. Speaking to the girl seems to calm her. I've been hallucinating, she thinks, and shudders, but the details of the near-dream are starting to fade. She wills them out of her mind. "No, I cast no curse," she says. "I'm not a witch. I asked him for his name so I could intercede for him on the Day of Judgment, since he is going to kill me unjustly in the name of God, which is a great sin."

She sees the girl's face twist in puzzlement. "Why would you do that?"

"Because I was taught to be merciful to my enemies and forgive them, as God forgives us."

"Only a fool would forgive an enemy. That would just give him another chance to attack you."

"And so? What if he attacks?"

"He might kill you."

"And so? We are called to be mujahideen, we are called to struggle for the sake of God. In the lesser jihad we struggle against the enemies of Islam and for justice, and if we fall we are taken to Paradise. In the greater jihad we struggle against ourselves. We strive to become like God, and what is God if not compassionate and merciful? If we fall in that struggle, the Prophet, peace be upon him, has told us that we gain a higher rank in Paradise than those who fell by the sword."

The girl looks down at her hands. She says, "I should not listen to you. You are a blasphemer. But look, I have had a dream."

"Tell it," says Sonia.

"I was on the bank of a river, a swift-flowing stream," says the girl. "On the other side was . . . a boy. He was holding a gold ring and beckoning to me, but I couldn't cross. Then I saw there were corpses in the water: oxen, horses, and some men, too. I was afraid, and I awakened."

Sonia says, "The river is the future, which flows ever toward us and cannot be stopped. The gold is the prospect of a successful marriage.

The corpses mean that the marriage cannot take place until someone, perhaps many, have died. And the boy is whom you love. What is his name?"

"Batur," says the girl immediately, and then gasps and holds her hand up to her mouth.

Sonia says, "Yes, Batur. He is from a good family in another village. He loves you and would marry you, but your father has promised you to someone else, an older man." It is only a guess, but Sonia knows such sorrows are the common lot of Pashtun village girls.

Rashida's eyes grow wide, glistening, reflecting the small yellow flame of the lamp. "How did you know that?"

"I know many things," says Sonia. "And this older man is ..."

"Khaliq Sumro. He has one eye and he stinks like a goat. He is of the mujahideen and advises Idris Ghulam. He has one wife in Peshawar but he wants one here."

"Never fear that you will marry him. His death is foretold and will come soon. Your father may have a dream. Tell your mother what I have told you, and she will use the ways of women to make him come and see me and I will interpret that dream as well."

The girl nods and assures Sonia she will do this and pushes forward a closed basket. She says there is food in it, and she will leave the oil lamp there, to stave off the rats. Then she darts up the ladder and closes the trapdoor. Sonia hears the bolt shoot home.

What a precious thing a little light is! Sonia thinks, and a little kindness as well. She cradles the small lamp in her hands. By its glow she can make out the shapes of the rats moving and from time to time the glow of their tiny fierce eyes. She wonders if the oil will last until dawn. Probably not. Perhaps that is part of the torment. Hope and some slight relief from the worst are the best weapons of any tormentor; the torturer smiles and offers a cigarette.

This adds incalculably to the most dreadful element in her situation, the anticipation of pain to come; anyone with an interior life knows that psychic pain is what breaks you. Sonia knows she is breaking. She is brave enough when free, with room to maneuver. She has confidence in her own cleverness, but now it is entirely gone. Her plan was a stupid one, and now here she is. She has always been a little claustrophobic, she has always sought the open skies, avoided tight spaces both physical and social; her life has been based on this preference, and now she is in this tiny grave packed with rats.

She sobs, letting the misery flow without constraint. She cannot bear the prospect of more pain. Easy to talk of torture, to discuss it as a phenomenon in a living room where the torturer is far away; one thinks on those occasions, perhaps, *Well, I could stand it, I'm no baby*, and then one sees people who have been tortured and they look the same as us; they laugh, they joke. How bad could it be? Secret, shameful thoughts, but there they are. Sonia has known any number of the tortured—they are common enough in Pakistan—and she has had these thoughts.

But now she knows they will take her out in front of the mosque tomorrow and lay her on the ground and tie her feet up to a chair and whip the skin from their soles. And a few hours later again, cutting the intricate weave of muscles and tendons into red jam and bringing her back to lie in this filth. Infection will set in immediately, she will die of septic shock, delirious and alone. She knows, too, that even this is not the worst. She knows that what utterly shatters the soul is this: when the pain is applied, sooner or later the victim feels in her deepest core that she would yield her place to anyone; she would say in her heart, *Torture my babies, torture my son, torture my husband, all my loved ones, but not me!* Thus the victory of the torturer is the absolute victory of the self: Hell incarnate.

Yes, the self, the nafs, what the Sufis spend their lives trying to control. Sonia thinks this, the word *nafs* is present in her mind, and all at once, astonishingly, her weeping turns into a bubbling laugh. So *this* is what you meant, my *murshid*!

℘

Now, in darkness, hungry for the brassy colossal skies of Asia, she thinks of her journey with Ismail, which she put into her first book and which made her enjoyably famous for a season, although Ismail had told her that fame was like wax dripping on the nafs from a great candle, thickening it and making the soul more than ever its prisoner. She thinks about warming his bedroll, which she did not put into that book. And most of all she thinks of his lessons, the Sufi training he gave her, for despite his lighthearted manner he was a hard master in the ways that the murshids of his order had, over six centuries, devised to strip the self from the body and allow God to burn it away to nothing.

From a pocket of her ruined kameez she takes a Sufi rosary of thirty-three beads, a *tasbi-e-Fatima*, the kind given by the angel to Hazrat Bibi Fatima, daughter of the Prophet and mother of all Sufis. Sonia rolls the wooden beads through her hands as she begins the recitation, the *zikr*, at the heart of Sufi practice. The zikr she recites is the Name of God. As she does so she visualizes the calligraphic representation of the Name, in Arabic, in the approved golden-wheat color. Before, when she was with Ismail, she never quite achieved the reported glow, her visualization flickered like the neon of a cheap motel sign. Somewhere after three hundred of the usual thousand repetitions, her concentration would flag and the self would issue forth like a fungus. She confessed this to her murshid. He told her not to worry. He told her to wait for God. He said God would find her when the conditions were right.

Now, obviously, the conditions are right, for the Name of God shines like the noon sun on a field of grain and she is also able to visualize her murshid. There he floats in the black cell, grinning, vastly amused, his face lit by the golden glow. The beads fly through her fingers; the Name echoes in her head like a gong. Apparently the right conditions for one such as her is the prospect of being tortured to death. Ismail thinks this is amusing and so does she, and all at once she understands that God is laughing too. Nothing is as she thought; everything familiar is now wonderful, and the esoteric is plain as bread. She understands that she is departing the *alam-e-nasuf,* the material world, and entering the *alam-e-malakut*, the realm of angels, the ground reality of the universe. In her ears, faint at first but growing louder, is a sound, indescribable, which is the *sout-e-sarmadi*, the eternal sound that permeates all the worlds, of which the most beautiful music is but a shadow.

Sonia chants without thinking, listening to the breath of God; the sound fills her, it removes the pain of her wounds, it banishes her fear—or not really, she thinks, looking back at herself as from a great distance, it's more like the pain is still there, but the being, the poor nafs, that feels it, the horrible person who behaved so badly to Farid and Theo and Wazir, who suffered under the whip and the rats and merited that torture, is not the real person.

I will never be able to explain this to anyone, she thinks, as Ismail was never able to explain it to me. I thought it was a trick to be learned, like legerdemain, but it's not. It's a grace. How peculiar not to have known it all along, although, now that she thinks of it, she *did* know it all along, but the nafs cast a cloud between her soul and the knowing, for it did not want to die.

The sound is still in her ears when the trapdoor swings open, letting in a flood of light and the guard, Mahmoud. She continues with the beads and smiles at Mahmoud. She realizes she can see the real person in him too, the image of his Maker, and she can also see, like an encrusting leprosy, the structure of pride, greed, lust, and folly that controls the man Mahmoud in the alam-e-nasuf. She climbs the ladder effortlessly, or so it seems, she feels like she floats on the rungs. Mahmoud seems taken aback now; he was expecting a cowed and beaten woman—the only sort of woman he has ever known, in fact—and now he sees something quite different and he is frightened, Sonia can see his fear, like worms roiling the shadows behind his eyes.

It is the time of Fajr, the dawn prayer. She is brought to the same wide place before the mosque, the same crowd of turbaned men are there, having just finished praising the Compassionate One and looking forward to seeing a woman tortured. Above, the sky is still pink, shading to the palest possible blue. Sonia is still handling her beads. She notices that the men have seen this, and there are murmurs. The mullah stands out of the crowd and gives a speech, in which he again describes Sonia's blasphemy and offers her a chance to confess. She answers in a loud but mild voice, as if explaining something to a child, that she has not been judged according to the sharia and therefore it is haram for her to be punished. She quotes the Qur'an on the wages of injustice.

The mullah shouts at her, although he does not quote from the Qur'an. Like most village mullahs he is an ignoramus on the subjects of sharia and Islamic theology, substituting a crude bullying style for both. Some men drag out a heavy wooden chair. Sonia is made to sit on the ground. Her legs are tied together and her ankles are lashed to the slats of the chair back. She is as modest now as could be wished. Mahmoud does this work and he is clumsy doing it, so she offers a word of encouragement.

"Mahmoud Saiyed, I forgive you your crime. In Hell you will be repaid for this, but although your feet will be lashed with red-hot wires forever, but I will look down from Paradise and beg the demon to temper the strokes."

Mahmoud is not quite trembling now, but he looks ill at ease. He takes up his bamboo cane and whisks it back and forth a few times, perhaps to pump himself up.

Sonia fingers her beads and increases the volume of her chanting. The praise of God echoes from the low buildings. The lash descends.

Sonia feels the agony and her body records the damage but it does not reach who she is now. The nafs suffers but she is no longer it. She shouts *"Haram!"* and continues her chanting Sufi prayer.

Another stroke, although this one seems to spend much of its force on the seat of the chair.

"Haram!"

The mullah calls out for Sonia to be gagged. This is done, with rags. A new murmur floats through the crowd. It is a grave sin in Islam to silence prayer.

On the next stroke a voice floats out past the shutters of a house, a woman's voice: *"Haram!"*

On the next stroke, there are more voices from the hidden, a chorus of voices, and the chilling ululation, a sound like the insanity of all the birds. *Forbidden! Shame!*

This is now the nightmare of the Pashtun male. The women are out of control and it is the women who have the honor of the men in their hands. The women know everything. They know who likes to fuck boys, and who is a drunk, and who can't get it up in the marriage bed, and for this reason they can never be allowed to escape the iron grip of the men.

Now, almost as one, the men trot off to their homes, including the mullah, who has two wives and a boy. Sonia thinks they will beat all the women now, but not very hard. She is left alone on the dusty street with poor Mahmoud, who looks like he is going to cry.

"It is over, Mahmoud," she says. "Untie me and carry me back to my room in the hujra. You have been saved from Hell today; God has been merciful to you. And when you have done that, I will interpret your dream for you."

Mahmoud carries her toward the hujra, but on the way he is stopped by two armed men with the look of seasoned mujahideen. There is a brief argument. The men don't want her returned to her prison; someone wants to see her. For the first time she hears the name Alakazai and it seems to be a significant one, for on hearing it Mahmoud stops arguing and follows the men. They go down several streets, the roar of the diesel generator grows louder as they walk. They go through a gate in a high mud wall and enter a house. Mahmoud is dismissed, protesting, at the door, and Sonia is forced to hobble on the edges of her feet, following the men, who make no effort to help her.

One of them grabs her arm and hustles her through an open door and into a small room with a high window. In it there are two charpoys and a low table, upon which is a tray with a tea service and a covered basket from which issues the smell of fresh naan. On one of the charpoys sits a man. Sonia collapses on the other. The guard goes to a corner and squats down with his rifle across his knees.

The man on the other charpoy indicates the tea with a flick of his hand.

"Would you like some tea, Mrs. Laghari?" he says in English.

"Yes, thank you," Sonia answers, and pours. To her surprise it is not the strong milky tea of the region but some herbal brew, flowery, like chamomile or jasmine. But it is hot and she drinks a whole cup and eats a piece of bread. The man watches her and she returns the favor.

He is a comfortably padded man, broad-shouldered, with a tan face and a neatly trimmed dark beard. His ethnic origins are not at once clear, for he has the hawk nose and the hazel eyes common among the Pashtuns, but his air of comfortable self-assurance, relaxed, faintly amused, is one she associates with the plains to the south. And there is something wrong about him, a cast of ill health; the whites of his eyes are yellowish, and there is a faint unpleasant odor in the room. That's why the herbal tea. The man's innards are not right.

"How are your feet?" he asks, after she has drunk the tea.

"How do you think?"

He shrugs. "That was a clever ploy. You almost started a riot there, among the women. Idris is very angry with you."

"It wasn't a ploy. I was perfectly sincere."

"Were you?" A look of amusement here. "You consider yourself a Muslim?"

"I am as much a Muslim as you are."

"Even though you wander around without your husband, unveiled?

Even though you are an infamous blasphemer and apostate?" He sips his tea, not taking his eyes off her. "You know, I saw you on television. It was quite a performance. I thought you seemed more an ally of our jihad than not."

"Really. Then you couldn't have been listening to what I said."

"Oh, I listened. And I was intrigued. Who was this American who spoke perfect Urdu and had such interesting ideas? Why had I never heard of her before? So I made inquiries, and of course I quickly learned that I *had* heard of her before; the whole umma had heard of her. And I was amazed that this Sonia Bailey would have the arrogance to lead a party of spies into a Muslim country."

Sonia surpasses a shudder of fear. She says, "We are not spies. We are scholars. And the Prophet, peace be upon him, says that the ink of scholars is more precious than the blood of martyrs."

The man waves his hand as if shooing flies. "Yes, yes, anyone can quote from the Hadith when it suits them, but the fact remains that you have already been condemned by competent judicial authorities. I could have you executed this minute."

"Yes, you could," she says agreeably. "Or you could have me beaten five times a day and locked in a filthy stable. I'd be dead in a few days from septic shock, and you wouldn't have to confront the women again."

"I'm not afraid of a few women."

"Nonsense, Mr. . . . ?"

"My name is Alakazai."

"Really? Then we are clan cousins of a sort. My son is an adopted clansman of the Barakzai."

A transient look of irritation passes over the man's face; Sonia observes it with interest and switches to English. "Although you're not a big one for clan connections, are you, Mr. Alakazai? You're not a real Pashtun at all. I suspect your father or grandfather was a detribalized Pashtun living in the south, what they call a Pathan in that country, and one or more of them must have intermarried with the locals, Punjabi or Sindhi perhaps, even Bengali. There is something of the babu about you, I think. Idris and the others are true Pashtuns; their lives revolve around honor, loot, and beating up any women or foreigners that come their way. But not you, and so we have to ask why they follow you. And the answer must be that you're the one with the connections. the paymaster, feeding money and arms from the Pakistanis. You might even be an actual ISI agent. On the other hand, I'm sure you have good connections with al-Qaeda as well. You're just the sort of deracinated, half-educated, semi-Westernized misogynist they like to recruit."

He regards her expressionlessly, tracing the line of his beard below his lip with a forefinger.

"And please don't tell me you're not afraid of women, Mr. Alakazai. Sexual terror is the motor of your entire movement. That's why you blow up girls' schools and toss acid in the faces of their students."

"Is that what you really believe? Remarkable, when you have traveled so much in the umma. You must be willfully blind."

"You don't blow up girls' schools?"

He made the fly-chasing motion again. "I have the greatest respect for women. A modest woman caring for her family is one of God's greatest creations. But it is also obvious that when the head is full the womb is empty, as we observe throughout the West. In whatever nations that accept the curse of women's education and freedom from the control of men, we see a rapid decline in population; we see pornography; we see sexual disease. Not a single one of the so-called advanced countries is reproducing its original population at replacement levels. In Europe, virtually all the population growth is Muslim, and it is clear now that in a certain number of years all these nations will have Muslim majorities. This is because we understand that the function of women is established by God and anything that seeks to destroy that function must be haram. Do you see? It's really very simple. Islam is a simple religion, and therefore it is the truest and most beautiful of all religions. So tell me, who are you working for, the CIA?"

"That's what everyone thinks, but I'm surprised you do too. I thought you would know that someone who speaks the local languages and is conversant with local culture couldn't possibly work for the CIA. The CIA is a bunch of white men in suits having cocktails at the American embassy, when they're not firing missiles into villages from drones, usually the wrong village."

"Very amusing. But if you're not a spy, what are you doing in the Northwest Frontier Province?"

"I was traveling to my brother-in-law's house in the Leepa Valley to participate in a conference about how to bring peace to this region."

"Oh? And how shall we bring peace to the region?"

"I have no idea. We didn't get a chance to hold the conference."

He makes a generous sweeping gesture. "Then by all means hold it. No one is stopping you."

"You don't mean that you're setting us free."

"Unfortunately not. But you can hold it here. The dining hall at the hujra will do very well. And I will attend. I too am a great lover of peace."

"You'll let me consult my colleagues."

"You may inform them that such is my will. We will all attend, and we will provide burqas for you and the other female hostage. Perhaps you will learn something about modesty in your last days. You know, there is a long tradition in this region of kings bringing scholars before them to dispute philosophical matters. And I am, as you have perhaps observed, a quite traditional man. I believe I will find your conference entirely interesting."

"In that case, I hope I can assure my colleagues that they will come to no harm while they are in your custody."

"Well, yes, providing that our demands our met. I hope Idris was clear on that score. All of you are hostages for the good behavior of the crusaders. On any day that innocent Muslims are killed by their forces we will be forced to behead one hostage. Of course, I should not want to execute anyone whose presentation I had not heard, so I will trust you to arrange the speakers however you choose, and I would also insist that you personally select the hostages to be executed."

Sonia stares at Alakazai and he returns her gaze blandly, as if he has just foretold the arrival of the next bus.

"Oh? Why me, if you don't mind my asking."

"Because you are the enemy. In you is distilled in the purest form everything against which we fight. You are worse than a mere infidel. You are a Muslim who perverts and dirties everything that is most sacred in Islam. You are woman, who destroys modesty and encourages others to do so. I have read your books, you know, yes I have. I read them when I was a student, when you caused this great furor and you were condemned by the ulema. I wished to find you and kill you then, as did many others, but you know how it is with the enthusiasms of youth, one forgets, one gets involved in work and marriage, and so forth. But always in the back of my mind I thought I would do it. And now God has placed you in my hands, all unknowing, like a gift. Don't you find that remarkable?"

"I do. And it is just as remarkable, don't you think, that a conference devoted to exploring the mental pathology that underlies terrorism should itself fall victim to someone who exhibits just such pathology in the most extravagant detail? You really should let us live, sir, so that we can study and write about you and your organization. Like the patients of Jung and Freud, you would achieve immortality in the pages of psychiatric textbooks."

He smiled. "You mean to provoke me, but I am not easily provoked, not like our Idris. I am a patient man and I *will* appear in books, but not because I am insane. You know, it is the victors who write the psychiatry books just as they write the history books. If the Germans had won the war, would the Nazi leaders be considered madmen? I don't think so."

"Perhaps, but moral relativism ill befits a supposed leader of mujahideen. If you really believe that, I would rather take my chances with Idris."

"And be beaten to death?"

"Perhaps, and perhaps he will remember that God is merciful and compassionate. At least he is still a Muslim. What you are, I leave to God, who knows all the secrets of our hearts. Death comes to everyone, and whether it comes today or in a week or in twenty years is of little account."

"You have no fear of the Hell that awaits you?"

"I do fear it. I have done wickedness and I will be punished for it. But I look forward to at least one pleasure in the next life, which will be to see you roasting below me in a far hotter fire."

"You really are a ridiculous woman, you know that? I am a mujahid and a leader of jihad, and God's word assures me a place in Paradise. I will be interested to see if you speak so brazenly after you have condemned your friends to death, when you are the last one and the knife comes for you."

"Not the knife, Alakazai: even you would not be so foolish as to behead a woman. But, as Rahman Baba says, 'All the world travels to the grave, as the caravan heads homeward; death reaps all souls, as the farmer cuts the ripened grain.' None of us can say what God has in store. You may kill me or you may not. For all you know, at this very minute a drone missile is being targeted on this house, or perhaps, since I am an important CIA agent, they are waiting until I leave."

She observes this last remark strike home: a little flicker of doubt, some fear in his eyes. She has spent much of her life reading the expressions on faces, in therapy and, before that, on her travels, when mistaking an expression, missing a lie, could be fatal. She is quite good at it, and even in this short interview she has learned more about her captor than he knows he has revealed.

He recovers his aplomb, makes a whisking gesture with his hand. "I assure you there is no chance of that; you will surely die, and your bones will be left to the dogs and birds. That will be your end. In the meantime, go and have your conference. There is little entertainment for a man such as myself in this place, and I look forward to seeing you perform." He speaks an order to the guard, who walks over and pokes Sonia in the ribs with the barrel of his AK.

"Out," he orders.

"I can't walk. Look at my feet."

"Crawl, then," he says, and pokes her again, harder.

She slides from the charpoy and crawls. Behind her she hears Alakazai laughing.

10

So what happened after that?" Gloria asked.

"You really want to know this? My war stories? Why?"

"It's interesting," she said. "Like I told you, most guys are totally boring. Your life is like a movie."

"You think? Okay, where was I?"

"Your grandfather and your sisters got blown up."

"Right."

And it happened at the worst possible time, not that there ever would have been a good time, but my mother was in Zurich. My uncle Nisar was studying in London, but it was some school break and he was off in the country with friends, out of touch for weeks. My uncle Seyd was with the army on maneuvers in occupied Kashmir, so he was also more or less out of the picture for days afterward. My aunt Rukhsana was a kid, although I have to say she paid more attention to me than anyone else. My father, who should have taken charge of the situation, he just collapsed, became practically catatonic, and had to be hospitalized, or so I heard later on. My grandmother didn't bother looking for me. She was probably already plotting to get Farid a new wife to replenish the gene pool.

Anyway, when the bomb went off I ran and hid in the storeroom. I wanted to be near my mother's tin trunk. Wazir found me there on the night after the disaster. When I saw him I started bawling and he told me to stop crying, and when I continued he slapped my face. He said, "Be a man! A man doesn't cry like a woman. If a man is injured he seeks revenge."

I stopped crying. I asked him against whom I should seek revenge and he said, "My father knows, and he is planning his revenge this minute."

I said, "It's my grandfather who was killed and my sisters. I should have a part in the revenge."

So he took me to his father. Gul Muhammed agreed that I should have a part, and he told me the story of why my grandfather had been assassinated. There was a zamindar, a wealthy landowner, who was cheating his peasants—which is to say he ate food, drank water, and breathed air—but in this case the peasants had somehow found the courage to bring a lawsuit against him, the case landed in the court-room of Laghari Sahib, and Laghari Sahib had refused the customary bribe and given justice to the peasants, at which point the zamindar, Babur Amir, threatened him aloud in his own courtroom, and Laghari Sahib had thrown him in jail—five days—for contempt of court. Babur Amir had waited and plotted the death of Laghari Sahib. There was a man who worked for Babur Amir and did his dirty work: beatings, shootings, and also bombs, because he had been with the jihad in Kash-mir and understood explosives. This man was Salim Malik.

I asked Gul Muhammed how he knew this and he said, in the way you explain something to a young child, "Everyone knows this. There would have been no point to Babur Amir's revenge if it were not known; also, having it known shows that Babur Amir has no fear of the police or the courts. Thus he can act after this with impunity, and no peasant will ever challenge him again."

Then I asked *why* the police didn't arrest these men for the murders, and he said, "Because Babur Amir is well with the government of Zia, and the government of Zia hated Laghari Sahib so they will do nothing." He made a gesture encompassing all of us. "But *we* will not do nothing, oh, no!"

He thought for a while, tapping his bearded chin. "You must stay here in my quarters and keep hidden."

"Why?" I asked.

"Because I say so. Wazir will bring you food. I leave tonight, and while I am gone you must not by seen by anyone but him. Say that you under-stand and will obey!"

I said this, happy to have someone strong in charge of me.

He smiled and patted my head. "Good. When you are older you will know why I do this."

꽃

The next morning, he was gone, Wazir did not know where, except that he had packed his pistol and his Enfield rifle in the sidecar of his ancient BSA motorcycle. A week and a day later I was sleeping when Wazir slipped into my room and awakened me.

"What's happening?"

"Quick. Get dressed. Wear your Pashtun clothes and take anything you want to take, but make sure you have blankets and warm clothes. One small bag only. We leave tonight."

I dressed in a black shalwar kameez and put a felt Pashtun hat on my head. I packed a bag: underwear, socks, sweater, a lined rain jacket, boots. And my mother's knife.

Gul Muhammed was waiting in the courtyard with his motorcycle. He pushed it out into the street and cranked it up, a sound shockingly loud in the night air. I climbed onto the pillion and we were off, through the warren of Anarkali and then past the Mayo Hospital and out onto Railway Road. We crossed through the deserted Landar Bazaar and by a tunnel under the tracks entered a part of the city I had never been in, an area of hulking godowns and small repair shops. Gul Muhammed threaded his motorcycle slowly through alleys where men pounded metal by the light of buzzing fluorescents and hissing gasoline lanterns; the work of Lahore never ends. At last he stopped in front of a godown. He unlocked and lifted a corrugated steel door, walked the idling motorcycle up a ramp, and closed the door behind us with a clang that echoed through the vast inner space of the warehouse. By the light of the motorcycle's headlamp I could see towers of crates and jute bags strapped to pallets. He steered the bike through the aisles of merchandise, the thumping motor sounding like a beating heart.

He stopped. Against the wall I could see the bound and gagged figure of a man. Gul Muhammed said, "Babur Amir is dead. I went to his haveli in Gulberg. He was well guarded. Three hundred meters from this house I found a tall tree, a cedar, that provided a view into the courtyard of the haveli. I climbed it and waited. Three days I waited, until Babur Amir came out to kick a ball around the courtyard with his sons. It was a long shot, but I didn't miss. This animal is Salim Malik, who set the bomb."

With that, he took his Webley out of the sidecar and handed it to me. I looked into the face of Salim Malik. It seemed to me that the resignation of death was already on it, but at the time I was not the expert I later became. I thought about what my grandfather and my sisters had looked like as they burned in the car, and what they looked like afterward, and what the smell was like. So it was not hard to cock the big pistol, set myself carefully so I wouldn't get hit in the face by the recoil, and shoot Salim Malik in the head like a good Pashtun.

≈

Gloria gave a small shriek. "You shot him? Oh, my God, how old were you?"

"Around nine. It was no big deal at the time. It was just like playing guns and Hindus with Wazir, which I guess is why those African militias recruit kids as soldiers. We numb up real fast and kill without thought. You want to hear the rest of this?"

She did, and I went on.

≈

An hour later I was stuffed uncomfortably into the sidecar of the motorcycle, along with a twenty-five-kilo bag of rice, plastic sacks of dal, oil and spices and salt, the Enfield with its ammo; a jerrican of water was lashed onto the hull forward of the little windscreen: the commissary and armory of our tiny army. Wazir was on the pillion, leaning back against our luggage. He looked at me with a wild delight. We were going to war, to jihad against the Russians. Gul Muhammed had been brief in his explanation: the infidels had invaded Afghanistan three months ago and all Pashtuns were obliged to heed the call of religion and tribe. Also, it was no longer safe for any of us in Lahore. I recall asking about my mother and how she would find me in Afghanistan, and he'd said war was not the business of women, which seemed a reasonable answer at the time.

So we sped through the night city to the Grand Trunk Road, north out of Lahore toward Peshawar and the border. I was exhausted, and after a while I arranged the dal sacks like beanbag pillows, and fell asleep on them. I recall I awoke once; it must have been near dawn. We had stopped for some reason, and I looked up and into the face of a boy about my own age in a white shalwar kameez. He was attending an all-night roadside tea stall. He smiled and waved and I returned the salute. I thought he envied me my adventure.

We got to Peshawar on the third day after two hundred and fifty miles of hard pounding, half choked by dust and fumes. The city was already full of Afghan refugees from the communist takeover and the brief civil war that followed, but not as crammed as it would be in future, when the war really bit in. Gul Muhammed had an address of a cousin, Bacha Khan, who offered us the customary hospitality. He was a fat man with a long beard, the first fat Pashtun I had ever seen. At the time, as I gathered from the conversations of the men, the resistance was fragmented into half a dozen squabbling parties, each with their own armed force and ideas about the future of the country, but which were temporarily united as the Islamic Unity of Afghan Mujahideen. I obviously didn't get the religious and political difference between the seven main mujahideen groups, but in the end it didn't matter much. The clan elders of the Barakzai were going with the National Islamic Front of Afghanistan, so that's where we went too.

The NIFA had a training camp outside of Peshawar in a village called Ali Shawr, so one day we packed up our stuff and went there. The original village had exploded into a vast improvised encampment on flat squishy land on either side of a trickling stream, thousands of people living a pickup kind of life in tents or shelters made of plastic tarpaulins, scrap wood, cardboard, and corrugated tin. Gul Muhammed found a shanty for us in the area occupied by members of his clan, and we slipped into the seething mass like a drop fallen into the sea. They say children are adaptable, and that was how it was for me. After a week or so, my life in the Laghari mansion was like a half-recalled dream; it was as if I had always lived here in the cold and the mud, with a dozen families, our neighbors, living out their lives in our laps, at full volume and odor.

A few days after we arrived, Gul Muhammed made his contacts with the NIFA command and went off to train as a guerrilla. We two boys, to our immense disappointment, discovered that we were to be sent to school at the village madrasa. I went along willingly enough, because they fed you a meal at the school, but Wazir rebelled, the first time I ever saw him defy his father, and he was savagely beaten for it, with an actual camel whip. Wazir was dying to go and kill Russians for God, although he had never seemed to be particularly religious up until then.

Before he left, though, Gul Muhammed formally adopted me into his clan and tribe, so I would have protection and be a real person. It was Wazir who convinced him to do it, a big deal among Pashtuns, so now I had two fathers and a brother.

Then he was gone and Wazir and I went to the school and were more or less looked after by the clan. The teacher was a half-deaf old man named Bazgar, and our education consisted entirely of memorizing the Qur'an, in classical Arabic, which none of us understood. I once asked Teacher Bazgar what it meant and he said, "It's the word of God, that should be enough for you," and swatted me for insolence.

Then came the endless winter—we huddled around the fires while old men told us stories of former wars and revenges—and after that the spring, wildflowers lighting up the slopes around the camp with color. When the passes and trails were clear of snow, an air of heightened feeling ran through the camp, for now convoys and caravans could be organized, to move supplies and reinforcements north to battle. Gul Muhammed came to see us one night to say farewell. He was armed, dressed for the mountains in boots, a quilted jacket, and a felt Pashtun cap, and carried an immense backpack.

"Why can't I go with you?" Wazir complained.

"Because I say not," his father replied. "Stay here and grow strong. This war will last a long time." Then he gave instructions about what to do if he should be killed, threading through his vast cousinage in succession, with contingencies: if such a one should die, go to that one, if he should die, then the next. With that, he gave us each a rough embrace and was gone into the night.

There were hundreds of similarly deserted children in that camp, yet we were all cared for in the manner of the Pashtuns. Our clan took care of us, and the clans of the others did the same. We formed wild bands, fighting battles in the rocky hills around the camp, practicing ambush, assault, escape. We hung around the mujahideen training grounds, yearning; we hitched rides into Peshawar and strolled the arms bazaars, ogling the wares like boys my own age in the States did in back rooms of magazine stands; pistols were our *Penthouse*, rifles our *Hustler*, weapons of all the world's armies over nearly a century: Mausers, Garands, Tokarevs, Enfields, Nagants, and, prized above all, the Kalashnikov AK-47, drool-making object! The bazaaris complained that prices were plunging disastrously, weapons were flooding in from all over the world; the Saudis were shipping, the Americans, the Pakistanis most of all. But the prices were still too high for boys with no money at all.

Summer, and the camp was a stove, it became unbearable to sit in a hot courtyard and chant suras, so we ditched school entirely. Refugees from the war continued to pour into the camp, and the crowding became insane, all the better accommodations taken by families with young children. We slept under a sheet of plastic propped up by sticks. In July the monsoon rains came, and the whole camp became a steaming mire. We found work building duckboards for a local guy and did that for a couple of months. We were restless and bored, and one day Wazir came to me saying, "I am tired of this life. We are not of the menial tribes, you and I, and this work disgraces us. But listen: there is a convoy leaving tonight. We can sneak onto one of the trucks and by the time they find us it will be too late. We will be in the jihad."

"But they'll send us back."

"They will not. I have spoken with men who have returned. They use Afghan boys just like us for carrying and for lookouts and for spies. We can do the same."

⁂

Wazir cleverly chose a truck loaded with blankets and medical supplies, or we would have frozen to death on the trip over the mountains. The mujahideen organizations supplied their fighters via a skein of caravan trails from their Pakistani bases, always switching routes to avoid patrols. We went north from Peshawar to Chitral and then took the Dorah Pass into Afghanistan, although at the time we had no idea where we were. It was cold. I was a kid from tropical Lahore and didn't know what cold was until that trip; winter in the camp had been nothing compared to it. We burrowed down in our nest of blankets in a tight embrace and pissed into jars. The convoy had to make several detours into side canyons and wait while patrols from the government army, the DRA, went by. It took us nearly a week to get to our destination, by which time Wazir and I would've fought for the Russians, almost, if they had given us something to eat or drink. We'd only brought enough food for a few days.

Anyway, they found us among the blankets when they unloaded our truck, and we got roughed up a little and cursed, and then we were taken to the leader of this particular band of mujahideen, Murad Habib, who was called the Colonel, because he had been one in the old Afghan army, before the communist coup. He looked us over and poked us to see if we were worth keeping as pack animals. Wazir was fairly well built at fourteen but I was a skinny little thing—I probably didn't weigh over seventy pounds at the time—and they were going to take him and send me back as baggage with the trucks, but Wazir said he wouldn't leave me and he told our clan lineage to them, and it turned out that the Colonel was a Barakzai just like us and he was distantly related to Gul Muhammed. So it was decided that we could stay with them and wash pots and carry things and dig holes, but if they ever ran into our father they would dump us with him and let him deal with us.

Wazir became a bearer, which meant that at least he went out on ambushes and raids, but I stayed in our village of Gumban and watched the unit's sheep. We had a flock of several hundred, for meat and milk and sheepskins, and also a herd of donkeys for haulage. The shepherd was Zorak, an older man, formerly a fighter, who had one eye and one leg. The first day he asked me if I wanted to hear how he lost them and naturally I did and he said he had been an RPG gunner and in the midst of a hot fight with a Russian column, he had fired so many rockets that he had fouled the tube of his launcher, and when that happens the tube kicks back when you shoot the next one and the rear sight rips out your eye. I asked him if it had hurt and he said he hadn't much felt it until later, but the blood had gummed up his other eye and while he was stumbling around in the open, a Russian machine-gunner had blown off his leg.

He was a friendly enough guy for a Pashtun and seemed glad of my company, and after a few unsuccessful attempts he left my young ass alone and resumed the love of sheep. Every day was the same. We both lived in a one-room stone hut at the edge of the village. At dawn we would eat our breakfast of bread and ewe's milk and, after morning prayer, feed the donkeys and drive the sheep up to pasture on the slopes of the Babur Valley and pray at noon and eat our lunch of bread and dal, then bring the sheep back at dusk, and pray again. When it snowed, we would feed them on hay and sit around the fire and sing songs and tell stories. Zorak knew the usual tales of kings and their clever daughters, of *deos* and fairies and man-eating devil-women, and I replied with what I could remember of the Arabian nights and Kipling and the plots of films I had seen. He was particularly fond of *Snow White and the Seven Dwarfs*. And we sang, to each other at night and to the sheep in their pastures. He knew a lot of traditional Pashto songs, mainly about love, and I responded with renditions of the ghazals I'd heard at Laghari Sahib's parties. The sheep seemed to like it. Actually, at the time I had a good, clear boy's voice and Zorak must have said something to someone in authority, because after a while I was invited to the celebrations the unit used to have after successful operations, to sing the ghazals of Ghalib and Mir and Nazir.

The NISA was a comparatively liberal organization, as things went in Pashtunistan. It attracted former Afghan army officers like the Colonel and other educated people. Their religion was the traditional mild Sufi-influenced Islam of the region. They loved music. Some of the younger guys had tape players on which they listened to Pashto pop songs from Pakistan, but the senior people liked the old ghazals and the old way of hanging out on a Thursday evening for a concert. I would come in from the sheepfold, wash, put on my one good shalwar kameez, wrap my turban neatly, and perform to the beat of the tabla and the plinking drone of the rubab, singing to my audience of rough, violent men about hopeless love and the great cosmic questions of life and death. I guess I became a kind of pet, especially of Colonel Habib's. He would ask for particular ghazals; I remember he liked the one that goes:

> We are bound by life and bound by grief,
> It is the same binding cord,
> Why should we look to be unbound from sorrow
> Before the day of death?

Once I asked the Colonel how long he thought the war would last, and without hesitating he said, "Ten years, just like Vietnam," and then he had to explain to me what Vietnam was and what had happened there. I got a good strategic education from the Colonel; he spent a lot more time with me than colonels typically spend with shepherd boys.

This connection helped ease my loneliness, because aside from Zorak I didn't talk to anyone for days on end, and often when I was in the high pastures I didn't even talk to him. Wazir had more or less dropped me, which is to say he would have given his life gladly to defend me, but he was a fighter and I wasn't. He'd moved up from bearer and now carried an Enfield—this was maybe in the spring of our second year with the mujahideen command—and he treated me with a condescension I found hard to take.

I was a shepherd for something like two and a half years, the first phase of the Russian war. When I started out I was the coddled, maybe even spoiled, child of a wealthy Lahori family and at the end I was a Pashtun shepherd, tough as the roots of a camel thorn, uncomplaining, rainproof, snowproof, uncaring of the cold or the heat, master of the hills. It was the work that did it, I think. It's no mystery why shepherds have featured so much in the great religions; being out in all weathers, under nothing but the sky, you can feel the eye of God on you all the time, and also the stupidity of the sheep, the constant worry over what they're getting into, makes you think you should try your hand at fixing the stupidity of men. That, and the land itself, the bony country of the Pashtun: looming hills, red and tan and black above the evergreen forests, and other colors I can't name, depending on the light and the season; and the softness of the floodplains, their green more gracious and lovely for the contrast with their setting of flint. The white of the apricot trees in spring, and in early summer the whole valley would be red with poppies, and in their midst you could see from the heights the glittering, braided river. And the air of the place, sharp as glass shards in the winter, like breathing live flame in deep summer, and the nights, ear-hissing silent except for the imbecile moaning of the sheep and the eternal wind in the stunted thornbushes, and overhead a million stars wheeling over the black rim of our canyon.

And I hated the Russians for stepping on my land and I hated any-one who wasn't us, and a month or so before my thirteenth birthday I got my chance to fight them. I started as a bearer for an RPG team, car-rying bags full of rockets and booster tubes. On an ambush, I would hang back a little from the team and hand a rocket and a booster to the loader. The RPG-7 is a terrific weapon and guerrilla warfare would be nearly impossible without it, but it has the disadvantage of being fairly slow to reload and of leaving a trail of blue-gray smoke that points right back to the shooter's position, which means you have to change position after you fire. But it's also hard to get a one-shot kill on an armored vehicle at any range and so we always had one team with two RPGs; its leader was Mirzal, our best shot with the weapon, and there was a loader, Bohrum Khan, and now I was a bearer.

ß

"Are you bored yet?" I asked Gloria.

"I'm riveted."

"Why? I wasn't riveted when I was doing it. War is pretty boring, especially guerrilla war. Most of it is hanging around and waiting for the other guys to send a convoy through so you can blow it up. And hiding. We did a lot of that."

"Okay, did you do any heroics? Let's cut to the chase here."

"Oh, heroics. The problem with heroics is that it all goes down so fast you can hardly remember what happened. Other people have to tell you what you did, after. Why do you want heroics?"

"Women love heroes; it's the secret shame of women's lib. We want our precious eggies to get sprayed by guys who can defend us. And also, you have all these scars on you. Don't you think I'm curious about how you got them? Surely you've been down this road before, the seductive powers of the hero and all."

"Not a lot. I'm not that experienced with women, to tell the truth."

"What? I thought soldiers were the horniest creatures on earth."

"Yes, soldiers, but I wasn't a soldier, I was a mujahid. A Pashtun mujahid. We didn't mess with the local women. It would've torn the jihad apart."

"So you were, like, celibate for the whole war? All of you?"

"No. There were plenty of sheep. Some of the big shots had boy harems. Others... well, for example, me and Wazir were an item after I became a fighter."

"You were *gay*?"

"That's the wrong language. I loved him and he loved me and we were warriors together. We shared our blankets. It was part of our war. It's hard to put in an American frame. He was a terrific person, a terrific fighter, much better than me, a real leader and smart as shit. It was very intense, a kind of love-hate thing going on there too."

"Because you thought he was smarter than you and a better soldier?"

"No, I admired the hell out of him for that. No, it was my mother at first. She sort of took him under her wing, spent a lot of time with him, and I wanted her for myself. "

"Why was she interested in him?"

"I don't know. We never talked about it. I was embarrassed, I guess, and she didn't volunteer anything. She was a very strange woman—is, I mean. They wouldn't—I mean the family wouldn't—really let her raise me; I was the eldest son of the eldest son, the heir. I guess that made her want to have someone of her own to form. You would've thought that Gul Muhammed would've objected, but for some reason he didn't. They had a funny relationship too, practically never talked, but he would stare at her when she walked by, like she had two heads. I never could figure it out. So then later, because I could sing and knew a lot of poetry, ghazals and Rahman Baba and all that, I became a favorite of the Colonel, and Wazir got crazy jealous."

"Why, did you do the Colonel too?"

"Of course. He was a great man. It was an honor to be asked. And Wazir found out about it and we had a knock-down drag-out fight and he kicked my ass. That was just before the Tsawkey operation—"

"Wait, what happened to him?"

"Wazir? I don't know. If he survived the war and the Taliban afterward, he's still up there. He might even be fighting against us."

"How come you left?"

"I'll get to that. Do you want to hear about my heroic deed?"

"After I pee," she said.

℞

I was still humping rockets for Mirzal and Bohrum Khan. We'd been hitting the outlying posts pretty regularly, shooting them up, killing DRA and stealing weapons, but now the Colonel wanted to take out the main post, which was set up in the two-story brick high school in Tsawkey town. We had about fifty mujahideen, with Kalashnikovs, Enfields, RPGs, and two PK light machine guns. They had a company of Democratic Republic of Afghanistan troops and a few Russian advisers.

We went in just before sunrise. I was part of a team under a commander named Sahak, twenty-one men and a boy, me, tasked to attack the south side of the school, and there were other teams going to hit the north and east sides simultaneously. I was carrying a satchel of rockets and boosters, a bag of Russian hand grenades, and an Enfield slung across my back, a load that weighed apporoximately as much as I did.

We had good cover in woods up until about a hundred meters off, where the enemy had cleared off the trees and brush. Our target was the heavy machine gun they had mounted on the roof, one of two up there in sandbagged positions. They also had a battery of 82mm Podnos mortars up there, so it was a pretty tough nut. We spread out along the tree line, and Mirzal, Bohrum, and I sneaked out and set up on a little rise a couple of dozen meters out. We were just aiming our first round when someone in one of the other attack groups must have stumbled or maybe he was just an asshole, of which we had a good number in our ranks, but there was a burst of fire off to our flank and immediately parachute flares shot up from the school and it was like we were in the movies, I could see the hairs in Mirzal's beard. He took aim, though, at the bulk of the huge machine gun and I dropped to the ground, and there was this enormous noise and something heavy and wet dropped on me. I struggled out from under it and found it was the top half of Mirzal's body, headless and trailing guts. He'd taken a full burst and the 12.7 had killed Bohrum too.

But the RPG was intact, all loaded, and when the flare went out and the rockets from the next one were just tracing a red pencil up into the night, I picked up the launcher without much thought and fired it at the machine gun. It was my first shot, but I'd seen it done often enough; the main thing is to remember that the rocket tends to fly into the wind and not away from it like a bullet. As soon as I shot I started running toward the school, because I knew I was dead if I stayed there and dead if I tried to make it back to the trees, and as it happened my shot just clipped the steel shield that protects a DShK machine gun from small-arms fire, and it exploded and one of the guns on the roof was out of action.

I heard a cheer behind me as the mujahideen swarmed out of the wood, and then the mortars started up and bombs fell among them but I didn't look back. I just ran toward the school and a door in the wall. Other DRA were shooting down from the roof and out of loopholes in the walls. I could hear the snap of rounds going by and felt a sharp blow on my side, but I figured it was from the tip of one of the rockets, it was always happening, and the other men were pouring in fire at the guys shooting at me so I stopped, knelt, loaded my tube, and shot one at the door. It blew down and I ran up to the doorway and pulled out a grenade and tossed it in, wondering why the grenade was all slippery, and then I dropped my tube and the bag of rockets and went into the building with my rifle.

I discovered I'd been dumb lucky, because the defenders had just been setting up a defensive position with a PK machine gun behind a pile of office desks in the corridor on the other side of the door just as my rocket hit, and the blast had killed or wounded half a dozen men. One of them tried to get up and I shot him with my rifle, my first face-to-face kill, not counting my boyhood revenge. The machine gun seemed all right so I picked it up and draped the belt of rounds over my shoulder and another one around my neck like a fashionable scarf. The PK is just a glorified Kalashnikov and weighs about fifteen pounds, so compared to what I usually carried I was floating on air. I went through a door and down a corridor. Three men came racing around a corner, pulling on equipment. They seemed surprised to see me and skidded to a halt, open-mouthed, and I shot them down.

Then I heard the sound of lots of men coming, pounding boots, so I ducked in a door, which turned out to be a stairway. I went up the stairs, past the second floor and up to the roof. Just as I got to the last flight up, the roof door opened and a man in Soviet camo gear appeared and yelled something. He was surprised to see me too, I guess.

After I shot him I stepped over his body and out onto the roof. There were the mortarmen loading rounds like crazy and an officer with night goggles standing by the parapet behind some sandbags yelling ranges and azimuths, and the other DShK machine gun was blasting away. So I set myself against the edge of the doorway I'd just come through and with one long burst shot everyone on the roof. There was still firing coming from the north side of the building, and I looked down and saw that the DRAs had set up a sandbagged position in front of the north door and they were holding up our guys attacking from that side, so I dropped a couple of grenades down on them. I was feeling a little bushed by then, so after making sure that everyone was dead and shooting them if they weren't, I sat down against the sandbags near the DShK gun and checked my weapon. My PK was nearly out of ammunition but I had lots of grenades. I remember seeing that the grenade bag was covered in blood, but it somehow didn't occur to me that it was mine.

I got up and began to futz around with the DShK, and figured out how to fire it, and did fire a short burst just for fun. As I was wondering what was keeping the rest of my people I heard sounds of boots and voices on the stairwell and out walked two DRA soldiers carrying crates of mortar bombs. They stopped and looked at the scene on the roof, stunned, I guess, and I turned the big machine gun around and blew them both to rags. Then I ran to the head of the stairs and threw a bunch of grenades down there, and the explosions must have set off the mortar bombs because the whole roof erupted like a volcano and knocked me on my ass.

When I came to again I was in bed back in our village and Wazir was sitting next to my charpoy holding my hand. There were tears in his eyes. He asked me to forgive him for his envy. He said the Prophet, on whom be peace, taught that envy eats up good actions as fire eats up wood. I asked him why he was envious of me—I had been a shepherd boy and a mere bearer while he had fought the jihad with arms and was accounted brave—and he answered, because the Colonel favored you. And then he went into a long story about something that had happened five hundred years ago, about the envy between the son and the adopted son of Ghoughusht and how this had brought calamities on their tribe, and this was the same thing and he was ashamed. He said he thought he could own me like a pet, which was very wrong, for all belong to God alone, especially we mujahideen, and this is proven by what you did with God's help two days ago; the Pashtuns will sing of it for a thousand years, how one boy captured a fort by himself and slew sixty men.

So I forgave him and said I loved him above all men and we were reconciled. It was interesting that I'd been out of it for two whole days. I didn't recall anything that happened after I fired the RPG, and it took days for me to recollect what I'd done. I'd taken a round through the flesh on my right side, my first battle scar. After that, people treated me with a kind of awed respect, since it was clear to them that I was under the special protection of God, or else I never could have captured a strongpoint almost single-handed and wiped out the better part of a company of soldiers. But the fact is that things like that happen from time to time in combat, call it God or inexplicable luck. You read, say,

Audie Murphy's Medal of Honor citation, and it sounds like someone made it up. For a whole hour this little guy holds off an entire company of Wehrmacht infantry, supported by six tanks, while standing upright in a burning vehicle firing a .50-caliber machine gun—and survives. He was eighteen when he did that. I was thirteen when I took the high school in Tsawkey. It makes no sense.

~

"Nothing makes any sense if you look at it that way," she said, when I'd laid all that out. "Why are we here? Why is there air? Is that where you got this scar?" She stroked it gently.

"No," I said. "Tsawkey's on the other side. That's a shrapnel wound."

"Is there another story?"

"Yes, but even I'm getting bored. And it's not very interesting. It was near the end of the war, a big operation. I was hiding behind a wreck. I shot a rocket at a Russian tank; the tank shot back. I should've died, but I didn't. I was out for ten days and woke up in a hospital with Gul Muhammed and Wazir holding a hand each. They told me I had been dead but came back to life according to the will of God, and I said *God can do all things* and asked how the battle had turned out. Gul Muhammed said it had been a great victory, with the greatest loot ever captured. The Russians were pulling out."

"And that was it, huh?" she said. "The end of the war. Or that war. How did you get back to the States?"

"That's another story," I said. "Time to sleep."

"Time to go," she said, hopping out of bed.

"You're not staying?"

"No, I have a shift that starts in about four hours. I'll barely have time to shower and change. Call me a cab, will you?"

I did and watched her hop into her clothes, all business now; whatever intimacy we had generated with our bodies and our talking was gone. It was an American hookup, about as serious as having a pleasant seatmate on a long-haul flight, and I've never gotten used to it.

Why don't you look at me properly?
Why do you magnify my suffering?

The torturer flays for a reason.
What's yours, beloved?

Ask your fierce eyes
Why they cut me to pieces.

Rahman Baba. We used to sing that one in the jihad as we marched through the dry hills. This came out of a culture where marriages are arranged and women are cattle. It makes you think.

After Gloria left, I slept for a few hours and then washed and dressed in my traveling clothes, packed up a small bag, and went downstairs.

My father was in the kitchen in white shirt and tie with the *Post* and a cup of tea. He must have heard me moving around upstairs because he'd made me a cup, strong, milky, and sweet.

I sat down and he reached into the pocket of his suit jacket where it hung behind his chair and handed me a thick envelope.

"Here is your ticket and your Pakistani passport and enough cash to keep you for a few days. You can always get more from Nisar."

I stowed it in my bag and said, "How are we doing?"

He removed his horn-rims and rubbed his eyes. He looked tired but brighter somehow, like he was plugged into a higher energy channel.

He said, "Well, we have laid the bait, as you know. The calls have been fabricated as we discussed."

"Jafar went for it?"

"No, of course not. I wouldn't dream of involving Jafar. He is a *govern-ment* man, and only family by marriage. No, Rukhsana sent her eldest to Kahuta and he borrowed his father's cell phone and made the call to her."

"This is Hassan?"

"Yes. He's turning out to be quite the conspirator. A very credible imitation of his father's voice."

"Who's in on it?" I asked.

"Just Rukhsana and her boys—and Nisar, of course. And us." He gave a sigh and put his glasses back on and looked at me through them, his owl look. He said, "I will tell you, Theo, if a month ago you had told me I would be involved in such a conspiracy, breaking the laws of my own and my

host nation, with the intent to bring about a military invasion of Pakistan—
well, I would have called you a lunatic. And now I have done these things—
me, Farid Bashir Laghari, full professor of law, LLD, by God."

"Why are you doing it then, if it bothers you?"

"You ask me why? You, who wept like a child in my arms when you
thought she was in danger, who has not wept in my presence since you
were small enough to carry? Because your mother makes me insane
and has since the moment I first laid eyes on her in Central Park. Who
could have known I would have such a weakness? I was always a good
boy, studious, obedient—my God, how obedient I was! Nisar was
always the rascal and Seyd was the spoiled baby, and I was the model
son, I assure you. And suddenly, in this foreign park I am in the midst of
a ghazal, I am Háfiz, I am Mir," and he recited in Urdu:

> "From the instant of the heart's creation,
> the body has been tinder,
> so fell this spark,
> the mantle burst into flames,
> now like the light of the full moon
> the fire has spread all over me."

I said in the same language, "Wracked with madness, the only sound
the rattle of my chains," which is a line from the same poem.

He smiled. "Yes, and I thought I could become sane again, by bringing her into my home. I had a fantasy, a fantasy that by some miracle
she might become a good Muslim wife."

"That was always a long shot."

"Yes, but hope is a mighty drug. You know the line—the same poem,
in fact—about ridding the terrified gazelle of wild despair? Those who
tamed her had done a miracle. I thought I had done it. We had a son, you,
and I thought she was settling in. I knew she didn't love me as I loved
her, but I imagined that as we grew older—"

He stopped and looked away from me. Maybe he was stunned by the
memories. I was stunned myself; I'd never had a conversation like this
with my father.

I said, "But she ran away."

"Yes. Can you imagine what it was like for the son of B. B. Laghari to have his wife run off and travel across half of Asia with that *faqir*? And then to *write* about it? My mother absolutely *commanded* me to divorce her. As you know, divorce is very easy in Islam, you say a few words, and it is done, and there is no question that it is the father who gets the children, but I could not. I simply could not do it. It would have strangled my heart. And so I waited and thought evil, unworthy thoughts. I prayed she would get into trouble out there and I would get a frantic call at three in the morning, *Oh, Farid, come save me with your law books and your money!* But the call never came, and then she became famous out of my disgrace, and then she went away again, on the haj, and this time she did something that scandalized even my father. Traipsing around Central Asia disguised as a man was bad enough, but on the haj! She had endangered the position of the whole family, so my father sent her into exile. And finally came the bomb and the catastrophe and I broke down and you vanished and what did I do? As soon as I recovered I could think of nothing else but finding her."

"In Zurich."

"Yes. Isn't it remarkable that we have never discussed these events, as father to son? I am ashamed of myself, but you know, Sonia draws a pall of secrecy behind her like a dark cloak."

"Yeah. I'm not entirely sure how she managed to find *me*. She was always pretty vague."

"Well, I can barely help you there. I was not a party to those doings; I was only the father, after all! But it happened very quickly. After I found her, I begged her to let me stay with her, I was pitiable, crying and all that, I said that I had lost everything; was she going to abandon me as well? And so on. Pitiable! My mother, you can imagine, was insane with fury. She cut me off entirely. I could not work in Switzerland, but Sonia still had some money left, so we were not absolutely destitute. We had a flat in the Kreuzstrasse, we took the trams in the morning, she to the Jung Institute, I to the Zentralbibliothek to do research for an article on international law I was trying to write, and we existed that way—I won't exactly call it living—like the war refugees you see on television. I did all the shopping and the housework, me who had never made a bed in his life! I made her tea, I massaged her feet, I thought if I turned myself into a servant she would acknowledge me, she would see my suffering and turn toward me with love. It was all I could think of doing."

"Did she? Turn to you with love?"

He was silent for a moment and then slowly nodded his head. "Yes, in her fashion, she did. It took some time, and I think that what she was doing, the therapy and all that, must have helped. I thought we might be able to repair things and start to live again. So some years passed. She completed her training and was certified as a Jungian analyst. I applied for jobs in the States, and the U.K., and so forth. I published a number of articles on international law that were well received and gave me a small reputation in this field. And then the American came to our flat. This was in 1987, late in the year. Or, at least, I assume he was an American; I only heard his voice in the foyer. So I am waiting there in our living room, and Sonia comes in with tears in her eyes, and says, *Oh, Farid, he's alive! Theo is alive!* This man had apparently found you in Afghanistan. Of course I was full of questions. Tears were in my eyes too. I wanted to rush out and question this man, whoever he was, but she stopped me; she said I must not tell anyone about this. It was a condition."

"A condition?"

"Yes, the gentleman in question had told her he could arrange to have you taken from Afghanistan provided the whole thing was kept completely dark."

"And you went along with that?"

"It was not a question of going along. Before I could say two words, she had taken her coat and disappeared from the flat. The next time I heard from her it was two months later, and she was calling from Washington, and she had you with her. So I forgave her that as well, and we made a life for ourselves here in this city, although she cannot bear to be with me for more than a few months at a time."

"But she stays married to you. That's something to think about." As I said that I was wondering, Who was the American in Zurich in 1987? It was something I planned to ask Sonia, if and when I got to see her again.

"Yes!" said Farid. "She does love me, in her way. When she's here, when we travel, she gives me the fullness of her presence, and it's only then that I feel truly alive. When she's gone, when I'm here alone, being looked after by a housekeeper and eating my meals in restaurants, I say to myself, *Farid, you are keeping a hawk; don't expect her to lay eggs like a chicken.*"

"You could get another wife. It's one of the advantages of the true faith."

My father shrugged and smiled a little sheepishly. "Yes, I could, but I am too modern for that. I'm almost as deracinated as you. Tell me, do I seem different to you, since this all started?"

"Yes. You seem like a completely different person."

"I *feel* like a different person. I find it hard to concentrate on my classes; I can no longer participate in university politics and all that rubbish. I ask myself why, and I can only arrive at one answer. At last the call has come! She needs my help. I feel that this is what I was meant for, my purpose on earth. You know, sometimes I feel as if I am one of those insect species where the male is tiny and the female gigantic. He lives for one single act, and when it is over he dies. But who knows what he feels in his brief moment of importance? Perhaps it is a concentrated ecstasy that, if translated into human terms, would rival the satisfactions of an unusually long and extraordinarily sensual life."

He stared at me, trying to read what was in my eyes. He asked, "You don't think this is perverse? To risk everything, perhaps even prison, for this?"

"No, I feel exactly the same way," I answered, "and I've spent a lot less time with her than you have. It's just Sonia. Also, sometimes you have to do crazy things for love."

He smiled then, a kind of smile I don't recall ever seeing on my father's face. He said, "Yes, at long last we're both turning into Sufis. I expect your mother will be quite pleased."

And then, after a second or so, we both laughed like maniacs for a good long time.

11

Mahmoud has waited in the lee of the wall outside the building, squatting, patient as a hound. When Sonia crawls out the door, he lets out a startled cry, picks her up in his arms, and carries her into the hujra, but not to the room she once shared with Annette Cosgrove. Instead she is taken to a somewhat larger room, which had once been the eating hall of the village inn. It seems to Sonia that all the captives have been assembled there and there is a stir among them as the guard brings her in and lays her carefully on a charpoy. When he leaves they all gather around her, all talking at once. Annette Cosgrove reaches her first, sees the condition of her feet, and cries out for water and cloths. She shouts at the others in a firm nurse's voice that Sonia has not heard her use before, telling them to go away and let Sonia breathe.

Annette bathes Sonia's feet, her touch professionally gentle, her movements efficient. She smears an ointment on the torn soles, and says, "I'm sorry, that must hurt."

"What is it?"

"Neosporin. We always travel with a medical kit, and I asked for it when they brought me in here. I said I would take care of their people too. Look at me, please. Have you had a concussion?"

"No. I fainted when they whipped my back."

"Let's take a look at it," says Annette. She helps Sonia off with her kameez, and peels back the bandages, after which she gives a small cry. "Oh, Jesus!"

"That bad?"

"Well, it may look worse than it is. You lost a lot of skin, but there doesn't seem to be any suppuration. Let me bandage you up again."

THE GOOD SON | 191

When she is done with this and Sonia's shirt is back in place, Annette says, "I don't know, I'd be howling if I had a back like that. Either you're incredibly stoic or . . . you're sure they didn't hit your head?"

"I'm fine, Annette. I had a religious experience. The pain is still there but it's not . . . engaging? It's hard to describe."

She looks around the little room. The group members are keeping their distance, but they are all watching her. She asks, "Is everyone here all right? Dr. Schildkraut?"

"He's fine, except for his bronchitis. The others . . . physically, they're all fine. A little smelly, maybe, but all healthy so far." A pause. Sonia is conscious of all the eyes on her and knows why. She's been outside, she's seen other faces, heard other voices, they are all dying for news of the rest of the world, even news from a village street. Well, she has news.

At last, Annette blurts out their desire. "What's happening? Did they tell you anything?"

"Yes, and we all need to hear this." She lifts herself up and gestures to the others and immediately the eight prisoners surround her, pressing close, kneeling or standing, or sitting on another charpoy hastily dragged over. Sonia is reminded of a baroque altarpiece: disciples surrounding a dying saint, their attention rapt.

She gives it to them straight. She has spoken to the man in charge. He has expressed interest in the conference and insists that they proceed here, but the threat made on the video is literal. On any day when there are civilian casualties in the so-called war on terror, Alakazai will execute one hostage. And Sonia herself is to choose each victim.

There is a silence, broken by Schildkraut. "Sonia, that is monstrous. You cannot possibly do such a thing, selecting the victims—"

"I don't think any of it is voluntary, Professor," says Ashton, and they all begin talking at once until Amin shouts for everyone to be quiet and enforces his demand by banging on the brass breakfast tray with a metal spoon.

"Thank you," he says, when they have settled down. "There is no need to lose our heads—in the figurative sense at least. Now, as to our situation. Obviously, we are at the mercy of this man, Alakazai, who clearly has no mercy at all. But we are not entirely helpless. We can at least relieve Sonia of this impossible responsibility by selecting the order of execution ourselves, in advance. We can draw straws—"

"I have a deck of cards," says Sonia.

"A deck of cards will do as well. Are we agreed on that score at least?"

"As if we had a choice," says Ashton.

Amin gives the Englishman a stern look. "No, we don't have a choice as to whether we will die, but we can choose if we will die like human beings. Our captor wishes to reduce us to a squabbling herd of animals and wishes to degrade Sonia by making her the mistress of our fate. He would like to see us begging her for another day of life, offering her money, favors, I don't know what. We can choose not to do that. We can choose to leave the order of our dying in the hands of fate—or God, if you will." He pauses to look each of them in the eye, then asks, "Are we agreed, then?"

Murmurs of assent, nods. Porter Cosgrove clears his throat. "But it's not certain that anyone will be killed, is it? I mean, it depends on whether any innocent Muslims are killed. Maybe they'll call some sort of truce while we're being held."

An incredulous laugh from Harold Ashton, and Amin says gently, "Porter, of course we all hope that, but I am afraid there is little chance that the various wars will cease just because nine people are being held hostage. Innocent Muslims are being killed every day by various armies, and the fact that most of them are dying at the hands of fellow Muslims can't affect our situation. The deaths will not stop—if not in Pakistan, then Kashmir, Afghanistan, Iraq, Chechnya. We can always hope for rescue, but there is no point in clutching at false hopes."

Sonia observes that Cosgrove has a lock on the prize for most demoralized captive. He seems to have lost two sizes since his expansive performance at the dinner party, was it four days ago? A lifetime ago, at any rate. His face has fallen into itself like a rotted white grape, and his eyes are a hurt child's: How can this be happening to wonderful charitable *me*? He sags against his wife's sturdy youth. Sonia catches Annette's troubled look but pulls her eyes away, feeling embarrassment, guilt.

Amin speaks again. He's also transformed himself, Sonia observes, from a slick, even oily, foundation professional into a death-camp leader. He's physically shrunken, like the others, but this has only exposed an unexpected core of moral steel.

"The other decision we must make is whether to hold our conference now. Sonia tells us it is our tyrant's desire. We must not suppose that he is really interested in what we have to say. It is most probable that he wishes to mock us. Nevertheless, I believe we should do it."

There is some outburst at this, but he holds his hand up until they are quiet again. "This is why," he continues. "We all stand for something and, if I may say it, different versions of the same thing. We stand for peace. We think it is possible in this world. We think intelligence, fair dealing, and moral clarity can help bring about peace, even in places where war is the only thing anyone remembers. Some of us have actually done this, so we understand that it is not merely a pious illusion. Some of us are inspired by religion. We think a compassionate God desires all His children to live in peace. Others of us are not religious, but believe that war is a crime against reason and humanity. None of us expected to be in this situation, with death hanging over all our heads. But consider our choices now. We can refuse to perform for this evil man, that is one way to look at it, or we can speak our truth, even in the face of death. This is what is meant by the word *martyr*, as I'm sure you know. Martyr means witness. And speaking only for myself, this is how I would prefer to die, with my truth on my lips to the last breath."

In the silence after this, Sonia begins to clap, and the others join in with enthusiasm, all except Porter Cosgrove, who sits stunned on the edge of a charpoy, like a stuffed doll. But Annette claps, as does Ashton, although Sonia notices he is looking at Annette as he does.

Schildkraut now rises as the applause fades and says, "Let me add, if I may, one observation to my colleague's remarks. I am the oldest person here, by a good measure. I was looking forward to my seventy-sixth birthday next month, and I suppose that in the normal course of things I would have volunteered to be the first to go to death. It would not be much of a sacrifice, I think, not of very much time anyway. But as it is, I will submit to the hand of fate, as Amin has suggested. I say *fate* and not *God*, you notice; I am one of Amin's atheists. And as the oldest of you, I suppose I have been to more conferences over the years than anyone else. That is what we intelligentsia do in the modern world, we travel and talk and confer, all paid for by people like Mr. Craig there. It is one of the perks of such a life, quite pleasant—the nice hotels, the beautiful conference centers—yes, and I agree with Amin that we must do this thing now, to speak our truth, and I would like to add that, should any of us survive, we should propose this arrangement as a general principle for conferences. At every conference there should be a card drawing and executions. Everyone should speak as if their speech were their last words on earth. I submit that this would make for shorter meetings and a good deal less bullshit."

He sits. After a frozen instant, Amin bursts into laughter and the rest of them join in, all except, again, Porter Cosgrove. He seems about to cry. Then he does cry, deep, almost soundless sobs. Annette talks to him softly, urges him to stand, moves him shuffling away from the others, and lays him down on a charpoy near the far wall.

Nobody comments on this. Instead they crowd around Sonia and Amin, seemingly reluctant to move away, as if these two have some powerful mana that will lift the curse of death, Amin because he is now the leader, and Sonia because . . . she doesn't quite understand it, but it has to do, she thinks, with the experience she had in the cellar stable. Maybe they sense it, the shadow of God; maybe they think, even the rationalists, the atheists, that she can work miracles as a result.

Sonia says, "There's something else you should know. I guess you've heard that I'm interpreting dreams for some of the locals, yes? Well, as Amin said, I'm not sure we can impress Alakazai with anything we do, but I have the sense that Bahram Alakazai is not well loved as a leader, and neither is his field commander, Idris Ghulam. It's hard to lead Pashtuns, even if they respect you, and respect ordinarily goes through khel and tribe. They'll take orders from people they don't know if they believe it's for a higher cause, like the jihad, but they don't like it. If the jihad for some reason proves illegitimate, the whole arrangement breaks down. If their violence is not authorized, they accrue blood guilt for the people they kill. And they need not take orders from someone not in their clan hierarchy, which I suspect is the case here. Alakazai is a half-breed, and Idris has the look of a *malang*, a man of one of the menial tribes."

"But even if this is true, Sonia," says Manjit Nara, "how is this to our advantage?"

"I'm not sure yet, but dreams are very important to these people. I think I've almost won over the guard Mahmoud. I mean he'll still torture me, but his heart's not in it. And Alakazai doesn't seem to want to go the full legal route to have me put to death under sharia law. Instead he's whipped up this supposed psychological torture for me.

That's not Muslim, that's simple sadism, and people won't like it when they find out about it, and Alakazai will lose face when we foil that by putting the choice in God's hands. Meanwhile, we can expect a big audience for the conference because Pashtuns love talk fests, and I intend to simultaneously translate the presentations into Pashto as you all speak. Among other things, we can make the case that murdering hostages is a violation of sharia law. Which it is."

This produces an unpleasant snort from Ashton. "But surely you don't imagine that nice legalities are going to stop these people from doing whatever they want. Mujahideen murder civilians all the time."

"People who call themselves mujahideen commit all kinds of atrocities, true, but they need some corrupt mullah to give them leave to behave like that. The kind of criticism that the liberal press in Western countries generates has no effect on them, they think it's hypocrisy. It follows that the only attack that might have some effect is from the *right*, so to speak, from real religion and not from what they consider Godless liberalism. These jihad mullahs are never challenged openly from within Islam, which is what I've done here and what I'll continue to do. These people can't stand to think of themselves as bandits, they can't stand to think that if they die they won't go to Paradise, and they won't if they're not in a real jihad."

Schildkraut turns to Father Shea. "What do you think of that, Mark?"

"You're asking *me*?"

"You're our expert on comparative religion."

The priest scratched at his newly bristling beard. "Yes, and as a Catholic I suppose you think I'm expert in both fanaticism and the furthest reaches of the right wing," which produces a scholarly chuckle among the group. "Well, I don't know that it's a religious issue at all. I believe it was a countryman of yours, Schildkraut, who said, 'Terrorism is the rage of the literati in its final stages.' Al-Qaeda and its offshoots are a disease of modernism, however much they dress themselves in traditional clothing. It's a kind of toxic nostalgia, which is something the Catholic Church only took about five hundred years to deal with, and we're still not past it yet. They see the modern world of technology and mass media and libertinism and consumerism, and they both desire and despise it. I mean, that's why we all came here, to talk about the diseased mental states that generate terrorism and violence in this part of the world. So I think it's something of a stretch to believe that what you call real religion can have an effect. In fact, whatever they say, they're not at all religious. *Thou shall not commit murder* is a pretty basic rule for the genuinely religious."

Manjit Nara laughs and says, "Ah, at last we are having our conference."

"Yes, and I believe, all things considered," says Amin, "that we would have been better off holding it at the hotel in Lahore. But I think Sonia has another arrow to her bow. I find it interesting about the dream work you are doing with our hosts. Have you ever done this for traditional Muslims?"

"No, but my practice in America includes a number of American Indians and Chicanos, and those are both highly traditional cultures. I'm assuming the same techniques apply."

"Perhaps," Amin says, frowning. "It's a risky enterprise. They already accuse you of witchcraft. What's your purpose?"

"To promote harmony and help those astray to return to the true path," says Sonia blandly.

Ashton says, "You mean you're manipulating them to serve your purposes, which, since I assume we all have the common purpose of staying alive here, I must heartily approve."

"No, I'm absolutely sincere. But I'm convinced the outcome will be the same."

"Oh, spare us! You sincerely believe that these maniacs, and I use the term literally, will respond to your messing about with their oedipal complexes?"

"Not at all. Psychotherapy is culture-bound. In Western society the psyche is considered to be individual, and the therapist works toward individuation. Even Jung, who understood that this was an illusion, worked this way in his practice. The basic stance of the Western therapist is to resolve interior conflicts within the different segments of the individual psyche. We observe, for example, a dominant father figure who limits the freedom of the client. If you're Freudian you try to bring the oedipal tension to consciousness; if you're a Jungian, you try to integrate the paternal introject, and other brands of therapies try to do the same thing under different names, but the goal is always the same: the freedom of the individual to fulfill his or her potential without neurotic limitations. This is not the case with traditional Muslims."

"It's not?" says Ashton. "You're suggesting they *like* being mad?"

"No, I'm saying it's a Western delusion that all psychological problems are reducible to restrictions on individual freedom. In other cultures, including the one we're talking about, the highest value is not freedom at all. It's harmony within the family and the tribe and the sense that the person is doing the right thing with respect to tradition."

"Are you serious? What if the family or the tribe or whatever is oppressive? Surely you wouldn't justify the way our hosts treat women."

"That's quite besides the point, Harold. My job is not to justify a culture or to encourage rebellion from it, but to enable a client to live as successfully as possible within it, without neurotic symptoms. In the West, that means reducing interior conflict. In the Muslim world, it means reducing exterior conflicts."

"If I may interpolate here, Harold," says Nara, "Sonia is quite correct. Among my own patients, both Hindu and Muslim, any attempt to strengthen the supposed ego at the expense of traditional structures of authority inevitably results in the failure of the therapy. The patients either leave or they sink into a paralyzing depression. In fact, the symptoms we commonly see in practice are the result of conflict between the patient's cultural expectations and his current situation. He has, for example, feelings of worthlessness because he tries to be a good Muslim and yet God does not favor him with success. Or a daughter feels she is being unjustly treated by her father or her mother-in-law. In such cases there is no point in trying to strengthen the autonomous ego because there *is* no autonomous ego, except of course in those who have been culturally Westernized, and they have a completely different set of issues. No, what we must do is to treat the situation, not the psyche as such."

"So you just tell them to knuckle under?"

"No," says Nara, "we try to restore harmony. We work with the family. We use quotations from the traditional scriptures. We don't probe the intimate details of family life because these patients think it's shameful to discuss such things. Instead, we use the unusually rich metaphoric life we find among such people and make suggestions that will result in real change and the alleviation of symptoms."

Ashton is not convinced; he shakes his head like a bull. "But the end result is that the woman remains a second-class citizen and the man slogs away in a corrupt and impoverished society. I can't believe you're really defending this sort of thing. Good Lord, you're all educated people! Surely you can't want the perpetuation of Muslim or Indian society as it now stands. It's the worst kind of patronization. It's like saying only white people have the right to democratic governance, honest administration, civil rights, a prosperous society, the lot."

Sonia, Nara, and Amin exchange looks. After a pause, Amin says, "This is the problem with cultural imperialism—"

"I beg your pardon! I am the furthest thing from a cultural imperialist."

"Please, let me finish! The problem, as I say, with cultural imperialism is that it can be completely unconscious, which I believe is the case here. For example, you used the phrase *knuckle under*. By that you mean it is wrong or unseemly for people to submit their will—their whim, even—to a traditional authority. Yet all of Muslim society is based on submission to the will of God, and everything follows from that. You look at us and you see oppression; we see stability and harmony. You see corruption; we see ties of family, friendship, and mutual support. You see feudalism, we see mutual responsibility. You see the oppression of women, we see the defense of modesty. But then you say, but *look* at you! See how poor and weak you are and how rich and strong we are, because of our culture, which prizes freedom above every other human value—no, that *destroys* every other human value to secure absolute freedom. In response to that, sir, I ask you to look at two things. First, yes, we are poor, but until sixty years ago, you Europeans owned all of us, we worked for you and not for ourselves. So of course we are poor—it took Europe eight centuries to recover from the yoke of Rome and its collapse. I say to you, sir, have a little patience! And the second thing is, for all but the last two and a half centuries, the traditional society you condemn was quite successful. A thousand years ago London was a wooden village occupied by starving barbarians and Baghdad was the greatest and richest city in the world. So perhaps it will be that way again; who can tell what God has planned?"

Ashton is about to launch into a rejoinder, a scarlet blotch stands out on his cheeks and his mouth gapes, but at that moment there is a clatter at the door. It opens and in comes Mahmoud and Rashida and an older woman, carrying trays of steaming naan bread and cans of tea.

Amin claps his hands, beaming. "Thank God! It is breakfast at last. I tell you, my doctor has told me these many years, 'Amin, you must drop ten kilos,' although I am almost sure he did not mean decapitation. If we survive this he will be most pleased."

~

Everyone except Manjit Nara and Sonia gathers around the trays, sits, and starts eating and drinking, as at a school picnic. Nara sits carefully on the edge of Sonia's charpoy and says, "I will bring you your breakfast and we will chat, yes?"

He does so. The naan is soaked in clarified butter and is warm, greasy, and delicious. The tea is thick, sweet, milky.

"You have a different look," he says. "At first I thought it was mere shock after what has been done to you, but now I don't believe so."

"No. They shut me in a dark stable and I thought I was going to die. Then I had a certain experience. It's hard to explain. I did spiritual exercises that I had been taught long ago, in despair, you understand, and it was as if I dissolved, and what was left didn't care about the pain and the fear. It was almost amusing. And now, sitting here, eating bread, talking about professional subjects, I feel I'm being drawn back into the world, and something in me doesn't want to return. Does that make any sense?"

"Indeed it does. Some people are broken by suffering and others transcend it and become more than they were before. The Christian martyrs are examples, but we also see it in daily life, especially in places like India, where we are among the world leaders in suffering. If there were an Olympics in suffering, India would take all the gold." He laughs nervously. "I must say, although it shames me, that I am glad we are to be chosen for death at random."

"Are you? Why is that?"

"Because otherwise I would have been the first, idolator that I am, and representative of the most hated nation."

"After the United States."

He smiled at that and coughed politely. "Yes, but al-Faran is a Kashmiri insurgent organization. Rest assured, they would have picked me. And I have been trying to prepare myself for death, to meet it with dignity, but I find I cannot. My insides turn to water when I think of the moment, having my head cut off. When they hold up the severed head, will there still be thoughts in it, even for a few seconds? What horror to imagine it!"

Sonia says, "The self slays not, neither is it slain."

"Yes, but I find the wisdom of the Bhagavad Gita is of little comfort to me now, knowing it is all a dream of Vishnu and I will be reborn, and so on. I have been poisoned by my education as a modern physician. The Brahmins are perhaps wise to avoid contact with the dead. Corpses are so undeniably real, it is hard to have lofty thoughts around corpses."

He shuddered and drank the rest of his tea greedily, as if it were an elixir of amnesia.

"But I didn't seek a private conversation with you only to expose my pathetic cowardice. I ask you to observe Mr. Ashton, over my right shoulder."

Sonia looks. Ashton has brought breakfast loaves and cups to where the Cosgroves are sitting. Annette seems to be urging her husband to eat but he has turned his face away from her. His shoulders are shaking. Ashton is sitting next to her, his hand lightly on her shoulder.

"See? A comforting gesture, perhaps, or something more? Mr. A is a bit of a ladies' man, yes? And the beautiful Mrs. Cosgrove may require a strong man to lean on in this time of trouble, with her husband having completely collapsed. I tell you, it was a surprise to me, this collapse, one would have thought that Cosgrove, with all of his oft-told adventures and dangers escaped, would have been the last to do so, but see, again, one can never tell."

"Perhaps he exaggerated," she suggests. "Perhaps the angel has never come quite this close."

"The angel! That is good. Or maybe it is being a prisoner, having no control of one's fate. It is the case that people who do all sorts of dangerous things on their own are terrified to fly in airplanes, and this may be an allied syndrome. And neither is Mr. A what he seems."

"What do you mean?"

"Oh, just persistent rumors among the community of subcontinental scholars. That Mr. Ashton has, let us say, official connections. That he is not unknown to MI-6."

"You think he's a spook?"

"Is that what you call them? Yes, a spook."

"Well, they said that about me too, you know," says Sonia. "After my trip through Soviet Central Asia. Perhaps we're all spooks, including Father Shea."

"Yes, but not the Cosgroves. Annette is as clear as water and Porter is a wreck."

"True, but perhaps that's part of their act. And whatever the actual case is, I suggest it would be better not to descend into that sort of paranoia. But now, Manjit, I believe Rashida would like to talk to me privately, or at least as privately as these conditions allow. Thank you for breakfast."

With a shrug and a smile Nara goes off, and Rashida, who has been hovering for some minutes, swoops in to sit at the edge of the pallet.

"So, Rashida, any more dreams?"

"No, but my father has had one and he will come to you tonight."

"How will he do that?"

"Tonight, Mahmoud will take you to an empty room. He has had a dream too, as you foretold him, and wants to know its meaning. Soon you will die and there are many who wish to have their dreams told before you are dead. They have given money to Mahmoud and so it will be done."

⁊ᴏ

It is done. In the night Mahmoud slips into the prison room, light-footed for such a large man, awakens Sonia, and leads her to an empty room of the hujra. It is dark except for starlight coming through a window and silent except for the sound of the diesel generator and a fainter high-pitched grinding noise, like the squeal of a rusty gate that never closes.

Sonia feels the faint breeze of an opening door on her cheek and then the loom of another person in the room. In a low voice he announces himself as Baryal Rostai, the father of Rashida.

"I have had a dream," he says and tells it, with many halts. Sonia considers it for a while, then speaks. "The well you fell into is the entrance to Hell; the rope you held on to is the Holy Qu'ran, that frees men from everlasting torment. As we read in the sura al-Imran, *Hold firmly to the rope of God and do not become divided.* This much is easy. But then you reached the top of the well and there was an angel there who handed you a string of pearls and pointed to the right side. The pearl indicates a young man, for it is written in the sura al-Insaan, *There will be young men of perpetual youth serving them; if you saw the youths you would think they were scattered pearls.* The right side indicates an escape from harm, as the Prophet, peace be upon him, interpreted it in a dream of his disciple, Ibn Umar. This is what it means. As you walk from this village there is a path that leads to the right and to another village. In this village there is a young man. To him you must marry your daughter."

"But I have already promised my daughter to Khaliq Sumro."

"I cannot help that. You have dreamed what you have dreamed. God in His mercy has given you this warning, and you are free to disregard it."

Baryal waits but she says nothing more and will not answer his questions. He leaves and before long there is another man in the room. Sonia interprets his dream according to the book of Muhammed ibn Sirin, who compiled an account by the Companion Abu Huraira of the dream interpretations of the Apostle of God. And then there is another and another, and this one is Idris Ghulam.

His voice is hoarse, exhausted. "Every night I have the same dream," he says. "I am in the mountains, fighting against the idolators. I am on jihad. I am pursued down a narrow canyon by five Indian soldiers. I set an ambush, and I kill all five of them with my rifle. Then I come out of hiding and look at their bodies, and I see that they are not Indian soldiers at all but my three brothers, my mother, and one other who is dear to me. Then I seem to wake from the dream with a cry. I am in my bed at home, with my brothers sleeping beside me and I am relieved. Then my mother comes into the room and says, 'What is wrong, my son? I heard you cry out,' and I tell her about the dream, and she reaches out to touch my face and I see and feel that her hand is a withered skeleton. I look at her face and I see a black corpse face, and I leap from the bed and I see my brothers are corpses too, blackened and rotting. And then I wake truly."

Sonia says, "God is sending you a warning. He is saying that you are not doing as you should, which is fighting the Indian soldiers. Instead, you are slaughtering Muslims, which is the same thing as murdering your family."

"What must I do to make it stop, then?"

"Hold fast to God and the true faith! Reform your life! You have been led astray by hypocrites who pervert religion. As it is written in the sura an-Nisa of the Holy Qu'ran: *And whoever kills a believer intentionally, his recompense is Hell to abide therein, and the wrath and the curse of God are upon him and a great punishment is prepared for him.* Does God speak falsely? And have I not seen you kill believers intentionally with my own eyes? God has cast you out, you have such dreams as a foretaste of Hell."

"That is a lie! I kill only those who oppose the jihad, and they cannot be true believers if they oppose the jihad."

"*If* it is a *true* jihad," she replies mildly.

"Of course it is a true jihad. All the mullahs have given their judgment."

"Well, perhaps you are right, Idris. What do I know? I am only a woman, although I am the mother of a hero in a jihad that everyone in the entire umma recognizes as being virtuous, and whose dead are surely in Paradise. And my son has told me that in the Russian jihad they did not murder innocent Muslims nor send women with bombs to blow up children. Perhaps the martyrs of the true jihad will welcome you as comrades. Perhaps they will ignore the blood of innocent children on your hands, and perhaps God will allow you to refresh yourself by the lake of Kausar and consort with the *hura* promised to true martyrs. No man knows these things, least of all ignorant village mullahs. But I was also for years the murid of a holy man, a true Sufi pir—"

"Impossible! No murshid would have a woman as a murid."

"True, but he prayed and God turned me into a boy for a space of time. Yes, even in the dark I can see you don't believe me, but it's true. I traveled with him through all the Muslim lands that were in former years oppressed by the godless Russians, and no man bothered us. He could make us invisible. Once we slept in Tashkent and in the morning awoke in Osh, where we prayed at the tomb of Solomon there. He had summoned a djinn, who carried us in the night."

Idris laughed. "You must think I am an ignorant peasant to believe such tales."

"No, but you believe mullahs who are just as ignorant, and about matters that affect your fate in the next world. Do you imagine that Mullah Latif has ever read the Holy Qur'an with understanding? Yes, he can mumble through the suras, but do you imagine he can understand classical Arabic? No, and neither can you, for which reason you are far from God's word and so do evil and dishonor the Pashtuns."

"You are a woman and an apostate. What do you know of honor?"

"Women know everything about honor, since you men kill us if you even suspect we have harmed it. But we can argue about who is right until the sun rises and never agree. The only fact here is that because of your dream you cannot sleep. Now I will bless you and you will sleep. You want to kill me, but I bless you all the same, and tell you that tonight you will have a good dream. And you will come tomorrow and tell it to me, and then I will interpret, God willing. Now, go and sleep, and let the others come."

For a moment the man is still, and then he says something she doesn't hear and she feels the wind of his movement on her face. The door slams. She hears angry voices from the corridor outside.

The door opens. Mahmoud enters silently and sits by her side; she can hear his heavy nervous breathing. After a moment, he clears his throat and begins.

"Idris has ordered that you interpret no more, but I have had a dream and you will interpret it for me. I was in the hills and my water bottle was empty and I was thirsty. A boy came down the path and I asked him if he had any water, and he laughed and leaned against a rock wall and his body become a flowing spring, and I drank from it."

She says, "The hills mean you will achieve the power you desire, for in the sura Saad we read, *Our servant David, that mighty man, was penitent. With him we subjected the mountain to give glory at dusk and at sunrise.* So you will have glory, but only if you reject your sins. A flowing spring means a reward for a good deed. So said God's Apostle, peace be upon him, when interpreting a flowing spring in a dream about a good man who had died. This good deed will concern a boy who is not a boy, as in your dream."

"I don't understand. How can a boy not be a boy?"

"Don't ask me that, Mahmoud. Only God sees the future, not God's Messenger, peace be upon him, as he attested many times as recorded in the Sunna, and certainly not me. But the dream says it is connected with such a thing. God will reveal it in His own time."

℞

Rashida brings news of the village along with the noon meal. Her father has suspended the marriage negotiations with the one-eyed Khaliq, so she regards Sonia with something close to worship. The following day is the seventh day of their captivity, and there is something even more astounding. Some Arab mujahideen are due to arrive that night, and they are bringing a very important person. He is the one they call the Engineer, who is in charge of building bombs for the jihad, but this is a great secret and musn't be told to anyone. Idris is so excited he is yelling at everyone.

Sonia asks, "It that what they are building all night in the house with the generator? Bombs?"

"Yes, so I hear, but they don't let any of us in there. That is what makes all this gray dust that falls everywhere. It gets in the food and the women complain. It is from the metal grinding, for the bombs."

"Who is making them?"

"They are all men from Dara who were brought here, and some others, foreigners."

"Not Pashtuns, you mean."

"Yes, but Muslims. These are big bombs that can even blow up American tanks, so it is very important. And we hear there will be beheadings. I would like to see them behead an infidel. They say that women cannot see it, but we will watch from the houses anyway."

"What if they behead me, Rashida? Will you still watch?"

Rashida laughed. "Oh, no, you they will not behead, only the infidel men. You they will only cut off one arm and one leg. They have talked to the Internet, and he has said you are guilty of great crimes against Islam so it will be done."

"Do you know what the Internet is?"

"Of course!" says Rashida in an offended tone. "I am not an ignorant girl. I have been to Mingaora. It is like the television but it shows beheadings and messages from the jihad."

"Yes, that is the Internet," says Sonia. "Well, I am happy that you will not be given to Khaliq. But tell me, what has happened to Patang? I have not seen him among the men when they let us walk out."

"Oh, that is a secret too, but everyone knows. He hurt his foot as you foretold, by dropping a heavy crate on it, so he can't be a mujahid anymore. He has gone off to Afghanistan to be *shahid*. First he goes to training and then *boom*! among the crusaders."

"I see. Well, God bless him. Did he desire this, do you know?"

"Yes, of course. It is an honor. And he did not want them to kill his mother. Instead she will get one hundred dollars. So of course he went."

In the hujra the following day the mood of the group is subdued, their minds concentrated—perhaps one of them will not live out the next day—but almost all are preparing for the strange conference they expect will soon commence. They speak quietly in small groups. The priest and the Hindu each pray more often in their separate ways. Sonia and Amin pray the required five times.

William Craig asks to borrow Sonia's deck of cards and with them he plays endless games of solitaire on his charpoy, not just the usual Klondike but a whole library of different games. Sonia thinks that this is as close as he can now get to having a computer. He seems perfectly calm, perhaps the calmest of all the prisoners, save Sonia herself. She tries to engage him in conversation, but he refuses to be drawn. He seems to have relapsed into a kind of nerd nirvana, re-creating the days of his youth, when he wrote the software that he would later turn into a business empire.

Porter Cosgrove neither plays nor prays, nor does he scribble notes. Instead, he suffers what appears to be a pronounced deterioration in his already shaky morale. He cries and moans almost continually. Sonia has heard the expression *shattered* used before this, most often ironically, but this is the thing itself. Annette tries her best but the man will not be comforted, nor have they calming drugs to give him, and it seems the therapeutic skills available to the group can not salve his terror.

That night Idris does not come. Perhaps he did not dream, or is afraid to come, or perhaps it was foolish to try to get inside his head in that way. God controls all things, she finds herself thinking, and laughs at herself. She has become acculturated again; the Sonia of Georgetown, of cocktails parties and seminars, the Sonia of the therapist's office, has quite faded. Again she is a Sufi murid, although her teacher is not visible to anyone else at present.

She is sleeping after interpreting a dozen dreams, herself deep in a dream of Mecca, circling the holy place with a vast crowd in white garments, a dream that supposedly indicates security and peace, from which she awakens to find a face hovering over hers; perhaps the sound of weeping has penetrated her sleep.

"Please, I'm going crazy," says Annette Cosgrove. "I don't know what to do."

"Your husband—"

"That's not my husband," says Annette, a fierce look appearing out of a face crumpled in misery. "I don't know *who* that is."

"Do you want me to try to talk to him?" Sonia asks.

"No, Father Shea is with him, although it doesn't seem to be doing any good." She shivers like a wet cat and, after a brief silence, says, "Did you ever read a book by Arthur Koestler, *The Call Girls*? It's about the international do-good community, the title says it all. I thought Porter was different, he really got his hands dirty, I thought. But what did I know? I didn't go to the important meetings, only the dinners and on the wives' tours, and once in a while they let me hold the sick babies for the cameras. It was a dream or something. Why is he acting like this? Everyone else is being so brave. It's killing me."

"I don't know, dear. Sometimes when a false self cracks, we find there's nothing inside. One of the sad things you learn in therapy is that there are some people who are beyond help, I mean direct help. They're like black holes. They can suck the life out of anyone who tries to help them. So you need to take care of yourself, yes?"

Annette cries some more and Sonia holds her and for a moment thinks of her dead daughters; Aisha would have been about Annette's age now, and she cries as well, but inwardly.

Now they hear the noise of trucks arriving and, briefly, the sound of many voices outside the hujra.

"What's that?" Annette whispers.

"Visitors," Sonia answers. "It's something to do with weapons. Maybe they'll attend the conference. That will be a change."

She hugs Annette and pats her back. "Sleep now, my dear. You know this can't go on. It'll be over in a few days."

"You think we'll be rescued?"

"Or dead. But in any case, over."

Annette has no response to this; she slumps away to her bed of misery. Sonia is at that stage of exhaustion when sleep will not come. She lies on the charpoy and listens to the night. The trucks outside depart; the generator stops its roar. Cosgrove's snuffling and weeping go on for a longer time, but even this eventually fades, and there is silence but for the coughs and snores of sleeping humans and the eternal wind of the hills. Or no: her ears pick up another sound, a deep, almost rhythmic voice in low register. It is Father Shea, praying.

Sonia moves now without significant thought, onto her feet and silently across the dark hall, following the sound, drawn to it as if by a fiber woven long ago. She finds the priest on his knees and waits quietly until he is finished. She moves then, attracting his attention. He does not seem surprised to see her in this wolf hour; it must be close to three by now. They sit on his charpoy and speak briefly about Porter and Annette, comparing notes, finding that they agree about the origin of the man's collapse, and then Sonia says abruptly, "I want to confess."

She cannot see his face in the dark, but his tone is mildly surprised. "Yes? What do you want to confess? An extra chapati filched?"

"No, I mean I want to *confess*. The sacrament."

"Oh, my, forgive me! I thought you were . . . and in any case I suppose I had forgotten you were so—what shall I say?—so *flexible* a worshipper. Okay, fine. I haven't got a stole, but perhaps God won't mind this once. Whenever you're ready."

Sonia kneels and composes her thoughts. She says, "The sin of pride. I get it from my mother, I think, the Polish aristocrat—I mean my special brand of it, not the kind from original sin. The idea that because I'm wonderful me I can get away with stuff, that I can manipulate the lives of people, that it won't all come back to bite me on the butt. I think you know my story, the public part of it anyway. I wanted to go on haj in the traditional way, by dhow across the Arabian Sea and then by caravan to Mecca, and of course I couldn't do that as an unaccompanied woman, so I went as a boy and wrote about it and the umma blew up in my face. I got kicked out of the family and the country, put on the first plane out of Lahore with the fanatics screaming for my blood. Farid—my sad, faithful man; oh, God, let me confess the misery I put him through, the uncharity of it!—Farid stayed with the children. I ended up in Zurich, but that's not what I want to talk about—"

"Excuse me," the priest said. "Why Zurich, of all places?"

"That's where the first plane out of Lahore stopped: British Air to Zurich direct and then change planes for London, where Farid had arranged with some friends to put me up, but when I got to the airport I didn't get on the connecting flight, I could not bear the thought of being with Pakistanis, however sympathetic, and I could not bear dealing with what I'd done, dealing with the press, with the publicity. I took a cab into the city and holed up. Zurich turned out to be a good place for someone like me to hide. The Swiss are incurious, and the umma was not well represented on its streets. And then my children were killed, my girls for real and my son as far as I knew, and I went crazy and that qualified me to be a shrink. No, I'm still avoiding." After a moment, she resumes. "This was something that began in Lahore, when my son was a baby. I fell in love."

"Yes?" says Father Shea in a certain tone, when the pause she made after this remark had gone on for a while.

"Oh, no, nothing like *that*!" she says quickly. "It was a child I fell in love with, not a man. A little boy; he was four at the time. He was the son of my father-in-law's bodyguard and his wife, who was the only real friend I had in my father-in-law's house. It's hard to explain. I had Theo, I had my own baby, but he wasn't really mine, he was the heir of the Lagharis, somehow alien and a reminder to me that I had done exactly the same thing as my mother had. I had married a man I didn't really love in gratitude for saving my life. Every time I looked at Theo I felt trapped, and it made me a terrible mother. I abandoned him twice— though I told myself it wasn't really abandonment because he had that gigantic, overwhelming family—and I *used* him. I tried to make him into an ally, or at least someone who wouldn't be smothered by the family as his father was, or almost was. I mean he married *me*, poor soul. But my real attention was focused on Wazir."

"The bodyguard's son," Shea says. "What was the attraction?"

"Oh, he was beautiful, first of all, just a knockout. And strong, athletic too, and very, very smart. When he was seven or so I found him in the courtyard with little piles of pebbles. He'd discovered prime numbers and he was scratching with a stick in the dirt trying to generate number theory. But more than that, there was this air about him, even as a little boy, that he was going to be something special, something really grand. And Theo, I have to admit, is a sweet enough man but nothing special; and I wanted to be part of something great. Pride, again, the ghosts of ten generations of impoverished aristocrats howling in my blood."

"What happened to him?"

So she tells him the story. Afterward he says, "I'm afraid I don't understand you when you say you *sold* Wazir to the CIA."

"In return for their help in getting Theo out of the war and bringing him back to the States. They were recruiting Pashtun mujahideen. They found out where Wazir was and brought me in there, and I convinced him and they took him away, back to America, and sent him to college, as I said. I made it sound like it was a great opportunity, and he went along with it. We were very close. His mother had died while he was on jihad and I was more than a mother to him. I don't know what they've done to or with him, but at the time that didn't bother me. I just wanted Theo out. Mother love? Or guilt. You tell me."

"I'm afraid that's not part of my job, Sonia. But I will say that in Guatemala I heard confessions from rebels and soldiers and paramilitary police officers during the dirty war there, and as a monster you don't stack up. What are you guilty of? Lack of singleminded devotion? Excessive interest in another woman's child? Betrayal? Yes, you meddle too much in the affairs of others. Cut it out. Trust in God more. Be easier on yourself. That's your penance, although being in this place would seem to be penance enough for worse sins than you've just told me about. Do you want a formal absolution?"

She did.

Father Shea said the magic words and made the motions, and Sonia thanked him and went back to her own cot. She did feel better. She had made a good act of contrition in her heart and wondered whether that would be sufficient for God. Because she hadn't told the priest anything near the whole truth.

12

They held another meeting of the GEARSHIFT group the following day, but Cynthia Lam was not invited to this one. Ernie Lotz went in her stead, and she understood why. She'd admitted her doubts to Ernie, not as devil's advocate but for real, and he had naturally passed them along to Morgan. She was now officially unreliable on the next phase of the project, which, according to Lotz, was bending every sinew of NSA to pinpoint the location of the supposed bomb factory. The president had given approval to start planning for a military option, but obviously they had to know where to invade. Satellites shifted their orbits to provide better coverage of the suspect terrain—the northwest frontier of Pakistan and the southern tier of Afghanistan—and hundreds of analysts dropped other projects to pore over the photographic catch. Drone aircraft were hastily fitted with radiation detection gear and flown low through the mountain valleys, although the area to be covered was so vast that no one expected a timely hit from the flights. The role of N Section was to expand the listening watch, on the theory that the supposed errors of the earlier cell phone ill-discipline would be repeated.

Cynthia believed this was a waste of time, because any calls they were likely to intercept would be fakes, like the others. She thought the original Abu Lais call was genuine, but whether or not it involved a nuclear conspiracy was at present unknown. N Section was also receiving feed from optical cable intercepts out of Pakistan; no Pakistani official could pick up a phone, she thought, without NSA listening in, although here, as always, the bottleneck was translation. She was particularly interested in traffic from the security services, because if there really had been a nuclear theft, these should be going mad. But they were not, or not that she could tell. It seemed to be business as usual in Islamabad and Rawalpindi, so either they were back to carrying messages in cleft sticks or there was nothing big going on.

Still, she logged her dutiful hours and even demonstrated zeal in the futile hunt, and at the same time she embarked on a covert venture of her own. First she searched NSA's secure intranet and found no reference to the code name Ringmaster. This was not particularly surprising. Security clearances at NSA are highly compartmented and her own Top Secret clearance gave her access only to those parts of NSA's vast trove of information that directly related to her work. Besides that, Ringmaster was a CIA operation and, despite changes in intel policy after the 9/11 events, Langley was not inclined to share. She would have to figure out some other way to discover what was going on.

It was, in contrast, no problem to research the nuclear scientist Jafar Baig Qasir, his family, and their connections. NSA's resources gave her every fragment of electronic information available about him: his bank records, his credit reports, his recent e-mails, the works. When she was done with that, and intrigued by what she had learned, she put in a call to Harry Anspach, got an answering system, and left a casual message— long time no see, let's have a drink.

He hadn't called back by the time she left work, at around seven, but she knew that Harry kept odd hours, spook hours. He'd rung her up occasionally in the middle of the night.

He might be one part of the thread she was beginning to tease out of the GEARSHIFT tangle. He was a consultant, so-called; he ran a tiny firm that provided undisclosed services for the U.S. intel community. Cynthia thought he might be close to seventy, although he looked a lot younger. Harry always had a nice tan and wore slightly rakish English-cut suits. He was, or claimed to be, an old CIA hand, a veteran of the glory days when the governments of nations lived or fell at Langley's pleasure. Harry had specialized in South Asia, he spoke the languages, knew the players face-to-face, and had a pile of stories. She'd met him at a training course early in her career at NSA. He'd been an instructor. It had been thought useful to give junior NSA staff some idea of how comint and humint worked together, and that was Harry's task. He'd begun by stating flatly that they did not, offered to leave the platform, and got a polite laugh. Then he'd launched into a brilliant analysis of the faults of the national intelligence effort from the point of view of the poor bastards who were out in the field, trying to make sense of the machinations of an alien culture. He talked about the difficulties the average American had in doing this, and of how hard it really was to weave the little bits derived from spies, intercepts, and open sources into a real understanding of what the bad guys were up to.

Cynthia thought it was the best presentation she'd ever heard during her training. Later that evening, when the trainees and their instructors were mingling in the facility's lounge, she'd heard a voice behind her say, "*The hard work of the foolish is all a waste, as rainless clouds make only dust.*" It was in Pashto. She turned around to find Harry Anspach grinning at her, and she'd asked what he meant in the same language.

"A line from Rahman Baba," he'd said. "The old guy might have been talking about U.S. intelligence."

And then they'd had a long conversation in Pashto about intelligence and Pashtun culture and the war against the Russians. He'd been there for nearly the whole thing, and before that, along with everyone else, he'd been in Southeast Asia. He had a lot of stories about both places, but somehow they never involved him; it was always "a guy I knew" or "someone told me that. . . ." She got the impression that Harry liked to go deep, that he wasn't an embassy cocktail party kind of agent, and that this had crimped his career. The CIA didn't like it when their people went native: intelligence was all well and good, but they didn't really want to hear stuff that conflicted with their prejudices or might embarrass their political masters. That evening Harry talked mainly about Afghanistan and the Pashtuns, those wonderful, horrible people. She got the impression he had gone *very* native, donning turban and shalwar kameez, growing his beard, living in the villages for weeks on end.

He was surprised that she'd never been there. She said she hadn't traveled much; she was a headquarters kind of person. He said she should go, and said her Pashto was excellent but a little schoolmarmish, it was stripped of colloquialism of the sort you could only pick up in a Pashtun village. He said he'd heard about her; she was a prize catch with her languages. And they talked about her for the rest of their conversation; whenever she tried to turn the talk back to his obviously far more interesting life, he diverted it back with a laugh and a joke.

Since that time, every so often they'd meet for a drink or a meal, and she'd tell him what was going on at the agency and in N Section. Cynthia understood that she was a source, he was using her to keep track of what that part of NSA was doing, and also maybe he was checking up for someone about how free she was with things she wasn't supposed to talk about—or even know. She didn't mind. She liked him. She thought they were two of a kind, both dedicated to the secret world, both alone, both a little lonely. It was like having a father who really understood what you were doing and approved and would help if he could, quite unlike her actual father, who wondered why Cynthia, with her grades, had not gone into medicine or law.

Anspach called just after six. She asked him where he was and he said he was in the street outside her apartment house and would she like to get something to eat? She said she would and he took her to their usual place, an Afghan restaurant on the other side of Dupont Circle. It was a tiny place, eight tables, only one of which was occupied when they came in, by a large noisy family, the men talking loudly in Pashto, the women, demure in *hijabs*, tending to the wriggling children. The proprietor greeted them like old friends, all smiles, handshakes, an embrace and two kisses for Harry, a bow for Cynthia. They sat and he fed them, not bothering with menus. They drank scalding sweet minted tea and ate: *kadu, aushak* dumplings, *fesenjan* chicken with Basmati rice, steaming slabs of Afghan naan bread. As usual Cynthia talked about herself, what was happening at NSA, nothing personal. They did not have that kind of relationship, and she had long since given up trying to get anything out of Harry, a worm-proof man.

Inevitably, GEARSHIFT and its discontents came up. She told him the whole story, probably in violation of innumerable security regulations, but she didn't care. She wanted to know if she was crazy or not. She told him about Abu Lais, and all the unlikelihoods, the phoninesses of the intercepts, and when she ran down he said, "That's pretty thin soup. Paranoia is a virtue in intel work, but it's got to be based on something more than hunches."

"It's not just hunches, Harry. First of all, I'm the language guy in this, and the language is fake. I know a staged conversation when I hear it. The original Abu Lais colloquy was genuine; I had no doubts at all about that one. But the others weren't. You can put that in the bank. The second thing is I did a little checking on Dr. Qasir. The woman he was supposedly talking to is Rukhsana Laghari Qasir, his wife. She's a journalist, works for a liberal English-language newspaper in Lahore. Have you been following this hostage thing in Pakistan? With Bill Craig?"

"What about it?"

"One of the hostages is Sonia Bailey Laghari, the writer. She's Rukhsana Qasir's sister-in-law."

"So?"

"So she's being held by a jihadi group. What if someone decided that this would be a good time to engineer a provocation, using the connection between Sonia Laghari and her brother-in-law, the nuclear engineer? Maybe the Laghari family is trying to fake up something. Maybe the point of this provocation has nothing to do with an actual bomb but is—I don't know—a way to get Sonia Laghari out of the hands of the mujahideen?"

"That's a big jump, Cynthia. A senior Pakistani scientist is going to commit treason to save his sister-in-law?"

"If it really *was* Jafar Qasir."

"You haven't checked?"

"No. I'm telling you, Morgan put this whole thing together on the fly. He finally gets to play in the bigs, he's not going to check every little detail. But I'm going to put in a call to Qasir tonight, and also to his wife, and I'll match the voiceprints to the intercept. Then we'll see."

Harry said, "I want more tea. Would you like dessert? I'm going to have the *phirnee*."

Cynthia shook her head, and Harry called the waiter over and had a brief Pashto conversation with him. When he went away, Harry said, "I assume if this voiceprint checks out the way you think it will, you'll go to Morgan and tell him to stop the train."

"Not Morgan. That's what I wanted to ask you about."

"You want to go around him."

"Or something. God, Harry, you have no idea what he's been like. He doesn't listen to me, he doesn't take me to the big meetings. . . . I honestly think that if I show him that the Qasir intercept is a fake, he'll suppress it or tell me I made it up or I don't know what. Whatever, I'll be finished at NSA."

"Uh-huh. Well, we can't let that happen." He smiled. "I'll tell you what. If it turns out the Qasir intercept is a scam, get your evidence written up, the voiceprints and all, and shoot it over to me by courier. I'll make sure it gets to the right people and that they know you saved the day."

She felt some tension drain. "Thanks, Harry. But there's something else." She explained about the acoustic freak in the meeting room, what she'd overheard, and her conclusion: "There's some other link between the hostages and this nuclear scam."

"What connection could there be?"

"That depends on who this Ringmaster is and what Showboat is. Anything ring a bell?"

Harry looked up at the approaching waiter. He said, "This is really good phirnee they make here. It's a kind of rice pudding with rose water and pistachio nuts. Want some?"

Cynthia took a fleck of the stuff on her spoon, to be polite. It tasted like cold cream.

He caught her look. "No? Well, it's an acquired taste. I ate a lot of it in Peshawar during the jihad." He started in on the dessert. Cynthia waited for what seemed like a long time and then said, "Harry? We were having a conversation."

He put his spoon down and dabbed his mouth with a napkin. "No, actually you were trying to pump me, which I thought we had an agreement you weren't going to do. My advice to you is to forget you ever heard those words."

As he said this, he gave her a look she did not recall ever seeing before on Harry Anspach's face, bleak and cold, the eyes blank and piti-less as a shark's. It lasted for only a second, but it stunned her; she felt her jaw slacken embarrassingly, like that of a schoolgirl caught at some naughtiness.

"You know, I just remembered," said Harry, in a different tone, as if that look and his comment had not occurred, "I ran into Sonia Laghari once, in Peshawar, back in—oh, gosh, it must've been 'eighty-seven. The war was winding down and we were tying things up, preparing to go back to ignoring Afghanistan and ditching all the people we'd been sup-porting, the usual American deal. You know, when I first started with the Agency, in the late sixties, when someone really fucked up, we used to roll our eyes and say, 'Afghanistan,' like he was going to get assigned to someplace of absolutely no importance. Anyway, I used to have an office, sort of, over a tea shop in the Meena Bazaar, and when I was in town I used to sit there all day drinking mint tea and people knew where to find me. So I'm sitting there one morning and in walks this woman in a burqa. Well, the place just froze, everybody stopped talking and stared, because women just don't stroll into tea shops in that part of Peshawar, and she walks up to me, hands me a piece of paper, and walks out. The note said she had to see me, matter of life and death, and she'd come by at ten that night, and it was signed Sonia Bailey. Of course I knew who Sonia Bailey was. After she wrote that book on Soviet Central Asia, half the Agency was trying to get next to her, to pump her about what she hadn't put in the book, but no dice. She said she was a writer and she didn't want to compromise herself, and so forth, so I gathered they gave up trying. And obviously I was interested. Did you ever read her books?"

"No. Are they any good?"

"Yeah, they are. But you're not that interested in travel. Or in the people who speak the languages you speak so well."

Cynthia was about to object to this remark but forbore. A personal revelation from Anspach was so rare she didn't want to stem his flow.

"So I'm in my room that night, and there's a knock, and in comes this little guy in the full Pashtun rig: shalwar kameez, waistcoat, turban, little mustache, never saw the guy before, and I jump up and the guy says in Pashto, 'Relax, Mr. Anspach, I'm Sonia Bailey.' Could've knocked me over. The mustache was phony, of course, but aside from that she *was* a Pashtun guy—language, gestures, the whole works. Better than me, as a matter of fact, and I'm pretty good. I mean, even though I *knew* she was an American woman, I totally *bought* her as a Pashtun man. Uncanny. And what she wanted to see me about was her kid, a teenager. Told me the damnedest story about how her kid had been kidnapped as a boy by this Pashtun bodyguard of her father-in-law's down in Lahore and had fought up in Afghanistan for years and she'd thought he was dead, and then she finally figured out that this legendary boy mujahid that everyone was talking about in Peshawar must be her son. And of course I'd heard of Kakay Ghazan; they were singing songs about him in the streets."

He motioned to the waiter, who was there in an instant with the check. Harry laid some bills on it, which Cynthia noted included a huge tip, and then the patron came out and they had some chat about wonderful to see you again and the best Afghan food in America, all smiles and embraces, and a special smile for Cynthia too, and then they were out in the street.

"So what happened?" Cynthia asked. "With the kid."

"What? Oh, I pointed her to some people and apparently they got him out of there. Interesting woman, though. Sad about what happened to her, getting kidnapped. I heard there was a fatwa out on her. The Muslims don't like mixing up the sexes, they like to know who's a woman and who's a man. Especially in Mecca."

"Do you think they'll kill her?"

"Oh, yeah. If they haven't already. So that idea you're developing about how this thing might be a Laghari family domestic intrigue probably isn't worth pursuing. The woman is toast." This thought seemed to depress him and they walked back to his car in silence. When they were driving, he said, "Look, Cynthia, I meant what I said about not messing with that stuff you overheard. I know you like to think you're a real insider, but there's some shit you don't want to get inside."

"Don't worry," she said, a little stiffly. "I've been put in my place."

"Yeah, and that attitude. It doesn't go with your chosen career path. You need to stay on the reservation, do your excellent work, and when the boss says jump, you say, 'How high, please, sir?'"

"You didn't."

"Right, and look where it got me. You notice I'm not running Langley these days."

"No, but you know all about Ringmaster."

"Never heard of it. And in the same vein you need to look again at this business about GEARSHIFT being a jihadist provocation. Do you really want to go ahead with rocking the boat? Morgan won't appreciate one of his people making an end run."

"But if it's a provocation, Morgan's finished anyway." She hadn't meant to say this. He slowed for a red light, and the red glare from above gave his face a devilish cast as he turned and looked at her.

"Yeah, I figured that was your plan, more or less. A chance for a big win and you kick your mentor in the ass, and not only your mentor but the guy you've been screwing for years; what does that say? That you're ruthless, that you won't let anything stand in the way of your devotion to the job? A very popular point of view around headquarters and why I couldn't ever stand working there for long. On the other hand I ended up in Afghanistan, where betrayal is a refined art, like calligraphy is in China."

"But I'm right! I mean, *if* I'm right it's not just about me or Morgan or who comes out on top. It's a national security issue."

"Yeah, that's what they always say. I wish I had a nickel for every time I heard that used as an excuse for doing something dirty."

"Oh, fuck it, Harry! Blowing the whistle on a serious mistake is not doing something dirty. You make it sound like getting us kicked out of Pakistan is ... is some kind of office politics I'm twisting for my own advantage. Jesus, wasn't the whole 9/11 fiasco and the whole Iraq war fiasco the result of people who knew better not standing up and telling the truth?"

"Yes, but in those cases, the people who knew better didn't want to risk career damage, so they stayed silent. You're speaking out because you think it will *advance* your career. You want to be famous as the little girl with her thumb in the dike, the one person who found what all the big shots missed, that GEARSHIFT was an enemy provocation."

"What does that matter," she snapped, "if it avoids a disaster?"

They had come to her apartment building on California Street, and Harry swung the car into an empty space by a fire hydrant. He shifted in his seat and looked her in the face.

"You *think* it'll be a disaster, but you don't know. We never know. You have no idea what will happen if a strike team goes in and shoots up a Pakistani village and there's no bomb factory there. Maybe it'll be a nine-day wonder. Maybe the Pakistani parliament gets blown up the same day and it drives the raid clean out of the headlines. Or suppose the worst case: there's an uproar, a national uprising, and the Islamists take over Pakistan and we have to evacuate Afghanistan. So fucking what? I can recall when it was going to be the end of the world if we lost Vietnam. Fifty-six thousand American dead, three million Vietnamese dead, two fucked-up countries, and now American tourists are sipping cocktails in Hue and the grandchildren of the Vietcong are lining up for jobs as busboys in Swiss hotels."

"I can't believe this. You're saying it doesn't matter if Islamists take over a nuclear-armed nation?"

"Why should it? I spent three-quarters of my working life fighting a completely amoral nation that had three thousand nuclear missiles targeted on American cities, and not one of them ever came close to being fired, so why should I worry about some mullahs having a dozen undeliverable nukes?"

"Unless one of them goes off in New York."

"Yes, the old bogeyman. Just think for second, Cynthia! No one is ever going to use nuclear weapons against a nation that has nuclear weapons. As soon as anyone has nuclear weapons they immediately become grown-ups. They become part of the balance of terror. Nuclear terrorism is something that happens in the movies."

"Al-Qaeda isn't a regular nation."

"No, and so what? The same rule applies. The al-Q leadership has been living underground for a decade because they knocked down two buildings. They'll be underground for the rest of their lives. If they used a nuclear weapon on us we'd kill everyone in Waziristan and no one in the world would utter a peep."

"Be serious, Harry."

"I am. The only people who can really destroy the United States are the Americans, just like the only people who could destroy the USSR were the Soviets, and they did, and we seem to be following in their footsteps. Modern nuclear-armed nations are essentially invulnerable. They can never be conquered in the sense that Hitler and Stalin conquered nations sixty years ago, but all our political stances and the intel that supports them are based on 1930s thinking. *We have to prevent another Munich.* How often have you heard that? We can't appease dictators? There *are* no dictators worth our trouble. It's all a fraud, Cynthia; I mean the high seriousness that attends all this statecraft, this strategizing. It's completely empty, down to the bones."

"Then why do you do it?"

"Because it's what I do. It's the only thing I know. It's a game, like tennis, existentially meaningless but amusing. It takes me—or took me, I should say—to interesting places, just like a tennis pro, and the possibility of being killed just added to the thrill. I'm a pro at this and I thought you were shaping up to be a pro too. A pro does his job, collects the data, makes an honest report. The people responsible make their decisions and if they're the wrong ones, in your view, it's none of your business. Your business is to keep faith with the people you work for, and the people who work for you, and let the chips fall wherever, because in the end the fate of nations doesn't depend on whatever bullshit passes for grand strategy."

"So you won't help me."

He paused and gave her a long stare, but in the dim car she couldn't quite make out his expression. He said, "Of course I'll help you. I'm your friend. But you need to think about it more than you have, okay?"

"Okay, Harry," she said. "I'll do that." She held out her hand and he took it and she leaned over and kissed his cheek. He smelled faintly of rose water.

Back in her apartment, confused and angry, she paced back and forth on the living room rug in front of her television set, turned to cable news with the sound off, and tried to make sense of what Harry had said. The content of his talk she dismissed as clearly nonsense—who could believe such a line? The problem lay in his intent. It was a smokescreen, it was *meant* to confuse, and it had started immediately after she'd mentioned Ringmaster and Showboat. No, SHOWBOAT, she thought, making the word appear uppercase on the screen of her thoughts, obviously an operation of some kind, something to do with nuclear weapons or nuclear theft, and Ringmaster, now held by the terrorists somewhere in the ungoverned wilds of Pakistan, must be an agent connected with it. Yes, she'd explained her theory that GEARSHIFT was a provocation, and he'd accepted it blandly, had even seemed pleased, and then she'd said the secret words and he went, *Cynthia, be a team player; it's all a game; don't rock the boat.*

But he'd forgotten how deep she was into the secrets of NSA. She had Top Secret clearance for all matters relating to nuclear theft, and therefore if SHOWBOAT had to do with nuclear theft (and what else could it be?) she *would* have known about it because *Morgan* would have known about it and he told her everything; she was sure of that. And suddenly there came the dawning of a new idea: what if SHOWBOAT was a *rogue* operation, what if the only people who knew about it were a small cabal at Langley—not the president, not the director of national intelligence, not the directors of NSA and DIA? A secret beyond secrecy! Immediately she felt a thrill race over her skin and sweat popped out on her forehead. *That's* what had gotten Harry so uncharacteristically upset; he was in on it too. It was a Pakistan-Afghanistan operation obviously, and nothing whatever went on in that region without Harry Anspach's thumbprints all over it.

What to do? What to do? Using Harry was now out of the question, and there was no one else she could think of who was both outside her normal chain of command and had the appropriate connections in the intel community—*and* whom she could trust. That was the problem. This thing had to be so big, that . . . okay, slow down, she told herself, she didn't yet have a lock on the scam. She needed one further piece of incontrovertible evidence.

She made herself relax. She switched on the sound and watched the news and then watched a late-night talk show. Gradually an alternative plan formed in her mind. She didn't have to knock off Morgan, not if she could use him, if her intel was so good, so undeniable, that *he* could carry it upstairs and save the day; he could be the hero, and he'd owe her big time. He might get a promotion out of it, and she'd make sure she got the credit for the save, and she'd move with him to the higher regions.

Cynthia felt a sense of relief and was in a strange way grateful to Harry for his odd little lecture on loyalty. Yes, a nice finesse. The show ended at midnight and she turned off the set and lit up her computer. She went to her bag and retrieved the small notebook where she'd written down the cell-phone numbers from the Qasir intercepts and also took out two pieces of contraband: the voiceprints of the two parties to the Qasir intercepts. It was a violation of strict NSA policy to remove anything from its premises, but she believed it was justified in exigent circumstances. Besides, no one would ever know.

She rigged the computer to make a digital recording of any conversations it might carry using voice-over-Internet protocol and then placed the first call, to Dr. Qasir's cell phone, at ten A.M. in Lahore. She got the answering service. In her fine Urdu she identified herself as an officer at his bank with an urgent question regarding his balance and a possible fraud. He called back ten minutes later and she engaged him in conversation for an additional five. Then she called his wife, got her right away, and had another five-minute conversation, posing as a potential source for a story about corruption in the Ministry of Finance.

After running a voice analysis program on both conversations, she made hard copies of the voiceprints and compared them to those from the original intercepts. Her sensitive ears had already told her what the voiceprints now revealed. The man in the original intercepts was *not* Jafar Baig Qasir; the woman definitely *was* his wife, Rukhsana.

So no one had stolen any uranium from Dr. Qasir's facility. That intercept was proved phony, and thus all the intercepts after the original Abu Lais one, all that stuff about moving shipments, had to be phony as well. It was the proverbial smoking gun. But she wasn't going to show it to Morgan yet, because what she'd now learned was bigger than N Section, maybe bigger than NSA. Nor would she send it to Anspach. Harry's response to her questions had confirmed that it was a major secret, involving the capture of hostages and the faked theft of uranium. Harry had tried to slam the door of the big boys' clubhouse in her face, but she was not having any of that, oh, no: she was going to find out what SHOWBOAT was all about and who Ringmaster was, and just at that instant it popped into her mind how she was going to do that as well. It had been triggered by the memory of the odd odor of roses that had come off Anspach. She was tapping away at the computer when it came to her: the unlikely smell and the computer. Borden.

13

Along with the rest of the village, Sonia awakens to the sound of the azan: *make haste to worship, make haste to the real triumph, prayer is better than sleep!* Agreeing, she shakes out of the really interesting dream she has been having, not even pausing to write it down, and goes to the prayer rug in the corner of the room marked with the qibla. She performs the ritual washing with the ewer and basin there and hears the sound of soft footsteps behind her. It is Amin. They wish each other peace, he washes, and they unroll the prayer rugs provided by the management and pray the Fajr, the dawn prayer.

Around them the infidels also arise, in their different ways. Father Shea kneels by his charpoy with his breviary, Manjit sits silently on his charpoy, perhaps in a meditative trance; Schildkraut sits slumped, coughing at intervals, staring at the ground; Ashton stomps heavily to the alcove where the slop pot is kept, trips over a blanket, curses vilely, and urinates with vigor, still cursing. Over this earthy noise they hear a sound that has become distressingly familiar: Porter Cosgrove has begun his groans and wails, and they can hear the soft strained murmur of his wife, trying to provide comfort.

"I thought Quakers were famous for being quiet," says Amin. "Shame on me! That is uncharitable. See how quickly the peace of prayer evaporates under these conditions?"

"Yes," says Sonia, "but isn't it strange then that every religion looks back to its time of persecution as one where the faithful practiced the purest religion with the most fervor? Perhaps it's different when one isn't being persecuted for the religion per se."

"No, I hardly think this captivity has to do with the religious beliefs of our hosts. It is a tribal matter entirely, in my view. On the other hand, I confess I have become more punctilious in my observances since we were taken. Perhaps the mind is concentrated by the prospect of eternity, except in cases like poor Cosgrove there, when it is utterly destroyed."

He cast a glance around the room, then stared for a moment at a particular vacant charpoy. He grabbed Sonia's arm. "Good God! Where is Mr. Craig?"

Ashton emerged from behind the curtain. "What's the matter?" he asked, when he saw Amin.

"Craig isn't here. Is he behind the curtain?"

"No, nothing back there but the old piss pot. What, you mean he's done a bunk?"

"I rather doubt that. They must have come in the night and taken him. My God, can they mean to kill him?"

"Why would they do that?" says Ashton. "He's worth millions to them alive. Isn't it obvious now why were were kidnapped? It's a simple ransom scheme. All of us were what they call side catch in the fisheries game. Although I daresay they'll find some propaganda use for us. Christ, I could kill for a drink! And I'd pick that weepy little bastard." He gives the Cosgroves an angry stare. "What an absolute waste of a beautiful woman. Can you credit it? I wonder what she ever saw in him."

"He did some heroic negotiations in Mozambique," Sonia says. "Apparently saved countless lives. It's an attractive trait, I suppose. Everyone responds to danger in a manner characteristic of their temperaments. Some grow stronger, like my friend Amin here, and some go to pieces."

"Is that so? And what do you do? Seek the comfort of religion?"

"Yes, I do. And you get nasty."

"Do I? Well, you can just kiss my arse, Miss Laghari, or Bailey, or whatever your name is. As I recall, it was you who concocted this brilliant idea of trekking through the most terrorist-strewn portion of the planet with a billionaire in tow. You might as well have taken out adverts—PARTY OF GORMLESS DO-GOODERS SEEKING YOUNG MEN WITH WEAPONS. MONEY NO OBJECT."

Amin said, "Enough, Harold. Let us not make enemies among ourselves. We have enough in the vicinity."

A short while later the point is proven, when the door flies open and a group of armed mujahideen storm into the room, Alakazai among them.

The men herd the captives roughly into a group against one wall and Alakazai tells them that a missile strike in Badaur last night has killed fourteen people, four of them children, and that as a result, in accordance with his threat, one of the captives will be executed today after the noon prayer. To Sonia he adds, "Make your selection!"

"I haven't decided yet," answers Sonia.

"Then decide by noon, or by God I will take two at once. And before the execution you will have your conference. We shall all attend."

With that, he leaves the room and his men follow after.

There is silence, except for Porter Cosgrove's dripping sobs. Amin says, "Gather around this bed, my friends and we will do what must be done. Sonia, you have the cards?"

Sonia brings out her deck and places it on a blanket pulled tight across the string bed. She says, "Everyone cut the deck once, and then I'll shuffle and deal out one card each. Low card loses, aces are high, repeat deal if there is a tie for lowest. Does everyone understand?"

Nods all around, and then, one by one, they cut the deck. Sonia gathers up the cards, gives them a thorough shuffle, and deals out one card to each. Ashton tosses his down first, turns and walks back to his bed. It is the ten of spades. Amin has the king of spades, Manjit the eight of hearts, Schildkraut the jack of clubs, Father Shea has the jack of diamonds, and Annette the six of clubs. Only Porter Cosgrove has not picked up his card. He is staring at it, like a bird at a cobra.

"Pick up your card, Porter," says Amin.

"I won't," croaks Cosgrove. "I didn't agree to this. This is not right. They have no right to do this to me."

His wife reaches out a hand to touch him. Sonia notices that her face looks bleached, the freckles standing out starkly, like the onset of a disease. "Porter, please," she says.

But he leaps to his feet and runs to the door, upsetting the blanket. The card flips and falls to the floor: the four of clubs. Instantly, Father Shea stands and runs after him, bringing him down with a football tackle. Annette lets out an un-Quakerish wail and moves toward her husband, but Sonia grabs her, folds her in a tight embrace. She resists, struggles a moment, then becomes soft, like a child, and from her throat comes the kind of hopeless keening that Sonia before this has heard only from Afghan women.

It takes the strength of Amin, Ashton, and the tiny contribution of Manjit to subdue Porter Cosgrove. He thrashes, he howls like an animal, he sprays thick saliva. At last, they use ropes torn from the charpoys to tie his hands and feet, and Ashton gags him with a strip of blanket, none too gently. But they can still hear him, cries like a distant bird and thumps as he strikes his head against the wall. In a civilized land he would, of course, be sedated, and his loved ones would not have to bear this, but here they must. Or she must.

Everyone goes to their own charpoy and lies down, exhausted, ashamed, except for Sonia, who sits with Annette and tries to comfort her. She is not good at it, she knows. Annette must sense this too, because she twitches her shoulders at the touch of Sonia's hands, snarls, and tells Sonia to go away, to leave her alone.

Sonia does not. Instead, she reaches out toward the source of all compassion; she slides off the charpoy, kneels, and begins the zikr that will take her deep into contemplative prayer.

After an undefined period of this, she hears in her mind's ear the laughter of her murshid. Of course she has time, all the time in the world. Through Ismail's spirit, now burned into her heart, she has access to eternity. The answers will come.

※

—You begin to learn patience, I see, says the voice of her guide. She can just make him out, a figure glowing with wheaten light.

—Yes, and I recall you used to say it takes patience to learn patience, so how can anyone learn?

—It's a mystery, he says, and laughs again.

—And is Paradise what you expected, my murshid? Is everything truly revealed?

—Indeed. Everything, including answers to questions we never thought to ask.

—And are there gardens and flowing streams and boys like strings of pearls?

—If I told you, you would not understand, but you would imagine that I described gardens and boys.

—Well, it won't be too long before I will see for myself. I am going to die very soon, I think, and I'm afraid.

—Do you recall when I passed from the world, my murid?

—I do. It was in a filthy town outside Bukhara. You asked for wine and I gave you tea. Then you recited from Rahman Baba: *If man's purpose and destination is God, then all the dead are guides for the living; if travelers shout at the time of departure, all their shouts are bells for the sleepers.* Oh, my murshid, I am awake now, be my guide! Help me to help this poor child!

—When pain exceeds its own bounds, it becomes the cure, he says, as the vision fades.

The line is from Ghalib. Strangely, Jung says almost the same thing, and Sonia has never before quite grasped the meaning, but she knows she would have a hard time explaining it to a suffering one. The panic and guilt she felt have now passed away. She feels a warm energy passing through her body and puts her hands on Annette's back; the woman stiffens, then relaxes. Something is going on, but Sonia does not understand what it is. She knows only that it is something beyond understanding and is as grateful as she has been at any other time of her life.

Now the door opens again, and they all flinch, but it is only Rashida with their meal. They are ashamed to eat after what has happened, but they are hungry. They pass the chapatis and tea. Only Annette does not eat; she takes a chapati from the tray, stares at it, leaking slow tears, and tears the bread into tiny pieces, small as confetti. After some silence, Amin says, "I am afraid the morning still has a store of unpleasantness for us. My sense was that the person chosen for death would be the one to speak at this so-called conference. My God! I cannot believe these words are issuing from my mouth."

"Yes, our ordinary language is quite inadequate for the situation," says Schildkraut, "but this does not produce in me a desire for silence. In fact, I find my thoughts are bursting out of me, so much I had not realized that I wanted to say. It is clear to me, and I speak as a psychiatrist here, that Porter has in a sense abandoned rational speech entirely and retreated to animal levels. It is impossible for him to speak, obviously, so I am prepared to go on in his place, if that is agreeable."

They start to make group-agreement noises, when Annette clears her throat and says, "No, I'll do it. I know what he has to say. I've written enough speeches for him, haven't I? I'll give this one."

They all gaze at her in amazement. Her eyes are red but crying no longer. She seems to have become a different person.

⁊

Some hours later, the room is packed to overflowing with the men of the village and the mujahideen troop. Sonia and the others are made to sit against the wall at the opposite end, ostentatiously guarded by rather too many armed men, as if they were dangerous criminals poised to escape. Porter Cosgrove has been released from his bonds and sits slumped over between his wife and Father Shea. Annette has been given a dark blue burqa, as has Sonia. Father Shea is speaking quietly to Cosgrove, a low confessional drone that Sonia cannot make out. Sonia wonders if he is seeking a last-minute conversion but dismisses this thought as unworthy. She wonders also what one actually says to a man about to die in an unjust execution, and whether Shea has ever done it before. Surely there can be no rubric for this office, but maybe there is. The Church has strange hidden depths.

Ashton is sitting on one side of her, Amin on the other. Ashton whispers to her, "I hadn't realized there were so many of the bastards. What do you think, over a hundred at least? We must be more important than I thought."

"It's not just us. There's a bomb factory in the village. It may be a major resupply depot."

"And those are quartermasters, I suppose. Those over on the left are Arabs."

All the charpoys have been moved to one end of the room, and upon these sit the dignitaries: Alakazai in the center, Mullah Latif on his right, Idris Ghulam Khan on his left. In the same row, also seated, is a group of men the prisoners have never seen before. They are darker and smaller than the locals. Sonia agrees with Ashcroft that they are Arabs. Their apparent leader is a wonderfully handsome young man of about thirty, with pale hazel eyes and a neatly trimmed black beard. The body language of the Pashtuns is easy to read, and Sonia observes that even the older men pay elaborate deference to him.

"Pretty Boy up there is no Arab," says Ashton. "That's odd."

"He's a Pashtun," says Sonia. "I think he's the one they call the Engineer."

Ashton says, "Who is he?" but Sonia doesn't answer because Mullah Latif has risen and raised his hands for silence. He invokes the blessings of God on this *jirga* and says they are gathered to hear the lies of infidels and apostates. Why should good Muslims and mujahideen hear lies? So they can resist them in their hearts, even as the Prophet, peace be upon him, heard the lies of Jews and Christians and made certain that they had rejected the holy word of God before he slew them. Thus, after the infidel speaks, our distinguished emir, Haji Bahram Pason Alakazai, will answer their lies and provide right guidance. Riotous applause, shouts: *Death to the infidels! Death to America, death to Israel!* When this dies down, the mullah withdraws and Alakazai rises. He describes the murder of innocents in the recent American missile strike and says that one of the hostages will be executed that day in revenge. More applause, the screams echoing off the low ceiling. He says that the choice of who will die will fall to the infamous apostate and blasphemer Sonia Bailey; as a punishment for her evil deeds she will send each of her companions to death. The assemblage loves this; it is such a Pashtun solution, redolent of the savage old tales, a clever trick to catch the evildoer in her own tangle and make her destroy her allies.

Two guards grab Sonia from the wall and pull her out into the room. One is a large man with a shaved head and a beard like a black bib reaching to his chest. His Kalashnikov is slung across his back. The other is a much smaller man in a black-striped turban and a Russian camo jacket, who has a scarred hook-nosed face like a nasty Western cartoon of a terrorist. He carries the AKMS version of the Kalashnikov, with the stock folded, and he likes to use it as a cattle prod. Sonia feels the muzzle jammed painfully into her ribs.

Alakazai says, "Choose!" and Sonia says, "I choose Porter Cosgrove," and points to the cringing man. The guards hustle him out to the center of the room, the little one grinning and poking the prisoner with his weapon. Cosgrove falls to his knees and starts crying again; urine darkens the front of his trousers and pools on the floor, to the vast amusement of the assembly. A few of the onlookers leap out balletically to deliver a kick, others beat him with their shoes. When this jolly uproar fades (and it takes a long time), Alakazai says, "Does this worm have anything to say?"

Sonia says, "Yes, but he has been driven mad by what has been done to him, just as Muslims in American prisons have been driven mad by what has been done to them. The shame is on you, as it is on the Americans. But his wife knows what he would say if he were able, and she will speak."

A babble of voices at this, with the mullah calling out that it is haram for a woman to speak to a jirga, but Sonia says in reply that Fatima, the daughter of the Prophet (peace be upon him) and his wife Aisha were both consulted after the Prophet's death by the rightly guided caliphs and spoke to assemblies of Muslims. They knew that women can be heard when they speak the words given to them by men, and so it is here.

There is some grumbling but in the end Alakazai allows it.

Annette comes forward and begins to speak. As they have agreed beforehand, she pauses after every phrase, and Sonia translates it into Pashto. She sees Alakazai frown at this—he had assumed that only a few of the assembly would be able to understand the doomsday speeches—but he does nothing now.

Annette says that she and her husband came to this country to speak about making peace. He has devoted his whole life to peace, and now he will be a martyr to peace. Why did they come into this country? Because every day a billion Muslims wish one another peace, yet from one end of the umma to the other, with few exceptions, there is no peace—there is dissension and riot, war, and calls for the death of this group or that—and they wished to learn why and to see if they could do something about it. Because, she says, peace is possible. It is not an idle dream of unrealistic people. She speaks about successful peace projects of the recent past, some of which she and her husband had helped bring about: Mozambique, Angola, South Africa, Ireland, Bosnia. In Bosnia, she says, the Americans and Europeans prevented the extermination of Muslims, and also in Kosovo. So peace is possible, even in places that have been fighting for years. Why then is there still so much war? There are two reasons, she says. First, many people find war beneficial. They are nobodies in peacetime and great men in wartime, admired, powerful, and rich. Naturally, they do not want to give that up, so nearly all successful peacemaking must address the ego needs of these warmongers. This can be done far more cheaply than most people realize, and she gives examples of warlords bought off or retired. The second reason is that war literally maddens. People do things to one another in wartime that they would never think of doing otherwise, psychopathic criminality becomes the norm, and people believe that only "victory" can make things right, can justify what they have done. So they fight on, even if—*especially* if—they have lost sight of the original purposes of the war. But this madness can be cured, and has been, in many places. She talks about how, even under the most oppressive regimes, peace movements can and have flourished and prevailed, and gives examples from different nations and periods of history.

Sonia thinks it is a good speech, cogent and spoken from the heart. No one listens to it, of course, since here in the heartland of misogyny no man ever listens to what a woman has to say, especially about war. War is the life of men here; the Pashtuns have always had war: clan war, tribal war, the war of nations and empires when available; peace means poverty and boredom to them. If Sonia had translated into Estonian instead of Pashto they could not have been less interested. Nevertheless, Alakazai rises now and explains why the woman is in error. The wars of the infidels are of no concern to the faithful, they are a just punishment on a people who disdain God's holy word and His prophet, peace be upon him. The jihad, on the other hand, is not war at all but a sacred duty and cannot and should not be stopped until the House of Peace, the umma, has won its final triumph over all unbelievers, which we rightly call the House of War. Everyone listens to this with respect and afterward they all shout the greatness of God and wave their weapons in the air.

Alazakai has been brief because the assembly is anxious to attend the next item on the agenda. He gives orders; the guards heave Cosgrove to his feet and drag him out, followed by the men and the prisoners. In the courtyard the prisoners are lined up against the wall as before. Sonia supports Annette, who does not seem to need much supporting; her face bears the thousand-yard stare of the combat veteran. The sky is overcast, as it often is this time of year, and a chill wind whips up small dust devils in the yard. Then, remarkably, the sun emerges from a small gap in the cloud cover, as if on order. A man holds what looks like a professional camcorder. One of the Arabs has a smaller camcorder and there are quite a number of cell-phone cameras in use. Sonia reflects that neither these people nor the culture they represent could ever have even dreamed up such a thing as a camcorder or a cell phone, far less the Internet along which they will send the images, but they are perfectly comfortable using them, rather as worms infest a larder without any idea of where the food came from. She realizes this is an imperialist thought; perhaps these toys are only a fair recompense for the zero, paper, and algebra—gifts of the umma and vital to the rise of the West—but just then she is not ashamed of it; she wishes a CIA drone would fire a missile and burn all of them to a crisp.

The guards bind Cosgrove's hands behind him and force him to his knees. There is no ceremony. A large man wearing a black ski mask comes forward carrying a *chora*, the thick-backed chopping knife of the Pashtuns, and strikes Porter Cosgrove's head off with one blow. Sonia makes herself look, and like everyone who sees this phenomenon for the first time she is amazed at the height of the blood fountain that shoots from the severed neck and how much red liquid is contained in a human body. The sad corpse topples slowly over, and the dusty smeared head is held up by the executioner, to a great shout from the crowd attesting once again to the greatness of God.

℞

Later, she is with Annette in the prison room, listening. The new widow is dry-eyed. "What's wrong with me?" she asks, "I can't feel anything. I mean, if we'd been *together,* if Porter hadn't—you know—collapsed like that, like he decided to die, to dissolve, before they killed him, maybe that would've been different; we could've talked about our lives and I could've held on to something, I could've felt that our life together wasn't meaningless. That pathetic thing they killed wasn't him. What I said in that speech was real; that was the real Porter. I loved him. I thought I loved him, but who was he? Was he really that . . . sad thing? I can't cry for that. Am I a monster? Why can't I cry?"

"You're in shock. Don't be hard on yourself."

"That's your advice? Okay, I won't be. I'll watch a little TV and catch up on my e-mails. Is that *Islamic,* by the way? Is that what God says? I see you talking to Him all the time. Is it like He's saying, Hey, when my servants cut off your husband's head, kick back, take it easy! Only in more elevated language, of course."

And more of this. Sonia endures it without demur, this outpouring of the poor woman's rage against fate, against God; because fate and God have left the building and there is only Sonia, the closest thing to a responsible party. The mujahideen have done exactly the same thing in response to their injuries real and imagined, if more violently, and if Annette had been able to swing a chora, she might have chopped off Sonia's head too.

"I know how you feel," says Sonia, inserting this at a break in the tirade. A banality, but at certain times in life only banalities are appropriate. Annette makes the expected response; she sneers contemptuously and says, "Oh, do you? You saw your husband's head get chopped off? Well, well, small world! Actually . . . actually, you have no *fucking idea* how I feel."

"No, I'm serious," says Sonia. "One day in Zurich, I received a telephone call telling me that my three children had been murdered in the assassination of their grandfather in Lahore. It was a bomb, and they were all burned beyond recognition. I didn't go to the funeral, I didn't even know about it until my niece thought to call me. I really was a monster at the time, certified monstrous by an Islamic court, exiled from my family and children. Would it have been worse if I actually saw them burn to death? I don't know, but I do know that at the moment I got the call I would've given anything to have been there. If it doesn't happen before your eyes, I think the human mind harbors the desperate illusion that maybe the loved ones survive; maybe they'll show up someday; it was all a mistake. And in my case, it *was* a mistake. My boy survived and I was able to find him again. But my little girls are still dead. Aisha was eight, Jamila was four. So I *do* know how you feel."

This revelation has the desired effect of snapping Annette—temporarily, at least—out of the downward spiral of self-pity and survivor's guilt. She says, "I'm sorry. That's awful."

"Yes, and I'll tell you the most awful thing about it . . . no, the second most awful thing. A little heads-up for you. Tomorrow morning the sun will rise despite the horrendous thing that it looked down on today. Almost all the rest of the people on the planet will go on with their lives in utter indifference to what has happened to you. The executioners will not be sorry, and it's odds-on they won't be punished for what they did. They're probably in the tea shop right now, laughing and joking about the day's events. We will all be sorry and supportive, whatever that word means exactly, but we won't be able to take any of your pain away, and everything we say to you will sound insincere. Because we didn't love Porter and we won't miss him, or at least not the way you do. And you'll go on, too. You'll fight it. You might not eat for a while, but sooner or later you'll be hungry and you'll eat, and the food will taste good, and in a shorter time than you imagine, someone will crack a joke and before you can recall that you're a grieving widow, you'll laugh. And assuming we survive this ordeal, you'll have a life. You'll drink cocktails and buy clothes and make love with a man. Yes, I can see the horror on your face, but you know I'm speaking the truth of my experience. From time to time, you'll despise yourself, but you'll have a life. What are you, thirty, thirty-two? You will not wear black until you fade away, mourning Porter Cosgrove. You will mourn for a time, and it'll take different forms. For a week after I got the news about my children I was numb, a sleep-walker. I didn't talk to anyone, wore the same soiled clothes. I ate from street vendors. One day I was on the Bahnhofstrasse in Zurich, down the street from Globus on my way to buy a sausage bun, when it hit me in a different way and I started to scream and tear at my hair and face. I fell down on my knees and pounded my head on the pavement. This is not allowed on the Bahnhofstrasse. The police came and took me away and I ended up in the Burghölzli mental hospital. That was how I became a psychoanalyst."

"I'll have to avoid sausage buns. Good advice, Sonia."

"See, you're making jokes already," Sonia says.

"Oh, shut up!" Annette replies and now it seems she does cry, not screaming or sobbing, but only a gentle liquid, snuffling sound, like a small defective pump. Sonia sacrifices the last of her precious tissue packs and waits.

"What's the other thing?" Annette asked. "You said the world going on despite poor you was the second worst thing."

"Yes. The worst thing is that at some level you welcome the loved one's death. A child dies, the most horrible thing that can happen, right? And some part of you is thinking, *Well, no more dirty diapers* or *Now I'll have more money* or *I can travel freely*. It's part of what we call the Shadow, all the dark parts of us we can't face. It's the thing that, if we don't deal with it, eventually poisons our lives. And no one is allowed to talk about that part of death. It's considered *insensitive*. But actually it's the height of sensitivity; you're sensing something even the bereaved is unconscious of feeling. So your husband is cruelly taken from you, and you're a good-looking, competent, talented woman of thirty, suddenly free of a much older man that most people found a little boring, whom even you were starting to find a little boring—"

"Stop it! God, you're horrible!" This in a voice loud enough to attract the attention of the others, Ashton in particular, who rises from his charpoy and seems about to come over to them.

"Yes, I am," says Sonia, "I'm horrible and you're horrible and the mujahideen are horrible; we're all horrible together, the only difference being I'm awake and you're all asleep in your various dreams of good-ness, them as holy warriors and you as innocent victim. Ah, I see Mr. Ashton has decided to join his comforting to mine. He'll be the first of a long line anxious to brighten your new life."

"Maybe I won't have a new life. I might pick the next low card."

"You won't."

"How can you be so sure?"

"Just the instincts of an old Jungian. Look, honestly, try not to worry. We'll be all right, don't ask me how, but we will. Now, here comes Harold with his consolations; take care. I'm going to check in with Schildkraut. I don't like the sound of that cough."

Ƥ

"It's the dust, I'm afraid," Schildkraut explains, when Sonia is by his side. "Where I come from, the mountain air is pure, but here not, it's filled with fine particles and the wind never stops blowing it about. And there is this peculiar metallic powder over everything. What do you suppose they are doing to produce it?"

"It's that grinding noise we hear all the time. Rashida says they're making weapons in the village. She says it's bombs that can blow up tanks, so I'm thinking some type of shaped penetrator. They use them in Iraq against American vehicles. Will you be all right? No, of course you won't, but I meant as far as your next breath goes."

"The next is fine," he says, smiling. "The one after that, not as certain. I am so unfortunate as to have a slight bronchial problem and I am sav-ing the last vapors of my inhaler for a true emergency. With any luck, I will draw the low card next time and bronchitis will be the least of my problems." In a more serious tone, he adds, "I could not help but overhear your conversation with Annette. You took a hard line."

"Because we're in a hard place. We can't have her dissolve into guilty tears."

"Why guilty? Perhaps she loved the man sincerely."

"Perhaps, but if so I would've said the same things. Doesn't the American sentimentality about death's tragedy and the cult of victimhood appall you? The whole sacredness of 9/11 and all the teddy bears and impromptu shrines whenever some act of violence occurs? It drives me nuts, frankly. It's the denial of death and the dark elements and it pollutes and trivializes the whole culture."

"Well, I'm a European, so it doesn't annoy me as much, and as an unbeliever I am not as bothered by these outbreaks of petty paganism. There is something of the ayatollah in you, Sonia, I believe."

"Yes, but one who draws the line at coercion. I say preposterous things to shake people up and bully a young woman who's just lost her surrogate daddy. Disgraceful, really, and worse to justify it under the name of group discipline. I should have let her cry on my shoulder as Harold is apparently doing right now."

The pair look across at Annette's charpoy, where the young woman is in close conversation with Ashton, their two pale heads separated by inches. "Speaking of group discipline," observes Schildkraut, "I expect our Harold is not so much comforting the widow as discussing plans for his escape scheme."

Sonia stared at him in surprise. "What escape scheme?"

"He brought it to me, strangely enough, the last person one would've thought interested, and I told him I would take my chances with the cards. I wondered why he would have thought that a coughing old man was the best escape companion, especially when he had a bull like Amin or an athlete like Shea to choose from, and then it came to me that I am the only other one among us who is not religious. Harold is outraged that we are being killed in the name of—what did he call it? The psychosis of an illiterate camel driver fifteen centuries ago. I think he would not mind so much if they were killing him in the name of moderate socialism."

"But Annette is a Christian."

"Oh, I suppose her vague do-good Quakerism is acceptable."

"Not to mention her more physical qualities. How does he intend to escape?"

"Well, he has noticed that Mahmoud comes to you in the night and takes you out for some hours to interpret dreams for people and then brings you back, escorting you into the room, when he checks to see everything is in order. Ashton has made a kind of cosh out of stones knotted into a sock, and with this he will lie in wait, and when you return he will lay out Mahmoud with a blow to the head, exchange clothes with him, and of course take his weapons. Annette will be in the burqa they gave her for the conference. They will slip out in the night, steal a vehicle, make their escape, and drive until they reach an army outpost or a patrol. He doesn't think anyone will notice they are gone until dawn prayers the following day. The perpetual roar of the diesel will cover the sound of his stolen truck. He thinks."

"Does he? Does he know that these people habitually disable their vehicles at night, just like they locked up their horses in the old days? Does he know that the area we're in is completely controlled by Taliban and mujahideen groups? We haven't even heard a helicopter since we've been here. And any military or police they may find might just as easily sell them back to the mujahideen. Does he have any idea what would happen to Annette, an unprotected woman and an American? They'd stake her down in a shed someplace and invite every man in the district to use her."

The old man shrugged. "Apparently he has high-level contacts in the security services here. He hinted rather broadly that he was some kind of agent and that as soon as he got free and made contact, all would be well. Do you think he was fabricating?"

"I don't know. Manjit thinks he's a spook, and Manjit's no fool."

"What will you do, Sonia, now that you have this information?"

"I don't know," she answers. "But Annette can't go with him."

℞

In the night, Sonia awakens to movement, the creak of a charpoy, a rustle of clothing. She does not sleep deeply now; sleep seems less necessary since Ismail came to her, there in the pit. She lies still and waits. Before long she hears the door open and feels moving air on her cheek, then a hand on her arm. It is Mahmoud. She rises, throws her dupatta over her head, and leaves with him. He takes her through the inn, but not to the same room. It is one closer to the sound of the diesel. There are rugs and cushions there and a dim oil lamp burning on a small table. He tells her to sit and wait, then leaves. He has an odd expression on his face, she thinks, frightened but also excited.

A few minutes pass, then Idris Ghulam enters. He sits on the cushions opposite her. His face, his black eyes, look fierce in the yellow lamplight. He says, "If you are a witch, then I am cursed. I gave orders that you should not interpret dreams, but everyone ignores this, and now even I am ignoring my own order. No one but Mahmoud knows I have come here, and he knows I will kill him if he tells, and to you I say the same thing. If I hear from anyone about this, on that day you die. Do you understand me?"

"You don't have to threaten me, Idris. I am trained to keep secrets. It is my honor to keep secrets. And besides, Alakazai will kill me whatever you do. So you need have nothing to fear from me. But you have come here to tell me your dream. You have had a dream, not like the one you had before, but a good dream."

He gasps and says, "How did you know?"

"Because I said it and it was so. I also say there was a woman in your dream."

"Yes, there was! A beautiful woman in an *abaya* made of gold. She was gigantic, as tall as a house. I was like a child next to her. She said she would lead me to Paradise. How did you know?"

"You would not understand if I told you," Sonia says. "Just tell me your dream, as much as you remember." It was a reasonable guess, she thinks, with some satisfaction. Men in patriarchal cultures who are under extreme psychological stress often have anima dreams, as the suppressed female principle in them struggles to break out.

Idris says, "I was in a room, in a palace, everything marble and gold, and fine rugs on the floor. The woman came and told me this was the porch of Paradise, and I was welcome to come in, but God had something He wanted me to do. Of course, I agreed. So she said I should follow her, and she led me through a door and down a grand stairway, down and down, and as we went lower, the stairway became poorer and narrower and lower, and it stank. It was dark, I could no longer see the woman, but I could hear her voice. At the bottom of the stairs was a small stone room and on the floor were three pots, one filled with sand and the other two empty. The light was dim, like candlelight, but there was no candle. The voice said, Idris, here is sand: you must separate the black grains from the white, putting the white grains in the right-hand pot and the black grains in the left. And take care not to put a single grain wrong, or you will be condemned to eternal fire, for this room is the gateway to Hell. Then I was alone, and I thought, I am doomed, because no one can do this task, not in a thousand years. Then I prayed in my despair, but there was no answer from God. After a while I heard a tapping sound, and footsteps, and into the room came a little girl, a beautiful little girl, but she had a stick; she was blind. She asked what I was doing there and I told her and she said, Oh, that is an easy task if you know the way of it. I will teach you. I said, how can *you* separate the black grains from the white? You are blind. She said, I am not really blind. It is a pretense, because my father wishes me to marry a man I don't like, so I pretend to be blind. Do you want me to help you or not?"

Here he pauses and passes a hand over his face. Sonia waits. A minute goes by and then he speaks again.

"Because I knew it was wrong to ask the help of a disobedient girl I said nothing. I thought, This is a test of God; this is the *real* test. But she seemed to know my thoughts; she said, Idris, don't be foolish. God does not play tricks. Do you want help or not? So I said yes, please help me, although the words stuck in my throat. She took my right hand in hers and plunged it into the sand, and I found I could feel the difference between the grains. The black grains felt as big as peas. In a short time I had separated all the grains perfectly. And as soon as the last grain fell, the room and the little girl disappeared and I awoke."

"This is a very good dream, Idris Ghulam. The great pir Najd ad-din Kubra writes of such a dream and calls it one of the greatest of dreams sent by God. Don't you feel that it is?"

"Yes. I felt very peaceful after I awoke, but also confused. Can you tell me what it means?"

"I can. But you will not like to hear it. You will cry out at me that I am making a false interpretation, even though in your deepest heart you will know it is true. Are you willing to hear it?"

"Yes," he says impatiently. "Get on with it!"

"Then listen, in the name of God the merciful, the compassionate! This is a dream about the greater jihad, the struggle within the human soul to reach God through right thinking and right actions. The woman is Wisdom, and she is an aspect of the divine presence. Wisdom is often a woman in dreams of men, because it comes through an inner part of them they do not listen to, in the way of men who think that women have nothing of importance to say. You are that kind of man. She says she can lead you to Paradise, which is true, but the way does not lead through fine furnishings and marble halls. These represent the goods of this world, gold and land and honor and reputation. Wisdom says you must turn your back on these and plunge downward into a filthy stairway. This represents evil, the dark things that you do and do not admit are wrong and against God's law. But God sees everything. The bowl of sand means all the actions you do in religion with an impure heart, all the hypocrisies, the insincere prayers, the false teachings that have infected your mind. It is as impossible to arrive in Paradise through these as it is to separate the black grains from the white in a bushel of sand. Now a helper comes, and she is a little girl, a disobedient little girl, who pretends blindness. The meaning of this is that you yourself are pretending blindness, and that also you have given your obedience in error."

Here he interrupts. "How? When did I ever pretend blindness?" But even in the dim lamplight she can see the worry in his eyes.

"You pretend not to see that Bahram Alakazai, whom you follow, is an unworthy leader. Where did he come from? What is his khel and tribe? When did the Pashtun ever follow such a man? Yet you follow him because he has money and weapons and promises you power, and at his command you make war on women and on the people of a Muslim nation."

"You lie, woman!"

"See? I told you you would say that, but I am not lying. It is my honor to tell the truth about dreams, and you know I am honorable, for didn't I endure the torture instead of falsely confessing to blasphemy? Now, do you want to hear the rest of the interpretation?"

He nods and makes a gesture with his hand and she continues. "A little girl shows you the secret of the sand, and this allows you to separate the black grains by touch. You could not have imagined such a thing, because no man can imagine God's mercy. This dream also says you must use a different sense than you thought, not vision, but touch. This means that all you thought was true must be considered again, to tell the good from the bad. After you accomplished the task, you had a feeling of peace, which is but a pale ghost of the feeling you will have when God takes you to Him. It is a promise, but only if you turn from the path of murder and pride and do the work of the greater jihad. That is the end of the interpretation."

He sits in silence, stroking his beard; she studies his face. For a moment the harsh Pashtun male mask he wears fades and a more contemplative person is revealed. They get that from the secret life they share with their mothers, she thinks. The poor women have only a single opportunity to acquire a fragment of power over their lives, and this is through their sons when they are small. But the women are stupid and beaten down, so they can rarely give their boys the spark of a strong opposite, the feminine introject that leads to individuation. And so the boys never grow up. They retain the brutality and carelessness of boys for their whole lives, living on boasts and the good opinion of their gang. And they have the short attention span of boys and the romantic wildness, building nothing, dumbfounded by the civilizations around them, knowing as little of how a political order or a modern economy is constructed as a six-year-old knows about what his father does at work. So they are doomed to poverty, the manipulations of others, and early death.

Idris utters something underneath his breath. She sees the mask drop into place and he rises with one swift motion. In a stiff, harsh voice he says, "But after all, it is only a dream and dreams are not real life. They are of no account in real life."

"Nor is the world to come a part of real life, yet the Prophet, peace be with him, told us to value it above every other thing. You have been given a great gift, Idris Ghulam. God will not be pleased with you if you throw it away."

The man's fists clench and he seems about to say something, but instead he turns away and leaves the room. There are six more clients that night, including Rashida's mother and several of the mujahideen. They relate the simple dreams of simple people, or so she decides to consider them. They want to know what will happen to them, should they sell a cow, will the child just started be a son? She answers as best she can in accordance with the ancient Sufi dream books. They seem satisfied and happy that there is no charge.

Mahmoud leads her back to prison. When they come to the door, Sonia turns and faces the guard. She says, "Mahmoud, wait! If I save your life now, will you promise me something?"

"What is it? And how will you save my life?"

"First swear by God and upon your head and the head of your son that you will do as I ask, if it does not soil your honor. I am an honest woman, as you know, and I swear by my honor that I am not trying to trick you. And recall your dream, that you would profit by helping a boy who was not a boy. This is the moment foretold, for that boy is me."

He goggles at her. "How is this possible?"

"It is a long story, Mahmoud, well known to others, but I do not have time to recount it here. Swear now, in the name of God."

The big man ruminates on this for some seconds and then nods. After the required oaths he asks, "So now, how will you save my life?"

She says, "Behind that door is a man with a club, and as soon as you step through it he will break your skull, take your clothes and weapons, and try to escape."

Mahmoud growls and moves forward, but she stands in his way. "No, you will do nothing to this man; that is my request. Recall that you promised to obey! Don't come through the door after me as you usually do. Let me slip in alone."

He glares; she holds him with her eye and hopes he was frightened of his mother. He relents, opens the door, she slides in, and he locks it. The room is utterly dark except for the dim sliver of light from the guard's lantern coming from under the door. She can see Ashton's bare feet as he waits with his weighted sock. She ignores him and his muffled curse, and the black shape, crouching there, Annette in a burqa.

14

How I got back to the States. That's an interesting story and one I usually leave out of my biography, especially when talking to women. I don't mind telling Billy Olin, though. I had a couple of hours to kill before my flight, so I dropped in to say good-bye on my way to the airport. He was the same. People change, they say, but not Rowboat Billy. He told me once, how he got the name—we were both of us drunk in an NCO club at Fort Bragg—and I assured him it was no big thing, as I'm sure he would have said about my little secrets. It was in the early weeks of the Iraq war and him and a bunch of Rangers were set up on the river near Tikrit, looking for insurgents running down the water from there, and one night Billy spotted a rowboat and challenged it and when they kept right on going he smoked it with his SAW. And wouldn't you know? It was a family with eight little kids. It happens. Pretty much everybody who's been downrange has a story like that.

Mine was a little different. After I'd got blown up in my final moment as a heroic mujahid, I woke up after maybe two weeks out of it, and there was Wazir again to praise me, eyes full of love, and tell me what happened. He didn't say that everyone else had thought I was dead and he'd carried me on his back for ten kilometers to the best doctor we had with us, Dr. Spin, and he'd fixed me up okay. I got that later from Gul Muhammed, because he was there too; we were in his home village of Barak Sharh, in Kunar Province, up near the Pakistani border.

Gul Muhammed told me that when I was fit to travel he was going to send me south with Wazir and a truckload of loot, guns, and equipment that we would sell in the bazaars of Peshawar and distribute the money to the families of the mujahideen in the camps. This trade was what had kept the resistance going. The CIA and the Saudis sent money and the Pakistanis provided support and took their cut, but it was up to the mujahideen themselves to support their families in the refugee camps, and they did it with Russian loot sold in the bazaars.

Peshawar was a different city from the one I had known in child-hood, huge now, even filthier, loud with motor scooters and cars, grown rich off the blood of Afghanistan. The nations that wanted Russia to lose up there had poured billions through Peshawar, and a lot of it had stuck. One of those it had stuck to was our cousin Bacha Khan, who was even fatter than before and now had a big house in the Khyber Colony and a Toyota pickup. He gave us good hospitality and said he'd help us sell our stuff; he knew all the merchants and their tricky ways.

I went with Bacha to the bazaar and was royally entertained by the various bazaaris. My reputation had preceded me, as they say. By that time I was known as Kakay Ghazan, which means little warrior of God. It's a big deal for a teenager to be treated as a man by older Pashtuns, and it seemed to me that my life had reached some kind of peak. Except for the admiration of girls, and access to them, it was exactly like being the best high school quarterback in Alabama.

᠊ᢧ

I said as much to Billy, because he'd played ball in Alabama, and I wanted him to understand the full impact of what happened next. But before I could go on, a guy came in and changed Billy's piss bag and I thought of that scene in the movie *Catch-22*, when the medic just switches the pee bag and the IV bag. The asshole gave me a look, like what was I doing talking to a broccoli? I gave *him* a look that sent him out of there in a hurry and picked up the story.

᠊ᢧ

We sold the stuff and got shitloads of money and then went to the hugely swollen refugee camps and looked up the relatives of the men whose loot we'd just sold, and I watched as Bacha handed over the money to the right people, and after that we had a feast, two sheep, and I ate more meat than I had in years, and there was wine, too, because the Pashtuns hadn't gone crazy yet over their religion like a lot of them did later. We both got drunk and Wazir recited some Sufi poetry I hadn't known he knew, and we got to talking some deep stuff about Sufi and Islam and so on, the kind of conversation we hadn't had before, and I asked him who he'd learned all that from and he smiled and said, "Your mother. Who else?"

I laughed because I thought it was a joke and I was drunk, so I just ruffled his hair and put my head on his shoulder, and fell asleep soon after that. In the middle of the night I got up with an urgent need to piss. I crawled over Wazir and walked out of the room Bacha had given us and went to the latrine, which was in an outhouse. I used it, and when I came out two guys, or maybe it was three, knocked me off my feet, taped my mouth, threw a bag on my head, tied my hands, rolled me into a tarp, and tossed me in the back of a van.

It was weird, because I honestly couldn't understand who would want to snatch me. It wasn't the Russians; by that point they were out of the picture. It could've been rival mujahideen, or some tribal beef, or just a kidnap for ransom. There was some of that starting to show up. And then I heard two of the guys say something in a foreign language, and then it hit me that I could understand what they were saying because it was English, and not Pakistani English. They were Americans. So then I was totally baffled.

We drove for maybe half an hour and I heard the sound of aircraft engines, a jet flying pretty low above, and the van stopped and the men dragged me out and put me on a stretcher, still wrapped in the tarp, and carried me up a ramp and set me down. Then there was a lot more airplane noise and I felt motion and knew I was in a plane, a big one, and I felt the floor tilt under me and heard the scream of engines on full power. Hands tugged at my tarp and I got unrolled from it and the bag came off my head and a hand ripped the tape off my mouth and I was looking up into a woman's face. The light in the plane was red so it took me a little while to recognize my mother.

⁊ₒ

Billy's eye was twitching and his mouth was opening and closing like a fish. His chalky tongue lolled out a little, so I picked up a squirt bottle that was there and squirted him a drink. I thought it would be interesting and maybe a good omen if he miraculously regained consciousness then, hearing the miraculous story of my reunion with Mom—but no.

℔

As I recall it, the main feeling I had when I recognized her was a kind of babyish annoyance, as if I'd been a nine-year-old playing cowboys or superheroes in a vacant lot and my mom had just dragged me in for supper. I'd been wounded in my dignity and she was the only one around to take it out on. The strange thing was that the last time I'd seen her I really *was* nine, and my relationship with her was frozen, like those insects you see trapped in amber.

I shouted at her, "What did you do? Why am I on this plane?"

She said in a calming voice, "It's okay, Theo, you're safe now. We're going home."

And I said I didn't want to go home to Lahore, I wanted to be with Wazir and Gul Muhammed and fight in the jihad. I said I was Kakay Ghazan and a famous fighter and what do I have to do with you, woman?

She switched her language to Urdu as well and told me that the jihad was over, the Russians were leaving, and now the mujahideen would turn on one another and there would be more war, but without the blessing of God, and she did not wish me to die in such a war. She said we were not going to Lahore at all; it was time for me to return to my real family in America. I went a little crazy then, screaming at her in three languages that I was a Pashtun and the son of Gul Muhammed and the brother of Wazir and I didn't want to go to America. I went on for a while but it was a long flight, and she had wisely left my hands and feet tied. Even though I was yelling at her she kept calm and talked in a low voice, about how I had always had two families and was a man of two nations and that this was a good thing—she didn't want me to lose that—and how proud she was of me that after I had lost my Pakistani family I had been so quick about finding a new one, because a man without his family is nothing. But now it was my fate to have a different life. God had willed that we be brought back together, she loved me, and I had to trust in God; the Prophet, peace be unto him, said that a man should trust his mother above all others.

And I recalled that and was calmer afterward. Then I asked her why she hadn't come to get me before this and she said because she thought I was dead. It turned out that a street boy had jumped up on the bumper of Laghari Sahib's Rolls-Royce just before the bomb exploded, and when they had found the charred and unrecognizable corpse of a boy among the wreckage, my grandmother Noor pronounced that it was me, a last little stab of revenge, and no one had the nerve to oppose her.

I told her that her daughters and my grandfather had been avenged because I had shot the man in the godown.

She touched my face lightly with her fingertips, just for an instant. She closed her eyes, tilted her head back, took in some breath, and made an *ah* sound. It was hard to read her face in the dim light. I thought then that she was expressing satisfaction, but looking back I think it was some kind of devastated grief.

Then I asked, "But how did you find me? How did you learn that I was alive?"

"Because I have friends in the jihad, and they told me of a boy there who was famous for his bravery, the younger of the two sons of Gul Muhammed, and my heart was lifted because I knew it was you and that you lived. So I planned with my friends to take you. I would have gone to Afghanistan but my friends learned you were to come to Peshawar, and so it was done."

"Why didn't you just ask me to come with you?"

"Would you have come?"

"No. But you should have asked, not tied me like an animal."

"I will untie you now, if you give me your word you will not try to escape when this plane lands."

"My word," I said, and she took out a knife and cut the cable ties at my hands and feet. I stretched and rubbed my wrists and stood up. She stood too, and I saw that I was taller than she was. A moment passed when we just stared at each other, and then we embraced. I was flooded with feelings I could not express and I thought of a ghazal of Ghalib's that goes, *My heart burns in a temple full of mysteries that, alas, have no voice to speak.*

I felt my eyes prickle with tears, but I did not cry. She cried. I asked her what she had done when she heard all three of her children were dead, and she asked me what Pashtun women do when their children die in the war and I said, They keen and tear their hair and clothes and fall on the ground and cast dust on their heads, and she said, That is what I did.

So I accepted my fate like a man, and besides she was my mother. I asked her what I would do in America, since I understood there was no jihad there, and that was the only thing I knew. She said I would go to school, and, according to what I liked to study, such would be my life. I said I would not stand to be beaten anymore, because I was a man now, and only my father could beat me. At that she smiled and said, No one will beat you; they don't beat children in American schools. This amazed me. I asked, How then do they learn anything? and she answered, They do not learn very much. She said Farid and she would teach me in our home, and when I had caught up they would put me in high school with others of my own age. I asked her what I would learn, and she said, to read and write English, and something about history and geography and also mathematics. She said, You have had an excellent fourth-grade education. It should not take more than six months to get you ready for your junior year in an American high school.

She had clothes for me. On the plane I pulled on my first ever pair of blue jeans. I had a Pearl Jam T-shirt, a quilted parka to go over it, and a pair of Nikes. The plane landed at a military airport in Germany, and we ate in a restaurant and took a commercial flight to Washington. So I entered my homeland through the various narrow gates, carrying a passport I'd never seen before. At the time I didn't find this strange.

I was taken to their house on Tracy Place in the Kalorama neighborhood of D.C., a white colonial on a green street lined with old sycamores. Farid was welcoming and nice enough, maybe a little distant, as might be expected. I was respectful and formal with him in my turn. He was a good teacher, patient and energetic. He gave me poetry to read at first, and then fiction, and then the school subjects I would have to know. I picked up math too, with little trouble. The only thing I had problems with was writing; I couldn't do an essay to save my ass. He worked hard, though, and so did I, and in the end he said that the inability to write was a characteristic of almost all American students, so I wouldn't stand out from the crowd.

My mother and I spent hours watching television together, so that I would learn how to be an American. All us immigrants watch as much TV as we can, it's the best way to learn the language and customs of the Americans. We watched soap operas because they spoke very clearly in simple sentences, and this gave me a good introduction to American idiom and sexual practices. We watched movies on the TV and game shows, to a background of my mother's commentary. By this means I learned that the true American religion was the pursuit of pleasure and money, although they professed to worship God, and this made them cruel, although they professed to be kindly. The other part of the American creed was redemption through violence, and that made me feel right at home. The good guy and the bad guy always meet up at the end of the film, and the good guy kills the bad guy in an interesting way, and that's the end of the movie: hug the girl and fade to black. My mother said that not all Americans were like the ones on TV, but it gave them pleasure to believe in what they saw.

There is a lot to learn in any culture, and I absorbed a good deal of this one, although, as it turned out, not quite enough. Maybe I saw the wrong movies. I liked being warm and well-fed, but there were still a few things that disturbed me about America. Cleaning your ass with dry paper instead of water, like we do in the part of the world I was from. And seeing people eating with their left hands; that still freaks me a little after all these years. And girls, the way they walked around with their sexual parts on display but weren't whores. Very, very strange, especially to someone like me who had no real experience with women.

But the worst thing was that I was no longer armed. I would walk in the streets and imagine someone insulting me or my mother and I would have no way of obtaining satisfaction or revenge. This thought obsessed me, and when the time came for me to leave the house and go alone to school I took care to arm myself with the dagger I'd taken from my mother's trunk. It seemed like a hundred years ago, but it was still very sharp.

Long story short, I got into a stupid argument with a football player in the cafeteria one day because he thought I was staring at his girlfriend, which I was. He pushed me and accused me of having sex with my mother, so I pulled out my knife and gutted him. A cultural misunderstanding, of the kind the U.S. government makes all the time, but that was not an excuse I could use.

I have to say Farid came through for me after I got arrested. He had a lot of contacts in the legal system, being a lawyer himself, and he got me charged as a juvenile, even though the commonwealth attorney wanted to charge me as an adult, because of the heinousness of the crime. My victim didn't die, although he had to quit football for the season, which I guess added to the heinous nature of my crime. So basically it was a year in Bon Aire Juvenile Corrections Facility, which would be a four-star hotel anywhere north of Peshawar, and where I was a model prisoner and completed my education in American culture and got a high school equivalency degree. I still couldn't write very well, but the standards were not high. They had job counselors there, and they were always saying that in order to succeed in life you had to have a skill set; just having a strong back and a willingness to work wasn't enough anymore. I took the message to heart. The week after my release I enlisted in the U.S. Army. I figured I had the necessary skill set for that already.

⁊ᴑ

I said good-bye to Billy and told him I wouldn't be seeing him for a while. He didn't show he cared, or maybe I just couldn't see it. I'm often like that myself, so I sort of understand.

It's a long flight to Lahore from D.C. through London, and I never learned to sleep on airplanes so I had a lot of time to think. The TV screen in the airport lounge had shown a news lady doing a story about Craig and the kidnap, with a logo that had Craig's face and the burned-out bus from the kidnap site on it. She said it had been a week since the event, and no word on what had happened to the hostages after the first video. So I thought about that and what I was going to do and what the army had to do with all of it. I figured my days as a soldier were coming to a close, even if I didn't get busted for this particular caper. I'm working against the interests of the United States here, no question, and I'm starting to feel funny about taking my paycheck.

No hard feelings or anything, the army does what it does, and I was reasonably happy in it, probably happier and more successful than I would've been in any other occupation, given my history. But I never got to love it, just like I never learned to love my mother's country. I know that's unusual; most immigrants, especially immigrants from the impoverished lands, turn out more patriotic than the native-born, but not me. Maybe it's because I never got to know America, only TV and a prison and the military, so you could say I did not see the best parts of it.

Also, because of my upbringing, I got along a lot better with the mujahideen than I did with the Americans. Most American troops are jocky overgrown schoolboys, mainly white kids from small towns and a good chunk of minority types, and after their unit's served together and been blooded there is unit cohesion, as they say, the men look after one another and sometimes they cry when one of their number gets blown up. But in most line units there are one or two who don't necessarily cohere, and don't cry at all, although otherwise they are excellent soldiers, efficient, self-sacrificing, and so on, but really they don't give a damn. That would be me.

᚛

The plane landed in Heathrow and we went through passport control. I got the fish eye because I was traveling on my Pakistani passport and because I'd been letting my beard grow for the past week or so. My Pakistani passport says I am Abdul Ismail Laghari, although I don't believe anyone ever called me Abdul. The name means "slave of God" and Theodore means "God-lover," which probably amounts to the same thing, and even my Pakistani family calls me Theo. I was actually baptized Theodore at the cathedral in Lahore, privately so as not to cause scandal. So I have been a kind of undercover person from birth almost, and I am bound to offend those who like neat classifications. The passport guy (one of those) looked at his computer for a few minutes to see whether I was the terrorist I seemed to be, but then he gave the passport back to me and moved his eyes to the next in line. I suppose I will have to get used to that when I travel now.

I bought half a dozen bottles of good scotch at the duty-free shop. I have a license to possess and consume booze within the borders of Pakistan, a state that's officially teetotal but whose citizens behave a lot like the Americans did when religious fanatics banned alcohol there some years back. My booze license is one advantage to having two identities, and bottles of scotch make a nice gift or bribe.

They called my flight and I got on with my yellow duty-free bag bulging and there was the usual boarding mess, because everyone else on the plane had been shopping too and the overheads were jammed tight. I had a seat in the next-to-last row in coach and there was a Pakistani family behind me with a five-year-old girl who insisted on sitting on her mother's lap and shrieked when the flight attendant made her buckle in for takeoff. As soon as the flight attendant turned her back, the dad took the belt off and put the kid back on the lap. This cycle went on several times until the flight attendant threatened to throw them off the plane, after which the kid howled and kicked the back of my chair until the plane was roaring down the runway and the flight attendants were belted in, at which point the dad blithely unstrapped the kid and returned her to the lap for good. I was back in Pakistan already, where no one pays attention to rules and family peace is the main goal of life. It felt just like home.

Customs in Lahore gave me some heat about the Scotch, but since I have a pale skin and spoke perfect Urdu (and had the booze license) the guy figured I was connected to the elite and let me through. My Auntie Rukhsana was waiting for me outside passport control, and I got a big hug from her, followed by a flood of tears—Oh, your poor mother, you poor boy—and so on, and I thought it was a little extreme, it's not like either my mother and I were the center of family life among the Lagharis. She asked me with a kind of hungry desperation how our plan was going, and I said it was going as well as could be expected but the thing now was to find out where the hostages were being held and I had to be here to do that, and she asked me how I was going to proceed, all business now, the tears dried, and I said I still had some contacts and I'd ask around. She pumped me a little then, like the good journalist she is, but I put her off, like the good secret agent I am, and at last she quit and flashed me a smile. "Little Theo, all grown up!" she said. "We're having a party for you tonight. I hope you are not too jet-lagged."

"Not too," I said. "I'm used to traveling. But I'm not exactly in the party mood."

"Yes, I understand, and we all, or almost all, feel the same way. But here the family is the most important thing; whenever something happens in your life, good or bad, the family gathers and we all eat, eat. You don't understand that maybe, but I think we must have such a gathering, because I think you will need our help in what you are going to do. So it is, in a sense, part of why you have come."

"Okay, got it," I said. I'm nothing if not culturally flexible. "Who all is going to be there?"

"Oh, just the immediate family, Jafar and our children and Nisar and his wife and children. They are dying to meet you."

"And Seyd? He's not coming?"

She made a face. "Oh, Seyd! That's all we would need, an ISI-wallah and you in the same room."

"Why not? I'm sort of an ISI-wallah myself. We could have an interesting conversation."

"You don't know what you're saying," said my aunt darkly, and then turned to snarl in Mahji dialect at the beggars and porters who had surrounded us as soon as we left the terminal building. Another sign I was back home, people willing to carry heavy loads for a few cents, and other people treating them like dogs, and me as one of the non-dog higher beings: the feelings connected with that, and the near-solidity of the humid air, a sticky sludge of diesel, sewage, and hot spicy oils.

We got into her Mini and Rukhsana gunned the engine and pressed the horn, trusting the dog people to scramble out of our way, which they did, apparently without resentment, and she whipped us out into the exit road traffic.

I said the expected *"Lahore Lahore hai,"* and she laughed and replied in Mahji Panjabi.

"Yes, and can you still speak your cradle tongue, or have you forgotten?"

I answered in the same language. "I have not forgotten, Auntie, although I think that even you are more comfortable in English or proper Urdu."

"Yes, but I am part of the cosmopolitan liberal elite that will be the ruin of pure Islamic Pakistan, according to my brother Seyd. I believe he has stopped using English entirely."

"Then, we'll have to speak Urdu when we meet."

"You intend to visit Seyd?" She seemed astounded.

"Sure," I said. "I need to find out what ISI knows about the kidnapping. I'm assuming he'll be forthcoming. One of his relatives by marriage is among the hostages."

"Whom he has always despised. Honestly, Theo, you cannot be so naïve. Don't you understand that the people who did this atrocity are ISI pawns? I would not be surprised to learn that ISI arranged the whole affair."

"Why would they do that?"

"A number of reasons. To embarrass the new government, who perhaps are not as bloodthirsty or purely Islamic as they would like. To discredit anyone working for peace with India. To curry favor with the mullahs. For money."

"How money?"

"Well, if you have kidnapped one of the richest men in the world, I assume there will be money involved. I have heard rumors of negotiations. I have heard of lunches up in Pindi between businessmen, strangers, and high officials of the military and Inter-Services Intelligence. Something is going on. It is well known the whole country is for sale, so why shouldn't our terrorists be for sale as well?"

"If that were true we'd have bin Laden by now. No one's collected the twenty-five million."

"Oh, well, those are Pashtuns. In any case, betraying a leader is a different affair entirely to selling a hostage." Then she yelled, "Get out my way, you shit-eater, go rape your sister!" out the window at a multicolored bus as she whipped across several lanes to make a left turn.

"You're not going to Model Town Park?" I said, as we changed direction.

"Oh, no, we are too fine for Model Town Park now. We have a house in Gulberg, which would have been quite convenient when the children were at school, but now we float around in it like fish in a tank. We have fifteen *marlas*, can you imagine?"

"That's a good-sized house," I said, falling easily back into the traditional calculations. A marla was 272 and a quarter square feet, so fifteen marlas was a big house for urban Pakistan.

"You must be doing very well, Auntie."

"Oh, well, I am working and the children are grown and Jafar was made head of his division, and we did well on the Model Town house and some investments. You know, most people have small houses full of elderly relatives so we all take one another out to restaurants. When you are able to entertain in your own home that is a big something."

"Yes, Auntie, I know. I was born here."

"Of course, I know that, but you look like such an American now. Anyway, it is now considered more chic to have others to one's house, and that was one reason we bought it. You'll see. Of course, it is not old Lahore, not like my father's house, but Gulberg is not nothing either."

She sounded sad when she said this, and I asked her, "And do you entertain very much, Auntie?"

"No, we do not, or rather not for some time, because when one is pro-moted to head of division one has no time for such things anymore. He is in Kahuta half the time, and I am by myself. And even when we did enter-tain it was all very stiff, the women on one side talking children's accom-plishments, the men on the other talking office politics. No conversation that any civilized person would recognize as such. Oh, Theo, do you remember those nights at my father's house? People from every part of Lahore, faquirs and generals, merchants, chemistry professors, journal-ists, ministers, and that wonderful music, with the ghazals floating up through the colored lanterns on strings. What happened to that world, that is what I want to know? We are richer than ever we were then, but somehow the taste has gone out of life. Or am I just getting old?"

I had nothing to contribute in that department, so I asked how her kids were doing, always a safe subject for a Punjabi woman, even a mod-ern one, and she told me about Shira, who was in the foreign service, a diplomat, if you can imagine, and Hassan, who was prepping for Cam-bridge, and the baby, Iqbal, not such a baby anymore; he is mad for computers and doesn't want to go to college but open his own software business, and Nisar is encouraging him, offering investments, and his father is going to shoot both of them; and we talked and argued about stuff like that for the rest of the trip to Gulberg.

The house was a new one, two floors, tan stucco, and a lot of sheet glass, with little Islamic details so you knew you weren't in L.A. My aunt showed me to a guest room and told me dinner would be at eight, she would be out and about getting ready, and if I wanted anything just ring.

I remembered that aspect of life in Pakistan too, and after unpacking my stuff, I rang. A young woman appeared, who seemed surprised when I addressed her in her native tongue and asked her to bring me tea and snacks. Upper-middle-class Americans don't usually have clusters of servants, but my aunt did, and I found I had not picked up any of the typical American discomfort with them. I guess you have to be born into a feudal society to understand what that's all about.

But I was gringo enough to ask the woman what her name was and how long she'd been working for the Lagharis and tried to start a little chat, but I saw she was not happy with that, was getting more and more nervous, and I realized that the only reason a male guest would normally engage a maid in conversation would be if he was planning to throw her down on the bed and fuck her, so I froze my face into a commanding mask and waved her out.

I fell on the bed alone and conked out for a couple of hours and then I had a bath and dressed in my one suit, a custom-made number I'd picked up in Dubai a few years ago for about what a pair of decent jeans would cost in the States. I'd bought some silk shirts and a tie at the same time just for the hell of it. I'd never owned an outfit like that, and I guess I'd put it on two or three times at weddings and the occasional party at the house in D.C., but I wore it to dinner that night because I didn't have any Pakistani clothes.

℞

When I got down to the living room, which looked like anything you might find in suburban Washington, I found that all the men were dressed Western-style like I was, and I guess they were doing it in honor of me, which I thought was pretty neat. I think there are about twelve cousins in my generation of the family, counting me, Rukhsana's three, and Nisar's three girls. Seyd's five kids were naturally absent. I was a little nervous about this gathering because of the current situation and the family history, my mom not being the pride of the clan, but it all went fine.

Better than fine, to tell the truth. I'm the senior cousin, the son of the oldest brother, which counts for something in Punjabi society; and it turned out they'd been hearing stories of my colorful exploits all their lives, mainly from Auntie R, and they were fascinated; and when it turned out I could speak their languages and wasn't a typical American asshole, was totally desi except for the skin tones, had manners, et cetera, it turned into a love fest. Rukhsana's three were as described, all good-looking and a lot smarter than me. Nisar's Yasmin, Zahra, and Miah were all in various schools; they chattered and tried out their flirting and used American slang they'd picked up from the Web and movies, just wrongly enough to be charming. Pakistanis of that class obviously travel a good deal nowadays and have total access to international media, but they're still psychologically sheltered, and now they had what amounted to a tame monster right in the family. I felt like I was coming out of a shell of my own devising into the sunlight of human life, that for the first time I could see a cure for the evil of my days, and I regretted having denied myself this for so long, nursing my isolation and loneliness, buried in the world of grunts, not that much better off than Billy Olin. What wonderful people, I thought: my family!

So we talked and laughed through a really terrific dinner, and they told me about their lives and I told them what I thought they could handle about mine, and the only things that weren't quite right was that Seyd had refused to come or let his kids come, and Jafar came in late, when we'd already sat down, and I could see that there was something not right between him and Rukhsana.

After dinner, the men walked out on the roof terrace for smoking and guy talk and I gave Nisar and Jafar the bottles of eighteen-year-old Macallan I'd bought, which they really seemed to appreciate, and Jafar got a servant to bring glasses and ice and we all had an illicit drink, with which we toasted Babaji, and Nisar said, "Scotch is not wine," and everyone laughed.

Then Jafar got into a discussion of the recent cricket test matches with his sons that I couldn't really follow and Nisar took the opportunity to pull me away for a private conversation.

"So what are your plans?" he asked.

"Obviously, I want to find out where they're holding my mother."

"Do you think you can do that?"

"I don't know, Uncle, but I have to try. It's not entirely hopeless, I think. I have contacts in the jihad, and something of a reputation."

"You'll go north?"

"Yes. I know people in Peshawar."

"From the jihad? How do you know they're still alive?"

"They were the kind of people that are hard to kill."

He chuckled at that and said, "Look, I don't want to tell you your business, but this is a difficult time for Pakistan. The general is out for now, which is a good thing in a way, but when the lion leaves, the hyenas fight over the carcass, you know? Ordinarily, I could ease your efforts in various ways; I too know a lot of people in the north. But nowadays it's difficult to know whom to trust. And I feel responsible, letting your dear mother and all of them go to Leepa . . . insane, really, but you know it's quite difficult to say no to your mother and my sister all in one go." He laughed sharply and then grew serious again. "It's also not a good thing that Seyd did not come tonight. You understand why?"

"Rukhsana suggested that ISI might have had something to do with the kidnapping."

"Oh, it's more than a mere suggestion, I can tell you. My God, this organization, this so-called al-Faran, was invented, bought, and paid for by ISI. Whether they are still following orders or have set up on their own, who can say?"

"What do you hear about ransom negotiations? I mean for Craig."

"I hear five crore—dollars, not rupees—is the asking price."

"That's a lot of money," I said. "It'll be hard to move fifty million dollars in Pakistan."

"Yes. I have interests in the largest bank in Pakistan, and now I am hearing discreet inquiries from people connected to ISI: how can they conceal an influx, an *unusual* influx, source unspecified? This country! Do you know, Theo, that my bribery bill is an insanely large percentage of my payroll? How can one run a nation this way? Look, I am not pure like my father. I do business, and to do business in Pakistan one must play along, but I am also my father's son and I say there is a limit. There is still decency."

He went on about the agony of Pakistan for a while before I brought him back to my immediate problem. "Can you get me in to see Seyd?"

"Not a good idea, Theo; he is a peculiar fellow, my dear brother. He is very proud and quite incompetent, which is a dangerous combination. He might even have you arrested or expelled. He owes me a great deal, but he would die before acknowledging how much of my influence has gone into supporting his position in the military. As for him knowing anything that could help you—well, let us just say that Seyd is not privy to the inner secrets of his organization."

"Yes, there are people like that in every army."

"And ours has more than most. Half our national budget goes to arms, and I ask you, have we ever won a war? The country is tearing itself apart, and these imbeciles spend and spend on nuclear weapons. Do you know the nuclear establishment employs over twenty thousand people?"

"Including Jafar. He seems to have done well out of it anyway."

"Yes, of course, but we have brownouts in Lahore every day. How can you run businesses this way, I ask you? And these nuclear bombs, what use are they? To frighten India? Don't make me laugh! Meanwhile, this war in the north—it could be the end of Pakistan, you know? And no one knows what the hell to do about it."

I couldn't help him there.

Then he asked, "Suppose you find out this location. What will you do? Because if you are thinking that the Pakistani authorities will help, I cannot encourage you. And this plan of yours—I can't say I have much confidence in it."

"I don't either, but it was all we could think of. As you say, we can't expect much help from the authorities here."

"Yes, but I wish you had come up with something that did not involve yet another violation of our sovereignty. Poor Pakistan: caught between monsters, and yet we persist in twisting all their tails."

He reached into a jacket pocket, removed a business card case, and wrote on the back of one of the cards with a gold ballpoint. Handing it to me he said, "This is a cell-phone number reserved for the family. If you need my help, do call, any hour. I have a very wide reach throughout Pakistan, and most problems can be solved with a proper infusion of money. It is, unfortunately, a national trait." He laughed and patted my shoulder. "Or fortunately, I should say, in the present case."

And then we drifted back over to the other group and the rest of the evening was devoted to talk about sports and stuff, and Nisar said he could offer me a car and a driver, if I wanted to travel north—it was safer, after all—which I gratefully declined. After a while the ladies came out and we chatted amiably under the stars. It was nice enough but it was not like an evening at Laghari Sahib's.

℞

The next morning I woke up early, the sky still bright pink, with little flags of the palest blue attached. I'd had a dream that the family party I'd just been at was my regular life, that the bomb had not gone off, that Laghari Sahib was still there at the head of the table and that I'd been raised and educated in Pakistan, and never been a mujahid or an American soldier, and that I was telling everyone at the table a dream I'd had, a nightmare, which was my real life and everyone thought it was awful, and for a few seconds when I woke up I didn't know which life was real.

I dressed in my American traveling clothes and went downstairs. I found Hassan and Iqbal having tea and *parathas* for breakfast, and I joined them. There's something intimate about breakfast; more than the other meals it reminds you of home and how your mother used to make your eggs and toast just right—if you had that kind of mother, which I didn't. These parathas and this tea tasted exactly like what I used to eat every morning when I was a kid in my grandfather's house, and waves of aching memory overcame me and I fell back into my dream a little until I realized that Iqbal was talking to me. Did I still follow cricket in the U.S.? So I snapped out of it and we talked about cricket and baseball, differences, similarities, and so on, a nice easy conversation. I said I needed a vehicle and Hassan asked if I could ride a motorcycle and I said I could, and just like that he handed me the keys to his and said I could use it as long as I wanted.

Iqbal said he had to go check his e-mail, to eye-rolling and jibes from his brother, and when he came back he had a piece of paper in his hand and a troubled expression on his face.

He handed me the paper and said, "It's from your father. It was encrypted so I decrypted it and printed it out for you. I hope you don't mind."

I read the note. Hassan asked, "Bad news?"

"Sort of. My father says someone in NSA seems to have almost sniffed out what we're doing. A woman, apparently, a translator named Cynthia Lam."

"How did she find out?" asked Iqbal.

"He doesn't say."

"And how did he find out she suspects us?" asked Hassan. "I thought NSA was the topmost of top secrets."

"It is," I said. "But everything has leaks. My dad says he got the tip from a man named Afridi, and Afridi got it from sources he won't reveal, as my father says discreetly. Afridi was some kind of CIA asset in the Russian jihad, and apparently he still has contacts with the spooks. But all that doesn't matter. The question is, what do we do about it?"

Iqbal was looking at the paper over my shoulder. "I noticed he has obtained her home e-mail and IP address. And her taxpayer ID number and bank information."

"Yeah, I'd sort of like to know where that came from. But obviously someone in Washington is supplying this information about her in the hopes that we'll figure out some way to distract her or discredit her long enough to pull this thing off. I'm open to suggestions, gentlemen. This is definitely not my department."

They had a number of suggestions, and I left the doing of them in their capable, devious hands. They seemed to regard it as some kind of game, which I guess it was for them, and I got myself together to do my part. It would not be nearly as gamelike.

℞

I went out to the garage and found Hassan's bike, a six-year-old Ducati ST in decent shape, and rode it back into the old city and the Urdu Bazaar in Anarkali. Lahore traffic was as I recalled it, maybe a little worse—more motorcycles, bigger trucks—but the same sense of riding in a circus parade operated by crazy people. Again I had the sense of dipping into an alternate existence, and also the feeling that I was comfortable in a way I was never comfortable when driving my rental through the streets of Washington—and even more at ease when I bought a Chinese fatigue jacket, a couple of shalwar kameez outfits, bull-hide sandals, and a scarf and kufi hat at a shop and changed my clothes in the back of it, wrapping my head with the scarf Pashtun style, my hands moving without thought.

Out on the street again, I swaggered around like a hill man in the big city and bought a couple of prepaid cell phones, a carton of Marlboros, and a tin hand mirror, so I could admire my beauty or kohl my eyes, and also a nylon duffel bag to put all that and my other clothes in. That done, I wandered through the bazaar and had tea and Afghan bread in a stall that Gul Muhammed used to like. The man there looked me over and addressed me in Pashto, we had the usual polite conversation, and once again memories rolled over me like heavy surf and I had to struggle not to drown in them.

After that I took the bike up Circular Road, around the old city walls to the M2, and took that north to the M1 at Pindi and on to Peshawar. Oh, the highways of my native land! Imagine an L.A. freeway's worth of traffic on a busted two-lane blacktop, and every truck is overloaded and painted like the calliope in a carousel, and the traffic laws are a legend no one believes in anymore, and instead of safety equipment they have inscriptions from the Qur'an painted all over the vehicles. I made good time, though, on Hassan's hot bike, not almost dying more than thrice, and reached Peshawar in the late afternoon.

To understand Peshawar you have to imagine that the crack wars they had in New York a few years ago never ended but got worse, and then the crack lords took over the whole city, and the main industries became dope, guns, and smuggling. They still get tourists, although it's one of the few places in the world where armed guards are a major sector of the hospitality industry. Again, I felt right at home.

I stuck to the Kohat Road, avoiding the tangle of the old city, and headed straight for the Cantonment, which is where the old Raj used to hang out and which is now occupied by the new ruling classes. My clan cousin Bacha Khan had bought a huge white bungalow behind a high white wall. When I told the guards who I was they showed me right in, with peculiar expressions on their faces. It's hard to impress a Pashtun, and I was glad to see what looked like awe on their faces, and that the name Kakay Ghazan was still remembered.

Bacha himself, I saw, remained in contention for the title of Fattest Pashtun. He bear-hugged me and sat me down on his right hand and plied me with mint tea and sweetmeats. After we had paid each other the usual compliments, asked about each other's sons, and him expressing shock and sorrow when I said I had none, he said, "I swear before God this is like a visit from a ghost. One day you are here and the next you are gone. We thought you were dead. And now, almost twenty years later, you appear at my door. It is like a story, with djinni. Tell me now, where have you been?"

I told him what had happened to me back then and how my life had progressed since. When I was done he said, "So now you fight for the Americans instead of God. Forgive me if I don't say that is a step in the right direction."

I said I was leaving the army, maybe leaving America as well.

He grinned widely, and I noticed he'd had a lot of expensive dental work done.

"Are you seeking work, then?" he asked. "Because if you are, I could find an honored place for you in my business. As you see, I am prospering in a modest way."

He gestured to the room, which was full of the kind of junk—ugly massive gilt furniture, enormous TVs and stereos—that you see across the world in the houses of very poor people who have come overnight into large sums of cash.

"What would that business be, cousin?"

"Oh, you know, import-export, various forms of trading."

That meant he was a drug dealer, an arms dealer, or both.

"I'm flattered that you should think to include an ordinary soldier such as myself in your business. Gul Muhammed my father would be very pleased, and honored too."

He nodded and asked, "And your father, he is well?"

"That is a question I hoped you could answer, cousin. It is a source of great shame to me that I have not seen or heard from Gul Muhammed all these many years. And unfortunately, in the times I have been in Afghanistan, my business was such that I could not make inquiries. But from what you say, he is alive?"

"I have not heard of his death, which is not the same thing," said Bacha Khan.

"Where is he? Do you know?"

Bacha Khan seemed to consider this question for a long time. He slurped tea. He put his cup down and said, "The last I heard he was in a safe place, or as safe as a man with as many enemies as Gul Muhammed can ever be."

"And can the son of Gul Muhammed know this place?"

I got a genial smile here. "Of course you can, although, you know, I would not like to misinform you. If God still preserves him, Gul Muhammed moves about a good deal. But I can get a message to him saying his son Kakay Ghazan has returned, and he will reply to me saying where and when you will meet. I am sure he will have great joy in hearing this news."

"I hope so," I said reverently, and asked, "And what of his son, my brother, Wazir? Is he still among the living?"

He shook his head sadly. "I think not. I think the war ate him—I mean the war after the Russian war. In any case he vanished, who knows how? It was a great blow to your father."

"Yes, and to me as well. Please, can you tell me where his grave lies? I would like to honor it with a visit."

He shrugged. "Who can tell? All of Afghanistan is a grave."

I understood the situation now. Of course he was not going to tell me where Wazir's grave was because that would be where Gul Muhammed was as well. Bacha Khan was a businessman; information has value, it's a kind of virtual heroin. He had to decide how best to turn the news of my arrival to his advantage. He was Gul Muhammed's kinsman, yes, but I had no idea what their relationship was at this point. Cousins kill one another all the time among the Pashtuns, and Pashtunistan has always been a place of infinitely tangled and conflicting loyalties. A man like Bacha Khan had to balance the government, which he bribed, against the Taliban, who more or less controlled the region, and whose various chiefs had to be bribed as well; and then there were the criminal bands, whose alliances and interests had to be considered, and he also had to take into account the various clan and personal vendettas that had been going on since forever. The thought of my American comrades trying to operate among these people made me smile.

My host took this as a good sign, and he smiled too and patted my knee. "I will send the message this very hour, God willing. Now, you will stay with me, of course. I have plenty of room."

"That's very generous, cousin, but I regret that urgent business calls me away."

"What! Not even for two days? Come, reconsider! I will kill a sheep for you; we'll have a feast, as in the old days of the Russian jihad."

"Perhaps another time, when my business is done," I said. "Nothing would give me greater pleasure."

He stopped smiling now. "What sort of business?"

"Personal business," I said. "An affair of the heart."

A smile bloomed again. "Oh, well, then, of course."

"Yes, and I will need some equipment, cousin. Tell me, does Masoud still keep his shop in Karkhani?"

"You require weapons? I can give you anything you need."

"Again, you're most generous, but I have special needs, and besides I would like to see Masoud again and remember our old times. And I would also like to go by Kachagari to see if I have any friends left there." This reminded him that I was a considerable person and might have connections in the refugee camps outside of his control.

"Well, then, do as you think best," he said lightly. "But, cousin, you will find things much changed in this part of the world. It is hard to know who to trust nowadays."

"As opposed to the past, when the Pashtuns were famous for their fidelity?"

266 | Michael Gruber

A brief confusion on his face, then he laughed, and for somewhat longer than the remark was worth.

After that I had to refuse an armed escort to Karkhani, and we parted good pals. I left him my new cell number and he agreed to call me about Gul Muhammed. Bacha Khan could not actually kill me himself, because he was bound by *pashtunwali* as my host, but he could certainly sell me to someone else, in the most indirect way possible. Or perhaps he was as he seemed, a kinsman who wished me and my father well. That I could not determine which of these two possibilities was true merely meant that I had entered once more into the chronic insecurity of Pashtun tribal culture. You just live with it; it can even get to be enjoyable in a funny way, especially to an adrenaline junkie like me. As Ghalib says:

> The steed of life gallops on
> Out of control.
> My hand no longer holds the reins,
> The stirrups are torn away.
> Who know where it will stop?
> Who cares?

Karkhani is the famous smuggler's bazaar of the Khyber Pass. It's run by Afridi Pashtuns and has been since the Raj, the deal here being that the Afridis undertake to keep the pass open and the government undertakes not to interfere with the sale of smuggled goods. It has two sections, one full of fairly ordinary shops selling appliances, electronics, and other homely products to tourists and Pakistanis (what we have instead of Costco, in other words), and a restricted section, closed to foreigners, where they sell guns, opium, heroin, and hashish. I walked right into the restricted section through the checkpoint, the guards didn't give me a second look, and directly over to Masoud's shop. I hadn't seen him in twenty years, but we recognized each other all right; we embraced, and he took me to the little terrace behind the shop where he entertained honored guests or special customers and suppliers. He had about a dozen sons by now and all of them gathered on the terrace and stared at us boldly while we drank tea, and the word spread through the neighbor- hood, and soon the mud walls around the terrace were lined with faces, all there to gawk at legendary me.

I brought up the subject of Gul Muhammed, and Masoud said he'd heard that he was living in Afghanistan, in hiding, more or less. He'd been active in the war against the Taliban and they'd put a price on his head. But he didn't know what village he was in. I asked him if he'd ever heard of al-Faran.

He stroked his beard. "Yes, I think so. There are so many groups it's hard to keep them straight. You would not believe what a good AK fetches now, even a Dara copy; the demand is out of control."

"It's the insurgency," I said.

"Yes, the jihad against the Americans, although in the Russian jihad we had the opposite problem, the Americans and the Saudis were sending so many weapons it was almost impossible to make a living."

"But as to al-Faran?"

"Yes, if I am not mistaken, this is a group based in Swat, I forget where, one of the groups doing jihad against the idolators in Kashmir. I think I sold them some rockets last year. Why do you want to know?"

"They kidnapped some foreigners. One of them is a relative of mine. I'd like to see if there is anything I can do to get them released."

"Oh, yes. That was on the news. Of course they used this al-Faran, but everyone knows that that was an ISI operation."

"Do they?"

"Of course. Al-Faran does not take a shit without ISI telling them where to drop it. It was that rich American they wanted. They will have a huge ransom and then they will use the money to fund a coup."

"And what about the others?"

He brought the edge of his hand sharply down on the back of his neck. "On videos. This is to show that al-Faran are true mujahideen and not merely pawns of ISI. And they will sell a lot of videos, too, with so many executions. I have some in my shop, if you would care to watch one."

"Not today, thank you," I said.

"Then how may I serve Kakay Ghazan?" All business now.

I asked him whether he had any of those Speznatz Stechkins left. He grinned and said he did, and we both talked about the day me and Wazir had brought him a case of twenty-four that our group had won in one of our ambushes.

The Stechkin is basically a machine gun you can put in your pocket, and this batch had been modified for the Soviet special forces to include folding wire stocks and silencers. They're rare now, and extremely expensive, but Masoud gave me the mujahid discount, and I also bought Makarov 9-mm ammunition for the thing, and five extra magazines.

We took my purchases out to the testing range, which was the roof. They don't do returns in Karkhani, so you have to make sure the gun works before you leave the shop. I fired the Stechkin on both single-shot and full auto, and it worked fine.

I loaded all the magazines and slung it in its odd wooden holster by a strap around my neck and shoulders, concealing it under my Chinese jacket. I skipped visiting the camp. It was getting late and my bad leg was acting up, complaining about the pounding I was taking from the bike on the bad roads. I went back into Peshawar to the Qissa Khwani Bazaar and had dinner at the Salateen Hotel, which makes the best mutton *karhai* in the world. I could've used a drink, but there wasn't one on offer, which I took as a bad sign for the future of Peshawar.

When I got back to my bike and paid off the street kids I had hired to watch it, I noticed a brown Toyota hatchback with a bent front bumper parked nearby, and I seemed to recall seeing it before, maybe in Kharkani, maybe earlier on the trip, but I was aching and tired now, and I didn't think much about it; there are lots of brown Toyotas. Leaning against it were two men. One was a burly guy, a Punjabi by the look of him, wearing a khaki safari shirt and slacks. He had cropped hair, aviator sunglasses, and a neat brush mustache, and I thought *soldier*. The man he was with was taller and thinner, a Pashtun, in a shalwar kameez and a round white hat. His beard was thick, long, and black, dropping from peculiar knobby cheekbones that stood out like a couple of golf balls in the rough. In Peshawar they don't wear T-shirts with TALIBAN written on them, but you can tell who they are.

They seemed to be arguing when I strolled up, but they stopped and the two of them stared at me, and I looked at them and gave them a polite nod. I got on the bike and rode off.

About twenty klicks south of the city, on the long grade up to the Kohat Pass, I saw the same brown Toyota again in my rearview mirror, coming up fast on my tail. I slowed a little and pulled to the left to let him pass, Sometimes in a combat situation you see a threat emerging, or rather you feel it's going to happen without really knowing how you know, your mind has just put together a bunch of unconscious details, and so you don't go through a door or stick your head up or whatever, and I had that feeling then.

So when the Toyota swerved violently toward me to knock me off the road, I jammed on the brakes and put the bike down and skidded for about forty feet, throwing sparks and tearing the leg off my trousers along with some patches of skin. I saw the hatchback screech to a halt in a cloud of dust and then pull a U-ey and come running back to where I was. It stopped and the passenger door and the two rear doors popped open and three guys got out, the military dude from the bazaar, hefting an AK, and two guys I'd never seen before, short wide men who had the dark skin and flat faces of Tajiks.

I pulled myself away from the motorcycle and got to one knee, my upper body bent over like I was hurting, and I lifted the Stechkin from its holster and thumbed it to full auto, and when they were about two yards from me I knocked the three of them over with one long burst.

I pointed the pistol at the driver and yelled out in Urdu to lift his hands from the wheel and get out of the car. After a brief hesitation he did so, and I made him sit on the ground with his hands behind his head. I looked him over: early twenties, shortish hair, a mustache. I figured him for a Punjabi soldier or cop of some kind. He was shaking slightly, like a bush in a faint breeze. I leaned over and checked out his hands.

I know guys who like this part, but I've never cared for it, it's not combat anymore, and it's embarrassing, to me at least, to have that kind of power over a human person. On the other hand, there are situations, like this one, where you need information.

I said, "What is this all about, brother? Why did you want to kill me?"

"Oh, God, are you going to shoot me now? Oh, God!"

"No, of course not. You are no threat to me, Naik. Is it naik?"

He dared a look up at my face. "Lance-naik. I am only a driver, sir."

"What's your name?"

"Shabbir Hussain."

"Very well, Lance-naik Hussain, why was your officer trying to kill me?"

"He wasn't trying to kill you! He was going to give you to those Afghans and they would take you away. He would put it out as a kidnapping. It happens all the time on these roads."

"And why was . . . this officer, what was his name and rank?"

"Captain Ahmed Waqar."

"What unit?"

He lowered his face. "I am not allowed to say."

"Don't be stupid, Shabbir. You have no choice, and no one will ever know what passed between us. I am trying to save your life, so help me, please. What unit?"

"Intelligence. But I am only a driver. I don't know anything."

"Thank you. And now, why was Captain Waqar of the ISI trying to have me kidnapped?"

"I told you, sir. I am only a driver."

"Yes, you keep saying. Would you like a cigarette?"

He would. I gave him one and let him smoke half of it in silence. Then I said, "Let's begin again, and let's not continue with this story that you're only a driver. An ISI captain on a mission like this would not take along a lance-naik driver. He would require someone who could take charge if he were out of action, perhaps a senior NCO, a *havildar* major or a *subedar*, and you are too young to be either of those, so I suspect you are a lieutenant. And by the way, lieutenant, drivers have little cuts and scars on their hands and grease around their fingernails. You have never changed even an oil filter with those soft hands."

He took in this comment and his shoulders sagged.

"Shoot me, if you like," he said sullenly. "I'm not saying anything more."

"Why not? Captain Waqar is dead, and your main problem will be figuring out what to tell Major Laghari when you return to Pindi. Fortunately, I understand he's not too bright, so you should have little difficulty making up a plausible story."

He stared up at me. "How did you know—" he began and then realized his mistake.

"How did I know you were sent by Major Laghari? Because, my friend, you have been suckered into a family affair. Major Seyd Laghari is my uncle. I bet he didn't tell you that."

He gaped at me. "No. He said you were an American spy."

"I'm sure. Well, the fact is I'm not here to spy on Pakistan. I'm here to look for my mother. She's one of the people kidnapped with William Craig. You'd know all about that, too, wouldn't you?"

I was looking into his eyes when I said that, and I saw them register surprise and something deeper too. Perhaps guilty knowledge. I thought then that Lieutenant Hussain did not have a shining future as an intelligence agent if he could not lie more convincingly.

"And the Taliban that Captain Waqar was talking to in Peshawar. What's his story?"

"I don't know," said the lieutenant sullenly. "Some Afghan."

"Name?"

"Baz Khatak."

"Who is he?"

"Nobody. An informant."

An insurgent was more like it, but I didn't press it because I thought I'd got everything I was going to get out of Lieutenant Hussain without actual torture. I made him drag his boss's body back to the Toyota and heave it into the back compartment, and all the time he was doing that he kept looking at me, like I was going to pull some fiendish trick of the kind we Americans are famous for, maybe shoot him at the last minute. But I did not, and instead made him toss the dead Tajiks and the AK down the dropoff and let him get in his car and drive away.

The Ducati had lost some of its fairing but it was still in running order and I used it to return to Peshawar, because I was not going to try to drive back to Lahore with ISI searching the roads, as they would be as soon as the lieutenant called in what had gone down. I should have capped the poor bastard, but I didn't have the heart; he looked too much like my cousin Hassan, even though I've shot dozens of people who resemble my relatives. It was just not his day to die.

15

When Rashida comes in the next morning with the eternal naan, dal, and tea, Ashton says, in reasonable Pashto, "Rashida, my gazelle, where are my eggs and bacon? I specifically ordered eggs and bacon this morning, and whole-wheat toast, and strong coffee."

Rashida ignores him as she always does. She does not acknowedge the presence of strange men; she places her tray and tugs her dupatta more tightly around her face.

"Well, if I can't get a decent breakfast, we're never stopping here again," he continues. "What do you say, Schildkraut? Next time we'll do the Pearl, I think. Baths, coffee, *and*, I believe, they don't do decapitations."

Schildkraut smiles thinly at this, and the captives all gather around the breakfast tray, except for Sonia. She has observed Rashida's subtle signal. She rises from her charpoy and follows the girl into a corner of the room.

Rashida raises her arm, flashing a clutch of gold bangles, and, grinning, says, "I am betrothed to Batur. God willing, we will be married as soon as my father has sold three cows and can pay the *walwër*. Perhaps it will be one week from now."

"God's blessings be on you and him and may you have twenty sons," says Sonia, embracing the girl.

"Thanks in the name of God," says Rashida, "but it will be a poor wedding, without sweetmeats and wedding clothes, if the emir does not open the road to Mingaora before then. We hear there will be another chop soon," she adds in a lowered voice.

"Why will there be another chop soon, Rashida?"

"Because the infidels have made an attack on a place where many of the leaders of the jihad are staying, I don't know where, and some may have been killed. Everyone is talking about this, and waiting to see if any were killed, God forbid. And if any were, one of you will be chopped. But it will not be you; you will be the last of all. Or that is what they say."

"I see. Then I will tell my friends. Is this the reason the roads are closed?"

"No, the road is closed because of the bombs. We have many strangers coming in trucks to take the bombs away to Afghanistan to destroy the tanks of the crusaders there, which is a very good thing. Even in Iraq they will use our bombs, they say. They are in silver cases with the name of God marked on the outside. It is a great secret, so they close the roads against spies like you. We are not supposed to look, but no one notices a girl."

She lets her dupatta slip away from her face, and Sonia can see that her perfect bisque forehead is knotted with worry.

"Anyway, that's not what I wanted to tell you. The emir is very angry with you. He is angry with Idris, but it is about you. He says if you do not stop interpreting dreams falsely he will put you back in the goat pen and beat you. And Idris says he shall not and they fought, and only Abu Lais stood in their way or their men would have spilt blood. My cousin Amira was cleaning in the house, and she heard it all."

"This Abu Lais must be a great man."

"Yes, they say so. He is a real Pashtun from a good family, not like the emir, who is a mongrel dog, my father says, although he buys loyalty with his money. Abu Lais has made the bombs, which is a good thing, but he eats with Arabs, whom no one likes. They cannot speak properly and they smell wrong, although they say they are Muslims. But everyone must respect Abu Lais, because he is a brother of the sheikh Osama and Mullah Omar. So now you are warned. I hope they don't whip you, because I don't think that the women can save you again."

Sonia thanks the girl, who gives a quick smile, veils herself, and leaves the room. Sonia goes back to the prisoners, who are still eating their breakfast. Manjit makes a place for her and shows that he has saved her four slabs of naan and a mound of dal. Her tea has cooled but she drinks it and eats the food gratefully, despite the tension she feels among her fellows. She tells Amin what she has learned from Rashida.

Amin waits until they have finished eating, then clears his throat and says, "Yesterday we lost our friend Porter Cosgrove. We now have information that there is to be another victim, so we must have another drawing of the cards."

"*Sonderkommando.*" This from Ashton, half underneath his breath.

"Excuse me?" says Amin, but Ashton shakes his head and looks nastily at Sonia. Amin continues to stare at him, waiting.

Schildkraut says into this silence, "I believe Harold was referring to those Jews in the Nazi camps who, in order to live a few months longer, managed the actual execution of their fellow inmates. They were called *sonderkommando.*"

"Well," says Amin. "Remarkable. I didn't know that. And you believe, Harold, that our moral situation is the same?"

Ashton shrugs. "How is it different? We're cooperating in our own destruction in order to live a little longer. We're participating in this obscene lottery for just that reason."

Manjit Nara says, "I thought we were turning cards to avoid an even more obscene situation, which is leaving Sonia with the task of choosing each of us for death. I thought it a gesture, you know, of human solidarity."

"Is that what it is? It seems to me more like sheep milling about and baaing over who's first for the chop. *Human* solidarity would be bending every nerve at a plan to get out of this fucking place. I was ready with such a plan, as some of you know, and had we been allowed to carry it out, Annette and I might have been miles away by now, armed and in a vehicle, quite possibly in contact with the authorities. A rescue mission might even now have been in the works. But *she* decided it would be preferable to curry favor with her co-religionists and betray us."

They all look at Sonia for an instant, like a literal flock when a predator steps into the fold, and then drop their eyes. Amin says, with exhaustion now showing in his voice, "Harold, really, you can dismiss that idea from your mind. I have known Sonia for years. She is the last one to sympathize with the Taliban, and I cannot for a moment believe that she, as you say, betrayed you."

"But I did," says Sonia; all eyes are on her again, their expressions range from puzzlement, through shocked amazement, to hatred on the part of both Ashton and the widow Cosgrove. "And I must disagree with Harold. If I'd let you go on with your plan, you would not now be either safe or even approaching safety. Harold would be dead, and probably not in a way anywhere near as quick as decapitation, Annette would be pegged out on the ground with her legs spread apart in a place with a very long line of men outside it, and the rest of us would have spent the remainder of our lives tied up with wires and lying in our own piss."

"It was our risk!" cries Annette. "You had no right to make that decision for us."

"I had every right, and a responsibility also, simply because I understand our situation and you don't. This area is completely controlled by the Taliban. That's why they brought us here, and that's why there's an important weapons factory next door. It obviously has reasonable cellphone service, because as you might have seen during our last outing every third man is talking into a cell phone. As far as vehicles go, you must know that in this country they pull the distributor rotors at night the way they used to hobble their horses, so you would not have been able to steal a truck. And even if you had, the region for a hundred square miles would have been raised against you, every track would've been blocked and guarded, and as far as leaving the roads and going cross-country, do you honestly believe that a slightly pudgy English academic and an American woman could escape across these mountains from a thousand armed Pashtuns? A pair of SAS commandos in peak training might have a ghost of a chance, but not you."

Ashton, red-faced, begins to object—he is making braying noises in the English manner—but Schildkraut places a restraining hand on his shoulder and says, "Enough, Harold! Sonia is perfectly correct. Her method stands a better chance of success than yours does."

"What method?" Ashton demands. "What are you talking about?"

"I am talking about where Sonia goes every night and what she does there. Are none of you curious?"

Ashton says, "On present evidence, she's telling tales about all our little doings—"

But Annette says, "She's interpreting dreams. She must've done half the village by now."

"Marvelous!" says Ashton. "Even more mumbo-jumbo. I don't see where that's to our advantage, unless you're telling them that their dreams mean they should let us all go. Are you?"

"No," says Sonia. "I give them as honest an interpretation as I can."

"Then what good is it?" says Ashton.

"I don't know," says Sonia, "but I'm certainly not going to try to manipulate them. They'd sniff that out in a minute. They're suspicious enough as it is."

Shea asks, "Then what did Karl-Heinz mean by success? What *did* you mean?"

Schildkraut answers, "You know, I have asked myself the same question many times in these empty hours we all have. And being Germanic, of course I have arrived at a theory. Would you like to hear it? Very well.

"We all had a discussion some little time ago about the psychological state of the people in this part of the world, in which it was argued that therapy here must consist of adjustments in external relationships, since the psyche in traditional Muslims is not a struggle among interior drives, as it has long been held to be in the West, but something much simpler. Here an individual's main drive is to fit in, to achieve harmony and satisfaction as a member of a family or larger group. True enough as far as it goes. But we must also remember that these people are believers. The unseen world is very real to them." He picks up a fragment of chapati. "It is as real as bread. And that is something that is difficult if not impossible for us unbelievers to comprehend."

"I beg your pardon," says Father Shea. "I am certainly not an unbeliever, nor is Amin. Nor Sonia."

"Ah, yes, but I meant we come from the unbelieving *world*. To be a believer in the West, one must continually swim upstream, as it were. The society around us has essentially returned to paganism, and we are quite content in it."

"Surely not in America," Shea objects. "It's one of the most religious societies on earth."

"Not at all. Sentimental churchgoing is not what I mean by belief. What America *believes* in is progress, money, sex, fame, and military strength, with a national philosophy based on pragmatism. This is a good thing, you know. You don't want a nation as powerful as the U.S. to be actually religious. But here we are still in the original state of religious intoxication; here we are still literally in the fifteenth century, as they reckon time, and arguments based on rationality are of no use. Appeals to our liberal icons—democracy, the rule of law, the open society, civil liberties—fall on deaf ears. So Sonia works at the other end of things. She inserts herself into their consciousness, she accepts their religious beliefs, their ideas about the nature of the world and their various roles in it, and so she exerts her influence. Am I correct in this, Sonia?"

All eyes turn now to Sonia. All the faces except Ashton's wear a distressingly hopeful look. She says, "To an extent. It's the case that our hosts are not susceptible to ordinary argument, and that they are in a psychic state where the unseen world is real, as Dr. Schildkraut pointed out. But I am not seeking to influence them. I'm trying to help them. It's what I do. It may turn out that by helping them I help us, but that's not my purpose. It's also true that I have entered, to the extent I can, into their psychic space. All real therapists do that as a matter of course. And what is this psychic state?

"At some level they must be deeply conflicted, because they are making war and murdering innocents in the name of a merciful and compassionate God. At some level they know that they are not engaged in a real jihad. No one is preventing them from the full practice of their religion and they are fighting the forces of a Muslim nation. Besides that, they are Pashtuns, and the sort of religion practiced by the Taliban is not congenial to them and never has been; this region is thick with the shrines of Sufi saints. In Afghanistan the people only accepted Taliban rule because the alternative was a naked and brutal anarchy. And their dreams reflect this. This morning Rashida told me that they are already arguing about me, but what effect this will have on our situation I can't say. It may get us killed faster, for all I know."

"Then for God's sake why don't you stop it!" Ashton snaps.

"I told you already. It's what I do. If these days are the final ones of my life, what else should I be doing? I've always tried to live my life so that if death arrived on a particular day it would find me doing nothing but what God had made me for. I sincerely hope all of you feel the same way."

There is an embarrassed silence. Amin breaks it. "You are right, of course. As the head of a charitable trust I hereby pledge one of my chapatis to be distributed to the poor. Annette is a nurse, and she has already started to comfort Karl-Heinz, who is ill. I'm sure he is contemplating ethical issues all the while. Father Shea, I observe, prays often. Manjit, I insist that you dispense me a powerful tranquilizer."

The Indian laughs. "If only I could! Although I would be happy to instruct you in yoga. A few exercises and I assure you that you will despise Haldol."

"Excellent! Well, now we must return to the business of the day, which I have already outlined. How shall we proceed in the matter of the cards?"

After a short discussion they decide to draw immediately, the loser to be the next victim when and if one is needed, that person to have the next presentation. As before, they each cut the deck and Sonia deals one card to each. As before, Ashton turns his over first. It is the deuce of clubs.

He says, "Well, fuck!"

Amin breaks the somber silence. "I am sorry, Harold. Truly sorry. You will give your presentation, I trust?"

"Oh, I'll give it. I'll give them an earful. You'll forgive me if I wait for the fatal day itself." With that he walks off.

All the others have middling cards, except Annette, who has drawn the queen of hearts. She goes over to where Ashton lies on his charpoy and speaks softly to him. The others do not hear what she says, but they hear Ashton's snarling, obscene reply. She walks to her own bed and lies on it, pulling a blanket over herself.

Amin gathers the cards from where they lie scattered, shuffles them idly, and then says, "Well, we must pass the time. Would anyone like to play bridge?"

It turns out that Shea, Nara, and Schildkraut are all bridge players. They push charpoys together, designate one as the table, and begin playing. Sonia walks to where Ashton is lying and stands over him.

"What in hell do you want?" he says.

"To talk to you."

"Oh, fuck off!"

She sits on the edge of his charpoy. "No. One of the disadvantages of prison is you can no longer select your visitors. I want to ask whether you intend to come apart like Cosgrove."

"You mean will I cry and wet myself? What business is it of yours?"

"Because how you die is important. It's important to this group, with respect to maintaining our spirits and our sanity and even more so with respect to how it's regarded by the Pashtuns."

"Oh, really? Is this a case for showing the flag in my last moments? The stiff upper lip? Bugger all that!"

"Yes, you're in the period of self-pity. *Oh, why me?* It's not attractive, Ashton, and unworthy of you. I'm prepared to wait until it dissipates."

Ashton's face reddens and he sits up and puts it close to hers. "You know what my chief regret is? Well, my two chief regrets. One is I've never had a fuck in an airliner toilet, and the other is that I'm not going to see you hacked into pieces. Isn't that what they do to blasphemers? A leg from one side and an arm from the other?"

"According to some interpretations of sharia. Other variants require crucifixion or stoning. And it's good that you're angry. Angry and brave is a good combination. I think you're a brave man, Ashton. It was brave to try to escape, stupid but brave, as you must have known. You're not a fool. You've been traveling in this area for years. Manjit thinks you're a spook, in fact. Are you?"

"If I were, you would be absolutely the last one I'd tell."

"I'll take that as a yes. So, since you're brave, I'm imagining that you're not afraid of dying per se, but object to the manner in which your death is going to be carried out. Is that it?"

Ashton stares at her. She meets his gaze. The staring goes on for what feels like a long time, after which she sees something change in his eyes, not resignation but a different form of anger, no longer directed at her but focused properly, on the guilty.

"Since you ask," he says, in an artificially perky tone, "I do object. I never thought I'd make old bones, and I have to say the thought of snuffing out now is preferable to the way my parents died, with the tubes and the stinks, but what I can't bear is being slaughtered like a sheep while those fuckers cheer. Isn't that odd? I mean, why should one care? But I do. It gripes me."

"I thought as much. It would gripe me too. Tell me, can you handle a Kalashnikov?"

For the first time in many days, she saw a smile flicker onto his face. "If I were a spy, I could, couldn't I? Do you have one tucked away?"

"No. But neither do you have to die like a sheep. Listen!"

They talk for some minutes and then Sonia goes back to the bridge players. The day wears on, but no one comes to the door to demand the next victim. Dhuhr and Ashr prayers are called, and the game pauses while Amin and Sonia pray. Schildkraut has a coughing fit that does not stop, and they make him lie down. Annette is roused from her lethargy by the call of her patient. She nurses him as best she can with the scant contents of her medical kit, but he is gray in the face, with blue lips. The bridge game resumes, with Sonia as a fourth. She is not a bridge player, but she knows the rules and some of the simpler conventions. Manjit, who is the best player among them, takes her as his partner. After the Maghrib prayer they are fed their second meal of the day. They play cards for an hour or so after that, until it gets too dark. The Isha'a sounds. Those who pray, pray, and they all go to bed.

ૐ

Some of them even sleep. Sonia, lying awake, continues to be surprised at the resilience of her fellow humans. In the house of death there is eating, sleeping, joking, and the playing of cards—with the same deck, as it happens, that condemns them one by one to death. She can identify the different sleep noises of her fellows by now. Amin, Manjit, and Shea are asleep, Annette and Ashton are not. She reflects on the wonderful differences in temperament among people, how these are often confused with the virtues and vices.

Schildkraut has a spasm of coughing. It ends and she hears him sigh and say something in German but she does not catch the meaning; her German is not as good as it was. She goes to his bed and kneels down.

"How are you, Karl-Heinz?"

"I have been better, thank you for asking. To be perfectly frank, I am dying. I cannot seem to get enough air."

"Is your inhaler completely gone?"

"No, there remains another dose or two, but I am saving it for my presentation. I may be able to hang on until then."

"You may outlive us all, given sufficient luck. What were you saying just now? It was in German."

"Oh, nothing. A poem by Hölderlin that once meant much to Elsa and me. *Wohl geh' ich täglich.* I seem to be reviewing my life, somewhat banal of course, but I am grateful that my brain is still capable of processing memory. That is the great fear, naturally, that we will fade away and never know it, but it is not my luck, so to speak, that I will exit with all my faculties intact. Do you know the poem? *Wie lang ist's! O wie lange! Der Jüngling ist gealtert, selbst die Erde, die mir damals gelächelt, ist anders worden.* 'How long ago it is, oh, how long! My youth has aged, and even the earth that once smiled upon me has changed.' Or something like that. We used to sit and read poetry to each other, and I recall you saying you did the same with your husband. Elsa liked you very much."

"I liked her. She was very kind to me."

"To everyone. An actual Christian, one of the few I've met. I wish I could believe all of that, you know: some kind of life beyond the grave. It's been twelve years since she died and not a day goes by that I do not miss her. I dream of her often, and in these dreams she seems wise in a way that she did not in life. So... projection, wishful thinking? Or does the psyche transform itself and survive, although in a way that's not given to us to know? You've read Jung's essay on the hereafter? Annoyingly vague in my view, but perhaps I didn't understand him. Perhaps I should have stuck to psychotherapy and not wandered off into philosophy. And you, do you expect a place in heaven?"

"Hell, more than likely. But I've never been much for thinking about those things. The Prophet was always going into detail about Paradise, which was fine for him, but I think it's not in general a good thing for believers. Saint Paul tells us not to bother. Jung says that the psyche is not merely what we think of as the self but a transcendent thing that does not strictly obey the ordinary material laws, and maybe that unknown part of us is what survives; maybe the rind of the ego shreds away and reveals something that will surprise and delight all of us. Or horrify us, in the case of our brothers of the jihad. I certainly hope so. And he says further that there's a great deal of evidence for this belief, although our civilization has chosen quite arbitrarily to classify such evidence as *not* evidence— hallucination, wish fulfillment fantasy, and so on. As a matter of fact, while I was being tortured recently I had a visit from my old Sufi guide that saved my sanity. Perhaps a fantasy, but like Elsa in your dreams he told me things I didn't know, and in fact my sanity was saved. It's a free choice in the end, and I happen to have chosen faith."

"Tell me more about the Sufi guide," he says, and they speak of this and other things of the spirit until the old man drifts off into an exhausted sleep.

Sonia returns to her bed and waits. Without meaning to she falls asleep. She dreams, but remembers nothing when she is shaken awake. It is Mahmoud. Silently she slips into her sandals, pulls her dupatta over her head, and follows him out of the room.

He leads her through the inn and briefly outside, just long enough to feel the night wind on her face, and then past a group of silent men and through a door. He leaves her. The room is small and windowless and smells of musty cloth and the crude oil lamp in a wall niche that provides its only light. There is a charpoy in it, on which is seated Idris Ghulam.

She wishes him peace; he makes the formal reply. She asks, "Have you had any more dreams?"

"Yes, but it was not as you promised. It was not a good dream, but a bad one. It was a dream sent by Satan, the worst possible dream."

"Tell it."

"I can't. It's too shameful."

"Nothing of God's is shameful."

"Foolish woman! I told you this was given by Satan."

"Listen to me. There are no dreams given by Satan. Only God sends dreams and only for our own good."

"No, the Prophet, peace be upon him, says Satan sends bad dreams."

"Then perhaps we now know things about dreams that were unrevealed to the Prophet, on whom be peace."

"That is blasphemy."

"It is *not* blasphemy. When God spoke through the Prophet, peace be on him, he spoke eternal truths: the law, and how men may please God, and the proper way to behave, and how we may win Paradise. But he was also a man of his own time with the knowledge of his own time. No one but a fool would look in the holy Qur'an or the Hadith for knowledge about how to fix a truck or shoot a rifle or fly a helicopter. Have some sense! And I tell you that the knowledge of dreams has also advanced since the time of the Prophet, peace be upon him, and I have that knowledge, as you have already seen. I have now told you something that you were not prepared to hear when you first came to me, but now you are. God sends all dreams, even the ones we think evil. You are a brave man, and I am only a woman, and besides I am soon to die. So have courage and speak!"

After a silence, he does. "I dreamed I was on haj. I walked in my white clothes with the other pilgrims to the Great Mosque in Mecca, and walked around the Ka'aba the required seven times, and shouted each time, and I felt a great peace; I felt one with God and with my fellow Muslims. And then . . . and then, as if I were at home in my village, and the Ka'aba were only a shed, I lifted my robe and urinated on the Ka'aba. And if you ever tell anyone I said this I will cut your nose and ears off and put out your eyes."

"These threats are tedious and unnecessary, Idris. I have told you before that my honor is to keep secret the dreams told to me. So then what?"

"In the dream?"

"Of course in the dream! After you had polluted the most sacred place in all Islam, what happened?"

"Nothing happened. No one noticed and I did not feel any shame, until I awakened. In the dream I left the mosque and then I was in a market where they sell souvenirs of the haj, and I bought some wooden beads. The man who sold them to me was wearing a black robe and there was something familiar about his face, but I couldn't recall what it was. Then I was at a time later in the haj when the pilgrims go to Muzdalifa, where they gather pebbles to stone the Devil on the next day. There was a great crowd, and it was moving very slowly, and it was very hot. Then the man from the bead stall appeared by my side and he said, Why not walk by the side of the road as I am doing? It will be faster. And I did, but I found that my feet sank into the ground. It was quicksand and I couldn't move, I was sinking down to my neck, and it became one of those dreams where you can't move, and then I woke up shouting."

"Yes, this is a famous dream. It is a Sufi dream and was first recorded by Bashir ad-din Khorezmi of Bukhara, in the sixth century after the Hijra, and many times after that, not the same in details, of course, but the theme of polluting a holy place. And be assured, if many holy men have had such a dream, it is not demonic but from God. You are blessed to have had it. Now I will tell you what it means.

"The first thing to understand is that God has given us the law, but God is *not* the law. God is not contained, not even in the holy Qur'an. He is endless and infinite and all-powerful. We say a hundred times a day, *God controls all things*, but we do not really believe it, and so we sin constantly. And because no one can bear this sin on their souls, we say to ourselves, I am a good Muslim, I pray the prayers, I fast, I go on haj, I give alms, I even make jihad; and therefore it does not matter that I am cruel and corrupt and murderous. What does Rahman Baba say? *Recall the piety of the Devil, when you grow arrogant about your abstinence and obedience.* This is what God tells you in this dream: that it does not matter how pious you are, how closely you observe the letter of the fiqh, if you are not compassionate and merciful you pollute Islam. You piss on the Ka'aba."

Even in the dimness she can see Idris's face working, frowning, grimacing, as he struggles to absorb this. People locked into the heart of a religion often have difficulty thinking about God, and so it is with this man. He asks, "And what of the man in black and the quicksand on the way to Muzdalifa?"

"Oh, that. The man in black is death, of course. You said you could not recognize his face, although it seemed familiar. Well, you have faced death many times, but each time you forget what he looks like or you could not live for a minute. The beads represent the Sufi way, which calls to you. Give up violence, practice mercy, contemplate and love only God, and your life will be preserved. I see you don't believe me. Well, believe this. Yesterday you had a quarrel with the emir, Alakazai. He hates you and is jealous of your fame and authority—"

"Wait! How do you come to know this?"

"Idris, do you think you are the only one to whom God sends dreams? And so I say to you that your death is already arranged and it will come sooner rather than later. Tell me, do you know a man, a small man in a black-striped turban and a Russian jacket, with a scar on his face, who carries a stockless AK? He will be close to the emir."

"Yes, that is Sarbaz Khalid Khan. What about him?"

"He is the one charged with your death. And you must do nothing against him, because if you were to kill him or send him away, Alakazai would only find another, and that one I might not know. Instead, you must make sure that the next time you require a victim to murder, he is one of the guards as he was before. This is very important."

"Why is it important? I don't understand." He pulls at his beard in frustration, he slams his fist into his palm, a shocking sound in the tiny room. "My God, I must be insane to be listening to a woman teach me how to fight!"

"You are a fool if you believe I am a woman, Idris. Of course a woman could not tell you anything important. But that is only the face and body you see. Who interprets these dreams is not a woman but a man, Ismail Raza Ali, a Sufi of the Naqshbandiyya order, who dwells in me, although he has been in Paradise almost thirty years. I am only the string he plucks. He speaks to you through me."

She sees the whites of his eyes flash in the lamplight. "That is impossible."

"Yes," she says. "We say God can do all things, but we don't believe it."

16

I drove the bike back toward Peshawar for a while until I found a place with good cell reception, and then I dug out the card Nisar had given me and called the number. He answered right away and I told him what had happened and what I'd learned from the ISI lieutenant. He assumed I'd shot him too, and there was a silence on the line when I told him I hadn't.

"Well, in that case," he said, "you can't travel by road back to Lahore. I can arrange a helicopter—"

I said, "Thanks, Uncle, but I don't want to go back to Lahore. I have some business in Afghanistan."

"Afghanistan! You are mad! The ISI has made an attempt on your life and you're going to Afghanistan? You will be a marked man from Herat to Kandahar."

"Nevertheless, I'm going. Can you help me?"

"Let me think." More silence on the line. "Yes. I do a good deal of business with a security firm with an office in Kabul. Force Eight, it's called. If you can get to the freight area of Peshawar airport, I can have them put you on a plane. They're in and out of there all the time."

"Thank you, Uncle. I think I can manage that. By the way, have you heard anything from Iqbal?"

"Oh, Iqbal! I tell you, Theo, you have revolutionized that boy's life. His parents were going mad with him spending his entire existence on that damn computer, and at least now he has something useful to do with it. I cannot follow the details, but he has tapped me for a good deal of money and I can only trust that I will get it back."

This was not a topic I wanted to discuss over a cell phone, so we said good-bye and I headed for the airport. As it happened, I knew something about Force Eight Security Services International, because people in my line of work are prime recruits for their kind of operation, which is providing private armies in nasty places. They mainly do bodyguarding and site security where our own military is either not engaged or stretched too thin and where the local cops are unreliable. I had received a few polite inquiries myself, usually around the time my enlistment was about to run out, and my sense was they had the kind of political connections that would make stop-loss orders go away. I always told them I wasn't interested.

At the airport I bribed my way into the secure freight area as any regular terrorist might have done and rode my bike right up to a black-painted Caribou with the Force Eight logo painted on it, just like the firm was a regular nation. I had no trouble hitching a ride, because Nisar had cleared it with the higher-ups, and also I happened to know the pilot, a guy named Arnie Havens, who used to be with the 106th, what they call the Night Stalkers, the people who insert Deltas and other special operations troops. Incredible pilots, and I almost asked him what they were paying him, but I found I was sort of embarrassed about it. He seemed a little embarrassed too, to be there.

While I waited, I called Cousin Bacha Khan and told him what had happened to me and he expressed delight at my narrow escape. He seemed sincere over the phone, and I figured that was because he wasn't up for a bonus if the snatch succeeded. Maybe he hadn't even set it up. I said I was going to Afghanistan to look for Gul Muhammed and did he have any thoughts on that since I'd seen him last? And he said, "Your father is where you would expect to find him." So that was all right, because I knew where that was.

We took off and made the short hop to Kabul, and when I got out of the plane I found, not to my complete surprise, Buck Claiborne. He gave me a big bear hug, and I guess he could see I was not that enthusiastic and hoo-ah, and he asked me what was wrong and I told him I thought that at least he could've given me a call when he was about to dump the army, and I didn't appreciate finding out from the first sergeant, and he hemmed and hawed and said he didn't want to bother me about it, seeing as I was wounded and recovering and all, but I could see he was a little ashamed. Buck is not devious like me.

So we had that out and then he led me into a new Denali, black with the tinted glass. There was some construction going on in Kabul but the place still looked as wrecked as it did the last time I was there; it never really recovered from the Russian war, and I remember my colonel going on about how beautiful and peaceful it was when he was growing up there.

Force Eight had leased a big guesthouse in Shari Haw, near downtown Kabul, and fixed it up with new plumbing, air-conditioning, fresh paint, the works. They had their own generator, you could have pizza and hamburgers delivered if you wanted, and the feel of the place was like you were in a pretty good motel in Arizona. They had a big room downstairs with a fifty-inch plasma TV with a satellite feed, lounge chairs, a pool table, and a bar. When Buck took me in to show me around there was a baseball game on the TV and a few men in black jumpsuits with the Force Eight flash on them sat at the bar or in the chairs. Some funny looks flew around when I walked in with Buck. I got the impression that the only Pashtuns who came through here were servants, and they relaxed when Buck told them I was a regular white guy in disguise. As he thinks.

Buck introduced me to the bartender, an Afghan he called Gus, who spoke English with an American accent. He'd spent six years in Fresno and was pretty much like any suburban bartender in the States. He served us ice-cold Buds.

Buck saw me take in the room and said, "Pretty fucking neat, huh? A far cry from."

"Yeah, it's pretty neat, all right," I agreed. "The company pays for all this?"

"Oh, yeah. They treat us real nice."

"What do you-all do?"

"Protect the diplomats, mainly. Kind of funny, a place occupied by the U.S. Army and they have to hire private guards to watch our people, but there it is. And, by the way, no fucking rules of engagement, either. Someone gets in our face, we waste them and nobody says boo, and that's because we also protect some big-shit Afghans, government people and such. They don't trust one another but they trust us, and we don't catch any flak from what passes for authorities in this shit hole. Nice business, and it's going to get bigger."

"Uh-huh. You got anyone speaks the language? Besides Gus, I mean."

"Not really. We got some Special Forces types who know a little Pashto, some Dari, but everyone speaks English so it's no big deal for most things. On the other hand, my friend, someone who *really* speaks the language and has the culture down and shit... fuck me! You can write your own ticket. I was telling the site supervisor about you—you remember Peisecki, he was a captain in Benning when we did that Ranger thing in '02? Yeah, him. An all-right guy, a good head; anyway, his mouth was watering."

"Because...?"

"Well, shit! The *negotiating*, man! We go in with a bunch of hajjis and they're all jabbering away, and the fucking translator just says whatever he wants, and we don't get any of the side play. Having you there has got to be worth serious cash. Man, you got no idea how much money is sloshing around this pissant country."

"Really? I thought it was a basket case."

"Oh, fuck, I don't mean the government. The government is fucked. I mean the warlords and the growers and processors. This place is smack central. Peisecki says it's the next big profit center."

"Protecting dope lords?"

"Hey, it's money. This is not the world, man, don't ever forget that."

I looked at him and then quickly away. The eagerness on his face made my belly twist. "Well, I'm happy for you," I said, "but personally I'd need to think about it for a while. I mean, I'm not sure I could make the jump from... you know, Thus be it ever when free men shall stand between their loved homes and the war's desolation."

Buck looked down at his beer and then gave me a defiant stare. "Yeah, well, I did that for twenty, bud, just like you; I got pins in my thigh and my ears are shot to hell; I hear fucking bacon frying every minute of my life, and I'm goddamned if I'm going to live in a double-wide on an E-7 pension. Uh-uh. Not when I got this opportunity. You'll see, Ice, it's the real deal here."

He finished his beer in two huge gulps and signaled for another round.

While I drank I thought about Buck and what he was doing and where he came from. Buck is a country boy from the western tail of Virginia, and his people have been fighting America's wars from way back before there *was* a country, an endless stream of officers and noncoms and grunts from all those little hollows and towns and farms, the heart of generations of American armies, and I thought it was a real bad sign when people like that started to talk like Buck was talking now; I thought it was bad for the country. *I* should be talking like that, not him, and I felt bad but hid it and we got pretty drunk that night.

In the morning, hung over, we went out to a joint down the road and ate parathas and drank sweet mint tea and he asked me what my plans were.

"I need to go to Kunar," I said. "I need that bike you got on the plane patched up and some Afghan ID."

"Hey, not a problem, but fuck, man, Kunar? That's deep in Apache country."

"I know," I said, "but I'm an Apache."

He laughed and slammed me on the back, and said, "Shit, I guess you are. You look like a goddamn Pashtun and you smell like one too."

꘎

All that took a couple of days to get ready. I lived at the Force Eight compound but spent most of my time in a tea shop off Flower Street. It was run by an enterprising young fellow named Atal, one of the innumerable class of fixers without whom life in Kabul would collapse more than it has already. He had a taste for the old poetry, and we would spend the afternoons examining the crowds on Flower Street, him pointing out to me who was a drug lord, who a terror chief, and who a CIA guy, quoting Rumi, Kabir, and Ghalib to each other as appropriate, and I sank so deep into pashtunwali that it was hard to remain civil when I returned to Little America at night. As Rumi says, *It is right to love your homeland, but first ask, where is it?*

Once I didn't go back at all but stayed up most of the night listening to a trio Atal had brought in, sarangi, *santoor*, and tabla, and I kept giving them dollars to play my favorite ghazals, and afterward I smoked opium in the back and Atal let me sleep there covered by a sheepskin.

When the bike was fixed and the papers were prepared, I asked Atal if he knew a reliable man to take the Ducati back to Lahore, a hundred bucks plus expenses and two hundred when he got back to Kabul with a note attesting it had been delivered in good order. Atal was surprised at the price being so high—there were people who would do it for nothing—and I explained that people were after me and there might be some danger. We would need a careful person, but not too careful, since he had to be seen leaving Kabul for the south on a red Ducati.

"Oh, in that case I know just the man. He goes back and forth quite often as a decoy."

"A decoy?"

"Yes, people smuggle, of course, and there are those who steal from smugglers, so the smugglers hire people to attract the attention of the thieves, but they don't carry much. Rangeen is one of these. And he is about your size and shape."

This man showed up that evening and was satisfactory in every way, and the next morning he left in my clothes and I in his, he on the motorcycle and I on a bus to Asadabad in Kunar Province.

Kabul to Asadabad is about two hundred kilometers, and even given the usual state of the roads the trip should take about five hours in peacetime. Our vehicle looked like a stumpy school bus painted vivid blue on the body, with the green and black national colors on its snout, plus a good deal of gold and silver paint, some of which was twirled into Qur'anic calligraphy, including *The greatest terrors shall not dismay them, and angels shall receive them*. I thought that made sense, given the state of the bus and the roads it was going to traverse.

My fellow passengers were mainly Kunar peasants back from shopping trips to the big city (their purchases towered on the roof rack), leathery men with missing teeth and sun-narrowed eyes, some with their burqa-clad wives and their children, plus a trio of musicians headed for a rural wedding, a schoolteacher, and three Afghan army soldiers in uniform going on leave. It was a fair cross-section of the people of Afghanistan, mainly Pashtuns, with some Tajiks and Hazaras. The bus had not left the outskirts of the city before we were a party, with people passing around food and tobacco, showing photos, registering their opinions, telling jokes. I sat in the front of the bus with the musicians on one side of the aisle and next to the schoolteacher. He was a soft-eyed man about my age with a neat spade beard and horn-rims. He was the one I had spotted as the suicide bomber, but he was not. He said he taught English in Asadabad, and I said I knew that language and if he liked we could practice on the way.

Up the narrow climbing road at unsafe speeds, and the terrors did not dismay us; we made good enough time to the Kunar border and then, because it was not peacetime at all, we were stopped by an Afghan army checkpoint. An hour baking in the oven of the little bus while the soldiers inspected our baggage and papers. I passed, no problem, but my schoolteacher was hassled, led off the bus; and returned forty minutes later, sweaty, red in the face, fuming. His name, Janat Gul Babori, was the same as or similar to that of someone the authorities wanted and he had to prove he wasn't that man, his argument being helped along by the usual bribe.

While we were waiting, another bus pulled up and the soldiers passed it right through without pulling people off or checking it out. I looked at Janat and he shook his head. Bribes again, the whole bus could've been packed with Taliban and weapons and dope, the whole country was bribed to the nipples, every public office was for sale, but what could you do? There *was* no Afghanistan the way there was a France or a Canada, there were only individuals and families and clans, and the Americans trying to make it different was like assembling a fighter plane out of wet toilet paper.

After that, when the bus was rolling again, we talked about the wretched state of the country and how bad it had been under the Taliban and what a mess the current masters had made of it and how tired we all were of the endless war. What didn't come up was anything personal. I've sat with people I've met by chance on airplanes and buses in the U.S., and sometimes you get their whole life story whether you want it or not.

But in this country reserve is the rule—no, it's more than reserve, it's a impenetrable thick mask—that prevents the expression of any genuine feeling. Maybe there *is* no genuine feeling; maybe the mask is all there is. I sometimes think that's the case, and it's one of the weirdest things about the transition from the West. My pal Claiborne is reticent for an American, he has the stoic uncomplaining humor of his mountain people, but Claiborne is an Oprah guest compared to the average Pashtun. Not making emotional waves is like the ruling passion of his life. The Americans see it as lying, as bad faith, but we think that the protection of honor, of the family, of the clan, is worth more than any mere veracity. Among the Pashtuns a man's front is everything; no one can penetrate it except, if you're lucky, you'll find a friend of the heart, and he'll be the only person in the world who will ever know what you really feel about things. For me this had been Wazir, and I for him.

It's impossible to explain this kind of friendship to people in the West; it gets all tangled up in the whole gay thing they have, and it's not like that at all. Or maybe it is, I wouldn't know. We loved each other up in the mountains, in the war; it was the core of my life then, and when I was stolen out of my life it was gone, which is why when Bacha Khan told me Wazir was dead it was like someone recounting a dream: interesting maybe, but not real life.

So we talked, Janat Gul and I, as the bus jounced over the potholes, communicating, if that's the word, in the veiled poetic Pashtun way, until we ran into another roadblock about ten miles outside of Asadabad, this one built around a couple of up-armored humvees and a squad of imperial storm troopers, my countrymen. The Americans were trying hard to be correct and do the rules-of-engagement thing, but you could see the drawn terror on their faces; they knew that any vehicle could be a bomb and, having been on the other side a time or two, I knew they would've preferred smoking any wheeled vehicle from a hundred meters away and fuck them if they can't take a joke.

They unloaded the whole bus and lined us up, and a uniformed translator helped the young lieutenant in charge question all of us, which was sort of amusing because the translator would ask a guy where he was going and what his business was, and the guy would say, indicating the American, "I am traveling to see his diseased whore of a mother fucked by dogs" or some such, and the translator would render it in English, "He is a shepherd returning home."

When it was my turn I took a long look at the lieutenant. He was in his early twenties, smooth-faced, wearing dark sunglasses. The translator, an older man, with the tired, cynical look of a city-bred Pashtun, took my papers and asked me where I was going.

I told him and added, "You have a pretty officer, brother. Does he let you fuck him in the ass?"

"He demands it," said the man. "All night long. I think they should pay me more than a hundred and twenty dollars a month."

"And have you caught any Taliban here?"

"You're joking," he said. "These sister-fuckers couldn't catch a terrorist if he was hanging by a rope from their balls."

"What are you saying?" asked the lieutenant.

"Nothing, sir," said the translator. "He's just another shepherd going home."

፠

Nor did they find any Taliban on the bus, although of course Janat Gul got the treatment again, because they were working off the same lists as the first guys. They were actually less rough on us than the Afghans, but the people were more pissed off when they finally let us go. It is just shitty to be questioned by foreign troops in your own country; there's no way you can make it right, no way in hell.

So when the bus started again our mood had turned dark. Some cursed the Americans and wished for the Taliban to return, and others asked those donkeys to recall what it was like under the Taliban; voices rose, fists shook. I leaned across to the nearest musician and offered a twenty-dollar bill, saying, "Brother, let's have some songs."

He smiled, shrugged, spoke to his compadres, they unlimbered their instruments—*dhol*, rubab, *toola*—and broke into a lively *attan*, which is to the Afghans what the samba is to Brazil. They were pretty good, and after they had got the bus jumping to the wild rhythms of the dhol, they segued into a ghazal, one voice wailing over the drone of the rubab with the waving toola tootling in counterpoint. I knew the song, it was one we'd sung in the jihad, and the next one too was an old one; they were recalling the old days, before the Taliban crushed the music and the spirit of the people in the name of an alien version of Islam preached by an Arabian maniac two hundred years ago.

And then they played one I didn't know, about a boy warrior who loved another boy warrior in the jihad and who had mysteriously vanished, leaving his abandoned lover to mourn alone, and it wasn't until they got to the refrain—where is my young lion, my little *ghazan*? I wait, I wait, I know he'll come back—that I realized that they were singing about me, me and Wazir.

I wanted to shrivel and I felt the blood rise to my face, but then I realized these people had no idea I was the guy in the song and I relaxed a little. It's a weird thing to find out you're a myth.

So we arrived, singing and dancing in the crowded aisle, at the town of Asadabad, having taken over eight hours on the trip. It was late in the afternoon by then and Janat Gul the schoolteacher insisted on giving me a meal and a bed for the night. His wife and sisters had to work like mad to clean out the room in his house where they sewed clothing to supplement his schoolteacher's wage, which I felt bad about, but you can't turn down hospitality among the Pashtuns and they are women after all; it is women's work.

In the morning the wife, upon whom I had not laid eyes, of course, supplied a big greasy bag full of parathas, fruit, and bread for my journey, and I started walking out of town, north and almost straight up. It was fifty-odd kilometers into the mountains of Nuristan and I'd figured on two or three days' travel, what with my bad leg, and that worried me, because my mother had been in captivity for seven days. On the other hand, no news was good news. Jihad groups had kept hostages alive for months—years—and I kept telling myself that my mother was a survivor, because if I wasn't thinking that I would be thinking really bad thoughts and getting crazy, and that would screw up any chance I had of getting her out.

As it turned out, I caught a lift from a Tajik in a truck hauling consumer goods and grocery items to Warna, which took me almost all the way I was going. The driver said the area was fairly prosperous since the dope trade picked up after the war, lots of orders for generators and TVs and cell phones. He asked me if I was going to the jirga at Barak Sharh, and I said I was going to Barak Sharh but I hadn't known there was a jirga, and he said yes, the Barakzai were having one, one of their clans anyway, and he hoped I was known there because they were very strict with strangers now. It was the opium trade and because the Arabs were killing all the *maliks*, them and the Taliban, the shit eaters, the pigs, the sister-rapers. The Tajiks don't like the Taliban.

We reached Warna a little after noon, and I walked up the track toward the ancestral village of my adopted ancestors. I passed the cemetery and the old Sufi shrine. The gravestones had all been smashed or toppled during the Taliban era and the shrine was a blackened shell. There was a group of armed men from the clan militia at the entrance to the village, and they braced me and asked me who I was and what I

wanted, and I said I was Kakay Ghazan, and I was here to see Gul
Muhammed Khan, my father.

Well, *that* caused a stir, and at first they didn't believe me. They held
me at gunpoint, scowling, and sent a messenger off to their honcho,
who turned out to be Sahak, my old commander from the assault on
Tsawkey, and he hugged me and lifted me off the ground and kissed me
on both cheeks, and then he took me in to see my father.

Who was lying on a charpoy in the courtyard of his house, which was
packed with armed men. And the usual thing: you haven't seen someone in twenty years, you still expect them to look more or less the same,
and it's a shock when they don't. Gul Muhammed the mighty had
turned into an old man, his white beard dyed with henna, his strong
hands reduced to chicken claws, his face stripped to sharp bones and
leathery deep-lined skin. Only his eyes seemed the same: under the
thick gray bristles of his brow they still had that hawkish look, but they
filled with tears when he saw me and learned who I was. I fell to my
knees before him and kissed his hands. We embraced while the hard
men of the tribe murmured around us.

So I was welcomed back into my clan, introduced to the many I did
not know, and kissed by those few I did. The clan had not loved the Taliban and had suffered for it, and they confirmed what the driver had
told me, that the insurgents were assassinating the maliks and the
tribal elders. This tribal jirga they had coming up was to plan a joint
response and to decide what the Barakzai position would be in the new
American war. They had been neutral, but with the killings this was no
longer possible.

After a while the others politely withdrew to allow Gul and me to
speak privately.

He smiled at me with his four teeth. "So, my son, you have grown
to a man. And how many sons have you now?"

"None, Father. I'm sorry."

"None? You have no woman?"

"I have had many women but none who wished to raise my sons."

"Then get one who will. Get two. Men will be fighting with knives to
wed their girls to Kakay Ghazan."

"Whatever you decide, Father."

"Good. You know Wazir has two boys. They are around here some-where."

"I am happy for you. I heard he has gone to Paradise."

"Ah! Where did you hear that?"

"From Bacha Khan."

"I see. Yes. Well, I miss him; he was a good boy."

"May I visit his grave?"

"His grave is not here. What do you do with yourself now?" he asked, changing the subject.

"I am a soldier for the Americans."

He gave me a sharp look. "And do you kill as they do, from far away, and never see the faces of those you slay, or whether they are enemies or children?"

"No, Father. The kind of soldier I am watches the enemy from very close, and if killing is necessary it is done silently and face to face."

He grunted to acknowledge this, that I was not utterly without shame.

"So will you do this for your whole life?"

"I don't know, Father. One reason why I've come here is to seek your counsel."

"Then my counsel is to leave the service of the infidels and join us here. We need good men, fighters, and there is no end of gold from the poppies."

Everyone wanted to get me into the dope business. I said, "I will consider it, Father, thank you. But before that I must do something. Some mujahideen have kidnapped my mother, and I have come to rescue her."

"Yes? I heard something about a kidnapping of foreigners. Your mother was among them?"

"She was. Have you heard anything about where they're holding them? It must be somewhere in Swat and perhaps even Kunar, close to the border."

"It is not Kunar, or I would know. I hear they got five crore dollars for one of them, and I did not see a rupee of it, and I would have if they were in Kunar."

He stroked his beard. For a while he seemed lost in thought. At last he said, "Your mother ... I never met a woman like her, before or since. Many times I thought of stealing her for myself, just to see ... but it was against my honor. I heard she took you herself, after the jihad."

"Yes. Who did you hear it from?"

"Oh, you know, bazaar rumors. But it was true, I see."

"Yes, she wanted me to be an American and be safe from the war here."

Now he gazed off into space again, like old men do. "A remarkable woman, a *devi* almost. She took both my sons—"

"Both, Father?"

"I mean she used to talk with Wazir in the evenings and filled his head with strange ideas. But in the end he was a Pashtun."

I was about to ask him what he meant, because there was something disturbing about the way Gul Muhammed was speaking, as if there were a message underneath his words that he wanted me to know but could not bring himself to voice. But now the courtyard was filling up with people; there was a continual rumble of trucks in the narrow streets outside, for the jirga was arriving, and my father had duties more important than chatting with a prodigal foster son about his mother. He asked me to sit down at his right hand, which I did, and there commenced a series of formal greetings of the assembled elders and chieftains. Tribal society is not efficient, which is one reason why it has faded over most of the earth, and I found that I was enough of an American to become bored by the pace of the proceedings. After an hour or so I excused myself and took a walk around the village.

It was a miserable little pile, with houses built of local stone and mud brick, more miniature forts than houses, surrounded by walls and dark and cramped within. In what passed for a market square, men were slaughtering sheep for the feast they'd laid on for the jirga, and I watched that for a while, but the sight of throats being cut and the gush of blood and the heads resting in the dust, swarmed with flies, reminded me of what I was trying to stop, and I moved on, back to Gul Muhammed's house.

Entering my father's courtyard, I waved to the guards there and they smiled and gestured for me to go through. The courtyard was more packed than before. I started to work my way through the mob and noticed that just in front of me two men were doing the same, so I stayed in their wake, like you do in a stadium or a concert. One of them was a thin Kiel with a heavy limp, probably eighteen or so, and the other was an older man in a turban; he had his hand on the kid's shoulder, guiding him, and I thought, father and son come to the big party from some village like this one, the kid probably hasn't seen this many big shots in his whole life.

But then the older guy gave the kid a little push and the kid moved out of sight into the crowd, and the older guy turned around to go back the other way and I saw his face, the beard, the knobby cheekbones. He looked right at me, I saw his eyes widen, and then he turned abruptly away and started to bull his way back toward the gate.

It was Baz Khatak, the man I'd seen in Peshawar talking to the ISI captain who'd run me off the road. I reached under my kameez and pulled my pistol out and started chasing him. He was pushing people aside—which is not wise in a Pashtun throng; they don't take kindly to that kind of treatment—and men were shouting curses and kicking at him, and I'd almost caught him by the time we both got to the courtyard gate.

I saw him fumbling under his kameez and my belly lurched because then I knew what he was going for and why he'd shoved the kid forward. I shot him in the back, and he went down. I was just bringing the front sight up on the back of his head when I saw the small black box in his fist and before I could get the round off he pushed the button and as my bullets smashed his head the kid exploded.

We had twenty-seven dead and forty-eight injured, including Gul Muhammed, who'd been hit in the chest and hip by bits of human shrapnel; the human body makes a pretty good frag grenade and there was a lot of metal junk in the kid's suicide vest in case that wasn't enough. They brought a doctor in from the government clinic in Asadabad, probably at gunpoint, and he got the shrapnel out of my father's stringy old body and I sat with him for a day and a night while he ran a fever and mumbled, talking to people who weren't there or were dead.

When he was well enough to eat I fed him beef broth with a spoon, and he spoke sense for the first time, asking me what happened. I told him the story, about the Taliban I'd spotted from Peshawar and the kid with him, the bomber, and asked him to forgive me for not seeing him sooner. He waved that off.

"If it had not been for you, the bomber would have pushed through and exploded in the midst of the jirga, and I would be dead along with all the elders of the clan. You know, the reason we Pashtun don't have a nation of our own is because no tribe can bear to see a man from another tribe above him, and so we are always under the heel of strangers. These Taliban say we should all be one people under the command of God and His holy Qur'an, as the Prophet, peace be on him, united the tribes of Arabia and conquered half the world. They are right in this, we should be united, as we were for a time against the Russians, and I do not like to see American soldiers in our country, but I have not heard that the tribes of Arabia were united by murdering their leaders."

"So the clan will turn against the Taliban now?"

"We will have our revenge, surely, but you know what we say: the right side is good but the winning side is better. No one thinks attacking America is a real jihad, not like the Russians, when they were using mosques as latrines. If the Americans have a blood feud with the Taliban, that's none of our affair. Let them kill each other!"

"I too have a blood feud with them, Father."

He nodded and looked at me, not with his regular sharp and challenging stare but almost tenderly. He said, "Yes, I know. It's what I would do and you are like me, although I didn't raise you. I have had few regrets in my life. I lived as a Pashtun and kept my honor and my land, and that is sufficient, but I regretted not having my sons by my side. Yet you are like her too, and that's not nothing. I have sworn an oath not to tell this, sworn it on naked steel, but I think it now touches the honor of my house, which comes before any oath, and when I swore it I did not think I would ever see you again, or that you would come with such a purpose, or that you would have saved my life, mine and these others of my kinsmen. So I will tell you, and let God judge me. They are holding these hostages in a village called Paidara, in the northern end of the Swat Valley. Until you told me, I did not know your mother was among them. But, son, let no one hear where you learned this. I would not have the Barakzai know that Gul Muhammed Khan has not kept his word."

I said I would keep this to myself at any cost, and then he closed his eyes and said, "Good. I hope you save her. God willing I will see you again, but if not, farewell. Come here so I can bless you."

So I leaned over and he took my head in his two hands and said a verse from the Qur'an,

"Surely those who say, 'Our Lord is God,' and then live righteously, no fear shall be on them, neither shall they sorrow. Those dwell in Paradise, dwelling forever as a recompense for their deeds."

Then he blessed me and I kissed him and said, *"O my Lord, dispose me that I may be thankful for Thy blessing wherewith Thou hast blessed me and my father and mother, and that I may do righteousness well-pleasing to Thee, and am among those that surrender."*

Sura 46, the Sand Dunes. Until the words came out of my mouth I had no idea I could recall them from when they had first been beaten into me in that dusty madrasa outside Peshawar long ago, when Gul Muhammed had been a mighty warrior and me a boy. I stayed with him until he fell asleep, and then got my gear and left the house, where I was mobbed by the clan notables wanting to know what was happening and whether I was going to make a claim for Gul Muhammed's land and status, and they were clearly relieved when I said it could all go to cousins and uncles for all I cared. That made me more popular immediately, and when I said I wanted to go back to Kabul, they arranged for a truck and a driver and six heavily armed clansmen.

To get around the roadblocks we went by tracks through the hills, some of which I recalled from the jihad. It took us about ten hours to reach Chaharbagh, and from there I took a bus for the rest of the trip, about seventy miles. It only took five hours and we weren't stopped once, perhaps by prior arrangement with the Afghan army. It's how the suicide bombers get in but it worked for me too.

I called my Uncle Nisar from Chaharbagh on his special cell phone and told him where I was, and he said he'd have a plane waiting for me when I got to Kabul, and he did, a neat little Bombardier turboprop, so by dawn the next day I was landing in Lahore, and there was a company car to meet me. The driver was holding a sign that said MR. T. LAGHARI so I walked up and told him who I was, but he ignored me and made a shooing motion with his hands, because people who looked and smelled like me were literally beneath the notice of N. B. Laghari's driver. But I was tired and pissed off so I used my command voice and called him a rude name in Panjabi, after which he looked at me again, with terror on his face this time, and almost tripped over himself ushering me into the Mercedes. A man unfamiliar with Kim and the Great Game, obviously.

Javed, my uncle Nisar's valet, didn't show by his expression that I was anything but an honored guest and a son of the house as he led me to the library. Javed was famous for not displaying any astonishment whatever, but Nisar was nearly as surprised as his driver when I walked through the door. He looked up from some papers on his desk and I could see his face change: first the contemptuous snarl, with which he was about to dismiss the ignorant sweeper who had stumbled into his room, and then the dawning surprise, tinged a little with fear, and finally the usual smiling mask snapped into place.

He rose to greet me—he even hugged me, which I considered pretty classy considering what I probably smelled like—and said, "My God, Theo, you gave me a shock. I thought I was being assaulted by terrorists from the Frontier. I would never have believed it. You look just like a Pashtun warrior—not just the fancy dress, mind you, but the stance, the expression . . . however do you do it?"

"The same way you manage to look like a Punjabi mogul. I *am* a Pashtun warrior."

He laughed, a little nervously, I thought, and said, "Yes, of course. Your famous adventure. Well, you have safely returned to civilization in any case. I suppose you'd like a bath and a change of clothes."

"Food first, if you don't mind, Uncle. I haven't eaten anything solid since I left Gul Muhammed in Kunar."

"Oh, of course, how stupid of me! Sit down at once, and I'll ring for a tray." He did, Javed entered, received his orders, and floated out. My uncle resumed his place behind what I kept thinking of as B.B.'s desk, and I recalled the last time I'd sat in front of it, when he'd chewed me out for that stupid thing with the pistol, just before he was murdered. Shit happens, as we say in the army, and I thought of that, and I also thought of what Rahman Baba has to say on the subject, which is:

> How long will the horse of the sky keep galloping,
> How long will it race across the roof peak?
> The business of the world is like a shadow,
> Which has no value to the sun.

Nisar got a phone call just then, and he picked it up and looked at me apologetically and said he had to take it, and I volunteered to leave and he motioned me to keep my seat; it was just some fools in Karachi who had to bother him about every little thing. It was something to do with export licenses for rayon, and although the word *bribery* was not mentioned I got the impression from his half of the conversation that someone paid to expedite these licenses had gotten greedy; Nisar closed the conversation by saying he would deal directly with the ministry involved. By the time he'd sorted this out, a servant had rolled in a tray laden with tea and steaming parathas and a covered dish of kedgeree and hot buttered chapatis.

I ate gratefully, and while I ate I told Nisar what I had learned in Kunar Province, without mentioning Gul Muhammed.

When I had finished, he said, "Well, that is an achievement. You know where your mother is being held. What will you do now?"

"Obviously, the first thing is to associate the village of Paidara with the nuclear theft we've concocted. I can do that with some cell calls, I think, and it'd be better if one of the calling parties was in Kahuta."

"You're thinking of going yourself?"

"I was thinking of sending Iqbal. My face is probably pinned up in every ISI office in the country, and it'd be annoying to get picked up and maybe disappeared. They tried once and they'll try again."

"Yes, very wise. In fact, I think you should stay here for the time being. I'll have someone go to Rukhsana's and get your things. If Iqbal is to go to Kahuta I can make a plane available to him. And the same for you. I don't want you flying commercial back to the States, it's too easy to be picked up out of an airport line, they ask you to step into a little room and you're never seen again. And, of course, any other way that I can be of service—"

"Hassan needs a new motorcycle."

He nodded and made a note on his desk pad. "Not a problem. I'll have someone see to it. Anything else?"

"Yes. Why are you doing this?"

An expression of innocent inquiry appeared on his face. It was well done, very nearly convincing. "I beg your pardon?"

"Just curious, is all. My mother's not exactly the family favorite, is she? And you don't know me from Adam, you were away at school for most of the time I was here as a kid, and then I show up and you open the wallet of Laghari Enterprises Ltd.: flights, money, and the breakage of any number of laws. I was wondering why. You didn't get to where you are now in Pakistani politics and business by being a sweetheart. No offense, Uncle."

"None taken. As to your question, your mother is the wife of the head of this family. I'm obliged to do everything in my power to secure her safety."

He looked at me to see how this was going over, and I guess my expression didn't quite close out the issue, so he continued, "That would be the official explanation. But in our Pakistan there is always an unofficial or actual explanation, and it is this. If the guests of Nisar Laghari are kidnapped by terrorists working under the aegis of the ISI, at least in part, then it becomes a significant signal in my world. It tells this world, among other things, that my brother Seyd, who owes everything to my patronage, has broken with me and has another patron, someone within the warmongering wing of ISI. I don't know who this person is yet—but I do assure you that I will find out—and let him beware! The same goes for Seyd himself, although I will continue to invite him to my house and to any family events, and no one will be able to tell that he is my enemy. Whatever feelings I may have about your mother or you—and I assure you that I *do* have genuine feelings for you both—are of no account in this business. It is an intolerable affront. If I were to let it pass, if my guests can be kidnapped with impunity, nothing I have would be safe; my children, my nieces and nephews, my own person and property would be, as you say, up for grabs. So you come along with this scheme, and I say to myself, Why not? And I may say now that you have not disappointed me. In fact, there is no one in my circle who could have brought it off. So you see, it is really I who owe you. Does that satisfy your curiosity?"

"Yes, it does," I said. "Thank you, Uncle. And thank you for not saying *if it works*."

His face turned grave. "Yes, that is the issue. And things are not as well as they could be. I assume you were not following the news on your journey."

"No. What happened?"

"I'm afraid it's not good news. First, Craig has been released. It was all over the news, although of course without details of the ransom. I have sources that tell me the funds have already fled the country, to various financial havens. This means the other hostages will be of no further interest to the authorities, if they ever were. In fact, it would benefit the people who set this damn thing up if they did not emerge from their captivity. Next, the terrorists have already executed one of the hostages—an American, I forget his name—in retaliation for one of your bombings. The video is all over the Internet and copies are for sale in every bazaar. There is therefore no doubt that they are serious in their threats. Finally, yesterday, a missile strike near Quetta killed the head of al-Qaeda operations in Pakistan, Khalid al-Zaydun, and about twenty other people. We can expect our terrorists to demonstrate their revenge. I'm sorry."

I was sorry too. I said, "So if this is going to work, it's going to have to launch right now. I should get over to Iqbal and Hassan and send the location out to where NSA can intercept it."

"I'll get my driver to take you, and may I suggest putting a note of urgency into it. You might say that the bomb is ready and about to be shipped to a target. The suicide plane is all prepared and so on."

I thought that was a good idea and got up to go.

"No bath?" my uncle asked.

"No time," I said, and thanked him, and went to call Hassan, and for the rest of the day we did all the necessary things. As it turned out, I didn't get a chance to change my clothes and clean up until late that night. I was particularly pleased with what Iqbal had done. Framing people on corruption charges is one of the minor arts in Pakistan, and I almost felt sorry for what we were doing to the woman at NSA. Collateral damage, as they say; shit happens.

Then I waited, which anyone who has been in combat will tell you is the hardest part, the death fantasies, the wound fantasies run nonstop on the interior TV, and here it was worse, because in combat you have to think that you're special, that you're the best trooper, with that special edge of survival, and you tell yourself that though ten thousand fall at your right hand it will not come nigh thee, this was worse because it was someone else: my mother. I couldn't sleep. I kept getting up and putting on clothes with crazy thoughts in my head—I was going to take a car and drive to Paidara and bust her out myself, like in the movies—and then undressing again and lying there in a sweat.

The next morning, unrested but at least clean and dressed for the West, I told my uncle that I couldn't stay in Lahore anymore, I'd done all I could and it would be best if I returned to my unit, because if the disinformation flew, and if Iqbal's operation to discredit Cynthia Lam worked, it was likely that we would be tasked to go in there and get the fictitious bomb. I wanted to be on the scene to control things to the extent I could, so the hostages didn't end up being collateral damage themselves.

A couple of hours later I was on a Laghari corporate jet flying to Dubai, where I'd pick up a commercial flight back to Washington, D.C. While I was on the plane I decided that this would be my last stunt as a soldier in the United States Army. I had betrayed America, there was no way around that, and I'd proved to myself that I was really a warrior and not a soldier, that tribe and family came before the chain of command, and wearing the uniform wasn't honorable anymore. That was one reason, and the other, which I didn't want to think about, was that if the bastards killed my mother I was going to have to go back into the hills and arm myself, and gather my clan, and go kill a really large number of people in revenge.

17

When Cynthia went to visit Borden she almost went right past his door. It was clean. All the nerd spoor had been removed, exposing an ordinary NSA slab. She paused outside with her hand on the knob and sniffed. No smell. A knock and Borden's voice answered; that hadn't changed. Borden was in.

Inside, she paused and let out a whistle. "What happened, Borden? Have you been born again?"

The tiny office had been stripped like the door—no junk, no decorations, no trash. Borden himself had obtained what appeared to be an expensive haircut, and he was wearing a cotton sports jacket over a striped button-down shirt and flannel trousers.

"No," he said, "the new me is nondenominational. I assume you approve, being fairly tight-assed yourself. So to speak."

"I'm amazed," she said. "You realize that you'll be barred for life from Star Trek conventions if this gets out. What happened?"

He looked at her, and she noticed that he had traded his greasy horn-rims for stylish aviators. He said, "Oh, you know, it was time. I turned thirty-five last week."

"I didn't know. Happy birthday."

"Thank you. No one knew. I say I have no life, but it's not just a throw-away line or a disguised boast, like I'm so busy and important that I have no time for trivia like relationships. It's simply the case. So it's my birthday and I go to Chicago Pizza and, like I always do to celebrate, I order a giant deep-dish pepperoni—mushroom, anchovy, and olive—and I'm scarfing it down when I see two girls at a table nearby sort of watching me, and I can tell they're grossed out; it's a classic, a fat, stringy-haired nerd pigging on pizza, nothing new about that; but just then I happen to notice that I'm sitting just where I can see my reflection in one of those mirrors they have on the columns and all of a sudden *I'm* grossed out too. It was like a revelation. Half my life is over and I'm alone on my birthday grossing out a couple of girls, and I realized that this was going to be it into the indefinite future: no life, no girls, nothing but video games and porn. No child porn, not yet, but I could see it was only a matter of time. It was like I'd been hit on the head and woke up a different person. And strangely enough I thought about you."

"Me?"

"Yeah. The way you come down here and get me to do you favors, and I pretend to sexually harass you and you flirt in a nonserious way, like an instinct, like one of the lower animals, and you let me look down your dress and get close enough for me to smell your perfume, and suddenly I could see myself from outside myself, like *you* probably see me, and it was, like, *appalling*. I stopped eating and practically ran out of there and I was thinking, What crime did I commit to be sentenced to this life? Was it just a matter of being overweight and interested in computers? Was it Asperger's? It's like in middle school we all lined up in the hallway and got issued a life: you got exotic beauty destined for world domination and I got pathetic fat nerd; it was like *Brave New World*, where all the Deltas are programmed to love their menial existence. I'm *glad* I'm a Delta, Deltas wear lovely brown uniforms, or whatever.

"I got into my car to drive home and the car was filthy, sticky from spilled drinks and full of wrappers, the foot well on the passenger side up to the seat rim in trash, because, what the hell, I never have a passenger, so why clean it? My skin was crawling, you know? And the same in my apartment: the junk, the filth, the spilled food, pizza boxes with roaches, no light or anything alive, except my tarantula. The banality of it! Ha ha, he's a nerd so *of course* he has a tarantula. Why the fuck do I have a tarantula in my *home*?

"There was this smell too, and I was, like, how can I have lived all my life with this *smell*? So I got a roll of thirty-gallon plastic bags and started to clean up, and once I started I couldn't stop. I took a couple of Adderall and worked all night. Not only did I clean out the junk, I threw everything away; clothes, towels, posters, everything but my comic book collection, and I put that in cartons and ran an ad on Craigslist to sell the whole thing. I'm fucking thirty-five and I'm still reading comic books?"

"The tarantula went too?"

"George? Get rid of George? I couldn't do *that*. If I got rid of George, I'd be *alone*. The next day I called in sick and took all the shit down to the Dumpster and went to Tyson's and got a haircut and shopped for regular grown-up-type clothes—not too many because I don't plan to be this shape forever—and then I went to Rock Creek Park and walked for hours, until my feet hurt, and looked at, you know, *normal* people, until it got dark and then I went and joined a gym near my house and went to an exercise class, twenty fat women and me, and bought a lot of fruit and salad stuff at the organic market and went to sleep early, and today I came in and cleaned this place up. And here *you* are but still the same."

"Not really. I'm scheduled for astronaut training right after I have the sex change operation."

Borden flashed an impatient smile, so unlike his usual ironic grin it startled her. "Still the same. I relate the most remarkable experience of my life, and you crack a joke. So, on to business: what's the favor?"

Cynthia felt her cheeks warm. "I'm sorry, Borden. I didn't mean to be flippant. It's just a little strange. The new you and all."

"It's strange for you, you can imagine how *I* feel. Have a seat. I cleaned it with a janitorial substance." She sat. The chair exuded a sharp astringent smell.

He said, "But really—what's on your mind?"

Cynthia had prepared an anodyne and amusing story about what she wanted done but on the instant decided, against her usual instincts, to tell Borden the plain truth.

"Okay, this is some serious shit, and I'm in trouble right now for telling you. You can't know this, and you're putting your career in jeopardy if you hear me out, and so am I, but more so. Are you up for that?"

Borden thought for a moment, then shrugged. "My career here is not as interesting to me as it was a couple of days ago. I think my era of staring at a screen in a tiny office, for however noble a purpose, may be coming to a close. What's the serious shit?"

So she told him about the provocation, and how everyone was being taken in by it except her, and about what she had overheard at the meeting, Ringmaster and SHOWBOAT, and how Anspach had stonewalled on that, and how there was no one else she could tell about it but him.

When she'd finished, he said, "That's an interesting story. You think there's some kind of rogue operation going on at Langley? That for some reason this operation *wants* us to get fooled into . . . what, invading Pakistan? Why would anyone want that?"

She said, "I don't care. Our only job is to find out what the truth is and send it up the line. This nuclear theft scam is not the truth. End of story."

"That's a fairly naïve expression of what we do. It'd be more accurate to say that we give our masters such information as they're willing to receive."

"Granted, and we can't do anything about a fraud concocted above us—WMD in Iraq and so on. But it's different when the fraud is concocted from below. It's a deeper violation. No one elected those guys. No one authorized them to drag us into another war."

"Why are you so sure these guys don't have authorization? Maybe it's another Iran-Contra. Someone way up high looks at Pakistan and thinks, This is a failed or failing state. It's got deliverable nuclear weapons. The Taliban have complete control of an area within a day's drive of the capital and the nuclear facilities, plus a good chunk of their army and intel apparatus seems to be in bed with the insurgents. So this someone thinks, let's prep the world for the idea that we better move in there and secure the nukes before the crazies do, and what better way to make that happen than by a big nuclear theft scandal?"

Cynthia was shaking her head during the last of this. "No. I was at the meeting. I know Morgan and I know Anspach. Morgan absolutely thinks it's genuine and so did everyone at that meeting, with the possible exception of the DDO of the CIA. That bunch of people are as secret as it gets in this country, so if a scam is in progress it has to be a small cabal. In fact, I would've thought it was nothing but an al-Q provocation if I hadn't overheard that business about Ringmaster."

"So what's your theory of the plot? Say there's no real theft. So our guys go in there, shoot up the place, and draw a blank. It's another Iraq, and no one is going to fall for that again. I mean, we're stupid, but not *that* stupid."

"But that's just the point, Borden! They can't *have* a fiasco. They have to find something, and that has to be what Ringmaster is about. Look, I'll tell you how I'd do it. First, you set up an agent, someone with the skills to infiltrate a mujahideen group. The conventional wisdom is that it can't be done, but that can't be right or else Muslim drifters from all over the world wouldn't be fighting in Afghanistan and Iraq. Christ, that gormless kid John Walker Lindh walked right into al-Qaeda a few weeks after 9/11 and no one said boo! So they set up a organization around this agent, who has all kinds of credentials that he can get hold of nuclear material. That shouldn't be hard to fake. And these guys are waiting in some village for the delivery; they're going to make a nuke or at minimum a dirty bomb. The inside agent leaks the location. Meanwhile, our cabal produces this scam, phony phone calls and so on, and the government panics and sends in a strike team, and of course they have to have a special unit to handle the nuclear material, and these are guys that none of the Deltas or whoever have ever seen before and they're carrying 'special equipment' in sealed crates."

She made quotation marks with her fingers as she said *special equipment*.

"They go to this village and blow up everyone, and lo and behold the special team finds nuclear material, which of course they've brought along with them in the sealed crates. Another triumph for the free world."

"But the Pakistanis will say they haven't lost any nuclear material."

"Oh, please! What would anyone expect them to say? Who on earth would believe the Pakistanis when we're showing off containers full of plutonium? And the beauty part is how covert the whole thing is. DOD, NSA, and the White House have full deniability. The president can get up there and announce with a straight face that we've averted a nuclear catastrophe and, by the way, the world has got to do something about Pakistan. Two days later the Indian army mobilizes on the border and U.S. missiles are retargeted."

Now Borden was shaking his head. "That's pretty rich, Lam. I mean, it's one thing to speculate outside, in the lefty press, about evil cabals, but we're in the belly of the beast. Did anyone ever ask *you* to join an evil cabal? Me neither. Something like this would leak like crazy; there'd be water on the floor."

"Then how do you explain what I've learned?"

He thought about that for a long minute. She studied his face, willing him to roll, willing him to see what she saw so clearly. At last he sighed and said, "Let's say I go with it. What specifically did you want me to do?"

"Use your AMICUS connections to trace any references to Ringmaster or SHOWBOAT in the CIA databases."

"*What?* That's . . . for God's sake, Lam, that's completely out of the question. I told you before, there *is* no AMICUS. It's a fucking committee! It's all bullshit coordination to make sure the different intel agencies aren't duplicating or stepping on one another's jockstraps. No one is going to let me wander through the CIA database, and even if they did, what should I look for? Do you think a search for *rogue operations* is going to yield many hits?"

"I didn't mean asking for permission. You've been telling me for a long time that a smart-enough computer guy on the inside could find out anything that anyone in the government ever put on a computer."

"You want me to *hack* the CIA?"

"Yes."

"Get out of here."

"You're saying it can't be done?"

"Of course it can be done, in principle. I'm over there for AMICUS meetings all the time, and they write their passwords on Post-its and stick them on their desks just like we do. I know the data architecture. And it's the government. Any operation spends money, and even a black budget has budget codes for different operations. But, frankly, I don't see any upside for me in this."

She stared at him until he dropped his eyes. He said, "What?" .

"What? You know, I always thought you had your problems, but I also thought you were a real person, not the night troll everyone else thought you were. So you cleaned up your act and got a haircut? Terrific. But when I ask you to do something that might prevent the deaths of thousands of people, including your own people, you ask me if there's some personal advantage? I'm putting my whole *life* on the line here, and you want to know what's in it for *you*? Well, fuck your upside and fuck you, troll!"

She turned and headed out of his office, quickly, but not so quickly that she missed the response she expected.

"No, wait!"

She faced him. "What?"

"I'll look into it. I'm over at the Agency for a meeting early tomorrow. I'll see if I can get a line into their budget system."

She waited a few beats and then strode over, slid easily onto his broad lap, and kissed him firmly on the mouth, a kiss just the tiniest bit south of platonic.

"Thank you, Borden. That was a very un-troll-like decision." She could see the sweat bubble up on his forehead.

"My pleasure, so to speak. I hope they give us adjoining cells in Guantánamo."

"It won't come to that," she said lightly, "you're smarter than all of them. I just want to find out what SHOWBOAT is, so I can make the case with Morgan. We're not selling secrets to the bad guys. Besides, the whole point is to share intel across the government. We'll be heroes if we stop this and no one will bother about the details of access protocol."

Borden did not respond to this; he just stared at her with the same concentration he paid to lines of code on his screen.

"What?" she said.

"Nothing," he replied. "Tell me, Lam, do you ever have any fun?"

"What do you mean, fun?"

"Oh, you know, like people do in movies or TV commercials. Happy family parties made better with adult diapers, and couples running through fields of flowers in slo-mo. Or clubbing. You know, sweaty dancing with colored lights. Do you ever do any of that?"

"I'm a grown-up, Borden. I don't go clubbing and my happy family consists of one unhappy person. But I'll tell you what: if this thing comes off, I will personally find a field of flowers and run through it with you, in slo-mo."

"I'd like that," he said, and turned to his screens as she left.

꽃

Cynthia walked back to her office thinking that it had gone rather well. She had been manipulating men with an adroit combination of sexuality and anger for many years; she knew she was good at it, and in this instance she hardly considered it manipulation. It was as natural as breathing. She had great hopes for Borden and his skills.

Some time with the headphones, then, where she found some interesting leads unrelated to the present scam, after which she composed the necessary reports and shipped them out via NSA's secure intranet. She checked her e-mail. That was odd: not a single message today from anyone in NSA. A slow day? It happened from time to time.

Feeling pretty pleased with herself after rolling Borden, she decided to go out for lunch. Cynthia did this several times a week and almost always at the same place, a Vietnamese restaurant located in a strip mall in Laurel, Maryland, a six-minute hop from the NSA parking lot. She took Fort Meade Road to Maryland 198, once a major north-south route along the eastern seaboard but now a continuous strip development of cheap restaurants, hot-sheet motels, used car lots, and marginal businesses selling things like secondhand batteries, videotapes, and truck parts. There was one point of historical interest on the way, however, an ugly tan eighty-unit lodging house with a mustard-colored sign out front, announcing it as the Valencia Motel. Here, during the summer of 2001, five men had stayed in room 343 and planned how to fly four passenger jet planes into American buildings. The events of 9/11, the single most devastating breach of America's national security, had been organized virtually in the shadow of the agency called National Security, and all its exquisitely sensitive instruments and magnificent computers had been powerless to stop it.

She passed that dismal monument and pulled into a undistinguished strip that contained an Arby's, a Firestone Tire store, a pet groomer, a mailing facility, a computer repair shop, and a restaurant called Pho Bac, which Cynthia considered one of the best Vietnamese restaurants in the Washington region, unlikely though it seemed. The patron and the waitresses all knew her; she got to keep up her Vietnamese; she was one of the family, without having to be one of the family. The spring rolls and the *pho* were wonderful, and she was able to comfort herself with these simple foods, so reminiscent of a warm and happy childhood that it almost didn't matter that she had never actually had one. It was an indulgence, one of the few she allowed herself, quite secret from anyone at work, and she had invented for the benefit of the staff at Pho Bac a wonderful Vietnamese-American family, about which she gaily chatted as she ate. The place, oddly enough, had a full bar and she occasionally treated herself to a drink, always a vodka martini, and she ordered one now.

After the spring rolls, she pulled her laptop out of her briefcase, which was the signal for the staff to leave her alone. No private device that can record or send electronic data is allowed within the buildings of NSA, so in order to check her personal e-mail during the day Cynthia had to leave Fort Meade for a place like this or one like it. The computer store had a powerful Wi-Fi signal and she had arranged with them, for a small fee, to use it whenever she was in the area. She logged on, found a note from someone she knew in school, answered it briefly, and deleted another message from a head-hunting firm looking for translators. She got a few of these every week. The rest of the inbox was junk mail—drugstores, sexual aids, a scam that asked her to contact a Swiss bank about her account—and two more of those peculiar encrypted messages. She'd received half a dozen of these in the past week, clearly from someone who had mistaken her for another person, or was it the backwash of another more obscure computer scam? She deleted all of it.

After lunch she went to the mail center and used her key to open the mailbox she kept there. It was usually stuffed with catalogs and magazines and mail-order merchandise. Cynthia was a big Internet shopper, and she lived in an apartment building where the postman or UPS guy had to leave packages on the lobby floor, from which they would occasionally disappear. Adams-Morgan was a neighborhood where such things still occasionally happened, hence this mailbox convenient to work.

She opened the box and was astonished to find it empty. It was never empty. She went to the clerk at the desk, a large tan woman with beads in her hair, and asked her if there had perhaps been some mistake. Perhaps the label with her name on it on the inside of the mailbox had come loose? The clerk checked and said it was right where it should be. But there *was* something wrong. The woman, usually cheerful and willing, often too willing, to chat and pass the time of day, was reserved, close-faced, avoiding Cynthia's eye. Had the woman stolen something? Cynthia dismissed this thought as unworthy, unlikely. She'd used the place for years without a problem.

Back at NSA, as she left her car, another car pulled into a nearby slot. Two men in suits got out, and as Cynthia walked by them she smiled and nodded in a friendly way. There was no response from the men; their faces stayed blank, as if they were looking at a telephone pole or a dog. Since passing through puberty Cynthia had seldom experienced this response to a social smile directed at a man, and it disturbed her. Was there something wrong with her face, cilantro on the teeth? When she returned to her office she checked herself out in a hand mirror. No, the same attractive face stared out at her but with worried eyes.

No, this was stupid; it was stupid to attribute meaning to a set of coincidences. She checked her office e-mail again and found a couple of routine circulars from administration, one about the schedule for annual evaluations and the other relating to changes in reimbursement for mileage in private vehicles. Ah, she still existed! She put the day's slight oddities out of mind and returned to her headphones and the dull conversations that might or might not be terror talk. Some were simple duds, people mouthing off about America or the Jews. These she erased with a few keystrokes. Even the vast storage facilities of NSA could not contain the far vaster flux of the intake. A few that seemed to fit certain predesignated patterns she saved in various files. Across the breadth of the great ear of the agency, scores of others were doing the same task, searching for patterns, specific words, the output of certain SIM cards, in hopes that significance might emerge from the buzz. Tedious work: she understood that it was necessary, but she hoped she would not, personally, be doing it much longer.

It was just after three when, with an almost physical shock, she heard it, a familiar voice, one she'd listened to dozens of times, the anonymous man who was pretending to be the nuclear engineer, Jafar Baig Qasir. Quickly she checked the log file. The call had been placed from Kahuta at 10:46 A.M the previous morning, near midnight on the East Coast of the United States. Both parties were speaking Urdu, and she did not recognize the other one, who was in Lahore. She listened to it again:

KAHUTA: Peace, brother. Any news?

LAHORE: Peace to you, brother. Yes, the best. The products are completed and ready to ship. The courier just arrived from Paidara.

KAHUTA: When will they leave Paidara?

LAHORE: Very soon, not more than a day or two, God willing. The trucks are moving as we speak.

KAHUTA: Wonderful! I would not like to be in Tel Aviv or New York next month. I assume the money has been distributed.

LAHORE: Yes, I made the wire transfers myself. It is all done, and soon the whole world will know it. Death to America!

KAHUTA: And to Israel! God is great!

LAHORE: God is great! God be with you, brother.

KAHUTA: And with you.

Cynthia felt her belly roll and had to take several deep breaths. This was insane, patently false, but the GEARSHIFT people would never stop to ask why men who had stolen weapons-grade nuclear material would reveal the location of their bomb factory over a cell phone. They'd bite so hard the hook would never work loose, the elite troops would go on full alert, the planes would spin up their engines on some midnight runway, and the invasion of Pakistan would be under way. Almost without volition her fingers flew to certain keys and the message disappeared. She knew it would reside in backup for thirty days and then be purged, but she didn't care. This whole thing would be over far sooner than that.

Could anyone else have seen or heard it? She checked the machine translation files. There it was, a little crude, as ever, but the gist was clear and the place-name Paidara hung there on the screen, the hook's juicy worm. But she was the chief translator and had certain privileges on the system. She had the authority to correct certain critical translations before they were distributed. It was necessary to log in to the system and leave her fingerprints on the changes she now made, but no one would notice that. She did it all the time. When she was done, the place-name was gone and the conversation made as anodyne as possible. Maybe bad guys were shifting money around, so what?

But maybe someone had seen it and recognized its supposed importance. She got up and found that her legs would hardly support her weight. Her face felt odd, and when she touched it her fingers came away wet. Sweat was running in streams from her hairline down to her neck, as if she had just completed a heavy workout. That was ridiculous. She hardly sweated even when she actually worked out. She ran from her office to the bathroom.

Who was this person in the mirror? What had happened to the famously cool Cynthia Lam? A wave of nausea griped her, and she fled to a stall and heaved futilely over the bowl, willing the attack to pass. After a quarter of an hour she felt calm enough to approach the mirror again, where she dried herself with paper towels, adjusted her hair and makeup, and realized that she was feeling this way because she had crossed a line for the first time in her life. Although she had no problem with dissimulation and the subtle lie, never before had she done anything frankly illegal. She had never shoplifted, cheated on exams, or inflated her résumé, nor had she ever even had a traffic ticket. She had been a good girl and had reserved a silent contempt for those who weren't, who committed impulsive and stupid acts.

She practiced a disarming smile. She thought it looked ghastly but it might do for Ernie Lotz. He answered her knock, she applied the smile, and asked him if he'd found anything hot in the recent traffic.

"Funny you should ask, I'm just about to go through the translations. I've been in Satcom meetings all afternoon about moving another bird to cover South Asia. Now if al-Q starts a branch in Tegucigalpa we'll never know. Hey, is something wrong? You look terrible."

"I think I ate something salmonella-ish at lunch. I'm going home," she said, and escaped.

℔

Cynthia had a lively interior-dialogue generator, by means of which she could usually convince herself that some course of action beneficial to her was the right thing to do, and she exercised this in turbo mode on the drive home. She played that last intercept over and over again through the headset of her memory and found she had not been mistaken in her initial judgment. The thing was so obviously a fraud, and using the same guy they'd used to fake Jafar Qasir was the capper, an easy proof of fraudulence. So why hadn't she immediately gone to Morgan with it? Because they wouldn't see it, they'd explain away the voiceprint comparisons. Morgan was maddened, they all were maddened by their own swelling importance, because at last, after the fiasco of Iraq, the intelligence community was actually going to find weapons of mass destruction in the hot hairy hands of terrorists. It justified their whole existence—unless it was a scam devised by a rogue element.

Which it was, which it *had* to be. And so she was justified in opposing it, heroic in opposing it, the little Dutch girl with her finger in the dike, preventing another stupid war, another catastrophe for the United States, better than the FBI woman who had almost caught the 9/11 conspirators, because there would be no *almost* about it. Borden would find the SHOWBOAT files, and she'd put the whole thing together in a neat package, the voiceprint comparisons, the CIA plotters, everything, and take it triumphantly to Morgan; and if he didn't buy it, she'd take it up the line, to the top of the agency. And the whole thing would wind down, the culprits would be exposed and canned, the intel world would breathe a great sigh, and everyone, right up to the director of national intelligence, would know that little Cynthia Lam had done it all by herself.

These thoughts relaxed her, and by the time she entered her apartment she was feeling as she normally did, which was a kind of irritable discontent. She changed into jeans and a T-shirt, made a salad of field greens with a squat cylinder of tuna from the can plopped in its center, drank a glass of white wine to wash this down, and watched cable news while she did so. Then some minutes at her computer, writing to distant strangers, checking e-mail, disposing of yet another request from a Swiss banker and yet another encrypted e-mail.

Her father called. She put his voice on the speaker while she cleaned her already clean apartment. He complained about his clients in terms that reflected the racism of a generation ago, complained about his health, asked when she was coming home, and asked for money. She listened and responded with meaningless sounds at appropriate intervals, promised a check, and got off as soon as she reasonably could. After that she watched two DVDs, one a steamy French one in which the couple rarely stopped having sexual intercourse and the other a frothy romantic comedy. She switched it off before the boy got the girl again, took a Xanax, and went to bed.

Before she fell asleep she thought about what Borden had said, about having fun. She thought he was right, in a way. After this was resolved she would ditch Morgan and find a suitable boyfriend. She would take some of the huge amount of leave she'd accumulated and go to the islands, a warm beach with palms, and have some.

ℛ

As was her occasional practice when arriving at work, Cynthia bought a couple of coffees and sticky treats at the canteen and knocked on Ernie Lotz's door. Ordinarily, she would hear a cheerful greeting, she'd enter, and the two of them would sit and have coffee and discuss the day's upcoming problems, or Ernie's personal problems if he had any that morning, and then she'd go back to her own office with a sugar-caffeine high adequate for the morning's labor. This morning, however, there was silence behind the door.

Could he be out sick? No, he would have called in and the group secretary would have put a Post-it on his door to that effect. She knocked again and tried the doorknob. The door was locked; then came Ernie's voice.

"I'm busy."

"I have cinnamon buns."

She heard movement within and the door opened just enough for Ernie's face to appear. It was not his usual morning face. It looked like he'd recently been gut-punched.

"What's wrong?" she asked.

"Nothing. I'm working on a rush thing for Morgan."

"Can I help?"

"No." He started to close the door and she said, "At least take your stuff!"

He hesitated for a second, then took the proffered breakfast and kicked the door shut. She heard the lock turning.

Very strange, she thought, Ernie was never like that in the morning. She was the grumpy one and he the ray of sunshine; it was a standing joke between them.

She shook off the feeling and turned to her work. People were still talking about wicked deeds in Urdu and Arabic and the great antennae were still sucking it in. She adjusted her headset and brought up the evening's catch of sound files.

As usual, there was nothing of vital interest. More significant was what was missing. She did not get a single call all morning, or any e-mails, and no one came to her door. It was as if she were working at a neutron bomb site. At noon, she knocked again on Lotz's door and asked him if he wanted to go for lunch in Laurel.

A muffled curt refusal through the door.

Something unpleasant was happening here and she felt the anxiety of the previous day return, stronger than before. She called Borden. He must be back from Langley by now and she was dying to learn what he'd found.

The phone rang twice and then she heard a strange voice say, "Dan Wilson."

"I'm sorry," she said, "I must have the wrong number."

"What number were you calling?"

"Extension 3988."

"This is 3988."

"It is? Look, I'm trying to reach Walter Borden. This is his number."

"Sorry, it's my number."

"Then what's his new number?"

"I have no idea. Have you tried the directory?"

"Wait a minute. Are you in Internet surveillance?"

"That's right. But there's no Walter Borden here."

"That's impossible."

"I'm sorry, ma'am, I can't help you," said the voice, and broke the connection.

Cynthia dashed out of her office, down the corridors, choosing the stairs over the elevators, and arrived panting at the door of Borden's office. It was covered with Dilbert cartoons and the name Daniel G. Wilson was in the slot next to it. She threw the door open. A young man with thinning sandy hair and wire-rimmed glasses turned in his chair and looked at her. She stared at him and his office, which was filled with books and manuals and personal memorabilia, as if this Wilson had been occupying it for years.

"Can I help you?" he asked.

She shut the door, turned, and ran. She ran out of the building and got into her car. She drove to Laurel, to the strip mall, and went into Pho Bac. The waitress gave her a peculiar look and asked her if there was anything wrong. Cynthia forced a smile. There was nothing wrong. But she needed a drink and she ordered a vodka martini. And comfort food, hot and spicy: *banh bop* dumplings, and a *bo kho* with lots of chili sauce. And another martini to help her think.

She stayed there for over an hour, going through her options. The main thing in her favor was that she was right. Yes, she had cut corners, and the business about roping Borden into looking for SHOWBOAT and Ringmaster was highly irregular, but agencies spied on one another in various ways all the time, and okay, she had violated security clearance protocol, but wasn't this a special case? She just might be able to make the argument. Suppressing the Paidara intercept was perhaps an actual misdemeanor, but she could not imagine that anyone would come down hard on her for that, if they even knew about it. And, most significantly, she was *right;* there *was* no bomb plot, and therefore the location of the fictitious bombs was a nullity, disinformation rather than intelligence. It wasn't as if she had compromised national security in any way. Perhaps a bit of a cowgirl, was Ms. Lam, inclined to go off on her own, but that was not entirely a bad thing in the intel game. Looked at positively, it might even be described as flair. After all, there was Harry Anspach. In any case, Anspach would understand, yes, and Morgan wouldn't dare come down too hard on her, having himself taken sexual advantage of a female subordinate and so forth, not a scandal NSA wanted to get into.

She drove back to NSA, angry with herself for the momentary panic but feeling confident that she would be able to brazen it out. She wondered briefly what had happened to Borden and then dismissed the thought. Borden was an adult with a million-dollar skill set. He would be fine, whatever the government chose to do. Again, it wasn't as if they had compromised national security.

She parked and walked through the lot to her building. There was a black car parked at the entrance. It had its rear door open and a couple of men in suits were standing in the road, watching her approach. She was composing a smile on her face when she recognized that they were the same two men who had been studying her in the parking lot yesterday, the ones who hadn't smiled back. They didn't smile back this time either. Instead, they flashed their ID: NSA Office of Security. Then they ushered her into the black car and out of her life.

18

At dawn, before the azan has sounded for the Fajr prayer, Bahram Alakazai sweeps into the prisoners' room with his usual guards and announces that an important al-Qaeda leader, Khalid ibn Hassan al-Zaydun, has been killed by an American missile strike, along with twenty innocents, as a result of which there will be an execution that day at noon. Before that, the people will gather to hear the lies of the infidels and apostates refuted by those who know the true word of God. He speaks for some time. When he leaves, Sonia asks Manjit what he thought of the speech and the man.

"I thought he was needlessly prolix and vehement," replies the Indian. "Why bother making such a passionate speech to his victims? We are certainly unlikely to convert to his way of thinking, and he need have no concern for what we think. I believe the real audience was his Praetorian guards."

"I believe you're right," says Sonia. "He has the sound of a man unsure of his authority."

"Your plan is working, then."

"There is no plan. I told you already, people come to me and I help them. If Alakazai came to me I would try to help him too."

"Do you think you could? He's a true believer, and in my experience true believers are essentially unreachable by ordinary therapeutic means. They don't suffer. Every setback or difficulty is projected onto others or onto the supposed enemy. Any offered help would appear as an assault on the perfection of his interior constructs, and we would undoubtedly see an abreaction, which, given the situation, might be personally dangerous."

She looks at him and sees the sly smile on his face. "Yes," she says, "and wouldn't it improve therapeutic practice immensely if all thera-pists were held hostage by heavily armed patients? It would at least limit the power games we so often play. But no, I think our host is beyond my help. It will require a miracle to penetrate the armor of his righteousness."

"And are you preparing such a miracle?"

"Manjit, what a conspirator you've become! Always seeing plots, with me in the center. Karl-Heinz is the same. Frankly, I almost wish there *was* some secret scheme to get us out of here, because I fear that the most likely outcome is that Alakazai will make a holocaust of all of us at once to reestablish his bona fides among his more bloodthirsty troops."

Before long these troops appear and once again herd the prisoners against one wall of the room, while others move the charpoys against two other walls, leaving the wall with the door in it clear. Sonia notices that Idris and the handsome man whom they had seen before Cos-grove's execution are seated on the wall opposite from where Alakazai sits, not in the seats of honor at his side where they had previously been placed.

From Sonia's right comes a whisper: Amin. "I see we have a full house again. And I notice Idris has fallen out of favor with Alakazai. He has been exiled to the opposite wall."

"Yes," says Sonia quietly, "and so have the Arabs and their leader."

"A Pashtun by his looks. What do you suppose they're doing in the village?"

"Making bombs, according to Rashida. The Pashtun calls himself Abu Lais."

"All of them are armed to the teeth. Do you notice a certain tension in the air? Perhaps this is your doing."

"I did not discourage it," says Sonia.

Now, again, the emir rises and voices the statement of grievance: the murder of a leader of jihad, and his family and friends, all innocents, by the weapons of the great Satan, and the consequent demand on the cursed apostate Sonia Laghari that she choose who should be killed in just revenge. Sonia names Harold Ashton, and he is duly pulled out into

324 | Michael Gruber

the center of the room by the man in the black striped turban, Sarbaz Khalid Khan, and his usual sidekick, the shaven-head with the bushy beard.

Ashton is pale but stands straight with his legs slightly apart and his hands clasped in the small of his back—parade rest, Sonia thinks; it is a military stance and must have some symbolism for the Englishman, a kind of defiance in his last moments. He addresses Alakazai directly, speaking good Pashto in a loud clear voice.

"Emir, noble Pashtuns, believers! I greet you as one of your enemies. My tribe is the Ingrezi, who ruled this land in your fathers' time. I was born here and my father and his father, and we drank the milk of your women from the breast when we were babies, the same milk as you drank. I tell you this so that you know I am not a stranger, but a milk brother to the Pashtuns. My grandfathers fought your grandfathers, and their fathers before them, two hundred years of fighting. Once you defeated us, and we defeated you every other time. Let others argue if we were good rulers or not, but I think we were not the worst. When we ruled, a child could walk unmolested from Peshawar to Kerala with a bag of gold in his fist, and perhaps that is no longer true. In any case, we were not thrown from the country by force of arms, but we grew tired and poor and changed our beliefs. We thought it was wrong for one man to go to another's house and rule him, even for some great good. I still believe it is wrong, even to do it in the name of God."

He pauses to see how this is going down and looks as though he finds it satisfactory. At least he is a man and is speaking to them in their own language, and in the kind of oratorical phrasing they are used to in their own jirgas.

"When I was a youth I was a warrior, as you are now, and killed and saw much death in different places. I am your prisoner now, but only because I came, as I thought, under a truce, as a maker of peace with these others, and had not thought the Pashtuns would make war on unarmed old men and women. But I was wrong. When I fought as a warrior, perhaps you would not have captured me and perhaps some of you would be dead. But no matter. I fought alongside your fathers, and even some of you perhaps, in the Russian jihad, although I am an unbeliever. And after what I saw there, being no longer a youth but a man and growing tired of war, I began to think. I thought about the Pashtuns, and how they loved freedom and how well they fought to defend their homelands, and how little they got from it, how for many, many years the great powers had used them as pawns. And in the Russian jihad you were pawns too, for you would not have won without the help of the Americans and the Pakistanis. And beyond the Pashtuns I looked at the whole of the umma and I saw what we see today and what has been true also for hundreds of years: a people who are weak and poor and backward and ignorant. From Pakistan to Morocco, the Muslims invent nothing, manufacture nothing that anyone wants to buy. Is there a Muslim cell phone? Is there a Muslim car? Is there even a Muslim gun or a Muslim bullet? You know there is not, although you use these things happily enough. Was this why the Holy Qur'an was given to you, so you could be like the birds who peck grains from the dung of cattle?"

Uproar: they did not like this, not so much for the analysis as for the use of "dung" and "Qur'an" in the same sentence, but he was not dismayed.

"Listen!" he cried in a parade-ground voice. "Listen, believers, and let no one say you were afraid of hearing the words of a dead man. These are my last words, and I do not lie."

They settled, and he resumed.

"Everyone knows this, but everyone disagrees about what should be done. Some say, abandon the traditional ways and become just like the rich countries, but no Muslim country has been able to do this except Turkey, which is a special case and only partly successful. Others say socialism—or said, because that has proven a false hope. Still others say, and you among them, let us return to living under the sharia, the law of God. If you meant that, no one would oppose you. Who in the West would give two pins if you all decided to live simply and be devoted to God? In America there are people, Christians called Amish, who live as their forefathers did, without electricity or machines, simple lives of peace, and everyone praises them and even envies them, a little. Or there are Jews who follow the exact law of Moses and dress as they did three hundred years ago, and who bothers them? But you don't want to live under sharia, if living so means living peacefully in a museum. No, not at all. You want to rule. You want all the goods of the West, you want Viagra and tanks and missiles and electricity and cell phones and computers. But you can't pay for these things because you also want to remain ignorant and uneducated, so you become tools of the oil sheikhs and sell drugs. You become the dogs of anyone who will buy you a gun. Is this the word of God? And who are these strangers you follow, from Arabia, from Egypt, who tell you it is forbidden to do things that your fathers and their fathers' fathers did for as long as there have been Pashtuns? Were your fathers infidels? O Pashtuns, who taught you to spit on the graves of your ancestors?"

Now a more violent pandemonium than before. Every mujahid in the room is up and shouting. One man draws a huge knife and runs at Ashton, jabbing and screaming insults. Ashton holds his ground and two men rush out from the throng and lead the enraged man away. Sonia looks at Alakazai. He is shouting for silence, but his voice does not carry; it is an office voice and grows shrill, like a girl's, when he puts power behind it. But now Idris Ghulan calls for silence with a voice of brass, and pulls out a pistol and fires two rounds into the ceiling.

Instant shocked silence, every ear rings from the shots, and all watch the sparkling dust float down from the bullet spalls and dance in the light bars streaming from the high windows.

"Let the man speak," says Idris, and Sonia sees that the emir looks like he has been struck. All the men sit, if they have a place, and Ashton speaks again, as if he had never been interrupted.

"Now as to this teaching. Where does it come from? None of you would drink from a stream unless you knew the water was pure and unpolluted, or eat meat that was not prepared according to the law of halal, but you don't take the same care of what you put into your minds, although the mind is the seat of the soul and it is the soul that will live in paradise, as you believe. Would you bring a polluted soul before God? So you must have a care with what you believe."

Sonia sees looks of puzzlement cross the faces of the assembly. The idea of questioning their received beliefs has never occurred to them. It is like thinking about whether air really sustains life. But Ashton launches forth, unconcerned, into a history of modern jihadism, starting with its godfather, Mohammed ibn Abd al-Wahab, in eighteenth-century Arabia, and his Salafist belief that the first three generations after the Prophet practiced the only pure form of Islam and that all Muslims must return to this purity. Then he moves forward by leaps through the period of colonialism and the discontents it caused, with a side trip through the Indian Mutiny, then on to the effects of the dissolution of the caliphate in 1924, the feelings of abandonment that spread through the umma as a result, the writings and influence of Abdul Ala el-Mawdudi here in what became Pakistan, his passionate appeal for a rejection of the Enlightenment and the modernity that followed it, establishing the premise for a new kind of jihad. Not only were Muslims to resist the colonial oppressors, for it was abominable for infidels to rule over them, but, even more important, they were to resist the interior colonialist, their admiration for the power of the infidels, their sneaking urge to imitate them and grow rich and powerful themselves. This was a form of idolatry, he wrote, as bad as the *jahiliya* that the Prophet had overthrown.

Now Sonia sees nodding heads—the infidel is starting to make sense. Ashton has loosened his stance; he is gesturing dramatically now, but only with his left hand. He keeps his right arm clenched to his side, as if it has been wounded.

He speaks further in the same vein, about the great Sayyid Qutb, the Egyptian who first extended these ideas to a condemnation not only of colonial regimes but also to supposed Muslim states that aped the infidels and pursued modernism, socialism, democracy, and liberalism. The poverty and weakness of the Muslim lands was their fault, Qutb said, because they had turned from the true religion. They were apostates, illegitimate, and every real Muslim was bound to resist them. The goal was nothing less than the restoration of the caliphate, a system in which state, religion, and society were again one, unfragmented, guided by the eternal word of God, embodied in the sharia. Qutb died a martyr, but his ideas could not be killed so easily. They spread, urged on by the shame of the Zionist usurpation of Palestine and the holy city, Al Quds, and the assaults on the umma by the Russians and the Americans. They were turned into action by al-Qaeda and the Taliban, and here Ashton tells the familiar story of triumph and defeat and renewal. He says, "These ideas now live on in you. This is why you are here."

Ashton pauses and looks out at the ring of dark, bearded faces. They are silent now, waiting, interested. He hitches up his right shoulder in a peculiar way and continues.

"The question now is whether you will succeed. Will you bring the caliphate to life again and erase five centuries of history? And the answer is that of course you will not. As the poet says, *The moving finger, having writ, moves on*; the Muslims may yet have another golden age, but it will not be like the last one, not at all. And your terrorism is futile. Terror is always futile, an announcement of impotence, the rage of a spoiled child. The powers of the earth will never allow a regime forged by terror to survive. The Palestinians have been crushed, the Chechens have been crushed, and the Russians left Afghanistan for the reason that all foreign powers leave Afghanistan, not because of the valor of the Pashtuns but because Afghanistan is worthless, a dry, rocky country that produces nothing but apricots and opium."

At these words the audience begins to rumble menacingly, but Ashton raises his voice and goes on.

"At some level you know this, and that knowledge is symbolized by the suicide bomber. In all history, no campaign of suicide has ever prevailed. It is the last stage of impotent fury—meaningless, insane. At last we come to that word, and the purpose of the conference you have held hostage, which was to examine the psychological basis of the jihad. I am not a psychologist, but I have a theory. Perhaps my colleagues will disagree and call me foolish, but I will not be around to hear it, and I speak, therefore, without fear of contradiction. The key lies, I believe, in the one feature that marks all Salafist regimes, from Saudi Arabia to the Taliban, and that is the oppression of women.

"Why should this be? The Prophet was respectful of women, of his wives, Khadija and Aisha, and his daughter, Fatima, and the rightly guided caliphs consulted them in Islam's early days, those days for which you pretend a deep and reverent nostalgia. The Qur'an is not notably against women, not even as much as the Bible. So I must conclude that the oppression of women is not a by-product of the jihad movement but its purpose. What drives you to murder and suicide is not the love of God but the fear of women, of educated women, of women released from the absolute domination of men. Because women are a true mirror. They are more sensible than you are, they want their children to flourish, and if they were free they would look at you all, and ask, 'O believers, why so poor, why so ignorant, why so despised by the world?' And they would despise you too. You fight to prevent this, you fight to preserve not the modesty but the *stupidity* of women, and where you succeed these stupid women produce even stupider sons—yourselves—and if there were a God he would be laughing in all your faces."

Sonia can barely hear the last of this peroration because of the enraged screaming echoing from the walls and ceiling of the room, the cry of a culture gored in its vitals. The roar coalesces into a chant: *Death, death, kill him, kill him!* Dispensing with reasoned rebuttal, the two guards dart toward Ashton. The big one raises his AK, clearly meaning to smash the Englishman in the face, but Ashton backs away from him, in the direction of the wall against which the prisoners sit. It looks like he is trying to hide behind one of the thick pillars that support the roof beams.

The other guard, Sarbaz, slips around between Ashton and the wall, and jabs him viciously in the small of his back with the muzzle of his stockless Kalashnikov. The crowd is on its feet. The noise is tremendous, like that at a bullfight and for the same reason.

Then Ashton whirls around to his left, knocking Sarbaz's muzzle aside with his left forearm. Sonia is only a few yards away and she sees the weighted sock he has held in his armpit drop into his right hand. A blur, as he swings it around, sending the stone crashing into Sarbaz's temple, at the same instant grabbing the barrel of the AK with his left hand. Sarbaz collapses. Ashton flips the weapon into firing position, comes around the pillar, shoots down the other guard, takes a few steps away from the wall, and directs an accurate stream of automatic fire at Bahram Alakazai and the people sitting near him.

He has certainly handled a Kalashnikov before, thinks Sonia, and it was wise of him to step away from the prisoners. He gets off most of a magazine before the crowd understands what is happening. Thirty or so weapons answer Mr. Ashton's arguments, and he falls, and the crowd rushes forward to fire more rounds into the heap of bloody rags and kick it and scream imprecations.

Now is the moment of greatest peril, Sonia knows, when the rage will turn toward the most convenient helpless objects, and all the hostages will be massacred. Several in the mob make just this suggestion, but a voice cries out, "The emir has been hurt, save the emir!" and this distracts them for a moment and they all rush over to surround the place where the emir and the group of his closest supporters lie in their blood. Within seconds of that cry, the Arab mujahideen dash forward, surround the hostages with weapons pointed, and hustle them out of the room, out of the inn, down a steep narrow street, and into a large private house, a two-story mud-brick structure surrounded by an eight-foot wall topped with rusty strands of barbed wire.

The prisoners are escorted to two rooms on the second level of the house, in the back, the men in one and Annette and Sonia in the other. The room holds two charpoys set at random in the middle of the floor, a pile of bedding, and a plastic water jug and basin. Light comes from a high window, a thin horizontal slit of blue. When the door is closed and locked, the two women look at each other, begin to weep, and fall together in a desperate hug. Their legs cannot hold them upright; clutched together, they slide to the floor. In two minutes the spasm is over. Sonia mops her face with her dupatta and grins.

"Well. We're still alive. Oh, God, that poor bastard! He said he didn't want to go out like a sheep and he didn't. The emir is turning on a spit in Hell and we're still here."

"Did you know what he was going to do?" asks Annette.

"More or less," Sonia admits.

"You *arranged* that massacre?" says Annette, her eyes widening.

"Of course not. How could I have arranged anything? I'm a helpless prisoner, just like you."

"But what about what Karl-Heinz said, about what you were doing with Idris? He wasn't killed. You must have told him what Ashton was going to do."

"No. What we just saw was the result of a rivalry between factions of the mujahideen. Idris and Alakazai were at odds and Alakazai was plotting to kill Idris, and this insight emerged in Idris's dreams. This happens all the time, but most people ignore it. I don't, and obviously neither did Idris. For all we know, Idris arranged the whole thing. As you point out, Idris was sitting on the other side of the room, away from the line of fire."

Sonia sees Annette nodding as she accepts this explanation. Sonia dislikes prevarication but she feels no need to dispense the truth in full to people who are better kept innocent. It is an ancient reflex of hers, and she has learned to live with it.

Annette says, "So what now? We seem to be in the hands of a different group of bastards. Are they going to kill us too?"

"It's hard to say. It may just be a temporary respite until the pecking order gets sorted out. My sense of these Abu Lais guys is that they're mainly interested in the bombs being made in the village. You've heard all the machine noises and the diesel cranking all night. I don't think they have much interest in being burdened down with hostages. Idris might demand our return or he might have sold us to these Arabs in a side deal. Maybe he decided he doesn't want to do any more executions, or maybe the Arabs would like to do them to spice up their own Web site, or maybe they have some kind of prisoner exchange in mind. I expect we'll find out in due time. Meanwhile, I'm interested in when we're getting fed. We would have had our postbeheading lunch by now, had it not been for Ashton's stunt . . . What?"

Annette was looking at her as at a video of a traffic accident. "I don't understand how you can be you. I mean, one minute you're kind and caring and say you want to help people and the next you're like, I don't know, some kind of calculating monster. We've just witnessed an unbelievable horror and we might die horribly at any minute and all you can think about is *lunch*?"

"One thing has nothing to do with the other," says Sonia, with a dismissive air. "Compassion is an obligation of the faith and I'm a therapist by inclination and training, and my instinct is to help where I can. All that is perfectly sincere. The other is me in my Islamic mode. Fate is in the hands of God and it's ignoble to worry about what might or might not happen. Also, I think existing in two cultures the way I do provides a different perspective on things. It inclines one to the long view."

"I don't understand."

"Well, take yourself, for example. By your own admission you're a corn-fed midwestern woman, and despite the fact that you've been around the world in some pretty rough places, you retain that basic American optimism: folks are the same all over, everyone wants the good things in life, and so on. Being American, and Protestant in the bargain, you're all for individual responsibility and the individual conscience that goes with it. You're basically in control. If you're in a church that doesn't suit you for some reason, you're out the door into another or you start your own. And you believe in progress. We can help people to advance, to be like us: bill of rights, elections, clean water, flush toilets, antibiotics, refrigerators and cars, the works."

"Don't you?"

"Up to a point. But as I said, I have the long view ingrained, along with all my co-religionists. Look at us now, locked up in what we think of as the ass-end of nowhere, but this area was once connected to a universal empire that stretched from Spain to Indonesia. A thousand years ago, Baghdad was the capital of the world, the richest city since the fall of Rome. Basra was the intellectual center of that world. Ever been to Basra? Today it's easily distinguishable from Silicon Valley, but back then they were inventing paper and mathematics based on Arabic numerals, and they had more books per capita than anywhere else. Hell, there were more books and scholars in Timbuktu than there were in Paris. Timbuktu! The metonym for isolation!

"I'll tell you a story. I'm in the middle of Central Asia, following my pir from shrine to shrine, all these decrepit little hovels watched over by shriveled men with no teeth. A devastated country, full of nothing but bones and blowing yellow sands—even the Soviets couldn't make much of it—and it looked like it had been that way forever. We'd had days of storms, the sand blowing so thick you couldn't see your hand, so we stopped outside a miserable village and pitched camp in the lee of some mounds, just a low brown scarp growing up near the track we were following.

"But in the middle of the night the wind dropped, fell off entirely, and it woke me up, the silence after days of that continual maddening howl, and I saw the most wonderful buttery light coming down from the sky. We were under a kind of tent, really just a crude windbreak, and I threw off my blankets and walked out. The sky was perfectly clear, thick with stars, and the moon was full, which we hadn't been able to see in days. And I walked away from our camp through those mounds, to take a pee, and suddenly I found myself walking on a solid floor, not crunching sand; I was walking on a mosaic. The wind had blown the sand away and I realized that the mounds I thought were some geological feature were actually ruins. The mosaic was exquisite, the work of real masters, I could see that even by the moon, and I took out my pocket flash and looked at it. It wasn't a floor at all, I saw; it was gently curved and it had calligraphy on it, worked out in mosaic tiles, black letters against a ground of lapis blue and gold. It said *believe in the Unseen*; that's from the Qur'an, the second sura: *That is the Book, wherein is no doubt, a guidance to the God-fearing who believe in the Unseen and perform the prayer*. It must have been part of the dome of an absolutely enormous mosque."

"Like in that poem."

"Yes, 'Ozymandias.' *Look on my works, ye Mighty, and despair!* But the thing here was that no one cared. It wasn't an archaeological dig. Central Asia is thick with the ruins of completely forgotten cities, and this was one of them. When the Mongols came through they just destroyed everything and killed everyone. They didn't like cities, the Mongols. So once you've had an experience like that, the cities of the West can't look the same, and by extension the whole culture seems almost provisional. There's nothing immortal about us either. Or you, I should say, the culture you represent."

"Yes, but what do you *do* with that? How can you keep that in your mind? I mean, you'd never bother to do laundry."

Sonia laughs at that. "Laundry is indeed one of the eternal things. Of course I live a daily life like anyone else, but always *sub specie aeternitatis*, if that makes sense. I'm religious, for one thing, and that helps; I suppose that's what attracted me to Jung, besides the fact that I went crazy in Zurich and needed help. Jung thought there was something real going on beyond the scrim of nature and that it was the most interesting thing in the universe; the playing out of consciousness, both divine consciousness and the little fragment that we're given to fool around with. Ah, the door opens! That has to be either lunch or death."

It is lunch. One of the Arabs leans in and, with a scowl but without a word, places a tray on the floor, on which sits a blackened metal pot, a steaming can of tea, and two chipped cups. When the door is closed behind him, Sonia washes her hands and kneels by the tray.

"What is it?" Annette asks, without interest.

Sonia reaches into the pot and tastes. "It's rice and peas and ... by God, it's mutton! Actual meat! I think we've received an upgrade, probably because we're such good customers. Come on, it's wonderful!"

The two women dip their fingers in the mess and eat, although Annette eats gingerly.

Sonia leaves off sucking on a small bone and asks, "What's the matter, no appetite?"

"Not really. All I can think about is poor Harold looking like something from a butcher shop. I might be off meat for a while."

"Suit yourself, but I intend to eat as much as I can, including your share." Which she does and leans back against the wall, nearly content, sipping tea.

"You're amazing," says Annette.

"Why? Because I eat after observing a massacre and the slaughter of a colleague? Consider this: it might well be my last meal, or someone else might get hold of us and not feed us for a week. Here's a tip: anytime you're cut loose from the groove of Western bourgeois life, eat anything you can until you can't eat anymore, just like four-fifths of humanity does every day. Uh-oh, I hope that's dessert."

A key rattles in the lock and the same guard steps in, holding a rifle. Both women stand. He gestures to Sonia. He says, "You come," and, to Annette, "You stay."

The man takes Sonia to another room. It is furnished with a charpoy, a simple wooden table, and a straight chair. In one corner sits a boxy shape the size of a small chest covered by a canvas tarpaulin. Sonia sits on the charpoy, and the Arab shuts the door behind him without a word.

Sonia waits. She is filled with a strange exultant expectation; she thinks it must be like waiting for a blind date who could be the one and only, or opening a fat envelope from a college admissions office, although she has never had these experiences. She reckons that nearly an hour must have passed when she hears steps outside. The door opens, and in walks the Engineer, Abu Lais. He looks at her and smiles and says, in barely accented English, "Well, Sonia, what the hell am I supposed to do with you now?"

19

In Dubai airport I checked my e-mail and found two significant messages, one from Farid and the other from First Sergeant Cheney. Farid's said, "Threat eliminated. Contact me as to your status." I found a pay phone, called him, and learned we'd got rid of Cynthia Lam and the government had completely bought the nuclear scam. Then I called Cheney and he told me that all leaves were canceled and to get my ass back to Fort Belvoir ASAP. Of course he couldn't give me operational details over the phone, but I assumed we were part of the government's commitment to go in and shoot up Pakistan, so I felt pretty good, and for the rest of my trip I managed not to think more than a little about some of our people getting killed chasing the phantom I'd created.

I cabbed in from Dulles, loaded up my gear, changed into my digital-camo battle-dress uniform, left a note for Farid, and drove to Belvoir. The second I walked into the orderly room, Cheney said, "Goddamn, Bailey, where the fuck were you? I said ASAP."

"I was in Dubai," I said.

"What the fuck were you doing in—oh, never mind. The old man wants to see you. He's been on my ass every half hour about you all day." He lifted his phone and shooed me away and I went down a couple of hallways to the company commander's office.

I saluted and Stoltz told me to sit down. He didn't ask me where I'd been, or why, which I thought was a good sign.

"Bailey, you recall that nuclear-threat clambake we went to last summer?"

"Yes, sir."

"Well, I hope it's still fresh in your mind, because it happened."

"No shit, sir? The terrorists have a bomb?"

"Maybe more than one. There's a shit storm over this from the White House on down: every resource we got, balls to the wall."

"Do we have a location?"

"As a matter of fact, we do, it's Pakistan, and we've apparently got some intel that the things won't be there for much longer, so everything's moving very fast. We have a manifest call for twenty-hundred hours."

"That's impossible."

"Tell me about it. But we're going, ready or not."

"Why us? There are all kinds of resources deployed downrange."

"*You're* why, my son, which was why we were going fucking crazy that you were off on leave. You remember that conversation we had in the car coming back from the conference? About how to handle a live nuke situation?"

"Yeah, I do. Don't tell me. I just volunteered for a dangerous solo mission."

"That's right. And now you and me are going to firm it up so it's not total amateur hour, and then we're going to go down the hall to Colonel Boone and present it to him and the battalion staff, and God have mercy on our souls."

So we firmed it up. Every army plan is the same, whether it's a platoon sergeant taking a strongpoint or a general leading an invasion: intelligence, operations, supplies, and communications, all laid out according to a fixed form. We had plenty of intel about this place, Paidara, which turned out to be a village of about a thousand people, high up a side valley of the Swat River, one little track going up to it, maybe a hundred buildings, a mosque, an inn; the Taliban were in complete control. We had close-up photographs of every building in town, natural light and infrared. One building in particular stood out on the infrared. It was unusually hot, and there was a big diesel generator outside it. They figured that was the bomb factory, which was a lucky break for me, something that gave a little extra credibility to my scam. For all I knew it *was* a place they were manufacturing weapons—half the villages in Taliban areas have shops like that—and I nodded and agreed it would be the first place to check out. Aside from that the operation was simple: insert one troop (me) in disguise. For supplies, I'd have a radio beacon and the usual weapons. If I couldn't actually get to the imaginary bomb I would secure the beacon at the building it was in, which would then be targeted from the air, with a really, really big piece of ordnance, reducing the nuke to tiny fragments and rendering the place uninhabitable for a thousand years, but tough shit on them. Before that, I was to get out and they'd send a chopper. On the other hand, if I secured the bomb, I'd contact by radio and the village would be taken by assault. Since the nuke was fictitious, that's the button I was going to push, right after I had my mother.

We tapped the whole thing out on Captain Stolz's computer, and one of our guys made a PowerPoint out of it, and we tweaked it right up to the time we had to go see Lieutenant Colonel Boone. Sergeants usually don't go to these officer briefings where our fates are decided by people smarter than we are, so I was pretty interested, and I thought it was kind of cool for them to invite me, my first and last officer briefing. Because obviously they were not going to find a bomb when they got to the beacon, only a slightly confused middle-aged American woman, who would tell them all about the scheme her son had devised that had brought them to this obscure place. The son by that time would be long gone, back into the hills, heading for wherever.

That's what I was thinking while the briefing was going on, and I was thinking also about the strange gravity of American soldiers, how isolated they are from their own society, where death is ignored or, when it comes, gets treated like an unfortunate mistake, or sentimentally, with the candles, the ribbons, the teddy bears, and how they struggle to make war safe for their guys, like it was pro football or something. And the heaviness of their wit, their American joshing, the sports talk, so different from that of my grandfather and his friends or my Pashtuns. They are terrific men; I admired them, but right there in that meeting I understood that I was not and never would be like that. I would never be easy with such men, nor they with me, and my American self sort of dribbled away. I looked out at the meeting through Pashtun eyes and felt like the oldest man in the room.

Forty hours after that I was the sole payload of an MC-130P Combat Shadow aircraft flying at twenty-two thousand feet over the Hindu Kush toward the Swat Valley. They'd decided on a HALO insert rather than trying to get me in by chopper because you never could tell when

338 | Michael Gruber

some goatherd might decide to take a leak in the middle of the night and see or hear the thing and raise an alarm. A couple of years back we'd lost a Chinook and sixteen men on a mission that way, and they didn't want to take any chance of the same thing happening on this one, especially not with that unique asset, me. I was feeling a little sausage-like because I had my Pashtun outfit on and over that a jumpsuit, and over that a heated suit. The crew chief let me know we were a half hour off the drop point, and I laid out my stuff and gave it the final check. I had an altimeter and a GPS that would clip to the front of my jumpsuit and I had my special beacon, a CIA unit that was rigged to look like a cheap Chinese portable radio, and it worked as a regular two-way radio in case I needed it. I had a big Pashtun knife, and my Stechkin too, and I cleaned and loaded that in the plane's red light.

Then my ears started popping, because the plane was descending, fast but carefully between the walls of the Swat Valley, which are around fifteen thousand feet high. We got the five-minute light from the flight deck. I stood up, switched to my portable oxygen bottle, put on my helmet, and attached my rucksack to the chute harness with a cord. I held the rucksack to my belly and clumped down the aisle of the plane. The rear clamshell opened, letting in the chill and the roar of the wind. The crew chief grabbed my shoulder hard and let go and I gave him the thumbs-up. In the red light he looked like a demon worried about the existence of goodness and I grinned at him, looking myself, I guess, like a more enterprising one. I walked past the line where you weren't supposed to go unless you were in a safety harness, and when the light next to the door turned from amber to green I stepped out into the clouds.

℞

I love doing this, I have to say. I've loved it since my first jump at Benning years ago, and I guess a month hasn't gone by since then that I haven't jumped out of an airplane, either at work or for fun. This particular jump was a high-altitude, low-opening jump, which means that I dropped free fall for a mile through cloudy damp freezing darkness, completely opaque, no light at all except the tiny glow from my instruments. It was like falling through the sea at the bottom of the ocean. It wasn't like a sky dive for amusement, where you can horse around in the air, but it had its own appeal, a jump like that you know you're really alive, you inhabit your skin the way you don't do any other way I know, sex maybe excepted.

Since it was a drop into mountains, I had to watch the altimeter and the GPS all the way down so that I would land in a flat place—a more or less flat place—in the Swat Valley and not on some rock, because altimeters work by measuring air pressure. It was going to give me distance above sea level but not distance above the random mountain, so it was dangerous as hell, but strangely enough I felt no fear at all. I was in the zone. I had the perfect confidence of the fanatic, and I thought of Ghalib's lines:

> I have become the dust in her street.
> O wind, let me down, I don't want to fly anymore.

As it happened, I came out of the clouds at about two thousand feet, in rain, and of course I couldn't see much and I popped the chute and the MT-5 opened up above me and I was flying. A modern military parachute is basically a controllable kite; subject to the wind, you can fly it as long as you like and land on a crate of eggs without much damage. So I watched my GPS, headed toward a tributary of the Swat River, and found it all right; I could see the white froth of its passage over rocks, and I landed nicely on a little gravelly beach.

I pulled my pack shovel from my rucksack, buried the flight suit and chute and helmet and boots, tossed the shovel in, and kicked gravel into the hole. I took my Stechkin in its wooden holster from the pack, strapped it on under my kameez, and wrapped my blankets over my shoulders against the thin rain. I found a sheltered place among the rocks that bordered the river, wrapped myself tightly in my blankets, and fell asleep.

In the morning sheep awakened me and for a second I was back in my youth, when I was herding for the jihad and the sound of sheep was always in my ears, especially in spring when the ewes call constantly to their new lambs, as they were now. I hoisted on my rucksack and knotted my blankets around my shoulders the way we do in that country and clambered up through the rocks until I came to a track on the east side of the river.

It was a good-sized flock, maybe eighty sheep guided by a middle-aged man and a boy. I approached the man and wished him peace and he did the same and I offered him a pinch of tobacco and a piece of newspaper and we both rolled and smoked and talked about sheep for a while. He was going to Kalam to sell his lambs and ram yearlings, and I said, "Brother, I see God is smiling on me today in meeting you."

He asked me how so, and I told him that I too was going to Kalam, but to buy sheep, not sell them. My brother's son was getting married this week in Paidara and I was going to give a feast for our whole clan, and if he would sell me half a dozen ewes and their lambs I would save a journey. He reflected on the providence of God and regretted that he was a poor man and could not give me a discount; I would have to pay the full Kalam market price, and he named a figure that, as an old shepherd myself, I reckoned was three times the sum that any sheep had ever sold for in any market from Herat to Lahore. I told him he had mistaken me for a rich man, or for someone in the market for sheep that had been especially trained to walk on wires or could talk in human tongues. I was only interested in ones that could be eaten, and I named a lower price.

He said that perhaps I had mistaken *him* for a charitable trust, but no, he was just a poor shepherd trying to earn a living, and I had to hear a story about the miseries of shepherding in these dark times, and we went around the block for a while in the good old way and finally I closed the deal for half a dozen ewes and their lambs for about 50 percent over market, and these the least desirable sheep in the flock, botflied, dull-eyed, and thin.

I used my Pashtun knife to cut a crook from a willow thicket and walked off with my flock toward Paidara. I had landed, by design, about ten klicks away, and dragging along with my sheep it took me until early afternoon to climb the high valley trail to the first mujahideen checkpoint outside the village. This was four beards with AKs and one on a Toyota pickup with a mounted Russian heavy machine gun. We had a nice chat, and I offered one of my ewes and her lamb as a gesture of my sincere support for the jihad. I passed through with smiles and good wishes.

Paidara was what I expected, a crumbled brick hamlet with some signs of recent prosperity: a shop selling cheap consumer goods, electric generators, fewer beggars than average, and scores of Taliban driving the narrow streets in mud-spattered brand-new trucks and SUVs. The jihad was good business, apparently. I asked a man on the street where the butchers were and sold off my sheep for about half what I'd paid for them. In the necessary chat with the butcher and his pals, and the curious Taliban passers-by, I gave a name and clan lineage out of Kunar in Afghanistan, which more or less protected me from undue suspicion. People cross the border all the time, of course, and when they found I was just a shepherd, not too bright, and had no smuggled goods, they all lost interest.

I went to the tea shop and drank sweet milky tea until it was coming out of my ears, and picked up the town gossip. Big doings recently in Paidara, I learned. The place had been Taliban for quite a while, and they were digging in, fortifying houses and tunneling; the Pakistani army had announced a truce, but no one trusted the Pakistani army, well known to be in the pay of the Americans. Besides that, Arab mujahideen had arrived, there were hostages, money had flowed, and more would flow from this. I asked where they kept the infidels. Oh, that was another good story. One of the infidels had grabbed a weapon and killed the Taliban emir and his chief men, and in the affray the Arabs had stolen the hostages. Did I know one of them was a witch? Yes, she had bewitched many in the village, telling them their dreams and what they meant, and some said she had bewitched the new emir, Idris Ghulam, of whom I had possibly heard, a local boy whose valor was famous throughout the Swat. He would deal with the treacherous Arabs, although there were complications having to do with a weapons factory the Arabs had set up in the village, and no one wanted to lose the money that brought in. Negotiations between the two groups was ongoing, and everyone hoped that soon they would start to chop heads again; everyone was looking forward to the fun.

Sheep for feasting were getting scarce, and I learned how much I'd gotten ripped off on my flock. Much laughter here—all Pashtuns love a fool. A man named Abdur took pity on the poor jerk me and offered a room for the night. I said I would be glad to accept, but I had a family duty. My aunt had recently been widowed in a village not too far away and I had promised I would bring her back to the family in Kunar Province. I couldn't impose on his hospitality with another guest.

He dismissed this airily: of course you can invite her, another woman is nothing, you are both welcome. I thanked him sincerely, saying that God would remember his generosity and threw in the quote about the blessedness of charity to the wayfarer from the Qur'an. So that was all set. I'd snatch my mother, bring her back here veiled, and get on with the rest of the mission. I walked home with my new pal, and we sat on rugs in the main room of his house and were fed by silent black shapes, and we talked of the terrible times. My man had no real objection to the Taliban, at least they kept crime under control and he thought the government was too harsh when it tried to uproot them. Bombs! Artillery! Many innocents had died. But of course the Taliban were wicked as well; they demanded that all rents be paid into their hands and not to the rightful landlords, of which he was one, and they murdered anyone who objected. Yes, it was a terrible time, but with God's help perhaps it would improve. Slowly, without seeming to, I turned the conversation to the captive infidels. I said I assumed the Arabs had them hidden away and no one knew where they were. Of course everyone knew; it was in the house of his wife's cousin, which he was renting to the Arabs, who at least paid dollars to the landlord. And he told me more than I needed to know about the house, how much his wife's cousin had paid for it, who had owned it before, and what improvements had been made since, and said his wife's cousin was a fool like all his family, since the man could've gotten far more for such a fine house if he had only known how to bargain.

Then I excused myself and said I had to go fetch my aunt and would probably be back quite late. Abdur wished me a safe journey and said his wife and daughters would be happy to receive the begum at any hour. I went out into the street. Perfectly black, overcast, a narrow alley like a mine shaft. I squatted down and screwed the silencer into my Stechkin and switched it to single shot. Then I strolled off to the wife's cousin's house. Paidara was shut down for the night, no one around, no sounds but the occasional dog barking and the purr of a generator. It had been a piece of good luck to meet Abdur, but anyone in the village could've given me information almost as good. Everyone knew everyone's business in a village like this, and it would never occur to any of them that an American soldier could pass as one of the tribe. I had a pretty good map of the village in my head from studying the satellite shots and I didn't have much trouble finding the house, a short street away from the inn.

It was a two-story building of the usual adobe brick and crumbling plaster, with an outside stairway up to the top floor and a high wall around it topped with a few strands of barbed wire. The gateway was closed with a wooden gate capped with spikes and faced with sheet-metal panels, and the windows were closed with louvered shutters. Bars of light strayed from the louvers in one of the upstairs windows, and I could see a ruddier flickering light coming from behind the closed gate. I stayed in the shadows across the little street and listened for a while. Men were talking in Arabic, softly: at least two, not more than four. I waited. They teach us to wait in my part of the army, and it's one of the hard things; you have to stop thinking you're in a movie, where action follows action.

Someone raised his voice, and there came an answering voice from the roof of the house. There was a man up there; I could just make out his silhouette. So figure three guys standing around a fire barrel in front and one up on the roof. He had to go first.

I walked through the darkness to the back of the house. Very good. A shedlike extension behind it with a tin chimney and a sloping tiled roof that connected with the rear wall of the house. It was not hard to get up on the tiles, and then it was a climb of maybe fifteen feet up the wall. Brick houses in this part of the world are not hard to scale; the brickwork is rough and often crumbling and the people are poor and slow to make repairs. I'd been climbing up walls like this since I could walk. I scrambled up and over the low parapet and crouched there in its shadow.

I heard steps. The roof guard had finished his conversation and was making his rounds, or maybe he was just moving because of the chill. He walked right by me and I stood up behind him and silently shot him through the head and grabbed his AK before it could hit the ground.

I slung the rifle over my shoulder and went down the outside stairway from the roof to the second floor. The door was unlocked and I entered the house. I was in a hallway with four doors. The only light came from under the door at the end of the hall; someone had a lamp going in there. It was enough light to see where they were keeping the hostages. It's hard to turn a private house into a jail. The interior doors of a house don't ordinarily lock from the outside, but the Arabs had attached two simple barrel bolts to each door, top and bottom. I chose one of the doors, pulled the bolts, and went in.

Two charpoys, each with a sleeping form under blankets. I bent my face closer to one sleeping head and sniffed. Unwashed woman. I took a lock of the invisible hair between my fingers. It was fine and when I walked my fingers down the strand I found that it was longer than my mother's hair. I went to the other sleeper and sniffed again and closed a deep unconscious switch, an animal relic. I knew my mother's smell. Gently, I touched her face. Her eyes popped open and her mouth opened to say something but I placed my hand over it.

"Quiet," I whispered. "It's me, Theo."

"Theo," she said and stared at me. She looked like she thought she was dreaming. "How did you get here?"

"Parachute."

"How did you know I was here?"

"It's a long story, Mother, and we haven't got time. We have to get out of here."

"Get out . . . you mean all the hostages?"

"No, just you. I came for you."

"Theo, I can't, I can't just leave all these people."

"You won't have to. There's a rescue operation on the way, but I want you where I can keep an eye on you. Put your shoes on."

The other woman stirred in her sleep and made a sound. After a moment's hesitation I heard my mother feeling around for her footwear and she stood up and I led her out of the room, bolting the door behind me.

Then someone shouted from outside. And again, more urgently. The men in front must have missed hearing from the guard on the roof. Footsteps and shouts on the outside stairway. I switched my machine pistol to full automatic.

A door opened. The hallway flooded with light. The black shape of a man in the doorway at the end of the hall. Everything was moving in slo-mo now as it does in a firefight. I had to take out the man in the doorway and then I'd go to the head of the stairs and shoot the guys coming up. I raised my Stechkin. I put the sight on the silhouette and squeezed the trigger, and as I did so, my mother struck my elbow an upward blow and the burst slammed into the ceiling.

"Theo!" she yelled. "Don't shoot him. It's Wazir!"

20

They took Cynthia to the basement of the main NSA building, OPS-2A, where the police force that monitors Crypto City has its headquarters. She was placed in the canonical windowless room with a table and two chairs, all bolted to the floor. There was no sound from outside, the only noise the whir from the overhead vent. At one corner of the ceiling hung a small closed-circuit TV camera.

She sat and avoided looking at the camera. The Dutch courage from the martinis was rapidly fading, and this vexed the martinis, so that they no longer wanted to dwell in this unprofitable belly. Along with her spicy lunch they were sending urgent messages that they wished to leave, perhaps to decorate the sterile top of that table, or the floor.

Cynthia took deep breaths; she attempted calming thoughts. A fine cool sweat bloomed on her forehead. The door to the room opened and the two security men who had lifted her walked in. One was a mild-looking Latino; the other was a taller man with a flat ugly face and small, deep-set, piggy blue eyes. The tall one, the obvious bad cop, walked around the table and stood just out of her peripheral vision, leaning against the wall. The Latino sat down on the chair opposite her. He extended his hand and she took it, aware of how clammy her own was.

"Gene Arbenz," he said. "That's Bill Cavanagh over there. We're here to explain your situation as it now stands."

"Can I make a phone call?"

"Not at this time, Cynthia."

"Well, when can I make one?"

"I don't have any information on that," said Arbenz.

"Then why don't you find someone who has that information?"

She felt the wind of movement behind her and Cavanagh leaped forward and slammed his hand down on the table with a shocking noise that made her bladder give way for a second, dampening her underwear.

His mouth was inches from her ear; she could smell his aftershave as he said, "Why don't you fucking shut up and listen!"

Arbenz cast an admonitory look at his colleague. "Bill? Let me handle this, okay?"

Cavanagh grunted and went back to the wall.

Arbenz smiled and said, "Look, Cynthia, in a little while this is going to be out of our hands. You know what we usually do in security; we put up posters and check bags, and we run like a small-town police force for the facilities here at Meade. We're not set up to, like, interrogate terrorists."

"I'm not a terrorist. I haven't done anything wrong." She heard the quaver in her voice.

"Yeah, well the bosses think you have, and I have to say it looks real bad for you. A terrorist mole in NSA? With Top Secret clearance? Holy shit, Cynthia, this is going to go all the way to the White House. So I'm advising you informally, speaking as part of the NSA family, if there's anything you're holding back, now's the time to let it out."

"I'm not holding anything back. I'm telling the truth."

"Maybe, but the best way to put everyone's mind at ease in that regard is to tell us about the money."

"What money?"

Arbenz sighed, as if he were so tired of hearing the pathetic lies of the guilty. "The money, Cynthia. In the Swiss account. Who paid it?"

"I don't know what you're talking about," she said. "I don't have any Swiss account."

"Yes, you do. Over fifty thousand dollars has been run through that account in the last week, sent in and drawn out in ten-thousand-dollar increments. We need to know the source and where it is now."

"I don't—"

"Who paid it, Cynthia?" snarled Cavanagh behind her. "Who paid you to sell out your country? Fucking little gook bitch, we let her into this country and this is how she acts."

Arbenz frowned at this. "Cavanagh, cut it out!"

Cavanagh cursed and walked to a corner of the room and slouched against the wall, an actor in a well-rehearsed play. Cynthia had seen the play too, like everyone else with a television, but that didn't mean it wasn't working.

"I'm sorry about that," said Arbenz gently. "There's never any need for that kind of language. But the problem, Cynthia, the problem is, we got you. I mean, we have this."

He reached into his pocket and took out a plastic evidence bag. In the bag was a thumb drive.

"You kept this in your mailbox. It's got the codes for your Swiss account and the decrypt code for the encrypted e-mails on your laptop. We've read them and they lay out the whole plot. How you were paid to convince NSA that there was no theft of nuclear material."

"There wasn't. The whole thing was a scam. And I never saw that drive before."

"Then what about Mr. Borden? Do you deny that you got him to hack into the CIA computers? Borden is being very cooperative, Cynthia. He told us everything."

Cynthia felt a pang of fear. "There's nothing to tell," she said. "I was trying to prevent a mistake. The intercepts were clearly phony and I can prove it with voiceprint analysis. The whole thing is part of a rogue CIA plot and I've been framed and you're falling for it."

"That's a little too fancy, honey, don't you think?" said Cavanagh.

"It's the truth," she said.

"Liar," said Cavanagh.

Arbenz let out a small sigh. "Okay, then, in that case let me tell you what's going to happen. In a few minutes a female officer will come in here and take all your clothes and jewelry, your watch, everything, and she will subject you to a full body-cavity search. You will be given other clothes to wear. You'll be taken to a holding cell in this building. After that, agents of another federal agency will remove you from this site and take you to another facility for further interrogation. Do you understand that?"

"Yes. What other agency?"

"I have no information on that," said Arbenz, "but you read the papers, you know what happens to suspected terrorists nowadays. They disappear. Stuff is done to them. And they talk; sooner or later, they all talk. So there's no point in holding out. Cynthia, I'm trying to help you here.

Please, for your own sake: Who's your contact? Where's the money? Who got you into this mess?"

Cynthia remained silent. After waiting a few long minutes, the two men left. She sat in the chair, trying to forget about her stomach and her bladder. She wondered what it would take to break her; not much, she thought, if they broke Arab terrorists they shouldn't have a bit of trouble with a stupid American girl who'd had things fairly easy her whole life and who really believed in nothing much except her own career.

A black woman came in, portly, blank-faced, carrying a large paper bag. She dumped a bright orange garment onto the table.

In a robotic voice she said, "Are you menstruating or pregnant at this time?"

"No."

"Are you currently infected with the HIV virus?"

"No."

"Take off all your clothes and jewelry and put them in this bag. Here is a marker. When you have removed your things and placed them in the bag, lick the tape, seal the bag, and sign your name on the tape. Then lean over and grasp the edge of the table."

Cynthia had often wondered in a vague way about how the monster regimes of the twentieth century got so many people—millions of them— to drop the human dignity that went with clothing and stand naked before men who were going to torture and murder them, but now she understood very well that there is hard-wired into the human psyche the false idea that someone who has absolute power over your body will be, must be, ultimately benevolent. Children are this way; human life would be impossible without that innate compact, and the evil ones of the earth exploit it to their ends. So children submit meekly to murder at the hands of their loved ones, and naked women march in orderly rows, holding their naked children's hands, to the edge of the execution pits.

So now she was naked, bent over, and the woman told her to spread her legs, wider, *wider*. Cynthia stared wildly over her shoulder and saw that the woman looked at her in a way she had never been looked at by another woman, as an object to be processed, and she did process her, shoving her glove into Cynthia's body cavities, first the mouth, and then, greased up, the vagina and rectum. Cynthia had heard that when rape occurred some women survived the horror by disassociating from their bodies, by making themselves believe it was not happening to them. She thought now that she would never be able to do this; she was failing now even in response to this lesser violation. Her body was too plainly importunate; it wanted to pee, to weep, and to puke, and it was all she could manage to keep these things from happening simultaneously.

The woman directed her to don the orange garment, and she did and placed the cotton slippers on her feet. She sat down again and waited, with legs crossed around her bursting bladder. Time passed, six minutes or six hours, she could not tell, and this was yet another way of announcing that she was cut off from the clock-bound society from which she issued; her time was now worth nothing, ergo she was nothing, an object, like a desk or a bar of metal.

The door opened after however long, and a small compact man and a quite large woman came in, both wearing gray suits, both with quite ordinary faces; she would not have spared a glance at them on the street. She asked to go to the toilet. They declined to answer but worked silently and swiftly to manacle her hands and feet, connecting the chains to a broad leather belt. They placed a cloth hood over her head and led her away.

A ride in some kind of truck ensued. The exhaust fumes and the motion of the vehicle overcame the last of Cynthia's physical resistance, her body betrayed her then and she wet herself and vomited into the hood, and the stench of this kept her stomach heaving long after it had been drained of its contents. No one helped her. Now she cried.

♫

They had to half-carry her out of the van; her feet tripped on a short flight of stairs and she lost a slipper. She heard the swish and hum of an elevator. A door opened. Someone removed her manacles and the hood. She stood unsteadily, blinking in a harsh light. She was in a small room lined with white tiles, like a bus station restroom. She tried not to breathe in her own stink. Vomit smeared her face and the chest of her prison suit and her crotch and thighs were soaked and starting to chill. Overhead a caged light fixture held two bare incandescent bulbs and next to it an eye bolt had been affixed to the ceiling, which was covered in what looked like gray foam panels. There was a steel drain in the concrete floor. Frigid air poured from low vents.

In front of her was a steel table and behind it, seated in a red plastic office chair, was a man: short brown hair with a widow's peak, dark interested eyes, the bland face of a middle manager. He had a folder and a pad in front of him, a government ballpoint in his hand. Behind him was a closed door with no knob or handle.

"Don't look at me," he ordered in a calm voice, a dog trainer's voice, a flat midwestern accent. "Look at the wall. There's a black spot on the wall. Look at that."

She looked at the spot and asked, "Can I get cleaned up?" Her voice sounded strange to her ears, as if she had become someone else in the last hour—if it was only an hour. She had no idea.

"Of course, after you've answered a few questions," said the man. "Satisfactorily answered. The way this works, Cynthia, is you give us a little and we give you a little, yes? So. Let's start. Name?"

She gave her name, address, social security number, phone number, date of birth, place of birth, education, residence history, marital status, occupation, job history, parents' names, their dates and places of birth, and then she asked, "Why do you need this? You know all this. It's all in my personnel jacket."

"No, Cynthia," said the man, "you don't ask the questions. You don't say anything unless you're asked a question. Let's start over. Name?"

Again he went through the same questions. She gave the same answers.

Then he asked, "When did you first have contact with a terrorist organization?"

"There is no terrorist organization. I'm being framed by rogue elements in the CIA."

"You're lying. Who paid you the money to conceal the uranium theft?"

"I'm not lying. There *was* no uranium theft. You're going to invade Pakistan for no reason and lose the war against the Taliban."

"That's not an answer to a question. Let's begin again. Name?"

She looked at him. She noticed he had a flesh-colored button in his ear. "I want to get clean," she said. "Please, won't you let me clean myself? I have to use the toilet."

"Look at the wall!" he said. "Name? Say your name!"

She said nothing. The man was also silent for a moment and then rose and, after gathering his materials, turned to the door behind him, which opened. He went through it, and in the door appeared a man in tan coveralls with a black hose nozzle in his hands. From this shot a powerful jet of freezing water. It knocked her down and played up and down her body. Water filled her mouth and she coughed violently and curled up, with her curved back facing the stream. The jet tore at the loose waistband of her prison trousers dragging them down, exposing her buttocks. The water blasted at this area for a long time.

The water shut off. She lay on the hard floor shivering, listening to the water gurgle down the drain. A voice said, "Get up!"

She pulled up her pants and stood on wobbling legs. There was a different man in the room, a heavier man with crisp sandy hair and damp blue eyes. He was dabbing at splashes on the table and chair with a white towel. He sat and said, "Don't look at me. Look at the wall." He opened his file. "What is your name?" he said.

She had long ago lost track of time. What followed could have lasted an hour, or three, or twenty-four. The questions were the same: who paid the money; who devised the plan; who were the other operatives in their cell?

For long periods she was mute. Twice she soiled herself and they hosed her down. At a certain point she could no longer stand, so they rigged a cable to the eye bolt in the ceiling, passed a loop of rope under her arms, and held her upright with that, so that it produced a tearing pain in the delicate flesh of her armpits if she did not stand on her feet.

At one point the interrogator started on her father. He'd been through a reeducation camp. Maybe he hated the United States. Had he taught her to hate her country? Maybe we should bring him in here and ask him. Was he involved in the plot? She must have told her father about it, a dutiful Vietnamese daughter. They would bring him in. Who was her contact? Who paid the money?

Cynthia had stopped shivering. She knew that was a bad sign, it was the beginning of hypothermia. Or maybe a good sign, maybe this would soon be over. The interrogator shouted at her. That was new. It was the sandy-haired one. She looked at him and saw that he looked worried, there was a furrow in his brow.

"Don't look at me!" he yelled "Look at the wall!"

Cynthia looked at the round black spot. It had grown larger, she saw, and it grew larger still until it blotted out the room. She sagged, she stopped feeling the cable cutting, she stopped feeling anything.

Now she was warm again. The ceiling over her head when she opened her eyes was made of ordinary acoustic tiles. She studied the pattern of the dots in the tiles for a while. Gradually, the rest of her environment came into focus. She was in some sort of hospital room. It had a window, with drawn venetian blinds on it, baby blue blinds. She was in a hospital bed and there was an IV bag hanging there with a tube that went into her arm. She wore a hospital gown and they had spread an electric blanket over her. She felt a little hungry, but not thirsty. Her armpits stung, but not too badly. She felt drowsy. They had given her drugs.

This was part of the torture, she knew. Get her comfortable and warm, relieve her pain. Then, after a while, they would come in again and ask her questions, and if this time she did not answer to their satisfaction they would take her back to the tile room. She would break then, she knew. She would tell them anything to make it stop; she would invent whole universes of terror, ingenious plots; she would name as accomplices anyone they cared to mention. She had nothing left in her to resist this. So she waited for the torturers to return, and after a while she drifted into sleep.

She awakened to the sound of the door opening. Harry Anspach entered. Why was she not surprised?

He pulled up a visitor's chair and sat down. "Well, Cynthia," he said, "this is quite a little mess you've made for yourself."

"Where am I?" she asked.

"In a secure location. How are you feeling?"

"Do you care?"

He looked startled and a little hurt. He was very good, she thought; the impersonation was wonderfully accurate.

"Of course I care. How can you ask that? That's why I'm here."

When she said nothing, he went on. "I used every chip I had to get in to see you. People are extremely annoyed at your . . . I don't know what to call it. Your interference. Why did you do it?"

"I did my job, Harry. The incercepts were fakes and I can prove it. There's a rogue unit in the CIA that will do anything to protect the operation called SHOWBOAT and they arranged to frame me with phony e-mails and Swiss bank accounts. That's the truth. And they had me tortured so I would confess to something that's not true."

"Oh, nonsense! You haven't been tortured. You're an American citizen and this is the United States. We don't torture Americans in this country."

She stared at him. He seemed genuinely shocked. "Whatever, Harry. So what happens now?"

"Well, there are people who think that rendition would be an appropriate disposition in your case. I've been arguing against it, of course, but you're not helping with this absurd story that some nonexistent operation in the CIA is having you framed."

"I was framed."

"Cynthia, listen to me! I shouldn't be telling you this, but the only thing I can think of that would make you act this way is some kind of psychotic break. You work so hard, you're so intense . . . well, it happens. The fact is, we have positive scientific evidence, irrefutable evidence, that nuclear material was stolen from the Pakistani facility at Kahuta."

"That can't be," said Cynthia. "What kind of irrefutable evidence?"

"William Craig. When he was released he was given a complete physical, and of course his clothes were minutely examined for traces that might suggest where the hostages he was with were being held. That analysis found definite traces of uranium dust on his clothes, and the composition of that uranium precisely matched that used by the Pakistanis as part of their nuclear bomb manufacturing process."

"I don't believe you. I don't believe that for one second. You're lying to me, because . . . because you're involved in SHOWBOAT too. And that's why you've been so nice to me, because you knew when you started your scam I was the only one who could figure it out. You've been manipulating me for years."

She stared into the perfect startled innocence of his face. He really is the best, she thought, I was playing way out of my league.

"And you ratted me out, didn't you? I'm here because you told someone I was on to your scam and they set up all this crap about secret messages and Swiss accounts."

"Cynthia, listen to yourself!" cried Anspach. "Do you hear how insane that sounds? Look, I know you're not a terrorist, not really. You had a little—let's say a lapse in judgment and maybe someone took advantage of it. Okay, but now's the time to recover. You need to tell us who set all this up. Do you even know? You must have had some contact. Come on, kid, give me something . . . anything."

She was silent. He leaned closer, his face inches away from hers. She couldn't look at it.

He said, "Cynthia! Look at me! You'll disappear. Have you any idea what will happen to you in Syria? In Egypt? You're a woman—do I have to draw you a picture? Please! Think of your father, your friends. What end could conceivably be worth imposing that kind of suffering on yourself and your loved ones?"

"Nothing could," she said. "Which is itself an argument that I'm telling the truth."

He sighed and drew away from her. "Well, I tried," he said, and it seemed to her that he was about to say something else, when the door opened and a man she didn't know stuck his head in and gestured urgently. Anspach rose and left the room.

Cynthia lay back and looked at the window. She couldn't see anything out of it from the bed, so she threw back the covers and the electric blanket and tottered over to the window, pulling the IV stand on its wheels. She opened the blinds to find that the window was made of milky translucent glass. She found this amusing, blinds over milky glass? Yes, too, too symbolic of the intelligence community.

She could see that it was daytime and that it was raining. The raindrops were visible as shadows running down, each making its own track against the glass. She watched them for a while, wondering whether she would ever again feel rain on her skin, until her legs grew wobbly and she returned to bed.

She dozed. A woman in blue scrubs entered and adjusted her IV. Cynthia asked what drug she was getting but the woman would not answer. Sometime later, the woman returned with a bag lunch: a prepackaged ham sandwich, a plastic bottle of water, and an apple. She ate everything. The window went gray and then became a dark mirror reflecting the room.

Some hours (she thought) after that occurred, the door opened and two women came in. They said nothing to her as they removed her hospital gown and shoved her arms into a canvas straitjacket, nor did they answer her increasingly frantic questions as they threw her back on the bed and put an adult diaper on her. They taped her mouth and placed opaque glasses on her eyes and padded earphones on her head, through which she heard nothing but loud static. They put her in a wheelchair, cuffed her ankles to it and wheeled her off.

She tried to keep track of time by counting, but lost the count somewhere in the tens of thousands and besides, what did it matter? She thought she might be on an airplane because she felt the kind of acceleration and shaking that you get on a plane, but there was no way to tell for sure. They might want her to think she was on one. She thought a lot about her life and how stupid and trivial it had been and how her highest desire had been to be one of the people who could do to human beings what was being done to her. She understood that her real interest in SHOWBOAT was not a good citizen's outrage but a kind of sick envy; *she* wanted to be included in the cabal; *she* wanted to know the innermost of innermost secrets, to get into the boys' clubhouse at last. She thought about being crazy and about the fake intercepts and whether it was in fact madness that had made her doubt them, and about whether or not Harry was lying about them finding uranium on Craig. She discovered she no longer cared. She was not filled with a lust for revenge. Her lust was only for having her diaper changed.

The wheelchair, after having been stationary for some incalculable time, now moved again. It rocked as if it were in a motor vehicle. It rolled again. It stopped. Someone ripped the tape from her mouth, and the earphones came off her ears. She felt a sharp pinch on her earlobe and then a more painful one in on the flesh of her inner thigh, and she knew what that meant and what was about to happen to her and her bladder gave way again as she shook in terror.

It did not take many shocks before she told them everything they wanted to know. She implicated every person she had ever known with a Muslim name: a friend from high school, her college Arabic teacher, the man who ran a falafel stand in Adams-Morgan, they were all part of the plot, and she told them who had paid her the money, and who her contact was and everything, using depths of creativity she had not known she possessed.

When they thought she had been sufficiently drained for the moment, they put her in a cell. They had taken off the diaper and given her rough cotton pajamas to wear, but they had not allowed her to clean herself. They had manacled her hands and chained her ankles together. The cell was as large as the bathroom in her apartment and contained a yellow plastic bucket. She did not think she was in the United States anymore.

They fed her twice a day, a rice gruel in the morning and two flat loaves like large pitas later in the day, and water in a can. This occurred twelve times. No one spoke to her and she was not interrogated again. On the thirteenth day her door opened and instead of the food there was a female warder with brown skin and a hijab on her head. She was holding a basin of soapy water, a washcloth, and a ragged towel. She pushed these into the cell with her foot and dropped a pair of fresh pajamas next to them. She unlocked Cynthia's shackles, and gestured silently to the materials, making motions indicating that the prisoner should clean herself and change clothes.

Cynthia wept with gratitude for a while and then did as she had been told. She wanted nothing more than to please this wonderful woman, she wanted it more than she had ever wanted to be the national security advisor. She waited, clean, smelling like laundry in her fresh pajamas. The woman relocked the manacles but left the ankle chains off. She placed a burlap sack over Cynthia's head and led her for a while, through doors, up a short flight of steps, into a room. The bag came off. She was in a small room with a steel grille on one wall and a wooden chair placed in front of the grille. On the other side of the grille was a middle-aged man in a dark suit, with thick, coarse, black hair graying at the temples and a gentle, intelligent face the color of doeskin.

When he saw her enter he said, "Ms. Lam? Ms. Cynthia Lam?"

Cythnia sat down in the chair. She felt tears start again at the sound of her full name and the honorific *Ms.*, at the prospect of being treated like a human person again, but she suppressed them, fearing it was one more interrogator's trick.

"Yes, that's my name. Who are you?"

"Oh, thank God!" exclaimed the man. "You have no idea how much trouble I have been through to find you. I have had not only to go through official channels but unofficial ones as well, if you understand my meaning, and in this country, unfortunately, unofficial channels are the only ones that work."

"What country is this?" she asked, staring at him through the grille.

"Why, you are in Egypt, my dear woman. And I am bending my every resource to get you out of it. It is just that you are so very unofficial, and they fear to take cognizance of holding you. I mean that until they admit they have you, they cannot very well release you. The Americans are, I believe, satisfied that they, and you, have been the victims of a hoax; the evidence is irrefutable, and of course they would very much like to forget it has ever happened. Such embarrassment for the government! But there is you, of course—"

"Who *are* you?" she demanded.

He smiled and issued a self-deprecating laugh. "Oh, forgive me," he said. "I am Farid B. Laghari, at your service. I am your lawyer."

21

Theo seems frozen. The footsteps and the rattle of armed men sound closer on the stairs. Ahead, Abu Lais beckons urgently to them. Sonia shoves Theo forward, putting all her weight behind it. His instincts take over and both of them dash into the room at the end of the hallway. Abu Lais shuts the door behind them. Theo is stunned, staring at the other man. He says, "It *is* you. They told me you were dead."

Wazir's face breaks out in his famous smile and Sonia sees her son throw his arms around his brother. The men embrace, and Theo begins to ask a string of questions in rapid Pashto that Sonia can barely follow, but this reunion is interrupted by a pounding on the door. Wazir motions them to the far corner of the room and opens it.

Sonia hears a brief conversation in Arabic and then heavy footfalls and shouted orders.

Wazir says, "The sentry on the roof was shot. They thought it was one of the locals, a sniper, because they thought it was impossible for anyone to get up on the roof without passing them. I told them to stay inside and that I doubted that anyone would try to assault the house."

He sits at the desk chair, as if normal business can now resume.

Theo asks, urgently, "Wazir, what are you doing here?"

Wazir shrugs. "I'm a Pashtun and this is Pashtunistan. Where else should I be? Let's say it's a long story. I don't have to ask what you're doing here—you came for her. But by God, I'm glad to see you!"

Theo is grinning and shaking his head in amazement. Then he sobers and says, "I'm sorry. I shot one of your friends."

"They are not my friends," Wazir says. "They are nominally under my orders, but in fact they were sent to watch me. The Arabs are very suspicious, especially of Pashtuns. You might even have done me a favor."

"I don't understand."

He looks at Sonia. "How much does he know?"

"I have no idea," she says. "I don't even know how he found this place."

"How did you?" asks Wazir.

"That's a long story, too," says Theo. Sonia studies his face as he looks at the other man. It is like flipping through one of those books that depicts the range of human expressions: love, anger, astonishment, confusion; each blooms, flickers, dies, and is succeeded by another. Her heart aches.

Theo says, "I can't believe it, Wazir, by God, it's been half a lifetime! Where did you learn English? You sound like an American."

"I practically am. I was in the States nearly as long as you. I was educated there, Case Western and Berkeley."

"How? The last time I saw you, you were a Pashtun mujahid. How in hell did you get a college education?"

"A Ph.D., actually."

"And you never tried to contact me in all those years?"

Wazir looked a little embarrassed at this and asks Sonia, "Can I tell him?"

"That's up to you, Wazir," she says. "I'm retired."

"Retired from what?" asks Theo. Now the confusion on his face gels, with an angry flush, a knotting of the brows. "Wazir, what is she talking about? What in hell is going on?"

Wazir leans back in his chair and takes a deep breath, lets it flow out. "Well, let's see—where to start? Let's start with your mother."

He makes a rotating motion with his fingers.

"The axis, the source of it all. Sonia's the reason I got an education in America. She pulled me out of the jihad just like she pulled you, but in my case I did a little better in school than you did. I can see you're about to ask why she did such a thing. Why me? Well, I'm smart, she knew that from Aitchison College and our many conversations up on the roof at your grandfather's house, and she needed a smart Pashtun with good mujahideen credentials."

"I don't understand," says Theo.

Wazir looks at Sonia, eyebrows elevated in surprise. "You never told him?"

She shakes her head.

"Told me what?"

After a considerate pause, Wazir answers, "Your mother has been an asset of the Central Intelligence Agency for a very long time, and she's been involved in a very deep Agency game, probably the deepest it has ever played."

"That's crazy," Theo says. "Sonia's not a CIA agent."

"Asset. There's a difference. Think about it for a minute, Theo. In 1973, Sonia Laghari probably knew more about Soviet Central Asia than any other American. She was an embarrassment to the KGB. Don't you think the CIA would've been interested in her? And they were. An agent approached her and she turned him down: oh, no, she was not going to spy for America. Then, what happened to your grandfather happened, and we did what we did. As I'm sure you know, she thought you were dead too, and when she found out you weren't, it was nearly as bad, because you were lost in the jihad. You, her last child; she was desperate to get you back. And they knew this. They contacted her in Zurich again, and this time she agreed to do anything they asked her to do if only they would get you out. They gave her a contact in Peshawar, and he arranged for you to be snatched and taken to America. So then it was time for the payoff, and the payoff was me."

"Why did they want you?" Theo asks. "They were funding the jihad all along, they had access to all the leaders, and you were just a foot soldier."

"Yes, then I was, but I was also young. I could be—how should I say it?—groomed for greater things."

"I don't understand. Are you saying the CIA educated you? For what, to spy on the jihad?"

"Not exactly. Let me give you a hint. My B.S. is in physics, and my doctorate is in nuclear engineering. My thesis was on new computational approaches to the analysis of nuclear explosions. The research was paid for by the Department of Energy, the people who manufacture nuclear weapons."

Sonia is silent, watching her son's face as he thinks this through. She feels a wave of shame, another blast of her failed-mother grief, and also compassion for what she has allowed to happen to him. He is not stupid, her boy, but neither is he Wazir; no, she has not groomed *him*.

At last Theo says, "You're a Trojan horse."

This provokes another sunny smile on the handsome face. "Exactly! I am Abu Lais, the great hope of the whole jihad to lay hands on nuclear weapons. Isn't that a joke?"

"Yeah, it's hilarious," says Theo, unsmiling.

Wazir does not notice this, his grin grows broader. "Yes, and the kind of joke only a Pashtun can really appreciate: Pashtunistan, the Brillo pad of intersecting betrayals."

"Why you?" Theo demands. "Why do you get this terrific education, courtesy of Uncle Sam?"

"As I said, it's a long story," Wazir says, not smiling now.

"We got time," says Theo. "I like long stories." He unslings the AK, props it against the wall, sits down on the charpoy. Sonia sits next to him.

"Theo . . . the gun," she says. "I think you can put it away, yes?"

He looks at the Stechkin in his hand, realizes he has been gesturing with it, gives her a quick annoyed look, replaces the pistol in its holster, and returns his attention to Wazir.

"Okay, brother," says Wazir. "So, it's 1987, the jihad is winding down, and the CIA is thick in Afghanistan. And what do they see? This Soviet threat they've been working against for their whole lives is crap. The great Red Army can't even provide bullets and food for its troops. The idea that this army could attack Europe or anywhere else against the wishes of the U.S. military is revealed as nonsense, Chad with rockets, and all that. So they start asking, Where's the next enemy? And what do they see? They see the jihad, the movement they helped to create, and at the center of this movement is a man they have built up into a great leader, and what a surprise! They find this great leader has no love for America; in fact he sees that America, far more than Russia, is the reason the Muslims are groaning under oppression. America is the prop for the Saudis, for the Egyptians—"

"Bin Laden," says Theo.

"Yes. And the CIA tells this to Washington, but Washington doesn't listen, communism has always been the enemy and always *will* be the enemy, and if, for some reason, communism falls, there will be an era of endless peace; democracy and capitalism will spread throughout the world, the end of history, and so forth. But one small group of operatives had their eyes open. They'd read the books bin Laden read—Sayyid Qutb and others in the same vein—and they understood that his goals were the destruction of the apostate regimes, the recovery of Palestine, and the re-creation of a caliphate that would unite the entire umma under one political roof. Well, of course this is ridiculous on the face of it—the Prophet, peace be upon him, was hardly dead before the umma fell apart into factions, where it has remained to this day. But uniting the world under a supposed Aryan master race was ridiculous, and the dictatorship of the proletariat was ridiculous too, yet the world paid dearly in blood for these two absurdities, and the same could happen again."

"Get to the fucking point, Wazir," says Theo. Sonia feels the atmosphere in the room changing, growing more tense. She can feel the anger pouring off her son like waves of heat from a stove; she has never seen this part of Theo before—he has always been careful to shield her from it, but not now—now she really understands that her boy kills people for a living.

Wazir makes an acquiescent gesture. "All right. Very simply: In 1987 elements in the CIA conceived a plan to recruit a mujahid and train him in the United States as an expert on nuclear weapons, so that if the jihad ever came close to getting nuclear material, they would have someone on the inside, a sleeper, as they say. The operation was codenamed SHOWBOAT and it was secret beyond secret, so secret that this person had to be recruited outside normal CIA channels. Not only the recruit, but the recruiter had to be perfectly secure. So they thought of your mother, who famously had turned down the CIA's overtures. A man named Harry Anspach, who had been deeply involved in the Russian jihad, had noticed a young warrior named Kakay Ghazan, and done the usual background check on him. Anspach was making a list of the future leaders of the jihad, should it ever turn against its sponsors, and in the course of this he was surprised to find the connection between you and your mother. I believe he thought you might be a candidate for his sleeper. He had your mother contacted in Zurich with the news that you were still alive and that Harry Anspach in Peshawar would be willing to help her get you out of Afghanistan, for a price. She immediately left for Peshawar, with the results you know. You were taken and returned to America,"

"But they didn't make me the sleeper," says Theo.

"No. I'm afraid your mother had another candidate for that role. I'm sorry, my brother, but you would not have been suitable. As I recall it, you were having problems with your studies at the age of ten. So I was recruited instead, and my existence is secret from all but a tiny handful of people. I am not on any list of assets, and my handler is not a CIA agent. My handler is codenamed Ringmaster, and I believe you can guess who she is."

Here he glances at Sonia and goes on, "Anspach understood the doomsday scenario was that al-Qaeda might get hold of nuclear material. India had exploded a nuclear weapon in 1974, and everyone knew Pakistan was working on one. Pakistan is a Muslim nation full of people sympathetic to the jihad. It was only a matter of time before doomsday arrived. So when the jihad gets hold of some plutonium or whatever, what do they do with it? You can't make a nuclear device in your kitchen like you do a roadside bomb. You need an expert, with excellent mujahideen credentials, who has kept contact with the movement throughout his education and who has been allowed to dig into classified material, despite those connections, protected of course by Anspach and his friends. Al-Qaeda needed someone like Abu Lais, and here he is, finished and packaged by the CIA. Naturally, such a figure is close to the leadership of al-Qaeda, but he doesn't betray them, not even for 9/11 does he betray them; oh, no, he is far too valuable. He waits for the moment when the jihad obtains nuclear material. Yes, Anspach is a farseeing man, Theo, farseeing and very covert. And here we all are."

The confusion is back on Theo's face, Sonia observes. He says, "But there *isn't* any nuclear material."

There is a silence now, and Wazir takes a long moment before responding. "Why would you think that, Theo?"

"Because I invented the whole thing. It's a scam. We needed a serious effort to rescue my mother, and the only way the U.S. was going to send a competent force into Pakistan was if they thought Pakistani weapons-grade uranium had gone missing. Farid and the family generated a set of fake conversations to convince NSA that there'd been a theft." He turns to his mother. "I had to do something. America wasn't going to try to rescue you, and the ISI was in with the kidnappers. I sent another phony message the other day saying the bomb was here in Paidara. I have a radio. In a minute I'm going to make a call saying that

I've located the nuke and the specials will come in and secure the area and that'll be it."

"Oh, Theo!" cries Sonia.

"What?" he says, and sees that Wazir is looking at him with a peculiar expression on his face: amazement, dismay, the kind of look one uses with madmen on the street.

"If true, that's actually quite amusing," Wazir says. "Because, you know, there *was* a theft. I have seventy-five kilograms of enriched uranium. And I made it into bombs."

"He's joking," Sonia says, looking at her son, wrenching a false smile onto her face.

"Are you?" Theo asks. He draws his terrible pistol and rises, changing his position, moving slightly on the charpoy so that his mother is not blocking a potential shot at Wazir.

Wazir seems unconcerned. "Of course not. Do you want to see one? I have it here."

He goes to the corner of the room, draws aside the tarp, and reveals a packing case. Theo's pistol comes up to cover him.

From the packing case Wazir takes a large stainless steel box, the kind mechanics use to store their valuable tools. It is obviously quite heavy, and Wazir has to strain at the handle with both hands to lift it out onto the table. He opens it with a key.

Theo rises and looks inside the box. It contains a steel cylinder eighteen inches wide by about thirty long that fills nearly the whole of the interior. The rest of the space is taken up by a small green plastic container the size of a lunch box, on top of which is a keypad and several small LED lights.

"It's based on the W-82/XM-785 artillery shell from the sixties," Wazir says, "but it's a little more advanced. My own design, really. Fifteen kilograms of fissionable material, beryllium reflector, weighs less than a hundred pounds. It's a linear implosion device. The fissile material is formed into an egg shape and it's surrounded by a cylinder of high explosive rigged for simultaneous detonation at each end. An inert wave-shaper channels the shock wave so as to compress the egg into a spheroid to achieve supercriticality. The calculated yield, best case, would be over two kilotons, but I'd be happy with one point five or even one. Of course I haven't tested it, but the math is right and the people I used for the assembly were all Dara artisans. I figured anyone who could manufacture a perfect working replica of a Beretta nine-millimeter out of an old crankshaft could do the job. The firing sequence runs off IGBT transistors rather than krytron tubes, not as efficient but a lot more available. I had the boards custom made in Malaysia and wrote the software myself. This is one of six."

He smiles like a schoolboy who has given the right answer. Then he sees that Theo is pointing the pistol at him and he frowns a little.

"Why are you pointing that at me, Theo?" he asks.

"Why? Fuck it, Wazir, you're my brother, but I'm not going to let you blow up an American city with that thing."

Wazir looks stunned; he gapes. "An American city? Why on earth would I do such a thing? That's crazy!"

"Thank you. That's a good description of al-Qaeda."

"Oh, for God's sake, Theo! There's no such thing as al-Qaeda. Was there such a thing as *the* jihad? You were there. It's just different factions. Sometimes they cooperate; sometimes they fight. Some of them are maniacs; some of them are perfectly reasonable people trying to fix an intolerable situation, which is the oppression and humiliation of the umma. Sure there are some who'd love to destroy New York or Tel Aviv, but I'd be a maniac myself if I listened to them. You saw what happened when those idiots knocked down two office buildings on 9/11. Can you imagine what America would do, what Israel would do, if we blew up one of their *cities*? They have *thousands* of nuclear missiles. They'd massacre every Muslim in the world."

"So what are you going to do with them?"

Sonia says, "He's going to blow up Ras Tanura."

"What?" says Theo.

"It's the Saudi oil terminal. Ten percent of the world's oil supply flows through it," she says.

"Yes," says Wazir, "and we will also take out the Khor-el-Amaya terminal in Iraq and Kharg Island in Iran. The other bombs will go to the giant Saudi fields, Ghawar and either Khurais or Manita, I haven't decided. All at once, of course. The world oil supply will be reduced for a period of several years by about forty percent. Yes, they can rebuild, but it's going to be hard to do in radiation suits in eighty centigrade heat."

Theo looks at his mother, remembering her television interview. "This was your idea."

"I was speaking theoretically," she says. "I had no idea he was going to put it into actual practice. He's going to kill thousands of people. Do you think I wanted *that*?"

Theo realizes that his gun is pointing at her and he moves it away. He says, "Mother, just once I wish you'd tell me the truth."

"That *is* the truth," she says. "Ask him."

Theo turns to Wazir. "Well?"

"Does it matter?" Wazir says. "Really? Ideas cause events. That's the story of the twentieth century. Do you think that the theoretical anti-Semites, respectable people all of them, all the intellectual race theorists, ever imagined Auschwitz? Or earnest European communists ever imagined the Gulag or Katyn Forest? What did I learn from her in all those years, Theo, when she was more my mother than she was yours? That oil is the curse of the umma; that it is inherently corrupting, worse than slavery; that Wahabi puritanism funded by oil is essentially a fraud, a fig leaf the Saudis use to salve their consciences while they live like emperors; that what the umma needs more than anything is to be left alone to find its way back to God; and that it will never be left alone as long as the oil flows smoothly out of the terminals. So that's one reason why I am going to turn off the taps."

"What's the other reason?" asks Theo, after a pause.

Wazir's face changes, and Sonia sees the mujahid boy flash out again, a startling resurrection, and in thick Pashto he says, "Revenge, of course. I am a Pashtun, after all."

"Revenge for what?"

"For *everything!*" cries Wazir. "Against being manipulated. Against being treated like a tool. Against the arrogance that believed I could be treated so. Against the arrogance that allows a tenth of the world to live in peace, comfort, and security, ignoring the miseries of the rest. Against the idea of collateral damage. Against the lazy stupidity of the Americans and the diligent hypocrisy of the oil sheikhs. That world has to be smashed. It can't go on. But I am only one man and that's all I could think of. Is that enough?"

"It's enough," says Theo. "But I can't let you do it, brother."

"Why not? Don't you feel the same way?"

"It doesn't matter what I feel. I'm a soldier and you're an enemy. It's an honor thing. Where are the other bombs?"

"What if I don't tell you? Will you torture me?"

"Don't be stupid, Wazir!"

"She knows," says Wazir, pointing at Sonia. "She helped me set up the networks under the noses of her CIA masters, and it was easy because none of them could imagine blowback on this scale. You could torture her as well."

Theo looks at his mother, and she thinks it is the same look he wore when he was a little boy and she came home from her long journeys, a look that said, *Why did you leave me? What did I do wrong?* A look that is a window into a heart that can never be healed.

"Is he right, Mom?" Theo asks. "Is he telling the truth?"

She says, "Why did you come, Theo? You're not supposed to be involved in this."

"Well, I'm sure as hell involved now. So tell me! He's blowing smoke, isn't he? I get the CIA connection, I get the whole Trojan horse thing. But you didn't know about the bombs, did you? You didn't help him plan this?"

Sonia remains silent. She can hear her own breathing and Theo's and the faint sounds of the village night, someone coughing, the distant rumble of a truck, a night creature calling, the wind. It goes on, this silence, for a long while, it is almost a contemplative silence, she thinks, waiting for God to speak, but at last it is Wazir who speaks.

"You know, Theo, I'm not sure you understand your mother. She's a very strange person, and I say this as someone who has met some very strange people indeed. Did you know she followed a Sufi pir all through the trip to Central Asia? She didn't put that into the book. An odd brand of Islam, really. They believe that everything written about God is in some sense wrong, because if you propose a complete picture of God, it's not God by definition, because God is beyond all human description. And it follows that Saint Paul was somewhat wrong and the Gospels are some-what wrong and the Prophet, peace be on him, was somewhat wrong too. God doesn't make deals with His creatures. He's always a surprise, and try-ing to chain Him to a human religion is folly. That's what she taught me and I believe it, because otherwise the world does not make a bit of sense."

He laughs, a little hysterically, Sonia thinks, but Theo doesn't even smile. Grimly, still covering Wazir with his pistol, he rummages in his pack and pulls out a coil of rope and what looks like a cheap portable radio.

"What are you doing, Theo?" she asks.

"I'm going to tie up Wazir, Mom. And then I'm going to call my control and tell them I've located the nuke and for them to come and get it. And us. Wazir, put your hands behind you."

Theo moves behind the chair with his rope, and the moment he is thus distracted, Sonia stands, snatches up the AK, and points it at her son.

"Let him go, Theo."

He looks at her blankly. "What're you doing?"

"I'm letting Wazir escape. The Americans will lock him up forever. They'll torture him."

Again she sees the emotions wash across the screen of his face. He really is a sweet boy at heart, she thinks; there is no real guile in him, or meanness. He says, calmly enough, "And if not, what are you going to do, shoot me?"

"I will certainly disable you. I'm a very good shot, as you know, and I am not going to have Wazir rot in an American prison. I would do exactly the same if the situation were reversed."

Theo nods and backs away. Wazir rises and speaks a few words to Theo, so softly that Sonia cannot hear them, and then he picks up the duffel bag.

To Sonia he says, grinning again, "I presume I can't take my bomb."

"Just go, Wazir," she says, "and may God protect you."

"And you also," he says and goes to the window. He tosses the duffel bag through it and climbs out.

Sonia watches her son raise his pistol and point it at Wazir. She puts the front sight of the AK on her son and her finger on the trigger.

They stand that way for a second or two, like a diorama of some awful historical event, and then Wazir is gone. They can hear his feet scrabbling as he descends the rough wall and the thump as he lands.

Theo clicks his pistol to safe and tosses it on the table.

"Would you really have shot me?" he asks.

"Of course not," she says. "Would you have shot Wazir?"

"No," he says, and shrugs helplessly. "Then what the hell was all that about?"

"Reflexes to satisfy our various codes of honor. Insect responses. What will you do now?"

"Like I just said, get on the radio, tell them I've secured the nuke, and call in the Rangers. They'll be here before dawn."

"They'll do a lot of damage."

"That's what they're for," he says, and fiddles with his fake Chinese radio. In a few moments it crackles with voices and Theo speaks cryptic words and numbers into it. He signs off and leaves the thing on the table, a green light glowing on its face.

He says, "This is the safest house in town as long as that beacon is on. They're going to be very, very careful with our gadget here."

They both look at the metal case. Sonia shudders and turns her eyes away from it. Theo says, "Yeah, the mind can't quite grasp it. Two thousand tons of TNT, did he say? It's like something from another universe. It shouldn't exist, but there it is. And he built it. I can hardly *look* at the fucking thing, and Wazir *built* it! Tell me, do you think he really has five other bombs out there somewhere?"

"I have no idea. I was astounded that he had even one."

"Uh-huh," he grunts: an unbelieving noise.

She sits on the charpoy. Suddenly, in the afterwash of violent emotion, she is exhausted. She would like to be far away from people now, even people she loves. Especially people she loves. Her son, who has done prodigies to rescue her, now leans against the wall, looking out the window from time to time, like a man waiting for a bus. He doesn't look at her. She knows he is thinking about Wazir, and what Wazir has done, and how she arranged for him to do it. It is a lot to take in; she sympathizes, she hurts with her boy, but her therapeutic skills do not help her now, the wonderful gearing of her empathic faculty will not turn in the thick gel of familial love. Still, there is the instinct to reach out.

"Theo," she says, "come sit by me. I want to talk with you."

He clumps over and sits, sullen.

"What are you thinking about?"

A shrug. He has regressed to sixteen.

"No, really, Theo," she presses.

"Really? Okay, I was thinking about Hughes."

"Who?"

"Wally Hughes. You know, from Special Forces. We went through jump school at Benning together and all through SFQC at Bragg. There was me and Buck Claiborne and Billy Olin and Hughes. I think you met him once, at Benning that time you came down, when I graduated."

"Oh, yes?"

"Yeah. Anyway, Hughes had a wife, Laura, and two little girls, one of them three years old and the other just a baby, and he was crazy about them: he had the picture in the helmet, he e-mailed every day when he could, the whole nine yards. This was in the early part of Iraq, the goat fuck. He kept getting extended. They'd give him fifteen-day leaves, but they wouldn't let him rotate home, because they were so short they were using Special Forces joes as regular line infantry, just to keep the lid on. Well, in the early part of '05, I think it was, Laura cracked. She wrote him a dear john, sorry and all that, but she'd met someone and she was moving away. She was frightened of him, frightened about the way he was when he came home. She was scared he was turning into one of the guys she'd heard about, who comes home and kills his family and himself. Hughes didn't say shit to any of us, just kept on trooping, except he started to volunteer for dangerous stuff. He was always on point, always the first one through the door. He got a Silver Star and a DSC."

"He was trying to commit suicide?"

"I don't know. I think he was going after the Medal of Honor, because that was the only way they'd let him out of the war. Anyway, we were in the area listening in on some al-Q comm, and we located a command center. This was in Samarra, and they tasked Hughes and his team to get them out of where they were, which was the top floor of a four-story apartment house, full of families, and the insurgents, of course, wouldn't let anyone out, because they kind of like it when we kill a lot of women and kids; it's good for their business. I think they were going to call in an air strike, but Hughes just runs in there all by himself with maybe twenty guys blazing away at him and he clears out the whole bunch of them. He must have been hit a dozen times, but he got them all. The damnedest thing you ever saw."

"Did he get his medal?"

"Posthumously, yes. And the reason I was thinking about him, which is what I know you're going to ask, is that I finally know how he felt when he lost the pin."

"The . . . ?"

"The pin that holds the wheel on the axle. Or the spoon on the grenade, whatever. Except for a few guys who are just stone killers, everyone who does war needs a pin: family, your buddies, ambition, honor, or . . . or *some-*

thing, because regular people aren't supposed to do what we do or see the stuff we see. Or no, I'm not saying this right: there has to be a place you can hide—what's the word? Existentially. You need an existential hide. Religion's a good one, it's real traditional, what those assholes out there have but we don't. We have our families, or a sense of the way things are, that defines us as not guys who blow innocent people up. For Hughes it was his family, and for me it was you and Wazir, even though I practically never saw you and I thought Wazir was dead. It was a set of memories that told me who Theo Bailey *was*. You know? And now I find that the base of my life was like a fantasy, a dream, that those people never existed."

"That's not so, Theo. People change."

"Oh, no kidding? People change! That's a terrific insight, Mother. Let me write that down so I don't forget. No, people *don't* change, not like that. I don't change like that, and Gul Muhammed doesn't, and Farid doesn't and Nisar doesn't. The only people who change like that are people who never were what they seemed in the first place. I had a friend, a brother, my brother-in-arms in a just war, and it turns out he was somebody else, because the Wazir I knew was not some crazy half-American nuclear-genius bomb builder; and my mother was a writer and a Sufi mystic and someone who did therapy in a charity clinic, not some fucking rogue CIA mastermind plotting to blow up the world."

"It must have been a real shock, seeing him again."

"She says in her calming therapist voice. It didn't work when I was seventeen and it's not working now. Because I want to *know*. I want to know my role in the game, because, you know, I can't believe that all this—all this *plotting*—was the result of them giving you help getting me out of Afghanistan. It doesn't compute, Mother. Because I'm not that important to you."

"Don't be ridiculous, Theo! Don't you think that, having lost two children, I'd do anything at all to protect you? Even this?"

She means the thing in its silvery casing on the table that neither of them can bear to look at; but now they look at it.

"Didn't *you* do what you had to do to find and rescue me?" she asks, in a gentler voice. "We're the same, we're mad in the same way, and Wazir makes a third. That's why you didn't shoot him and that's why you're not going to tell anyone about him being here or what his plans are."

"I won't?"

"No. Because your love is only for your family. You've already betrayed your country and your army to organize this rescue. The fact that there happens to be a real bomb doesn't signify. And you'll do it again, as will I. We do everything for each other, because that's all there is for people like us, it's the curse of us primitives, it's why the bureaucracies lord it over us, why the earth is ruled by people whose loyalties are to abstractions. I had a dream about this on the flight over here, and I just this minute realized what it meant. Would you like to hear it?"

He nods, and she tells him about the warped little boy in the circus yard and about smashing the nests of baby birds or squirrels and the stern woman in spangles and her horrible magic.

"What does it mean?"

"It means that in a world ruled by violence, you can't protect love without becoming warped and injured in some way. My mother taught me that, which is why she—or rather her introject—is in that dream: it's the lesson of her glorious but unsuccessful nation. When I was a girl we had a poster in our trailer, one that had appeared all over Eastern Europe, first in Prague during the Soviet suppression and then in Warsaw and Budapest and East Germany. Ours was in Polish, of course, and it said:

> "We have not learned anything, we don't know anything, we
> don't have anything, we don't understand anything, we don't sell
> anything, we don't help, we don't betray, and we will not forget.

"I was a just a kid, so that even though my mother translated the words, I didn't understand what they meant. But I think I knew the meaning in some *deep* way and that it would be a guide for my life; I was to be a resistant, a subversive. And perhaps if my mother had lived I would have been a respectable subversive, like they have in America, educated and in the chattering classes, but this was not my fate, as you know; she died, and my father was weak. Did you know he actually sold me to Guido Armelini for *cash*? Even *I* didn't know it for years; I had completely suppressed it until it came out in therapy, in Zurich, after the girls died. I remembered then how Guido used to feel me up—I was sixteen at the time—and whisper about what he was going to do to me when I was legal. He was very afraid of jail, old Guido, at least he was afraid of jail for statutory rape. For card-sharping not so much. Then I found Farid and made him fall in love with me, and I took the money and made sure Guido's gangsters would think it was Guido who took it, and they killed him; and I told Farid I had to get out of the country right away, which might even have been true. Yes, well may you stare! All these revelations! Did you ever read a story by Flannery O'Connor called 'A Good Man Is Hard to Find'? No, of course you didn't, you're not a reader. But there's a line in it that goes something like *She would've been a good woman if someone had held a gun to her head her whole life.*"

She looks again at Wazir's shiny case.

"I feel that way now. It's that bomb, it's hard to tell lies in its presence; it's what the West has instead of God; it's what America *really* believes in, despite our constant churchgoing."

She sighs heavily, it turns into a sob, she clutches at her son, and they stay that way for a long time until gradually, without really understanding when it began, they become aware of a sound.

"That's them," says Theo, gently breaking her grip. He removes a night-vision scope from his pack, adjusts it over his right eye, slings the AK, and extinguishes the oil lamp. In the darkness she hears him say, "You should get back to that room. It'd be better if they discovered you by accident. You'll be Sonia Laghari. There's no reason anyone on the mission should know you're my mother."

He takes her back down the hallway, pistol at the ready, but as they pass a door she hears a familiar cough.

"I want to go in here for a minute and check on Dr. Schildkraut."

"Yes, but make it fast," he says, and as if to confirm the urgency of the moment they hear shouts and warning gunshots from outside. The mujahideen have also heard the thrumming of massed helicopters.

Sonia goes into the room. It is lightless and she follows her ears to where Karl-Heinz is huddled against the wall.

"Sonia, is that you?" he wheezes.

"Yes. How are you feeling?"

"Wonderful. Sonia, will you do me one last favor? On the next draw of cards, use your tricks so that I am low card. Can you do that, please? Because I wish to use the last gasp of my inhaler now. I wish to feel like a human again and not a pathetic coughing wretch when they cut my head off. I should have demanded it before, but I was a coward."

It comes into Sonia's mind, like a reflex, to lie, to pretend she has not fixed the drawing of the cards, but of course Karl-Heinz, the old friend, has known all along.

"There will be no more drawing," she says. "We are being rescued. You can hear the helicopters. But Karl-Heinz? I would appreciate it if the others were not told."

He says nothing to this. She feels him move and then hears the hiss of the inhaler and a deep sigh, and then shouts and heavy footsteps. The sound of helicopters also increases.

She feels a motion in the doorway and hears Theo's voice shouting, "Everyone down on the floor, get down!"

After that, the sound of automatic fire at close range, colossal, penetrating the body like the promise of wounds. By the flash of his weapon she sees for the first time her boy practicing his profession. He is fighting off Wazir's Arab team. Her ears grow numb, but oddly she can still hear the snap of the return fire, the thud of bullets hitting, and the tinkle of brass falling. Theo is firing the AK now, but in another minute all the sounds of gunfire are drowned in the roar of a helicopter directly overhead. Theo stops firing and pulls the door closed, but the gunfire does not cease, it grows, she can see bright flashes come from under the door and through the many bullet holes pierced through it, like red and green lasers in the dark.

The nearby firing fades. The door to the room is kicked open. By the faint ruddy glow of some distant blaze arriving through the window of the room down the hall Sonia sees the shapes of armed men, she hears urgent shouts to lie down and put their hands behind their heads.

So she is captured one final time, now by her fellow countrymen. Theo makes himself known to the Special Forces officer in charge, he tells about the bomb and explains the hostage situation. The officer insists that the hostages be removed immediately; only certain people can stay in the house of the bomb; he has his orders, no exceptions. The former hostages are led out of the building, surrounded by a protective cordon of elite troops. Sonia supports Schildkraut and Annette, who has endured the recent firefight alone and in the dark and is shaking uncontrollably. Theo is not with them.

Outside, there is war. The night sky above Paidara is studded with aircraft of all types, the Americans are not stinting on the Invasion of

Pakistan. Sheets of fire rain from above, overwhelming the few feeble green tracers that rise from the guns of the mujahideen. They pass exploded, burning houses; by the light of one of them Sonia sees Amin's stunned expression, his mouth gapes open.

"What are they doing?" he cries out. "This is insanity. They are killing everything."

"It is the bomb, Amin," she says. "There was a nuclear bomb in the village, made with material stolen from Pakistan. It gives them all the excuse they need." Amin, that strong confident man, bursts into tears.

They are hustled into an intact house some streets away, the door forced open, the terrified family confined to one room, and the hostages are examined by a Special Forces medic, who recommends the immediate evacuation of Dr. Schildkraut. The old man is carried off and flown away.

The others are interrogated by men in jumpsuits without name tags or military insignia. Sonia tells her story to one of these. Not the true story, of course; he is not cleared to hear it. Has she ever told the true story? Probably not. Would she even recognize the true story if she heard it? Probably not. It is, she concludes, like the advice she received when first learning how to ride the circus horses. If the horse bolts, they told her, hang on and ride it out. Eventually the horse will get tired and stop. No matter how frightened you are, never try to jump off. Sonia has been riding this particular runaway for over twenty years, and she detects a slowing in the pace; these last events have an air of sweat and hard breathing. Soon, she thinks, she will step lightly off the steaming back and resume her real life. Her interrogator wonders why she smiles like that.

She passes Annette Cosgrove in the hall of the house of interrogation and offers a friendly look, but Annette stares straight ahead and passes by without a word. Someone not dead must take the blame for all this, Sonia thinks, and Annette has apparently included her in this group. Somewhat later she happens upon Father Shea and Manjit Nara. They are cordial but distant. There will be no joyful hugs among the released, and Sonia accepts this. No one wants to touch the death dealer.

ॐ

The sounds of battle fade. The dawn comes, a chill one, with a wind that fills the air with the stink of burning and tosses the rich drifts of fresh debris into stinging clouds. Sonia and the other hostages are led out to

376 | Michael Gruber

view the prisoners and the wounded and slain, to identify those who were involved with the mujahideen and the kidnapping. They have placed the corpses in neat military rows in the street in front of the ruined mosque, where Sonia has twice been whipped. Mahmoud is there, and the man who cut Cosgrove's head off, and the older man with the hennaed beard who wanted Rashida, and many other mujahideen, who were just faces in the crowd to the hostages but obviously had been wicked indeed, deserving of this fate. Rashida, who was not a mujahid, is also there, a little pile of bloodied rags, her wedding bangles gleaming on her thin wrists, and there is her father too, and a woman who may have been her mother or someone else's mother, lines and lines of collateral damagees lying under a shifting, buzzing scrim of flies.

Idris Ghulam is not there, however; he has survived. He was blown through a window in the first moments of the battle and landed well; he has broken bones and his body is peppered with pieces of metal, many and painful, but he is not dead. She identifies him to her interrogator like a good citizen, and then kneels beside him.

"Peace be with you, Idris, and I am sorry to see you hurt," she says in Pashto, "but I am happy to see you alive."

He glares at her for an instant, then looks away. "Did you see this in your dreams?"

"Oh, yes," she replies, "and if you recall I tried to warn you, but, as Rahman says, *Like a child you put your hand in the fire, hoping for something good, unconscious of the pain to come.*"

"They did all this, made all this death, just to save you?"

"No, there was another reason, but what does that matter? The dead are still dead, including those you killed yourself. It would have been better not to start the killing."

"Will they kill me?"

"No, they will confine you, and perhaps you will be tortured in some way, not as badly, however, as what awaits you in Hell, unless you repent and change your life. There is still a lot of time. When I was your age I was a begum in a great house in Lahore, but after that I led a very different kind of life. Trust God and follow His commandments, Idris, and may you have peace."

Now the interrogator demands to know what they've been saying. "We were just discussing religion," says Sonia, and walks away.

22

Night in Lahore at the start of Ramadan. The Muslims have been fasting all day, and roasting too, because it's August, and the crowds are thick, up and down the Mall and in Anarkali, where I am. I live here now, working for the family business. Like I figured, the army tried to stop-loss me when my enlistment ran out, but a call to Major Lepinski fixed that up pretty good. I was not that indispensable for national security, it turned out, and I was able to take Uncle Nisar up on his standing offer.

We're sitting in Koh's Tea Shop in Anarkali, on the terrace there, down the Mall from the museum. Koh's is a tourist trap—no Lahori with any pretension to elite status would be caught dead there, among the Japanese tour groups and the backpacking blond girls—but I like it. I like it because it is near my house in Anarkali, and because if any of the elite ever do show up at Koh's it's because they want to see me without an appointment, in a place where none of their peers would be caught dead, and because the barman has an American generosity with the ice, which he makes from distilled water, and because if you look down the Mall you can just pick out through the haze the great gun Zam-Zammah on its stupid little traffic island across from the Lahore Museum, and also because Koh's terrace has a low wall of solid concrete separating it from the street and affords excellent fields of fire in several directions.

I look down the road and see that, as usual, some kids are climbing on the gun, as is forbidden. It warms my heart, after a lifetime of following orders, to be in a place where laws are barely suggestions, are more like lists of actions that you can get rich by transgressing.

Yet we are not lawless here in Pakistan, we are feudal, a big difference, although our many lawyers don't see it that way. Everyone loves
feudalism in their hearts, which is why *The Godfather* and *The Sopranos*
were huge hits; there is yet to be a movie about legislative markup or the
courageous agents of the federal elections commission. We also have
democracy here now, which means I vote for whomever Nisar tells me
to, along with all the other thousands of his people, and I make sure my
people vote right too. Nisar is a genius with the smooth aspects of the
business world, while I am in charge of the rough parts.

Every big Pakistani firm does some rough work or has to defend
against the rough work of rivals. There is extortion. Everybody has
trucks, for instance, and what do you do if somebody wants money for
not burning your trucks or beating your drivers? Forget the cops; the cops
have been paid off or maybe they're moonlighting as muscle in the same
racket, so you have to show you're tougher, that you won't be intimi-
dated. Maybe you make an example of the extortionist. Maybe you bribe
a senior police official to pull the protection the extortionist is buying. It
depends on the situation. I try to avoid violence where I can, but where I
can't I go in with the max, shock and awe, just like I learned from the
Americans. I had to do a lot more of it when I first got here, so no one
would think I was an asshole who just got the job because he was the
sahib's nephew. During that period I introduced kneecapping as a tool of
Pakistani commerce, and it has worked pretty well for us. I am known
around town as Bhatija Sahib, which means Mister Nephew—without
irony, I believe.

There is that woman again. I point her out to Malang, my chief bodyguard, who sits beside me on the terrace, and he turns his head slightly
to bring her into view. She has just walked by, dressed as she always is, in
a black kurta and shalwar, with a gold-colored scarf over her head. Not a
Pakistani woman, I thought when she first walked by, but a European or
an American. You can tell: the walk is different and the way they hold
their bodies is more relaxed—sloppy, some would say, but not I. She is
beautiful in a gaunt way, and she is a Eurasian of some kind, like me. Of
course, I sent my boys to find out who she was.

Because any number of people would like to see me dead. There have
been several attempts so far, but fortunately the ineptitude that afflicts
our society has reached even into the assassination business. Even gang-

sters have incompetent relatives who require jobs, and I have not been harmed, although that hasn't prevented me from taking revenge. They have never tried with a woman before; if they are using this one, it would at least be an original twist.

I am assembling a private army, too. Gul Muhammed sends me likely Pashtun boys from our tribe, and I train them up as my personal guard. I also tour the few dozen Punjabi villages the family owns, look over the crop of teenagers, and pick the ones who remind me of myself: tough and smart but not bookish. I educate them at my own expense with the understanding that they will have lifetime jobs defending the Laghari interests.

I intend to stay here when the place falls apart. I've gone around this issue a couple of times with Nisar, who is patriotic enough for a Lahori, but when the news is bad he always thinks first about moving resources offshore, so that when the Taliban take over Punjab the family can have a comfortable exile in London or New York. I tell him we can resist. If we have a loyal force and if we treat our peasants like human beings, we will not have Taliban in our villages, and when they try we can strike back at them. He asks me how you can fight people who use suicide bombers, and I say it is very easy; suicide bombing is a sign of weakness, not strength. If you are attacked in this way, you find out who the bomber was and then you go to where he comes from and kill every male member of his family, all the way out to the cousins. I have done this once already, and there has not been another suicide-bomb attempt. No one likes killing children, but we do it all the time in my former land, and the main difference between doing it from ten thousand feet and doing it from two feet is a strong stomach and a dislike of hypocrisy.

I make it a point to get reports of what is being taught in our mosques and madrasas, and when I don't like what's going down I have a talk with the mullah. My intel service is not as good as it should be, but it is getting better. I want to know who's oppressing and who's oppressed. I don't like my employees to use their power over those lower than they are in ways I would not approve. No raping girls, for example, and no cheating on wages. Often a little talk is all that's necessary to resolve these problems. They are amazed that anyone in Lahore cares what happens in some village south of Multan, but I do. Nisar thinks this is an American eccentricity, but it is not. It is the foundation of our kingdom.

If Nisar is correct, and my father Farid is correct, we will travel through this period of strife and establish the rule of law. Farid points out that England was once a lawless land full of religious wars, and look at what it became. This is his great dream and I admire him for it, but Gul Muhammed is my father too, and his dream is different and more modest: that his tribe might be secure in their little valleys and grow fruits and tend animals and sing their songs and be left alone by the world, and leave the world alone, except maybe for a little plunder. That dream seems more realistic for this part of the world, and so I plot and deal out violence and charity in about equal measure, like any good lord, fair but cruel. I never thought I was much of a plotter, but it turns out I am. In this at least I am my mother's son.

Wazir has vanished. At the last moment he whispered into my ear that, despite all, he still loved me and that God was merciful and would not keep us apart forever. I try to believe him. Strangely enough, that belief is a big part of what keeps me safe from the sadistic megalomaniac of my fellow warlords, or such is my hope. He has not set off any of his bombs, so the traffic still rushes along the Mall and along all the streets of the world. I did not tell anyone about the other bombs or about his plans to rid the Middle East of the oil curse. It's none of my business, and my mother agrees.

She's temporarily here in Lahore, as a matter of fact, and perfectly secure in my house; it would take a reinforced company with heavy weapons to get in there. This is one of the advantages of being a warlord. I think the whole thing amuses her; when she's back in Washington she works hard to convince poor Farid that I have not become a complete monster.

℞

My mother is not a Punjabi matron, but she still would like grandchildren, and quite aside from that I need to think about founding my dynasty. Nisar has only daughters, and Seyd has taken himself and his family out of contention (after the events of last year, Nisar arranged to have Seyd assigned to Jidda as military attaché to our embassy there, in the hope that a little soaking in true Islam will knock some sense into him), leaving only Rukhsana's boys and me. Or only me, since Hassan and Iqbal are going the traditional professional route and will eventually join the great diaspora. I am not the most eligible bachelor in my circle by any means. High Pakistan does not like to dwell on the means by which it is kept in power, and I am too thuggy by far for the best matches, plus there is the scandal of my mother. High Pakistan has a long memory.

But my skin is nice and pale, comparatively, and I have good manners and speak perfect English, and I'm rich and I'm a Laghari, which are all enough to win me a suitable girl. I have not met one so far that I like, and I am American enough to want that in my official wife. I kind of miss Gloria, or a Gloria-type thing. I go to the Hira Mandi as often as any other man in my position and have had several interesting relationships with women in the house my uncle patronizes, but I do not have that whole wife-and-mistress thing in my DNA. Maybe another gift from Mom.

❧

The woman is crossing the street, weaving through the tangled traffic on the Mall. She is walking directly toward us. I feel Malang stir, and he signals to the two boys on perimeter duty. Shuja walks into her path and engages her in some conversation while Tofan comes up behind her and tells her he has a gun and he will either shoot her now or she will allow him to make sure she is not carrying a weapon or wearing a suicide vest, and sorry for the indignity. Malang stands up and positions himself between me and the blast, if any, but there is no blast and the woman walks toward our table. I stand up and indicate a vacant chair.

I say, "Please sit, Ms. Lam, and tell me what I can do for you."

She sits and looks at me. Terrific eyes, almonds with chocolate centers, showing a complex, ironic intelligence. She says, "What was that all about with the pat-down? You knew who I was; did you think I would try to kill you?"

"Standard procedure. Although you have more reason than most to want to kill me."

"Oh? Why is that?"

"I framed you and ruined your life. I got you tortured and made into a stateless fugitive. Those are pretty good reasons."

"Except that if my life was no good at heart, then ruining it did me a favor."

"And why was it not good at heart?"

She shrugged. "Because there's something inherently disgusting about clawing your way to power in a bureaucracy, don't you think?"

"I wouldn't know. I claw my way to power in a nonbureaucratic environment."

"So I've heard. The dreaded Bhatija Sahib."

"Would you like some refreshment, Ms. Lam?"

"Please, it's Cynthia. Yes, I would love an iced mint tea." I motion to Malang and he motions at large, and in three milliseconds there is a waiter there to take our order. Another reason I like Koh's Tea House.

"So what have you been doing since your life was or was not ruined?" I ask her. "It's been well over a year."

"I've been traveling. Your father was extremely generous. I have a Pakistani diplomatic passport and a black credit card that never seems to send me the bill."

"Yes, the Lagharis are inclined to be generous to the people they chew up. It saves trouble in the long run."

"Does it? I've stopped thinking in the long run." She sips her tea, then leans back in her chair and looks at me with a cool regard, very unlike the looks I get from the Pakistani possibles. She is not afraid of me, for one thing.

I say, "You have no plans? You intend to wander the earth indefinitely?"

In Urdu she quotes from the the first *dirwan* of Mir:

"How long will you wander thus
and live in desolation?
Isn't death better than this deadness,
the grave to this living decay?"

I say, "Well, I didn't mean *that*," and she gives me the first smile, and I say, "But now you lack all ambition? You shouldn't have much trouble if you wanted work. You have the languages, firsthand knowledge of the U.S. intel system, Laghari connections, and you're easy on the eye."

"Are you offering me a job, Bhatija Sahib?"

"It's not impossible, if you wanted to settle down. Lahore's an interesting place, especially if you're expecting the end of the world. It's a society heavy with risk and the joy that comes along with desperation."

"Well, I'll certainly consider it. But I have some more traveling to do. I want to see Afghanistan. And Central Asia. And Burma and Cambodia and Vietnam."

"But you're not leaving this minute for all those places, are you? I mean, you'll let me buy you a meal?"

"You buy all my meals."

"I meant as Theo Bailey, not the dreaded Bhatija Sahib."

She nods and gives the second smile. I utter a command: "Malang, the car."

He pulls out his cell phone.

I get up and tell her, "We'll go to Gulberg, I think, and dine with the elite at a place with no menus and no sign outside, and then we'll come back here to Anarkali, to my house. It's just around the corner."

"Yes, I know. And why would we do that?"

"I want you to meet my mother," I say. "I think you have a lot in common."

Acknowledgments

I would like to acknowledge the help of my editor, Marjorie Braman of Henry Holt, and of my agent, Simon Lipskar of Writers House, in the development of this novel. Novels are reputed to be the work of a single author, but what you have just read is a fourth draft, and whatever faults it retains, it is a lot better than the first three, the result of Marjorie's and Simon's careful reading and comments.

The real (as opposed to invented) poetry quoted in the novel are my own versions of translations from Pashto and Urdu originals derived from the following books:

The Poetry of Rahman Baba: Poet of the Pukhtuns by Robert Sampson and Momin Khan, University Book Agency, Peshawar, 2005, and *The Golden Tradition: An Anthology of Urdu Poetry*, edited by Ahmed Ali, Columbia University Press, New York, 1973.

THE GOOD SON

by Michael Gruber

In His Own Words

- A Conversation with Michael Gruber

Behind the Novel

- "Consciousness, Culture, and Creativity: Writing *The Good Son*" An Original Essay by the Author

Keep on Reading

- Recommended Reading
- Reading Group Questions

For more reading group suggestions, visit www.readinggroupgold.com.

🦁 ST. MARTIN'S GRIFFIN

📖 A Conversation with Michael Gruber

This is your seventh novel and you have been praised for being able to write on a wide variety of subjects. In what ways does *The Good Son* represent your exploration into new territory as a writer?

I've never done a classic international intrigue novel before and I wanted to take a stab. I started thinking about this book five or so years back when the situation in Pakistan had not become what it is now. Today, *The Good Son* has a ripped-from-the-headlines feel to it that was not my original intent. I was thinking more of a modern version of *Kim*.

But now the novel appears more relevant than you expected?

Yes, the fate of the U.S. expedition in Afghanistan and our resistance to terrorism in general appears ever more dependent on the stability and goodwill of Pakistan. We are assured that the nuclear capabilities of Pakistan are secure, but we also know that the director of Pakistan's nuclear program was selling nuclear technology practically on the open market. We also know that the safeguards against corruption in that country are not all they should be (Pakistan stands toward the bottom of Transparency International's list of the most corrupt countries) and we have to take in faith that the people guarding nuclear material are tremendously unlike their compatriots with respect to corruption. My novel is a work of fiction, of course, but the events described in it seem a good deal more plausible now than they were when I thought them up.

You live in Seattle, yet write with such knowledge about Pakistan. Tell us about your research and how you were able to write characters that are part of the Islamic Jihad Movement.

The best way I've found to imagine a different place and culture is through novels written by writers from

that place and culture. I read a lot of fiction written
by Pakistanis and Afghans, including, for example:
The Kite Runner and *A Thousand Splendid Suns* by
Khaled Hosseini; *The Reluctant Fundamentalist* and
Moth Smoke by Mohsin Hamid; *In Other Rooms, Other
Wonders* by Daniyal Mueenuddin; and *The Pakistani
Bride* and *The Ice-Candy Man* by Bapsi Sidhwa. Besides
that, the Internet is a trove of information about dif-
ferent cultures. If you want to know what jihadists or
Muslim women are thinking, it's all there on the web.
Some sites I looked in on include muttaqun.com/
Muttaqun Online—for information about Islamic life
in general and the religion; Khyber.org—for a view of
Pashtun life; sufi-psychology.org—to get the Sufi take
on the psychology of terrorism; forumpakistan.com—
for contemporary desi lifestyles; and islamfortoday.com
as a gateway to a discussion of Muslim women's issues.
This tour d'horizon did not make me into any kind of
expert, but did, I think, guard against the more obvious
errors. What works on such information, finally, is sheer
imagination.

**In addition to your research, you also had inspiration
for the book from a personal situation. Similar to the
mother and son character in the book, your wife has
been through the Jung Institute and your son was in the
Navy. Can you talk about how your family life directly
inspired these characters?**

The idea for this book popped into my head during a
time in 2004 when our son was with the military in
Iraq and was just about to start SEAL training, and
my wife was the head of a peace organization. Despite
their differences they had and have a close relationship
and I thought that odd connection was a good premise
for a novel. My wife did train at the Jung Institute and
although she is an artist and not a therapist, I thought
that was a good thing to throw into the mix.

*In His Own
Words*

Why did you decide to title the book *The Good Son*?

Because it's basically about mother-son relationships. The mother gets in trouble and "The Good Son" naturally wants to get her out of it.

What might you say to your current fans about the direction you are taking with this novel and what makes *The Good Son* similar or different from your body of work?

My work really has two main themes. One is thinking about the underlying nature of reality, the uncanny, religion, how we each decide what's real and what isn't. The other is deracination, or what happens when cultures interact, either in the heart of a particular person or as a function of the enormous increase in emigration that characterizes the modern world. *The Good Son* is just another take on what I started doing in *Tropic of Night*.

You're talking about what happens when cultures interact and the three major characters who narrate the book are multicultural. How are their diverse backgrounds important in understanding their view of reality?

Our view of reality is interpreted through culture and the signal fact about the current age is that cultures are in flux, through deracination, through mixing of populations with varying cultural baggage, and the globalization of culture. The symbol of this is that for the first time the president of the United States is a deracinated individual. Something new is happening in America and the world and I wanted to write about it. I also wanted to say something about cultural imperialism, the idea that the way we see the world is essentially real and the way that others see it is warped. We say, if only others would see the right way to do things—democracy, civil rights, equality of women, secular humanism,

whatever, all would be well. I thought it would be inter-
esting to start from a different premise, to accept other
realities as just as valid as our own. I wanted to do a
little mindbending.

**Though your work is fiction, your book can also serve to
educate readers on America's present conflict with parts
of the Islamic world. What political lessons or insights
do you hope your readers will take away from the book?**

The lesson for the American reader would be to
suspend self-righteousness for a moment and to see
the world through the eyes of the other.

***Booklist's* starred review of *The Good Son* says "if only
governments were half as interested in the psychology
of violence, maybe war itself might become a work
of fiction." Do you think psychological insights could
indeed get through to a terrorist?**

Yes, in that war of any kind (with the exception of literal
defense against patent attack on the literal homeland) is
a form of madness. Islamic terrorism, in particular, has
nothing to do with the actual tenets of Islam. People in
Muslim countries are literally driven mad by personal
and social conditions and pursue terrorism as a result.
The insanity on our side is more subtle and we don't
see it as easily because we take it that our leaders are
sane by definition. But they're not. The foreign policy
of the United States has often been conducted with as
much respect for reality as that presented by someone
who thinks he's Jesus or Napoleon. But we're all inside
that crazy fantasy, and accept it as the way things are.

**How has the experience of writing *The Good Son*
affected you as a person?**

I read the news from South Asia and the Middle East
with enough grains of salt to promote hypertension.

 *An Original Essay*
by the Author

"Consciousness, Culture, and Creativity:
Writing *The Good Son*"

There's a note in my notebook from around three
years ago that says: "Woman, peace worker, Jungian,
kidnapped by terrorists, SEAL son tries to rescue
her." I have a lot of notes like that, some of them get
turned into novels and others don't. Most of them just
pop into my head but this particular one came out
of my life. At the time, my wife was an organizer in
the Catholic Peace Movement at the beginning of the
Iraq War and studied dreamwork with the Jungian-
influenced Process Work Institute based in Zurich.
Her son was in the Navy and about to embark on
SEAL training, because he wanted to become a bomb
disposal guy and the training is largely the same as it is
for the SEALs. I thought it was an interesting situation,
quite apart from the tension and terror in our house,
the warrior son and the peacenik mother. After some
years, with the young man safely back home from Iraq,
I decided to turn the idea into a novel.

My fiction has two major themes. One is how culture
influences our view of reality, especially in people who
are the product of two very different cultures, deracinated people, if you will, and the other is the underlying nature of human consciousness, especially as that
relates to what may be called the unseen world. Given
the current world situation, I also wanted to place the
characters in a context where they could explore our
present conflict with parts of the Islamic world.

So I decided to make the mother eclectically religious,
a Jungian, a Catholic, married to a Muslim and an

occasional and heterodox practitioner of that faith. The
son would be the product of an upper-class Pakistani,
raised in Lahore, and an American mother with a speck-
led past. And then I worked out a series of events that
brought the boy into the jihad against the Russians
in Afghanistan, because I wanted him to be not only
an elite American soldier, but someone having deep
contacts with mujahideen, someone who understood
Islamic jihadism from the inside.

The problem with this basic story, man seeks captive
mother, is that it wants to slide into the old melodra-
matic mold, where the hero is terribly good, and brave
and noble, and the victim is innocent, and the villains
are very evil indeed. Melodrama always arises from the
unexamined assumptions of a culture; its purpose is to
affirm those assumptions rather than prompt any deep
examination of the culture's values, far less to penetrate
them to the layers where the deeper feelings are engen-
dered.

*Behind the
Novel*

But one of the uses of fiction is to take the received
wisdom of a writer's society and hold it up to a hard
light, and so we have the imperfect hero, even the anti-
hero, and the villain who inspires sympathy. What I've
tried to do in *The Good Son* is a version of that effort.
The society in which I am located is loosely known as
the West. It is a liberal (in the original sense of the
word) democracy, with a free-enterprise economy, the
rule of law, equal rights, freedom of speech and religion, and is characterized (at least in its leadership) by a
scientific worldview and, especially, an almost religious
devotion to material progress. It further believes that
these qualities have made it both powerful and rich. As
members of this society, we naturally assume that it is
inherently right, and that all rational human beings will
aspire to live in such societies, and that the only reason

they do not is either a defect in the minds or education of people who live otherwise or the malign influence of wicked rulers. This assumption is called cultural imperialism, and it is very deep, even subconscious in most of us. How, we ask, can anyone not want to be rich in things? How can anyone not want freedom? And further, since all people are the same (another unexamined assumption), it is insulting to these all-the-same folks to believe they might want something different.

It is, however, an obvious fact that some people do want something different, and are willing to fight and die for it. Across the Islamic world, the *umma*, or community of believers, rejects the basic cultural assumptions of the West. The primary value here is not political freedom or material progress but submission to the will of God, as expressed in the Qur'an, in the sayings of the Prophet Mohammed, and in the codification of these writings in sharia law. Those who cherish such values look not ahead to material progress, but back in time, to an era when, they believe, the umma had attained a perfect relationship with God and His laws, the time of the Prophet and the "rightly guided" caliphs, when Islam was the most advanced and powerful culture on earth. Education or exposure to Western ways does not seem to have much of an effect on this way of seeing the world; quite the opposite in many cases. It is one of the horrible ironies of the 9/11 events that the leader of the attack was a man with an advanced degree in (what else?) urban planning.

Criticizing or condemning the political or psychological aspects of this view is beside the point. It is a real difference in consciousness, and since the relationship

of consciousness to culture is, in my view, at the core of any novel, I wanted to see what happened if I took this strange and alien consciousness seriously, on its own terms. In the book, this central theme is played out in two theaters: a struggle within the mind of the young soldier, and between the mother and the terrorist leader who holds her life in his hands. In the latter of these, I try to show what happens if we were to take the deep religious impulses of Islamic jihadism seriously, instead of treating them like a kind of nostalgic psychosis.

Good novels are supposed to make us look at ourselves and our culture through fresh eyes, and almost nothing does this as well as getting into the head of a character who shares not one of the assumptions on which we have constructed our own lives. (Of course, the actual way that novels do this is by packing all that sort of thing in what the author hopes is a ripping good yarn, and I have tried to do that as well.) In order to write this book I had to read a lot of material about Islam and its culture, and novels set in that culture, and the works of writers who thought that nothing I believed was true, and that death and murder were better than accepting a world that I was entirely at home in. I gained at least partial entry to a world that is, as one book I read has it, "lost in the sacred." The experience shook me; I hope *The Good Son* does the same for its readers.

Recommended Reading

Here are just some of the books I read in preparation for writing *The Good Son*. Each one of these books was eye-opening in its own way and added a layer of complexity in what I hope turned out to be a book that not only entertains but illuminates a subject about which I learned so much from my own reading.

Counseling and Psychotherapy with Arabs and Muslims

Marwan Dwairy

The case for believing that the psychology of people from traditional Muslim cultures is very different from what we understand the psyche to be in Western psychotherapy. The goals and practice of therapy are entirely different—assuming "they are just like us" leads not to understanding but to confusion and failure.

Afghan Guerilla Warfare: In the Words of the Mujaheddin Fighters

Ali Ahmad Jalali and Lester W. Grau

The anti-Russian jihad described through interviews with the men who fought the Soviet Union to a standstill. The best oral history of this war.

The Soviet-Afghan War: How a Superpower Fought and Lost

Translated and Edited by Lester W. Grau and Michael A. Gress

The same conflict from the Soviet side, based on the after-action reports from Soviet commanders.

*Killer Elite: The Inside Story of America's Most
Secret Special Operations Team*

Michael Smith

A nameless organization acting as the Army's private
CIA. The unit Theo belonged to is based on these guys.

City of Sin and Splendour: Writings on Lahore

Edited by Bapsi Sidhwa

A collection of writings about the Punjabi city in which
much of *The Good Son* takes place.

In Other Rooms, Other Wonders

Daniyal Mueenuddin

A wonderfully vivid evocation of modern Pakistani
culture, told in linked stories.

Pashtun Tales

Aishe Ahmad and Roger Boase

If you want to understand a people, a good place to
start is with the stories they tell about themselves, and
the tales they tell their children. What the Pashtuns
have instead of Snow White and Goldilocks.

Body of Secrets

James Banford

An anatomy of the supersecret National Security
Agency, the people who track electronic signals worldwide. Why bin Laden can't use his cell phone.

Reading Group Questions

1. What role does America play in this novel? As a character, how does it influence the course of the story?

2. This novel introduces many different archetypal women—Gloria, Rashida, Cynthia, Sonia, and all the unnamed "black figures" that appear throughout. What are their main differences? Similarities? What do all of these women bring out in Theo?

3. In the beginning of the novel, we are presented with the image of a hawk swooping down and killing a pigeon. How is this image carried throughout the rest of the story, and what are some of its possible interpretations?

4. Throughout *The Good Son* we are shown many scenes of torture—the mujahideen torturing Sonia and the prisoners, the U.S. agents torturing Cynthia, and the many scenes of torture in Hell that we see through the dreams Sonia interprets. How do each of these kinds of persuasion tactics differ and what do they tell us about the people behind them?

5. How does this novel touch upon relevant current events? How does it relate to your experiences in the aftermath of 9/11?

6. What can we learn about the world—and ourselves—from Theo's story? From Sonia's?

7. Is there a moral to be taken from *The Good Son*?

8. The role of family is very important throughout Theo's life. Discuss his relationship with his father, mother, and women in general.

9. What do you think is the next chapter for Cynthia and Theo—do you think they will, in fact, work together? Would you have ended the book the same way the author did?